THE
GENESIS
FLAME

The Genesis Flame © 2018 by Ryan Dalton. All rights reserved. No part of this book may be used or reproduced in any manner whatsoever, including Internet usage, without written permission from Jolly Fish Press, except in the case of brief quotations embodied in critical articles and reviews.

First Edition
First Printing, 2018

Book design by Jake Slavik
Cover design by Jake Slavik
Cover images by Jg_cuz/Shutterstock, da-kuk/iStockphoto, szefei/ Shutterstock

Jolly Fish Press, an imprint of North Star Editions, Inc.

This is a work of fiction. Names, characters, places, and incidents are either the product of the author's imagination or are used fictitiously, and any resemblance to actual persons living or dead, business establishments, events, or locales is entirely coincidental. Cover models used for illustrative purposes only and may not endorse or represent the book's subject.

Library of Congress Cataloging-in-Publication Data (Pending)
978-1-63163-170-2

Jolly Fish Press
North Star Editions, Inc.
2297 Waters Drive
Mendota Heights, MN 55120
www.jollyfishpress.com

Printed in the United States of America

For Miss Weber, my eighth grade science teacher.
You were right.
I did grow up to be a writer.
Thanks for believing.

Dalton, Ryan(Young adult author)
Genesis flame

2018
33305242660722
sa   05/08/18

GENESIS FLAME

THE TIME SHIFT TRILOGY

BOOK THREE

RYAN DALTON

JOLLY
FiSH
PRESS

Mendota Heights, Minnesota

CHAPTER 1

October, A.D. 3088

The shackles dug into her wrists. She twisted and struggled to break free of her captor's grip. The humanoid machine just kept walking, never wavering as it pulled her down the hallway of perfect white quartz.

"Let me go. I didn't do anything!" she shouted.

With a lurch, she swung her shackled fists at its white-and-chrome face . . . and missed completely. Her unkempt, dark hair flailed as she toppled to the floor. The Cyonic kept its stride, and she scrambled to her feet rather than be dragged.

"Stupid Cyonic. Since when do you bring people to the Pyre for one bar fight?"

"Thirty-fourth bar fight," the Cyonic corrected in that infuriatingly soothing voice.

Abruptly, it turned to face a random section of the wall. Or it seemed random until the glowing outline of a doorway appeared.

"Rectify," the machine intoned.

The outline pulsed, and then the wall was gone. She blinked. Nothing had phased out or folded away—the wall had just been there and then *not*. Beyond it was a pitch-black chamber.

She swallowed. "I have the right to speak to *aah!*"

The Cyonic flicked its wrist and sent her flying into the chamber. She tumbled to the floor as the doorway closed. Darkness enveloped her.

"Yeah, you better run," she said.

"Are you so angry at the world that you would hurl yourself against it until one of you breaks?"

The voice echoed, coming from everywhere at once. She leapt to her feet and spun, searching.

"Who are you? What do you want?"

A beam of light pierced the dark, illuminating her from above.

"What is your name?"

"You're the mystery man in a dark room. Why don't you tell me?"

"I suppose it doesn't matter. That name is dead. Soon you will have a new one."

That caught her off guard. She hid it by scoffing. "And why would I want a new name?"

"Because with a new name comes a new purpose."

Out in the blackness, a screen glowed to life, displaying two faces. Faces that made her tremble with hate. She clenched her fists.

"You know who they are?"

"Yes," she said through gritted teeth.

"The atrocity you endured at their hands . . . it is unthinkable. An act so terrible that you have spent the last six months seeking death."

She flinched.

"Have you not? The constant drinking, the brawls night after night. I know the face of one longing for oblivion."

She stared down at her feet, tears burning behind her eyes. "What else do I have? Vengeance? No one can fight people like that."

"What if you could?"

Slowly she looked up.

"What if there was a chance to set all the wrongs right? Would you take it?"

What could a nobody like her do? Nothing.

But if there was even one chance, didn't she owe it to Maya? Tears came again, and this time she let them spill down her cheeks.

"Yes. I would."

"Be warned. The very core of you will be broken and re-made. The woman you are now—she will cease to exist."

She snarled. "Give me a way, and I promise I will die with my hands around their throat."

The chamber became bathed in bright light. It was big, maybe thirty meters by fifty. Emblazoned across one wall in massive chrome letters was a word.

RECTIFY.

Someone cleared their throat. She whirled to see a man standing before her, clad in a black suit. Tall and lean, with a narrow face and dark hair, he stood with his hands clasped behind his back.

"Do you know who I am?" he said.

"Y-you're the Regent."

The supreme leader of their world government nodded, stepping toward her with sinewy grace. As he moved, the light bent subtly around him.

"And did you mean what you said?"

"Every word."

As the Regent came within arm's reach, she tensed to keep from trembling. His stare sliced through her. For an eternal moment, he seemed to examine her insides. Then, finally . . .

"Are you ready to begin?"

A dark thrill raced through her. "Now?"

"Welcome to Project Rectify . . . Calypso."

Agony . . .

 . . . searing . . .

 . . . blinding . . .

 . . . burning . . .

 . . . freezing . . .

 . . . slicing, digging . . .

Reaching . . .

 . . . stretching, bending . . .

 . . . *breaking* . . .

time blurs,

day after day, month after month . . .

More. Give me more! I can take it.

anguish

one year

stretching into forever

And then . . .

Train.

Run.

Jump.

Faster. Higher.

Faster. Higher.

Punch.
Kick.
Again.
Faster. Harder.
  Again.
  Again.
  AGAIN.
    Slice.
    Shoot.
    Don't stop.
    Don't miss.
    Don't question.
    Target, sight, *shoot.*
    Target, stalk, own the shadows,
      slice

      Charm
      ??????
        Smile.
        Flirt.
        Slink.
        Seduce.
        Listen. Learn.

        You're almost there, Calypso.
You almost have it.
Keep going.
  Don't stop.
    Don't give in.

Our world needs you.
Our time needs you.
I need you.
THAT'S IT
YOU'RE

"I'm ready."

CHAPTER 2

Present Day
Two years after the Frost Hammer's defeat

"He's on the move!"

Malcolm Gilbert barreled down the alley, carving between buildings in downtown Emmett's Bluff. Fifty yards ahead, a hulking man in copper armor sprinted away, his horned helmet bouncing.

"Mine's running, too." Valentine's voice rang through the comm device in his ear.

"They all are," John said. *"Satellite shows them moving in the same direction."*

"Do you know where the, uh, whatever they call themselves are heading?" Valentine said.

"Not yet," John replied. *"And the translator said they call themselves Techno-Vikings."*

Malcolm grimaced. These guys only looked like Vikings for someone casting a ridiculous action movie. Braided beards, giant axes and war hammers, and those stupid horned helmets.

"That's not even historically accurate," he said, vaulting over a stack of empty pallets. "Vikings never dressed like that, and—"

"Maybe save the history lesson for later?" Valentine said.

Malcolm chuckled. She had a point, and historical accuracy was hardly the biggest problem. Though these guys dressed like movie extras, their tech was way beyond that of the Vikings. Like the Time travel device that had brought them here a week ago.

They had been quite a nuisance. Something about traveling the "waves of Time" and conquering like their ancestors had done across the ocean. Malcolm rolled his eyes.

Was the warrior drawing his weapon? It was hard to tell at this distance. Malcolm willed the Time flowing through his body to move faster. The alley became a blur, and a microsecond later he'd closed the distance to his target. The warrior glanced over his shoulder, shouted in alarm, and threw his considerable mass around a sharp corner.

Malcolm stretched out his Chronauri senses, awareness extending along the currents of the Time stream. The brick walls around him were aging—he could feel them crumbling ever so slowly as Time took its toll. An ant colony glowed with thousands of tiny pulses of light, the temporal batteries of each insect.

The Techno-Viking's presence pulsed like a heartbeat. Malcolm felt the unique signature of his internal Time battery, sensed the subtle shift of the Time stream as the currents flowed around him. The man was young, retaining at least two-thirds of the Time in his battery. All of this, and more, was how Malcolm knew the warrior had stopped around the corner and prepared an ambush.

Grinning, Malcolm dropped into a somersault. A gleaming axe blade *whooshed* overhead to clang against the wall, throwing sparks and shattered bricks.

Malcolm leapt back to his feet and skidded to a halt, facing his prey. The Techno-Viking whirled, shouting in the Old Norse language.

"He's threatening to eat your fish," John said. *"Wait, no—face. He's threatening to eat your face. Sorry, this translation program isn't perfect."*

Malcolm laughed, which his foe did not appreciate. Growling, the Techno-Viking pressed a button on his bracer.

Thousands of shiny nanobots streamed across his body and interlocked to form a layer of high-tech armor. Blue flames burst from the warrior, threatening his enemies while the man remained protected inside.

Two years ago, this would have been terrifying. Now Malcolm stood his ground, watching calmly as the huge man lifted his flaming axe.

The Techno-Viking bellowed and launched a vicious overhead swing. Malcolm held up his right hand, and a razor-thin distortion shimmered around his fingers like a blade. With a flick of his wrist, the axe flew to pieces.

Sheathed in fast Time, Malcolm dashed around his opponent like a rushing wind, carving laser-precise lines in the flaming armor. Half a blink later, he nodded in satisfaction and kicked behind the warrior's knees.

The Techno-Viking crashed to the ground. His armor fell off like a banana peel, leaving him with only a cotton under-layer for protection. He growled, rolled onto his back, and tried sitting up. Malcolm kicked him hard in the chest, sending him back to the ground, and pressed a boot down on his shoulder.

"Trust me, your axe can't match my Entropy Blade," he said. Valentine kept arguing the name wasn't scientifically accurate, but how could he give it up when it sounded so cool? "Now, don't you feel like leaving my town?"

The Techno-Viking barked in his language.

"Anything useful?" Malcolm asked.

"He'll kill your family, take you as a slave, pain, death, world domination, et cetera," John replied.

"So, just the usual?"

"So far."

Shaking his head, Malcolm drew a modified paintball pistol from his utility belt. He pressed the first of three buttons. Four red laser dots clustered on the Techno-Viking's chest.

"Sure that's all you want to say?"

The warrior spat on his boot.

"Okay, then."

He pressed the second button. With a *foomp,* a metal sphere the size of a Ping-Pong ball smacked against the Techno-Viking's chest and unfolded. Black outer segments lay flat and latched on, while the silver inner layer awakened.

Eyes wide, the warrior grabbed for it. Malcolm kicked his hand away. On the Viking's chest a tiny mechanical ring was spinning, cradled by magnetic coils and an array of mirrored surfaces. Seconds later the ring disappeared, replaced by a tiny, blue vortex.

"Say hi to Tyrathorn for me."

Malcolm pressed the third button. The vortex expanded with a *whoosh,* wrapped around the warrior, then folded back on itself and disappeared.

Malcolm took a moment to savor the victory, then tapped his comm.

"They've got flame mods and nanotech armor. Nothing to worry about, but be alert."

"Too bad Fred is halfway around the world," John said. *"He would have loved taking these guys down."*

Malcolm agreed. "How many are left? Seven?"

"*Six*," Valentine said. "*Just sent Thorn another one.*"

"Good. Anyone have eyes on Asha?"

As if in answer, Asha Corvonian's Time signature pulsed behind him. Malcolm whipped around to see her leap from a roof, cartwheel across a dumpster, and sprint past him. He couldn't help admiring the way her form undulated underneath the fine mesh armor and silver plating. The metallic grays glowed with shimmering waves of red light, evoking the image of a burning ember.

"*Now five*," Asha's melodic accent came through the comm. "*And they're on my tail.*"

Malcolm's jaw dropped. "What?"

"*I'll trick them into cornering me. Then we take them all.*"

Malcolm could hear clatters and shouts approaching. Grinning, he shook his head. Asha lived for days like this.

"What do you need?" he said.

"*Disappear. If you distract them, they won't come after me.*"

Malcolm backed into a corner and fished a small device from his belt. When he pressed the red button, nearby shadows stretched and wrapped around him like living creatures. Soon after, five gigantic warriors crashed down and ran after Asha.

"They're coming," he said. "John, can you find a choke point?"

"*Already sending coordinates.*"

Malcolm's mobile beeped and his navigation app displayed a pulsing dot.

"*Meet you on the roof of Oswald Library, Mal,*" Valentine said.

Malcolm vaulted up a fire escape, reached the roof, and took off. Valentine appeared at his side soon after, leaping across rooftops with him. They arrived early. Crouched behind the roof's parapet, the twins peered down at the dead-end alley behind Oswald Library.

Asha skidded around the corner, her long, black hair flying. She stopped short at the dead end, spinning as if desperate to find an escape route.

Right on cue, the Techno-Vikings arrived to block her in. The largest advanced on her, the others a step behind. Malcolm noted that the largest wore the most gilded armor. *There's the leader.*

Valentine tensed as they closed around Asha. Malcolm put a staying hand on her arm.

"Wait," he whispered. "I love this part."

The Techno-Vikings' armor caught fire, and they drew weapons. The leader pointed at Asha and barked a challenge. Malcolm had to admit, these guys put on a good show. Lesser opponents would have cowered in fear.

Asha drew her own weapons with a metallic *shing*. Throwing back her shoulders, she lifted her chin, and the warrior became the warrior princess.

"You dare threaten me?" she demanded. "I am Ashandara Corvonian, princess of Everwatch and High Protector of the Ember Guard. Attack me, and from the dawn of the universe to the dwindling of Time itself, there will not be a moment in which you can hide from us." She stepped forward, blazing red, the air around her sizzling. "Come to me, fools! Come and meet your doom!"

The leader hesitated.

A thrill surged through Malcolm. *That's my girl.*

"You're hopeless," Valentine whispered.

He shrugged. "I'm okay with it."

"Don't you think it's time?"

"Yeah, probably so."

Asha could handle herself, but there was no sense waiting. In unison, the twins vaulted over the parapet.

As he fell, Malcolm opened his being to the universe and drew in a rush of Time. Splitting the energy into multiple streams, he channeled them outward to prepare for a grand entrance. Valentine's corona glowed like a white star as she did the same.

The Techno-Vikings spun as one to see the twins land, crouch, and punch the ground. As their fists hit home, each called a bolt of lightning to strike the pavement behind them. With a burst of light, the ground trembled. The warriors stumbled back.

The Techno-Vikings' armor generated flows of fast Time to conjure their fire. Two years ago, the twins would have countered with slowed Time, covering their enemies in ice to smother the flames.

Since reaching the impossible Sixth-*sev*, they had transcended such rudimentary methods.

Malcolm seized the Vikings' flows of fast Time and willed them to unravel like so many loose threads. The flames died instantly. Back-tracing the flows' path, he found the tiny pulsing machine inside each warrior's armor. With a satisfied grin, he sent spikes of hyper-fast Time through the machines and melted them to slag.

Asha leapt at the leader, becoming a red blur of motion. The Viking's broadsword split in half, his chest plate fell away in pieces, and with a great clatter he collapsed onto his back. Asha stood above him, blade point resting under his chin.

At the sight of their leader in danger, the underlings shook out of their stupor and charged Asha. Or they tried.

Valentine lifted her hand and the flow of Time *shifted*. Thousands of tiny *pops* filled the air at the warriors' feet. Microscopic ultra-fast Time bubbles weren't so useful on their own, but when used the right way, they created localized gravity wells—a little trick they'd learned from fighting Charlotte Corday.

The Techno-Vikings found themselves unable to attack, then unable to walk, then unable to move. In short order, they were on their backs and groaning at the heavy weight.

Malcolm conjured Entropy Blades. The shimmering distortions raced back and forth over the warriors' armor, slicing through metal as if it were shiny wrapping paper.

The twins approached amid threats and curses from all except for one man, who was crying about his ruined equipment.

"Oh, stop whining," Valentine said. "You're supposed to be tough."

"Not like you'll need that stuff where you're going," Malcolm added.

Drawing his device again, he aimed and fired with four identical *foomp*s. Four tiny portals spun to life, and the four henchmen disappeared in flashes of light, leaving only their leader.

"*I see you're enjoying the Portalizer,*" John said.

"I'd enjoy it more with a better name."

"*Those are fighting words, sir.*"

Malcolm chuckled, then put on a stern face as they gathered around the leader. "What are you here for?"

The leader spat at Malcolm. The extra gravity seized the

spit and pulled it back to splatter across his own face. Malcolm worked harder to appear serious.

"You didn't get here randomly," Valentine pressed. "Why here and now? Help us, and maybe we can help you."

He understood them. Malcolm could see it in his eyes. Yet, when he responded, it was still in his own language.

"He says you're not as smart as you think you are," John said, the worry evident in his voice. *"What could that mean?"*

Pondering, Malcolm leaned closer to study the leader's face. So he caught it when the man's eyes flicked over his shoulder. He felt it then—a faint presence in the Time stream.

"Get down!" he shouted, yanking Valentine and Asha to the pavement.

As they dropped, a puff of wind ruffled his hair. Dozens of steel projectiles slammed into the far wall, having barely missed their heads. Malcolm rolled, pulse pounding, as more steel chewed into the pavement.

He regained his feet, and flows of Time burst from him to prepare a dozen dangerous responses. Valentine and Asha mirrored him, standing ready.

At the alley's mouth, the air rippled like the surface of a pond, and a new figure stepped into view. Malcolm felt no *shifts* in Time—whoever this was, their tech wasn't powered by temporal energy.

Small and lithe, this new player moved with a catlike grace. *Possibly a woman.* Though her armor bore similar styling to the Techno-Vikings, it was sleeker and more finely crafted, displaying its futuristic origins openly.

The Future-Viking pointed toward them. Small compartments raised from her gauntlets, and Malcolm could see them reloading the spikes.

"Release the Konungr and escape with your lives." Her voice came out digitized, as if modulated by the helmet.

Malcolm shook his head. "He attacked our home, and we've got questions."

The gauntlets whined, preparing to fire. "I will not ask again."

As she spoke, a shadow emerged from a dark corner behind her back. Malcolm tensed. Another surprise player—one with their shadow-manipulating tech? He prepared to face them both.

But instead of joining the Future-Viking, the shadow lunged and enveloped her. Sounds of struggle echoed from the darkness. Malcolm exchanged uncertain glances with his companions.

With a heavy *clang,* the Future-Viking's helmet flew from the shadows. She stumbled back into the light and then toppled over, unconscious.

This is getting crazy, Malcolm thought. *Time to simplify.*

Hefting the Portalizer, he fired twice. The Techno-Viking and the Future-Viking both disappeared.

He aimed at the mass of shadows. Then they unraveled, leaving a familiar face.

"I guess you—" The newcomer stopped, crestfallen. "Aw, man, y'all sent her away too fast. I had a good victory line."

"Fred!" Malcolm said.

His old friend flashed a cocky grin. "In the flesh, dawg."

The four friends bunched together, exchanging greetings and volleying questions. Though there was much to catch up on, the reunion felt instantly like old times.

"You changed your hair," Valentine said, ruffling Fred's platinum-blond locks. Where before it had been longer and spiked in every direction, now it was cropped close. "Look at you, all sophisticated."

"New clothes, too," Malcolm observed, noting the unique cut of Fred's jacket. "You look like a world traveler."

"You're standing differently." Asha appraised Fred, then gripped his forearm in an old-style Roman handshake. "And you're stronger."

Fred gave an embarrassed grin. "Yeah, well, uh . . . two years can change a lot, I guess."

Malcolm gave him a second appraisal. Asha was right; the change went deeper than wardrobe.

Two years ago, not long after Winter found a new life in Everwatch, Fred had announced that he was leaving. Not forever, but something inside him had needed to go.

Everyone had understood. It was plain how badly he missed his friend. With his father globe-trotting nonstop for business, it was a perfect chance to see something new, and maybe figure out a few things. Though they kept in touch, Fred had not set foot in Emmett's Bluff for two years. Until today.

"How'd you find us?" Valentine asked.

Fred unzipped the jacket to reveal his gear belt from two years ago, designed by their dear, lost friend Clive Jessop.

"Still had it in my closet with the earpiece. Y'all still use the same comm frequency. Figured, why not crash the party?"

"*Welcome home, Fred,*" John said. "*Nice to have you back.*"

"Yo, thanks, brother," Fred said.

That reminded Malcolm. "Good game out there, John. Thanks for running overwatch."

"*Happy to do my part, as always.*"

"I'll thank you when I see you," Valentine said, a glint in her eye.

Malcolm gagged. "I did not need to hear that."

Valentine stuck her tongue out at him.

"We should leave," Asha said, taking Malcolm's hand. "Someone might have heard us."

"Let's get to the car," Malcolm said. "It's dinner time anyway. Want to come, Fred?"

"Your grandma cooking?"

"Yep."

"Sweet. You know I'm down," Fred said. "Hey, who were these dudes? It's like this town is flypaper for Time travelers."

"They were new," Valentine said. "Called themselves Techno-Vikings."

Fred rolled his eyes. "Lame."

"Yeah, and they weren't even close to being accurate," Malcolm said. "More like Tech-*Faux* Vikings, right?"

His laughter met with blank stares.

"Faux as in fake. You know?"

Fred snapped his fingers in recognition. "History nerd humor, right?"

"Uh, yeah. Guess it's not funny if I have to explain it."

Asha squeezed his hand. "I liked your joke."

He brightened. "So, you got it?"

"No."

Everyone did laugh at that.

Valentine. Malcolm. Asha. Now Fred. They would never notice her, but she kept her cloaking field active anyway.

Callie de la Vega—more recently, Callie Gilbert—lay atop a water tower a half-mile away, watching through the scope of a high-powered railgun, one of the few items she'd brought to this century with her.

Hacked into the little group's comm frequency, she

eavesdropped as they walked toward an old Honda. It was cute how much they loved that junk heap.

Callie squashed the smile. *Remember why you're doing this.*

The memories were buried deep, raw emotions suppressed under layers of training, layers acquired over five years of grueling work, plus more than two years in Emmett's Bluff. Layers that Callie peeled back now, allowing the memories to touch her again.

Darkness crept along her bones, seeping from the gaping wound of her memories. As Callie watched the twins climb into their old Civic, pure hate darkened the edges of her vision.

Her finger hovered over the trigger.

Don't, another part of her said. *You've seen the truth. You made your choice.*

Despite what the Regent had taught her—even what she had seen with her own eyes—Malcolm and Valentine could not be what everyone in her century thought them to be.

Still, Callie had lived with that conviction for so long, the hatred had baked into her bones. Even now, as she watched the twins she'd grown to love, an ancient part of her screamed to pull the trigger.

That was why she still watched them. Because, *what if.* What if she was wrong about them?

Her hands trembled as Valentine put the car in gear and drove out of sight. With a relieved sigh, Callie deflated.

An alert blinked at the corner of the HUD—her armor's Heads-Up Display. Her report was late again. She stared at the icon with dread, knowing she was about to lie again. Because she had to.

At her command, the report draft appeared before her eyes. She forced as much conviction into the lie as she could.

Regent,

The twins have evaded our justice again. They have proven

uncommonly intelligent and skilled, and their power is growing.

Still, I remain confident that the final solution is within my reach.

I will not fail you. I will chase them across the globe until our

people are safe.

Faithfully,

Calypso

As she hit *Send,* Callie's conscience ached. The Regent had rescued her, remade her, given her purpose again. Every false report betrayed him.

He would discover the truth eventually. When that day arrived, Callie hoped she could explain herself before he sent another assassin. She hoped he would understand.

A different alert broke her chain of thought. Neil's face appeared in the top left of her HUD. Callie forced a smile and accepted the call.

"Hello, dear."

"Hey, sweetie," Neil said. "Just checking when you'll be home. Mom's got the cornbread in the oven, and the twins are on their way."

Callie glanced at her chronograph and grimaced. She had lingered too long. Someone would have questions about her unusually long day. Even innocent questions could lead down a bad path.

"Oh, how nice. Do we have dessert? Maybe the twins could stop for ice cream."

"Good idea. I'll send them a text. You'll be home soon?"

"Just finishing up at the gym."

"Still? Wow, long run today."

"Well, if I'm going to eat ice cream *and* fit into that little dress you bought me . . ."

Neil chuckled. "Love you, babe."

"Love you. Bye."

Callie sprang to her feet. As her weapon folded away, she leapt from the tower and raced toward home at inhuman speed. By the time she arrived, Calypso would be buried underneath Callie Gilbert—journalist, new wife, devoted stepmother.

And nothing else.

CHAPTER 3

"Tech-*Faux* Vikings?" Neil Gilbert chuckled. "That's funny."

"It's really not," Valentine said.

From the kitchen table, Malcolm shot a pointed look at Valentine. "We both think it's funny, so you're outnumbered."

"No, she ain't, dude," Fred said.

Valentine grinned at the near-offended look on her brother's face, then at the way it softened when Asha wrapped his hand in both of hers. She seemed to love holding his hand that way. As if, even in this small gesture, she was committing all of herself.

The oven buzzed, and Valentine pulled out a sheet pan covered with cornbread. The smell made her mouth water almost as much as Oma Grace's stew—which Fred was currently trying to steal a spoonful of. Her grandmother appeared and swatted his arm.

"No thievery in this house, young man," she said. "You can wait like all the others."

Fred scooted away with a full spoon. "Sorry, can't hear ya. Whoa, what's this doing in my hand? Aw, no, not again." He brought the spoon to his lips, arm shaking as if he were resisting. "What's happening? It's coming for me!"

He gulped the spoonful, a satisfied grin on his face. Oma Grace gave one of her own.

"And now I know who's helping me with the dishes."

"Worth it," Fred said around the mouthful. "Missed ya, Oma."

Oma Grace patted his cheek. "Welcome home, my boy."

"I can hardly blame him," John said. That smells amazing."

He approached Valentine's side as she sliced the cornbread. His hand rested on her hip.

"Would you like help?" he whispered in her ear, sending warm tingles through her.

She shook her head. "Almost done. You can go relax."

Turning her head, she gazed into his deep brown eyes. His lips hovered inches from hers, so soft and tempting, so . . . she leaned in and stole a kiss. A girl could resist only so much temptation. John favored her with a deliriously happy smile and moved to the table where everyone was congregating.

"So, these Techno-Vikings," Neil said. "You took care of them pretty quickly."

Valentine considered. "Guess so. It's not like they were our first supervillains."

"That's one advantage to doing this so much," Malcolm said. "We're a better team now."

"Our tactics and coordination have improved," Asha agreed.

"Right on," Fred said. "Those Nerd-Vikings never stood a chance."

"Techno-Vikings," Valentine corrected.

"Whatever."

"You won?" Callie appeared, wrapped in a silk robe and shaking out still-damp hair. "Those warriors, they're gone?"

"Yep, problem solved," Malcolm said.

Callie smiled, her relief palpable. "Good. I'm glad you're all safe. Maybe things will be quieter now."

"Hope springs eternal," Neil replied. Moving toward Callie, he squeezed Valentine's shoulder as he passed by. "I'm proud of you kids. This town has no clue how much it owes you."

"Hear, hear!" Oma Grace cheered, holding her ladle high.

"Have a good workout?" Neil asked Callie as they came together.

She nodded, stroking the side of his face affectionately. They kept talking, but among the bustle of the kitchen, their conversation fell to whispers and flirty smiles.

Valentine grinned. Moments like this made it plain that the two of them were still newlyweds, happy just to be near each other. It warmed her heart to see their father like this again.

The improvement wasn't a one-way street, either. Early on, Valentine had accidentally seen Callie crying when she thought no one was looking. That hadn't happened in a long while. Not that Callie wasn't entitled to hard moments, but her inner glow had increased over the last two years.

It was nice. As far as Valentine was concerned, they'd all earned a little happiness.

"Five minutes, everyone," Oma Grace called. "Take your seats."

Plates and flatware clattered, glasses clinked, chairs scraped. Callie accidentally bumped an empty tea pitcher and gasped as it tumbled toward the floor, only to be snatched out of the air by Fred. Callie marveled at his reflexes, but he gave a nonchalant shrug. Soon they were gathered, awaiting Oma Grace and her culinary masterpiece.

"We did all right today," Malcolm said, tapping his chin. "But we could've done better."

Ah, yes, the source of their constant disappointment. Valentine sighed.

"The Chrona still hasn't showed, huh?" Fred asked.

Valentine shook her head. "We've tried everything to get her attention. I wonder if she's just ignoring us."

"Do you really need her?" Callie said. "You're doing great on your own."

"We're getting by," Malcolm said. "We're stronger than when we fought Corday, and we've figured out some new tricks. But . . ."

He trailed off, looking to Asha.

"In Everwatch, some of the Chrona's exploits are known," she said. "The feats she accomplished are legendary. You have achieved Sixth-*sev*, like her, and that would indicate . . ."

She, too, trailed off, but the implication was clear. If they were technically the same level as the Chrona—the ultimate authority over Time—then a huge gap in power and skill existed between them. They were missing something, and the only person who could show them wasn't taking their calls.

Only two others had achieved Sixth-*sev*. The Chrona's siblings had ascended with her, turned dark, and died long ago. Without the right guidance, Valentine doubted the twins could ever achieve their full potential.

"Still, we should celebrate the progress you *have* made," their dad said.

Valentine gave him a grateful smile. "We do. I just feel like we've been given something amazing, but without an instruction manual."

"We never know what skills we'll need in the future," Malcolm added. "There are more bad guys out there."

"Speaking of futures," Oma Grace called from the stove.

"Senior year is approaching. Have you all given thought to what comes after?"

"Good question," Neil said. "A year's not long to plan, after all."

Valentine exchanged a knowing look with Malcolm. Of course this subject was coming—it was inevitable. The twins had spent many nights talking about this very thing. She had also spent time with John, searching for colleges they could both attend. It was important to them all that they do something real with their lives. And yet it was hard to know exactly what that meant.

Before the silence could turn awkward, Fred jumped in. "One thing's for sure—now that I've seen some of the world, I wanna see more."

"I've known my calling since I was small," Asha said. "I consider High Protector of the Ember Guard to be my only profession."

Valentine wondered at the steel in the girl's voice, and how it contrasted with the tenderness in her ice-blue eyes when she gazed at Malcolm. No matter how she was dressed, her armor only truly came off in his presence.

Even more pleasing was the enchantment on Malcolm's face, his fingers gently twirling a lock of Asha's long black hair. *Two years ago, he thought he'd be alone forever.*

John spoke next. "Since my profession is decided, thanks to Clive, I'll attend college to further my passion. I don't know what major that will translate to yet."

That made sense. In his will, Clive had left his prestigious—and surprisingly lucrative—auto restoration shop to John, who had taken to it with more excitement than Valentine expected. Then again, it was no regular shop.

John would probably choose something like electrical or mechanical engineering. He was never happier than when he was building some new gadget.

He looked to Valentine, which meant it was her turn.

"Physics," she said. "Not sure what application, but yeah. I love it too much to leave it behind when school ends." She squeezed John's hand. "So, we'll be a couple of science geeks our whole lives."

John gave a warm smile and squeezed back. The table grew quiet again as all eyes drifted to Malcolm, who stared wide-eyed at his plate.

"Uh," he said. "Uhhhh . . ."

"Something with history, maybe?" Callie offered.

"Aw, yeah, that's totally your thing, bro," Fred said.

"Uh, well, maybe." Malcolm shrugged. "Honestly, right now I just want to learn to fly."

Valentine studied him quizzically. "Like, in a plane?"

"No. Like, with what we can do."

She smirked. "Fly. Right."

"I mean it, Val. We can already play with gravity a little bit, so why not?"

"Mal, that's basic at best. We can't actually warp gravity; we just play some tricks with Time and it works out that way."

His face fell. "Yeah. One more reason we need a teacher. I mean, even with all we can do now, the day may come when someone doesn't go down so easily."

Neil's expression clouded. "You really think that could happen?"

"It has happened before," Valentine admitted.

"Given how many temporal disturbances occur here, it's best to be prepared," Asha said. "I've spoken with Everwatch, and even they don't know why Emmett's Bluff attracts all this activity."

"If more show up, we'll send 'em to the Pendulum like all the rest." Fred gave the table an enthusiastic thump. "Right, y'all?"

With that comment, the conversation steered back to a brighter tone. Valentine gave Fred a grateful nod, and he returned a knowing wink.

The twins were fortunate to have all this. Watching everyone, Valentine reminded herself how rare it was. Family and friends that trusted each other, no dark secrets waiting to catch them unawares.

Their extended family even transcended Time and space. Hidden over a thousand years in the past, Everwatch was home to more. Winter had sent a few letters to update them on her life, assuring them that she'd found real happiness. Asha's brother Tyrathorn lived there as well, and from what they'd learned through Asha, the people of Everwatch were rebuilding their trust in him.

With the approval of King Jerrik and Queen Meliora, he had even worked with the twins to form a stronger partnership. One result was the Pendulum, a highly advanced prison built underneath the Eon Palace in Everwatch.

They had needed somewhere to contain the time-traveling criminals and psychopaths the twins defeated. Soon after it was built, the Ember Guard began adding to the population. It felt good to work together on something that would protect more people across the Timeline.

Oma Grace's huge red pot *thunk*ed down on the table, interrupting Valentine's thoughts. A heavenly smell wafted toward her.

"Enjoy, everyone!"

As they reached for the food, Neil suddenly stood. "Hold on. Just one more thing."

Valentine sat back, exchanging a curious glance with her brother. *Well, this is new.*

"I just want to say, um . . ." He paused, suddenly unsure. Callie quietly reached out to take his hand. With one look at her, his hesitation evaporated. "Through Time travel and supervillains, through what we've lost and gained along the way, nothing will be more important than what's in this room right now. We're family. No matter what this universe throws at us, we'll always be family. You all make me proud, and I love you." With his free hand, he grasped teary-eyed Oma Grace's shoulder. "So, let's remember tonight, okay? Because moments like this, they're what really matter."

This time, a different kind of quiet enveloped the table. Not one of awkwardness, but of gratitude, and a tidal wave of other happy emotions. Valentine felt a pleasant sting behind her eyes and dabbed at them with her napkin. The Neil Gilbert of two years ago could never have done that. Then again, the Valentine Gilbert of two years ago couldn't have appreciated it.

"Okay, enough sappiness. Let's eat!" Neil said, which drew a laugh from everyone.

On John's other side, Fred gave a subtle sniff and turned away to wipe his eyes.

John eyed his friend. "Are you crying?"

"No! *You're* crying!" Fred said. "I mean . . . yeah, okay? That was beautiful, or whatever. Fight me, bro."

Valentine laughed until her sides hurt.

"They're so beautiful," Valentine said.

She leaned against John's car in her driveway. Stroking the back of his neck, she stared up at the stars. Here in Emmett's Bluff, the clear night sky glittered like a field of diamonds.

"They're perfect," John said.

He wasn't looking up. He had never stopped gazing at her. She studied the ground, suddenly bashful.

John slid his hands around her waist, and instinctively she leaned into his embrace. Butterflies danced in her stomach. *How can he still do that to me?*

Just before their lips touched, the front door of Valentine's house opened.

"Nice!" Fred said. "Keepin' the romance alive."

Valentine giggled. As Fred stepped across the lawn, a shiny, black limousine rolled up to the curb. Fred threw them a wave before diving inside.

"Later, y'all. Yo, what up, Jeeves? Back to the pad."

"When will he adopt slang from this century?" Valentine said.

"I would guess never," John said. "It's good to have him back."

"Yeah. All that travel was good for him, too." Valentine snuggled tighter against John, luxuriating in his scent, the calm baritone of his voice.

John brushed a lock of wavy, red hair away from her eyes. "So, physics, hm?"

"Yeah," she said. "When they asked, it just came out. But the more I think about it, the more it feels right. I mean, whatever happens with all this Chronauri stuff, I'll always be a science geek. I figure, why not embrace it?"

John kissed the tip of her nose. "I like it. Find a school you like?"

"Not yet. I know, I'm a bad nerd, right? I should have a road map for how I'm going to dominate the scientific world."

He grinned. "Well, you've been busy. Saving your town twice is a good excuse."

"Think I can put that on scholarship applications?"

"If only."

"I figure the Chronauri stuff will always be there, no matter what else I do. Always a new threat to put down." Valentine's expression turned wistful. "Don't get me wrong, I love what we can do. I want to keep doing it. I just don't want it to be all I'm about. You know?"

"I do." John's finger traced a line down her chin, then her neck, and circled her collarbone, sending sparks through her. "What we're doing is important, but we deserve to have real lives, too. Be real people."

She smiled in relief. Until now, she hadn't realized she'd been worried about whether or not they still wanted the same things. After all, it wasn't like many teenage romances lasted. Hearing his words now, on the cusp of so many big life decisions—it felt like coming home.

"One thing I do know: I'll take any future, as long as you're in it." Valentine pulled him closer and whispered. "I love you, John."

She lost herself in him for a blissful slice of eternity.

Asha loved to dance.

Malcolm knew she wouldn't openly admit it, but whenever they could steal a few moments for themselves, this was what she asked for. They stood in his backyard now, arms around each other while their favorite slow song played from his phone.

No other feeling could equal these moments, when his Chronauri and her Ember Guard slipped away, leaving two teenagers who'd met across Time and fallen in love.

Inside one of his Time-conjured snow globes, Malcolm swayed with Asha. He drank in her scent. The feel of her hands as one caressed the back of his neck while the other rested on his chest. The warmth in her ice-blue eyes as she gazed up at him like he was the only thing in her world.

As snowflakes swirled around them, Malcolm beheld the girl who'd run away with his heart. The look in her eyes filled him inside, like fire and gentle rain all at once.

"You're just too beautiful," he said. "Stop it right now."

Laughing, Asha drew closer. The song finished, repeated, and she started to sway again. He thrilled in the sensation of her pressed against him.

"Did you mean what you said?" she asked. "Not knowing about your future."

Malcolm nodded. "I admire you. You've known all along what you were meant to do. Wish I could be the same."

"Maybe we can figure it out together."

Malcolm brushed his fingers through her hair. "I'd like that. Right now, I just don't want my life to feel small. When I look at colleges, it's not like I hate them, it's just that they don't fit. The thought of picking *one* thing to do with my future—it's like pulling on a shirt that's three sizes too small. Sure, you could wear it, but you'd never forget that it wasn't made for you." He glanced at the ground. "Sorry, I know that's not a satisfying answer."

"Hey." Slipping both hands behind his neck, Asha pulled

him into a soft, tender kiss that spread warmth all the way to his toes. "It's *you* I want, not your profession. If I have you to the end of my days, I'm happy."

Malcolm wrapped both arms around her waist. She melded to his touch as if their bodies had been created for each other.

"How in Eternity did I deserve you?"

"Shut up," she whispered. "And come here."

He didn't remember when they started kissing. All at once her lips filled him with life. Her touch wrapped him in this moment, and he wished only that it would never end. Maybe this was why people craved love and feared it. Because once you have it, nothing else feels like enough.

Malcolm felt a *shift* nearby. Breaking off their kiss, he absorbed a rush of Time and prepared to defend. The snow globe shattered. He tried to step in front of Asha, while she tried to step in front of him.

A new presence glowed in Malcolm's Chronauri senses. He felt—almost saw—the Time stream flowing around it. Then its signature became clear, and he stopped struggling with Asha over who was protecting whom. Instead, he peered toward a row of tall hedges near the back door.

"Val?"

Sheepishly, his sister stepped into view.

"Sorry," she said. "Didn't want to interrupt. John left a few minutes ago, and I thought maybe we could . . ."

Malcolm caught her meaning. "Try looking for her again?"

"We probably should, yeah. Sorry."

"It's all right. This is important," Asha said. Untangling from Malcolm, she placed a last kiss on his cheek before moving toward her house. Technically, it was Walter's old house, but they had made it her home for the past two years. "Good night. I hope you find her."

Malcolm watched her leave, acutely feeling the empty space she left between his arms. Giving himself a shake, he forced his thoughts back to their quest.

"Okay. I'm ready."

Wind howled through the night, buffeting trees and rattling the shutters on the twins' house. Their clothes and hair flapped wildly in the gale. Somewhere, a branch groaned and snapped.

Malcolm pushed harder.

Closing his eyes, he opened his being more than ever before. It ached as if he were trying to stretch a limb too far, but he refused to let up. Vast quantities of Time poured through him as if he were a funnel trying to redirect a river. Each time he did this, that funnel grew a little bigger. Every night he drove himself harder, channeling a little more energy than he could before.

Beside him, he could feel a constant Time *shift* the size of a mountain. Valentine's actions mirrored his own, her corona glowing a bright, silvery white.

They didn't manipulate the energy. Just opened themselves like living conduits and let it flow through them, then back into the Timeline. Having tried everything else, the twins had conceived this last, desperate strategy: Channel so much Time that the Chrona couldn't help but notice them.

It had been more than a month now, and nothing. Still, they couldn't stop trying.

"More, Mal," Valentine said, straining. "We need more."

Malcolm gave a reluctant grunt, dreading the bone-deep discomfort he was about to ask for. "Alright. *Now.*"

They pushed themselves up another level, gasping as torrents of temporal energy poured through them. A tremor passed through the Timeline, radiating out for weeks in both directions—which explained the weird anomaly they had felt several weeks back, on the last day of junior year. Thunder cracked overhead and lighting arced from cloud to cloud.

Malcolm felt a sensation that had become familiar over the past months. As their ability to wield Time expanded, so did their awareness, their ability to stretch their consciousness along the Timeline. At first it had been days, then months, then years. Now they could cast their thoughts more than a century into the past or the future.

They forbade themselves from studying future events too closely. That kind of knowledge was scary. Instead they let Time flash by and concentrated on broadcasting their signatures out to the universe.

"It feels so old. So worn," Valentine said. "The Timeline."

Malcolm felt it, too. A black spiderweb of cracks slowly spread across the Aegis—what Everwatch called the boundary that contained the Time stream. As if it bore a heavy strain and was slowly breaking under the weight. How much could it crack before breaking completely?

"Yeah," he said. "The Chrona ignores us, and it seems like she's ignoring the Timeline. So, where is she?"

"And what's she doing? Even Everwatch is worried."

"They say it wasn't always like this. All the cracks, the Time travelers causing trouble."

"Would Time travelers be part of the problem? They've got to be damaging the Timeline."

A light bulb went on in Malcolm's head. He'd been puzzling over something for weeks, and Valentine's words finally brought it all together. Casting his thoughts further, he traced along the curves of the Aegis. It was wildly uneven, solid as steel in some places, weak and cracking like an eggshell in others.

"That's what's been bothering me," he said. "The Chrona built controls over Time, right?"

"That's what Everwatch says."

"If that's true, then I think she made mistakes."

Even through the howling winds and thundering sky, Malcolm felt his sister turn toward him, radiating disbelief.

"She pretty much saved all of Time."

"Yeah, but the way it's built, it's like she assumed no one else would try to Time travel. She made controls that were supposed to prevent it, but those are failing, and the Aegis can't handle it."

Valentine's voice grew heavy. "So, now, when someone manipulates Time the wrong way, a little bit of the universe cracks."

"And you can only crack something so much before it shatters."

"So . . . can we fix it?"

Malcolm gave a bleak chuckle. "I don't have the faintest clue." He felt further along the Timeline, his consciousness touching a day 112 years in the future. "Would we be strong enough to—"

He stopped, alarm bells ringing in his head.

"Whoa," Valentine said. "Do you feel that?"

He did, and his throat went dry. "What . . . what is that?"

"I don't know." He heard Valentine swallow hard. "I guess we should, um, take a closer look."

With every fiber of his being, Malcolm wished he could avoid that. A wave of unnatural dread sank into his bones, begging him to turn and run. He squashed it as best he could.

"Yeah. Guess so."

With a slow, deep breath, he forced his Chronauri senses to extend just a little more. A nearby ripple touched him as Valentine did the same. The dread grew like a weight around his neck.

The sensation started as a *wrongness*. Malcolm's instincts knew that something was not right with the Timeline here. That the universe itself was in pain. He had felt cracks forming before, but this . . . this was something else entirely.

"We need to get closer," he said, even as his heart pounded a drum beat. He felt Valentine's hand searching for his and grasped it.

"Okay," she said. "*Now.*"

They leapt forward, awareness extended now to 116 years in the future. They gasped as a wave washed over them—like intense heat, but from flames burning on a deeper level of perception. As if they had turned a corner in the Timeline and discovered a raging wall of fire.

Hand in hand, the twins took another temporal step forward. Then they could advance no farther, but still the wall of fire drew closer.

"Whatever it is," Valentine said, "it's moving backward through Time."

Like a burning storm front, the wall of flame continued rolling toward them from the future. They stood their ground as the heat grew unbearably intense.

This close to it, Malcolm suddenly understood why it had filled him with dread. Beneath the heat, there was a sound only his Chronauri senses could hear. A terrible sound like screaming, as if something in the distance wailed in agony and despair.

The wall of fire came within reach. Those screams raked at his heart. Malcolm almost fell sobbing to his knees, overwhelmed by the feeling of souls dying hopeless and terrified. Only the solidity of Valentine's hand kept him anchored.

"Mal, the black," Valentine said urgently. "The black. Do you see it?"

He saw it now. Whatever hid behind that wall of flames wasn't just making a tunnel as their enemies had before. It was literally burning through Time, destroying temporal energy and leaving a scorched wake of destruction in its path.

"Oh, God," Malcolm breathed. "What could do this?"

Valentine's only response was panicked breathing.

They were face to face with it now. Could they stop it here? End the destruction before it reached its destination, whenever that may be?

They had to try.

Anchoring his presence at that point in the Timeline, Malcolm summoned a wave of Time energy to his side. A nearby *shift* signaled Valentine doing the same. He clenched his jaw in determination. *Unstoppable force, meet immovable objects.* The twins reached out together, pressing their energy against the flames and willing them to stop.

Agony. Burning, intense, bone-charring.

Terror.

Despair.

Hopeless.   Alone.   Dying.

Over and over again, dying.

A wave of force burst from the fire, blasting them back through the Timeline until they crashed into their bodies.

Malcolm's hand tore free of Valentine's as they were blown

off their feet. They tumbled to the grass, groaning as residual heat burned under their skin. Every muscle ached. For a long moment, they lay there catching their breath.

Slowly the agonizing sensation faded. The sky above calmed. Malcolm found just enough strength to rub his face.

"Ow," he said through his fingers.

"Yeah," Valentine croaked. "Ow."

Eventually, he pulled up to his knees. Valentine followed, and as she did, their eyes locked. It had been two years since Malcolm had seen that kind of fear in his sister. She must have seen the same fear in him. Staring at each other now, they spoke in unison.

"What was that?"

CHAPTER 4

The flames kept getting closer.

In the den of Walter's house, Valentine sat curled up in his old leather recliner. Cradling her head, she rubbed her temples and wished the headache away yet again. Ever since they had touched that . . . thing . . . a week ago, it had lingered in the back of her head like a bad dream.

What started as subtle pressure was building to a dull throb. Each day it grew worse as that wall of fire loomed closer.

Malcolm stirred on Walter's couch. He looked like she felt: his eyes were glassy and unfocused with dark circles underneath. He moved sluggishly, but brightened as Asha appeared with steaming cups of tea.

"Everwatch cannot decipher it," she said, sitting next to Malcolm. "They are finding Time travel more difficult, and my communication link with them has become unstable. This must be the phenomenon Winter warned us about."

"I figured as much," Valentine said.

"It doesn't matter what we do," Malcolm said. "The same thing happens every time."

Valentine winced at the memories. Multiple times now, the

twins had stretched out their perceptions to explore it. Each time, they had been thrown back with overwhelming force.

"We don't even know where it's going, or when," she added, "much less how to stop it."

"Maybe we won't need to," Malcolm said, forcing hope into his voice. "Maybe it'll just pass us by. It's not really hurting anyone."

"No," Asha replied, ruffling his hair. "Just blazing across Time, leaving a burnt trail of temporal ash in its wake. Perhaps it wants to be friends."

"You've been here too long," Malcolm said. "Now you're learning our sarcasm."

"We may be flying blind," Valentine said, "but we still need a strategy in case something bad happens."

"Agreed," Asha said. "Some manner of—"

A knock at the front door interrupted her. Then, unbidden, the door opened. Instantly the twins were on their feet, and Asha flew across the room to draw her *qamas*. Valentine opened herself, and Time's radiance rushed in. There was a *shift* next to her, and Malcolm's corona glowed.

"Valentine?" a familiar voice called.

They froze, eyeing each other, and burst into laughter.

"It's possible," Malcolm said, "that we're a little on edge."

"Back here, Callie," Valentine called. She added with a whisper, "Crap, we were supposed to go clothes shopping. I totally forgot."

"You should go," Malcolm said. "We need a break."

Asha agreed. "Just keep this to yourself."

Valentine nodded. They had decided that after their first encounter. No sense worrying everyone until it became something to worry about.

Callie appeared in the doorway, wearing a stunning combination of dark jeans, red high heels, a silk top that wrapped around her lithe torso, and the thousand-watt smile their dad had fallen for.

She had taken an interest in teaching Valentine how to dress fashionably, which Valentine had resisted. That is, until John saw Valentine modeling one outfit and practically had to scoop his jaw off the floor. Her resistance had melted that day.

"Hey, guys," Callie said, then focused on Valentine. "Ready?"

"I can't pull this off."

"You totally can."

"I look ridiculous."

"You haven't even looked in the mirror."

"Dad will totally hate it."

"John will totally love it. And soon enough, your dad will realize you're growing up."

"Are you sure we can't—?"

Callie grasped Valentine by the shoulders. The intricate silver bracelet on her left wrist jangled, its red gems catching the light as she turned Valentine toward the mirror. Valentine caught sight of herself.

"Ooooh," she said, stunned.

She wore a short, green sundress, the kind that cinched and flowed in all the right places. High heels—higher than she had ever owned—that shouldn't have worked with the dress but somehow totally did. Had her eyes always popped like that? Even distracted, with visions of fire gnawing inside her skull, she felt beautiful.

Callie peered over Valentine's shoulder, catching her eye in the mirror. "Say it."

She sighed contentedly. "John will love it."

Callie's eyes sparkled. "And yes, your father will hate it. But in this case, that may not be a bad thing, right?"

Valentine's throat tightened as she held back tears. *I've missed this so much.* Two years ago, she never would have believed someone could fill the void in her family. Callie wasn't her mother, but she had become something irreplaceable. Eyes stinging, she placed her hand over her stepmother's.

"Thank you," she said, a whisper all she could manage.

Callie smiled—a different one than the red-carpet flash of glamour she used with everyone else. This one was deeper. She bit her lip, holding back her own tears, and cleared her throat.

"Let's get you checked out. We have one more stop."

Ten minutes later, they exited with bags in hand and turned to walk farther along the strip mall. A surprising number of nice boutiques had sprung up recently. Although Emmett's Bluff was still recovering from Lucius Carmichael's energy beams and Charlotte Corday's ice monsters, it was going to come back even better.

Lost in conversation, Valentine almost forgot the throbbing in her head. The pressure had moved so far into the background that she stopped in shock as it roared back to life.

Stronger than ever, it squeezed her temples like a red-hot vise. Her Chronauri senses screamed, the wall of flames flaring brighter, hotter. In her mind, she saw a beam of fire lance out from the wall and burn across Time like a missile.

Distantly she heard Callie's voice, tight and concerned. *It's moving so fast!* The universe was hurting. She could almost hear its cries. The fire missile loomed in her mind, filling her senses and . . .

Somewhere in Emmett's Bluff, the Timeline burst open.

As the cries of the universe turned to screams, Valentine's bags dropped from her hands. Whatever this thing was, it had just torn through a portal into today.

Callie's voice begged to know what was wrong. Valentine forced her eyes open.

"Something's here," she croaked. "Something bad."

Callie came instantly alert. "What is it? What do you need?"

"Don't know, but it's . . . aaah!"

She winced as the wall flared again, then again, sending two more fire missiles through the Timeline. Somewhere on the north side of town, another portal ripped open.

The third one didn't veer away. With sinking dread, Valentine knew why. She stepped in front of Callie and steeled herself.

The fire missile blew a hole in the Timeline right in the parking lot. The opening roared like a predator, a gaping maw of blackness wreathed in flames. Spiderwebs of pitch-black cracks spread out from it, as if the fabric of the universe were scorching like dried paper.

Valentine clutched her temples. The screams of a universe were a nauseating punch to the gut. Then there were human screams as shoppers ran for shelter inside the shops.

From inside the portal, there came a heavy *clank*. Then another. The pavement vibrated as a giant metal foot stomped through the maelstrom.

"Oh, no," Callie said. "No, please not this."

A second foot appeared, cracking the pavement.

Disoriented as she was, Valentine didn't know whether to stare at the portal or Callie. *Why is she saying that?*

Her questions died as a fifteen-foot-tall machine burst through the portal. No, not just a machine—a walking, robotic tank. A triangle of green laser beams erupted from its shoulder and traced over its surroundings, as if searching.

"Stonewall-class Destroyer. Val, run!"

Callie grabbed Valentine and dragged her away. Aching and disoriented, Valentine dug in her heels and pointed back at the robot.

"Callie, what—?"

Callie grabbed her by both arms. "Val, you've got to run *now*."

"Why?"

"Because it's here for—"

A glowing green triangle appeared on Valentine's chest. For an instant, both women stared in shock. Then came a cold, robotic voice.

"*ACQUIRED.*"

Callie swore as the machine pointed in their direction. Its left arm split open to reveal a massive cannon.

Valentine absorbed Time and formed a fast-moving bubble around them. Searing pain lanced into her head like a white-hot poker, shattering her focus. Valentine cried out and the bubble burst.

With a high-pitched whine, energy projectiles burst from the Destroyer's cannon, leaving light trails in their wake. Valentine could only watch as they loomed closer.

Is this it? she thought in the instant she had left. *Is this how it ends?*

Throwing her arms around Valentine, Callie spun. The projectiles struck her between the shoulder blades and exploded.

Then they were flying, thrown by a concussion wave. They crashed through a plateglass window into a boutique, reducing a rack of wooden shelves to splinters before tumbling to the carpet in a heap.

Callie groaned as debris piled on top of them. Valentine tried to stand. Stars filled her vision and she fell back to hands and knees.

"Holy crap," she said, struggling for a full breath. "H-how did we survive that?"

Outside, a car exploded. Then another. She could hear people screaming. The town needed her! But right now, her limbs were made of gelatin.

The Destroyer appeared at the broken window, green lasers searching. As they swept toward Valentine, Callie plucked her off the floor and ran at the nearest wall.

Without breaking stride, she gave a shout and punched the drywall. The sheetrock caved and she flung them both through the opening. A blast filled the shop behind them as they rolled into the adjacent shop.

Valentine flopped onto her back and stared through the hole in the wall. The shop they had vacated was no longer a shop; it was a war zone.

"It's not supposed to happen like this," Callie muttered, scrambling to her feet.

"What do you mean? And how are you doing this?"

"This was supposed to be a last resort!" Callie stared up at the ceiling, looking lost. Then her eyes went wide. "He knows. He knows I lied, and now they've come!"

"Who?"

Tremors in the ground interrupted: the metallic clunk of approaching footsteps.

"Someone's going to get killed," Valentine said. "I've got to—"

Halfway to her feet, her vision swam. She found herself back on the floor, dazed from concussive blasts and the burning in her head. She commanded her body to move, to—

A strong hand gripped her shoulder.

"No, Val. Stay down," Callie said. "I've got this."

Valentine stared up at her, more confused than ever.

The Destroyer rounded into view, beams sweeping back and forth, searching for them. As Callie stepped toward it, her face changed.

Callie Gilbert, always sweet and glamorous, melted away. In her place was someone Valentine had never met. Someone with death in her eyes. She tensed like a coiled snake . . .

. . . then ran at the machine.

"No!" Valentine cried.

Moving at inhuman speed, Callie flung herself through the open window. As her feet left the ground, she pressed a jewel on her bracelet.

Somehow, it unfolded. While Callie sailed toward the parking lot, the trinket multiplied and expanded. Shiny segments, deep purple with accents of silver and black, spread out from her wrist and raced across her body and locked together.

Callie's hands touched the ground. She flipped forward, then landed on her feet and skidded to a halt as the last segments locked into place. The Destroyer paused, noting her in its path, clad head-to-toe in . . .

Armor. Valentine gaped. *Callie has super-advanced armor hidden in her bracelet?*

A thousand questions collided in her dazed mind. Before she could get them all straight, the Destroyer attacked.

More weapons popped out from the behemoth, spewing light and fire and steel. Everything in a fifty-foot radius turned to ash or debris. Except for Callie, who raced around the walking tank with astonishing speed and agility.

The Destroyer's arm cannon glowed, firing round after round. Callie danced aside, then grabbed hold of the outstretched arm and vaulted up the machine as if it were a jungle gym.

As she scrambled toward its domelike helmet, light traced over the segments of her armor and collected at her gauntlets. She slapped her hands over the Destroyer's mechanical "eyes," and with a *whoosh* she fired two concentrated blasts.

The Destroyer stumbled back, disoriented. Callie climbed down the arm cannon and hugged it tightly, then fired her boosters in opposite directions. She became a blur, spinning like a tornado as a deafening metal screech filled the air. The arm cannon ripped free and fell to the ground.

Even with her head pounding, Valentine whooped with joy. Just as quickly, her whoop choked off.

As Callie disentangled herself from the cannon, the Destroyer's shoulder-mounted railgun spun to life. Steel projectiles raked across her left flank with staccato pings.

Callie flew backward, skipped and rolled across the pavement, and disappeared.

What? Valentine looked in all directions, finding no trace of her stepmother. If she tried searching with Chronauri senses, would she even be able to right now?

Before she could decide, she caught a hint of movement

beside the Destroyer. A small device appeared on its right flank, seemingly from nowhere. A single red light blinked.

Three heartbeats later, the device exploded. The Destroyer lurched to the side, flailing and firing its railgun but hitting nothing.

Twin beams of red energy burst from nowhere to hit the same spot. Armor plating that had buckled was now boiling away.

It dawned on Valentine then. *A cloaking device.* Callie was fighting firepower with stealth and agility. *And so far, she's winning.*

As if it heard her thoughts, the Destroyer reversed a half-dozen steps and leaned back to face the sky. Its chest unfolded to reveal a bank of six missiles. In a blink, all six launched into the air, only to turn back and slam into the ground around the machine.

The explosion was deafening. Valentine hugged the ground as flames and debris and hot wind flew overhead. When they passed, she saw with horror that the tactic had worked. Callie's cloak probably worked by bending light around her. What it couldn't bend was fire and shrapnel, and so, the wave of destruction outlined her hidden form.

The Destroyer appeared through the flames. Grabbing Callie with its remaining hand, the machine cocked back and drove its fist through the pavement. Arms pinned, steel and concrete hemming her in, Callie struggled but could not break free.

Valentine's heart froze. *No!*

The Destroyer moved slowly now, as if it wanted Callie to feel what was about to happen. The laser points glowed on her chest, then moved up to her helmet. The railgun began to spin.

Valentine heard someone scream. It might have been her. *No. No, you can't take her, too.*

Somehow she found her feet. Beckoning to Time, she screamed as its power filled her.

Intent on turning the railgun to superheated slag, Valentine trapped the weapon inside a bubble of fast Time and drove it with every ounce of her will, forcing Time inside it to spin faster and faster until the bubble transformed.

The *shift* deepened, taking on a life of its own. The Time bubble collapsed into a pinpoint of light. Then the light became the deepest black she had ever seen.

Slowly it expanded again, becoming the size of a tangerine, then a baseball. Gauzy waves of blackness wafted from the black orb, cresting and swirling and collapsing again.

As the orb gained strength, the foreign feeling inside Valentine grew with it. Somehow, while Time streamed around this thing as normal, inside all that blackness was nothing. A deeper nothing than she thought existed. This wasn't a Time *shift.*

It was a Time *void.*

When it reached the size of a softball, everything changed. It touched the railgun and the weapon crumpled, warping and bending toward the orb as if it were a cosmic black hole. With an earsplitting screech, the railgun tore free and plunged into the inky depths.

The orb grew. The Destroyer's frame warped toward it now, sucked in by the strange and unstoppable power.

Now Valentine had a new problem. *What happens if it keeps getting bigger?* She couldn't afford to wait and find out. *If it's a void, then it can't be popped like a bubble.* It would have to be closed.

Valentine focused her will to create a shell of Time around the black orb. Opening herself, she channeled a raging river of temporal energy into the shell, filling it until the pressure of all that focused Time began to impose itself on the black orb.

It works! Valentine pushed harder, awash in relief as the orb shrank, and then collapsed and disappeared. With a sigh of relief, she released her shell and focused on the original problem.

But the Destroyer was badly damaged—twisted, misshapen, barely able to move. Its fighting days were over. Valentine reached out, intending to conjure one of Malcolm's Entropy Blades and cut Callie free.

Before she could, a *shing-hum* echoed from the hole in the pavement. A glowing plasma blade extended from Callie's forearm and sliced through the hand that held her captive. As the mechanical fingers fell away in pieces, Callie gave a savage shout and leapt.

Her boosters pulsed and she flew straight up, swinging the plasma blade like a reaper's scythe. Metal screeched and melted as Callie cleaved through the Destroyer from bottom to top, leaving a glowing trail in her wake.

The war machine split into halves and toppled. It lay there smoking and silent. Callie landed among the wreckage and deactivated the plasma blade with a flourish.

The fiery portal collapsed, taking Valentine's agony with it. She breathed a sigh and staggered out of the boutique. Callie turned as she approached.

On closer inspection, the armor Callie wore wasn't metal. *Some kind of ceramic?* The overlapping plates moved with both rigidity and flexibility, almost like scales. It hugged Callie's athletic form, yet somehow had enough room to hide weapons and who knew what else.

The three gems that had adorned her bracelet now glowed at the center of her chest plate. Despite her questions, and her fear of what the answers might reveal, the science geek inside Valentine couldn't help but marvel.

She stopped at arm's length. Then she noticed Callie wasn't looking at her. Valentine peered in the same direction and her insides lurched.

Inside the Destroyer's armor was a cockpit.

"Was someone inside that thing?"

"Destroyers have pilots. The smaller models don't," Callie replied, her voice strangely digitized. "They're pulled through portals when the rig is compromised. Like an ejector seat."

Valentine faced her stepmother squarely now. "What the . . . how in . . . I mean . . ."

With subtle *whirring*, Callie's helmet peeled open and folded away. Waves of conflicting emotions crashed over her face. Her lips worked as she searched for words. Valentine waited, desperate to hear anything that would make sense of this.

"Valentine, I—"

Police sirens wailed in the distance. Valentine noticed then that they had drawn a crowd. Though they kept their distance, those who hadn't fled the Destroyer now gawked at the women who'd taken it down.

She gave a frustrated huff. *So much for getting answers now.*

"We have to go," Callie said with regret. "I'll answer everything, but right now there's more to worry about. This won't be the only one they sent. Okay?"

Pursing her lips, Valentine nodded. "Did our car get blown up?"

"Too slow."

Deploying her helmet, she moved behind Valentine and looped an arm around her waist.

"Trust me," Callie whispered.

Boosters fired. They rocketed into the sky, warm winds whipping Valentine's red hair as Emmett's Bluff sank away. She fought down a thrill of excitement. *You're not supposed to be enjoying this!* Yet, as they raced toward the clouds and split the air with a sonic boom, she couldn't help herself.

In less than a minute their neighborhood came into view. As Callie slowed and they descended, Valentine caught sight of their house.

Her heart dropped into her stomach.

"Oh, no."

CHAPTER 5

Malcolm stood on his front lawn as flaming chunks of steel rained down. He closed his eyes to savor the fact that everyone had survived.

He and Asha had stepped outside to greet John as he arrived when the universe had screamed and a fiery portal had burned its way through Time. If that wasn't shock enough, the giant battle robot and its two human-sized robot sidekicks made up the difference.

John appeared through the dissipating smoke, all his gadgetry powering down. The bow he had taken from Charlotte Corday's minion came in handy. He stopped at Malcolm's side and removed his glowing goggles.

"Something tells me this wasn't an isolated incident."

"It wasn't. I felt two more portals," Malcolm said. "The ring of fire, the black cracks. I've never seen one like that."

"Nor have I," Asha said.

She approached from what remained of the street, the red glow fading from her *qamas* and armor. As she passed a human-sized robot, it suddenly lurched. Without looking down, she flicked her blade and its head flew away in pieces.

"Why would someone make a portal this way?" she continued. "It almost appeared deliberately destructive."

Valentine's Time signature sliced through their perception and cut off Malcom's reply. She approached from a direction he didn't expect. He peered skyward.

"More coming?" Asha raised her weapons.

"It's Val," Malcolm said as a distant figure burst through the clouds.

"And someone else." John slid his goggles on, tapped the side, and stiffened. "It's a machine."

Malcolm opened to Time once again, willing Entropy Blades to form around his hands.

"If something took her hostage . . ." he began.

"I'll slice it to shreds," Asha finished.

John quietly selected an arrow, nocked it, and waited.

But as Valentine drew closer, something struck Malcolm. He held up a hand. "Wait. She's not struggling."

A moment later, Valentine's feet touched the grass. She rushed toward them.

"Oh, thank God. I felt the other portal open here."

"It was a shock, but we're good," Malcolm said.

"They weren't ready for us," Asha said, standing tall.

Valentine gave them quick hugs, then held onto John, sharing comforting whispers.

Malcolm nudged Asha and nodded toward Valentine's mysterious companion. It differed from the other machines. They had been white and chrome, with pleasant faces and soft voices that ran counter to their ferocity.

This one, though, was midnight purple with splashes of silver and black. Instead of smooth armor, it was more segmented and layered, like futuristic dragon scales. Something about the red gems on its chest tickled Malcolm's memory. And this machine had been molded to appear female.

Malcolm and Asha moved to flank the machine. It noticed, and instead of resisting it held up its hands in surrender.

"I'm not your enemy. I promise."

Malcolm's eyes narrowed. *That voice.*

With a faint whirring, the helmet folded back. The woman inside watched Malcolm, equal parts wary and nervous.

His brain exploded. "Wha . . . how?"

"By Eternity," Asha muttered.

"Holy . . ." Malcolm heard John say.

"Mal," Valentine said.

Her voice barely penetrated. He stood rooted, drowning in questions.

The sound of the front door broke the spell. All eyes turned as Neil and Oma Grace appeared on the porch. Malcolm yearned to push his dad back inside. Yet he could only stand there with his heart breaking as his father saw Callie.

Neil examined his wife in confusion. Then his expression clouded over.

"Neil," Callie said. "I was going to tell you. I've *wanted* to tell you for so long."

Stunned, he leaned against the doorway. "Tell me what?"

"How did these things know where to attack?" Asha said.

Malcolm shot her a look, and her eyes widened.

"Forgive me," Asha said. "I only meant to think it."

"First strike protocol," Callie said. "Small forces sent in as a vanguard. They take out known threats to clear the way."

Oma Grace wrung her hands. "Clear the way for what?"

"For an invasion."

"How?" Staggering down the porch steps, Neil approached

his wife. He reached toward her, but forced his hand down. "How do you know this?"

"Because," Callie swallowed, looking as if she'd rather be anywhere else, saying any other words, "I was the first one they sent."

The tense silence was palpable.

Ever the soldier, Asha cut through it with the right question. "If they're targeting all known threats, what about Fred?"

Malcolm's insides turned to ice. He saw the same alarm on everyone's faces.

"The third portal," Valentine said.

Malcolm nodded. "We have to get to Fred's place, now."

If there had been a more awkward car ride in the history of the world, Malcolm wasn't aware of it.

John drove one of several huge antique vehicles Clive had willed to him, and Valentine sat by his side. Malcolm and Asha occupied the rear seat while Callie sat in the middle alone.

Each had come ready to fight. Along with her usual battle gear, Asha wore a streamlined version of the gear belt Clive had designed for them. John had taken his ideas and advanced them, customizing the gear for each person. He wore his own, his bow across his lap.

The twins wore no special equipment. Their protection became clear when they embraced Time. Still, it left Malcolm feeling strangely underdressed. *Maybe we should have a uniform or something.*

Valentine had confiscated Callie's armor. Watching it fold back into a bracelet had blown Malcolm's mind. Now Callie wore a gray leotard of sorts, with an "encounter suit" worn underneath.

Their dad had been caught between anger, worry, and betrayal. It didn't help that they'd had to rush off, giving Callie long enough to promise an explanation. To insist she hadn't betrayed them.

Asha hadn't wanted her to come. As the agent of an invading enemy, she was a tactical liability. The twins had overruled her. Like it or not, Callie had valuable knowledge.

John veered onto Fred's mile-long driveway.

"We should stop here," Callie said. "By now, they know the other attacks failed. They'll be watching for threats."

John braked. "The truck has surveillance countermeasures."

"It won't be enough," Callie said. "I'm sorry, but my future is a thousand years from now. They have tech that would seem like magic to you. My armor can create a dampening field to mask our approach."

Valentine scoffed. "You're not getting your armor back."

"That armor may mean the difference between saving Fred and losing him," Callie said. "I'm not your enemy, Valentine. You know me."

Malcolm bristled. "We know Callie de la Vega, a journalist from the Dominican Republic. Not a spy from the future."

Callie stared down at her lap. Malcolm could see her fighting to contain tears.

"Callie Gilbert," she whispered.

"What?" Malcolm said.

Swallowing, she looked up at him. Her eyes still glistened and her voice was thick, but it came out strong.

"Gilbert. Callie Gilbert," she said. "That's my name."

Regret warred with Malcolm's sense of betrayal. The part of him that loved Callie hated being this way with her. But he couldn't afford to ignore another part of him, one that had been betrayed by friends and had watched other friends die.

"No armor," Valentine stated. "Find another way."

Callie pursed her lips. "I suppose I could activate its passive mode. That's how I took those first hits from the Destroyer. Even deactivated, it gives some protection."

"How can it counteract your people's surveillance?" Asha asked.

Callie hesitated. "My armor isn't exactly standard issue. It's designed more for stealth and speed than heavy combat, which means lots of digital countermeasures. Believe me, I'm good at this. They used to call me—"

She cut off, showing instant regret.

"Call you what?" John prodded.

With a sigh, Callie closed her eyes. "They used to call me Oblivion's Kiss."

Malcolm fell back in his seat. He had seen enough movies to know what a name like that meant. "You're an assassin."

"I *was* an assassin."

Another bombshell. Yet, the biggest thing Malcolm felt was regret, knowing what his dad's face would look like on hearing the truth. Right now, though, they had a friend to save.

"Do you have to wear the bracelet for it to work?"

"No."

The twins exchanged a look, and Valentine handed the device to Callie. With a few taps on seemingly random spots, she finished by pressing the second red gem and handed it back.

"We'll need to walk from here, and stay close together. That field's only meant to mask one person."

It wasn't just that the front door was gone. It was that a hole now gaped in the front wall of Fred's house. Splintered wood and broken bricks littered the foyer.

From their vantage point in a cluster of trees, the group surveyed the scene.

"Gee, I wonder if they're here," Malcolm said.

"How many times is Fred going to have to fix his house?" Valentine said.

Quelling his nerves, Malcolm darted across the lawn and ducked inside the broken doorway. The others entered on his heels, just as Malcolm caught the echo of voices.

On tiptoes, he crossed the tile and crouched next to the railing. On the other side was a drop-off to Fred's gigantic living room below. *I forget how big this place is.* Half the twins' house could fit in the foyer.

The voices were louder now, coming from below.

"Where are you friends?" an angry voice blared. "Where would they hide?"

"I dunno. How 'bout your mama's house?"

Malcolm suppressed laughter. Fred was definitely here.

"What are the Gilbert twins' weaknesses?"

"They're allergic to jackass fools, so y'all should be safe."

Malcolm glanced back. Valentine covered her mouth to muffle her own laughter. Grinning, he placed a finger over his lips and leaned forward.

Fred sat in a wooden chair, hands tied behind his back, looking as relaxed as if he were lounging around the house. He still wore a robe. Two humanoid robots stood beside him, one on either side, each holding a futuristic gun. "Cyonics," Callie had called them.

Across the room, a Destroyer towered over Fred. The angry voice came from there.

"It doesn't matter whether you help us," the pilot said. "Eventually they'll come for you. Then they're finished."

Fred snorted. "Whatever, dawg. Try not to pee your pants when they send you cryin' back to daddy."

With a frustrated growl, the pilot punched a hole in the floor and fired his railgun into the ceiling.

As debris rained down, Fred fixed the Destroyer with a flat stare. "So, do I send the repair bill to you, or your evil boss?"

The Destroyer stomped closer, shaking the house. "My instructions were to keep you alive. But maybe you resisted." Its left arm peeled open to reveal the cannon inside. "Any last words?"

"Yeah. I always get the same nightmare when a school project's due. I dream that everyone in class got a bird to take care of all year. Last day of school rolls around, everyone's in class with their birds, alive and healthy, all proud and whatever. And I'm sitting there with nothing but a piece of fried chicken." Fred looked around at the machines. "Never told anyone that before. I feel real close to y'all now."

The Destroyer aimed at Fred's head. "I will enjoy this, you dark-age hillbilly."

Alarmed, Malcolm drank in a rush of Time. He felt a *shift* as Valentine did the same. But instead of backing down, Fred laughed.

"Yo, I don't think so, Tin Man. See, you made two mistakes. One, you threatened my friends." His grin turned dark. "And two, you assumed that just 'cause I ain't like them, it means I'm helpless."

He leapt from the chair, the rope falling from his wrists. In one smooth action, he kicked the chair into Cyonic One at his left, reached into his robe and drew what looked like the handle of a katana. A curved blade unfolded and locked into place.

Fred swung at Cyonic Two to his right. With a metallic *shing-crack* he chopped its arm off at the elbow. The gun flew free of its robotic hand, and Fred snatched it out of the air.

As Malcolm gaped, Fred unleashed chaos.

Aiming at Cyonic Two with its own gun, he opened fire. Bursts of green energy riddled its torso with holes. The robot convulsed until a bolt blew its head to pieces. As if surprised by its own demise, it locked up hard and stood like a statue.

Fred dropped to the floor and rolled between the dead machine's legs, coming to his feet behind it. Now Cyonic Two was his shield.

Cyonic One took aim and fired. Cyonic Two rattled as staccato blasts pummeled its chassis. Fred reached around it and flicked his wrist. The katana flew like a javelin to skewer Cyonic One through its left eye.

The robot fired wildly, hitting the Destroyer as its pilot tried to lock onto Fred. The big machine stumbled back.

Cyonic Two's frame collapsed. Fred somersaulted over it before charging Cyonic One, firing green energy with every step. As the machine fell dead, he plucked his katana from its skull in a shower of sparks.

Malcolm stared wide-eyed. It had taken seconds and Fred moved like winged death. Blade and gun proficiency, battle tactics, acrobatics—he wielded them as if they were old habit. What had their friend been up to for two years?

Turning now, Fred faced off with the massive Destroyer. As its targeting lasers finally found him, he raised gun and sword high, refusing to back down.

That woke Malcolm up.

Time blazed through his veins as he leapt over the rail and flung a wave of super-slowed Time at the Destroyer. The machine slowed to a fraction of normal speed, decreased molecular activity freezing it solid.

As Malcolm dropped, he conjured an Entropy Blade and cleaved straight through the middle. The machine's two halves split apart and then shattered like frozen glass.

The pilot disappeared through a black maw ringed with flames. A spike of agony shot through Malcolm before the portal disappeared. He hit the floor and crouched, clutching his temples until the pain faded.

The rest of the team arrived from the stairs, walking through iced-over debris to join Malcolm as he stood. In stunned silence, they faced their long-lost friend.

Fred's cheeks colored under the weight of their stares. He scratched his ear.

"Uh, hey guys. When'd you get here?"

Malcolm had no words. None of them did.

Fred gave a nervous chuckle. "Crazy what you can pick up playing video games, right?"

"Fred," Valentine said.

"Yeah?"

"Explain."

CHAPTER 6

John steered the old truck with one hand while speaking into his phone with the other.

"You're welcome. I'm glad you like it," he said.

Next to him, Valentine spoke into hers. "That's where we're all meeting. Can you get there now?"

"Your flight leaves tonight," John said. "The hotel in Hawaii is expecting you."

"Just drive across the lawn. We'll get the road fixed later," Valentine said into the phone. Malcolm could hear the eye-roll in her voice. "Fine. Okay, bye."

"See you in a week. I love you, too." John finished his call.

Valentine squeezed his hand. "Bill and Nancy?" she said, referring to his adoptive parents.

John nodded. "They'll be out of danger now, and they think I'm going camping in the foothills."

"Maybe we all should," Malcolm quipped. He gazed at their town as it passed by, worried for it once again. "When this hits the news, all the conspiracy nuts will come flooding back."

Fred chuckled. "We should let *them* fight the bad guys for once."

John's idea had been a good one, though, Malcolm reflected.

His adoptive parents knew nothing about what John did with the twins. With what might be coming, it was better for them to go on a surprise vacation.

There were perks to being the new owner of a world-class auto restoration shop. John wasn't quite eighteen, so he hadn't fully taken over, but money would not be a concern. As they had found in his will, Clive had been wealthier than he'd ever let on.

"That was Dad on the phone?" Malcolm said.

Valentine nodded. "They'll meet us at the shop."

The enemy obviously knew where they lived. Hopefully the shop would escape notice.

With family taken care of, all eyes turned to Fred. He had changed into jeans and heavy lace-up boots. The katana rested at his feet, in a bag with some exotic tactical armor.

"My turn now, huh?" He tried to force laughter, which became an awkward throat-clear. "Well, uh, wow. Where do I start?"

"Perhaps with how and why," John said.

"Right. How and why." Fred tapped his chin, trying to look thoughtful but looking lost instead. "How. Why."

Finally, he gave a frustrated huff and just began.

"You know how you start doing a thing and you think it's for one reason, but then you realize, duh, there's another reason? Well, that's what happened. Know what I mean?"

He met a sea of blank stares.

"Naw, course you don't." He tapped his forehead, his brow scrunched. "So, I left to travel with my dad two years ago. He builds stuff all over the world, man, like crazy stuff. Told y'all I missed Winter and wanted to see the world. That was true, but not, like, the whole truth. I just didn't realize 'til I left."

When he looked at Malcolm, his expression grew more serious.

"You and Val, you got this whole Lords of Time thing going on. John's a super genius. Asha's the scariest girl I've ever met. Y'all might as well be the Avengers. And here I am, just a dude with a smart mouth who somehow keeps surviving."

"That's not true, Fred," Valentine said. "We couldn't have done all this without you."

"Thanks, girl. But when the Frost Hammer went down, I realized something. I would do anything to protect my friends, but there was only so much I *could* do."

Fred hesitated, then lifted his shirt sleeve to reveal a tattoo emblazoned across his shoulder. Or rather, several small tattoos wrapped together. One of them looked similar to the sword Fred had used against the Cyonics.

"As we traveled, I found people who would train me. Fighters, monks, swordsmen, marksmen, even acrobats. I told 'em to push me harder'n I thought I could handle, then push more, so that when the next bad guy came around, I could stand beside y'all and fight."

"How did you know another threat would come?" Asha said.

Fred smirked. "Come on, girl. You've been around Mal and Val for, what, two years? Tell me you don't think trouble orbits 'em like the sun. Of course something else would come, so I made up my mind to be better. For them."

Malcolm couldn't help feeling touched. Fred, his goofy, loudmouthed, unbreakably loyal friend, had literally traveled the globe and transformed himself for them. But still . . .

"Did we do something, Fred?" he asked. "We never meant to make you feel like less."

"Nothing like that, dawg. This was for me."

"Judging by today's performance," John said, "I'd say you succeeded."

Fred flashed a grin.

"Gotta admit, that was fun. And check this out!" Pulling up his sleeve again, he flexed to display taut and corded muscles. "Got me a tight body. Look out, ladies of the world! Am I right?"

Malcolm laughed. He may have some added layers now, but their old friend Fred was still very much *Fred*.

Oma Grace and their dad were waiting for them outside the shop. John led everyone through the office, then to the far end of the property.

One by one, they filed through the door into John's private workshop. Malcolm came last and shut the door behind them.

"Stand in this square, everyone, if you don't mind," John said, indicating the section of concrete flooring that met the front door. As they scrunched together, something chimed.

"Welcome back, Boss," said a cheerful female voice with an Irish accent. *"Company today, I see?"*

"Hello, Jane," John said. "And yes. Visitor Configuration, please."

With another chime, the entire room changed.

Clive had always divided the workshop into quadrants: work area, kitchen, lounge, and open, with *open* usually meaning "space to test something fun but dangerous." John had taken the idea and drop-kicked it into the future.

Mechanical *clunks* and *whirrs* vibrated under their feet. While the group stood stationary within their concrete square, the rest of the workshop floor lifted, separated into segments, and rearranged.

The kitchen and lounge shuffled to the far left corner, opening up more floor space. The work area, cluttered with a dozen lab tables and crazy equipment, spread out to accommodate their large group.

The most exotic machinery moved toward the back, no doubt to prevent curious visitors from unwittingly destroying the universe. Floor segments locked together again, settling into a semicircle configuration with a large open circle in the center of the workshop.

The group's collective jaw hit the floor. Malcolm had seen much of this before, and it awed him every time. Only Callie seemed unmoved.

Neil recovered first. "Uh, what's the big open spot for?"

"Ah, right," John said. "Jane, *Trusted* Visitor Configuration."

The center segments lifted and separated. With a loud *hiss* like compressed air, they flipped over so that their bottom sides faced up. As they clicked back together and sank to floor-level again, a circular command station appeared.

It was bursting with racks of high-powered computers, rows of high-definition monitors, joysticks, haptic gloves, and even VR headgear. This was the heart of John's operation, the nest from which he monitored and communicated with the team during missions.

"So," Malcolm said, eyebrows raised. "Jane? You created an artificial intelligence?"

"Just clever tricks," John replied. "She's helpful, but the veneer of a programmed personality makes her seem more advanced than she is."

John always downplayed his abilities. One look at this place, though, at what he'd accomplished with Clive's spectacles and his own mind, and there was no mistaking who carried the biggest intellectual hammer. The twins were smart. This was another level.

"Who's Jane?" Asha said.

John gave a wry smile. "Just Another New Endeavor— J.A.N.E. I know, it's silly."

Valentine grinned. "Remember when you didn't even own a cell phone?"

That got a laugh from everyone.

John gestured at an empty lab table encircled by chairs. "Have a seat. I know it's been a long day, but . . ."

Valentine nodded heavily. "Yeah. Lots to talk about."

"It's the threat Winter warned us about, isn't it?" John said, a shadow behind his eyes.

"Sorta has to be, right?" Fred said. "It's doing weird stuff to the Timeline."

"Not just weird," Asha said. "Destructive."

"I don't know how," Malcolm said, "but that wall of fire literally hurts to think about. And it's always getting closer."

"Has Winter indicated why these things keep happening here?" Oma Grace asked.

"Actually, we think we know," Valentine said. "The fabric of the Timeline has gotten weaker here."

"Yeah, our little patch of Timeline has taken a beating," Malcolm added. "I don't think it was built to handle it."

John tapped his chin. "Like a trampoline. Jump on one spot too much, and eventually the weave there sags."

"Exactly," Valentine said. "Now, imagine setting a ball on that trampoline. If you let it go, it's going to roll right to the spot that's sagging."

Malcolm huffed. "Whatever the Chrona did, it's sure not helping us now."

At that, he felt the weight of everyone's stares.

"Dude," Fred said. "Didn't she, like, save the Timeline?"

"Yes, Fred," Valentine said, shooting Malcolm a sharp look. "And as far as we know, she's part of the reason we're Chronauri in the first place."

"Come on, Val, you know I agree," Malcolm returned. "But it doesn't mean she did everything perfectly. However she structured the Timeline, it's like she assumed no one else would try to use it. So whenever someone does, it cracks more. Apparently she's accepted that, because she's ignoring us and Everwatch."

"What would you have done differently, my boy?" Oma Grace asked.

It was the earnestness in her voice that took Malcolm aback. What *would* he have done in the Chrona's place? His thoughts had never gotten that far—he had only seen the problem, not how to fix it. That kind of solution would have to happen on a cosmic scale, which was way above his pay grade.

He shrugged. "I don't know."

Maybe it was the despair in his voice, but Valentine softened. "I know it sucks, but right now we have a more immediate threat."

Malcolm acquiesced. "Yeah. We need to plan, and without knowing what we're facing."

"But we do know, don't we?" Neil asked, focusing on a dark corner of the workshop. "At least, *one* of us does."

All eyes locked onto Callie, who had done a masterful job of occupying an inconspicuous space. Malcolm had almost forgotten she was there. Even surrounded by people who knew her, she had an assassin's gift for avoiding notice.

The fight-or-flight instinct came alive in Callie's eyes. Malcolm could see her weighing options—she could either run or stay and fight through this. For an instant she teetered. Then . . .

"What do you want to know?"

"Everything you do," Valentine said. "Let's start with your name."

"I barely remember my old name." Her eyes clouded over. "That person doesn't exist anymore. After she was gone, they only called me Calypso."

No one responded, so she plowed ahead.

"My century has one world government, led by a great but mysterious man. We call him the Regent. Against all odds he managed to pull the world together. Poverty is rare, science and medicine have leapt forward, and people in general feel safe. We even live quite a bit longer. Things were better. *We* were better."

She paused, staring into the middle distance. Malcolm noted her breaths coming shorter, as if anxiety was filling her up.

Neil cleared his throat expectantly. Callie snapped back to the present.

"We assumed it would go on forever." She shook her head ruefully. "But, of course, it couldn't last. Things were about to get much, much worse."

CHAPTER 7

April, A.D. 3088

The open-air market teemed with life. She wandered between booths, soaking up the festive atmosphere. Live music interwove with cheerful chatter and the scents of a hundred cuisines.

The impossibly tall skyscrapers of Eldurfall knifed into the sky above them, but for now they went unnoticed. The market, with booths covered in bright patterns from every corner of the globe, stole all their attention.

Cyonics of all configurations wove through the crowd, running errands for their owners. Children played beneath parents who bargained with vendors. Negotiations were never aggressive. No one did this because they needed the money anymore; they did it to share their skills and passions with the world.

"Pretty lady!" a sonorous voice called.

She turned. A swarthy man in robes waved from a table piled with flowers. Smiling, he plucked a small blossom and tossed it her way.

When she caught it, the flower glowed, sky-blue petals pulsing gently in time with her heartbeat. *A Starburst Lily.*

The man tossed a second flower, this one with red petals and deep purple light.

"For your little one," he said with a bow.

She responded with a dazzling smile, which sent a flush of color across his cheeks, and handed the red flower to the little girl at her side. Her eyes sparkled in delight as it filled her palms with an ethereal glow.

"Maya, what do you say?"

"Thank you, sir!" Her four-year-old voice barely carried over the crowd. Dark-brown curls bounced as she waved.

"Okay, now hold it by the stem. Careful! That's it. Now give me your other hand."

"Why?"

"Because it's a big crowd and I don't want you to get lost."

Maya giggled. "Mommy, you have my finder code!"

"All right, you caught me. I just like holding your hand. Is that okay?"

Maya's smile brightened everything in a hundred-foot radius. Reaching up, she clutched her mother's hand as they wandered farther down the side street.

"Oooh!" Maya pointed at a booth. "Can I have a cinnamon spark? Pleeease?"

She tried to look stern, as a mother should. Maya had already snuck a few from the pantry. But that excited face . . .

Her resistance melted. "You have to promise not to argue about bedtime tonight. Deal? Spring break is over tomorrow, and mommy has to be a teacher again."

"I promise, I promise!"

Five minutes later, they were approaching the end of this arm of the market, Maya skipping along and swinging her arms. The flower was tucked in her pocket now, with the sweet taking its place in her hand. Every few seconds she held it up to her lips, and with a pop-flash the most delicious roasted-cinnamon scent filled the air.

"Pace yourself, honey. You want it to last, don't you?"

"I want it to last foreeeeever!"

She laughed. "Okay, let's walk the other way now. We should get home soon."

Happily focused on the candy, Maya would agree to anything now. They turned, and the view changed from a dwindling side street to a massive spectacle covering multiple city blocks.

"Can we live at the market?" Maya asked.

"How about we visit once a week, like always? Deal?"

"Deal!"

"Good, because we—"

With an earsplitting *boom*, the sky above them ripped open. A shock wave struck, and the world became a spinning blur.

She was flying. Smacking into the ground. Tumbling end over end. Smashing through something, hearing wood splinter. Tangling in a stretch of fabric. Then, finally, rolling to a stop.

She floated in a haze, distantly registering the sounds of chaos, yet wanting nothing more than to sleep. *Yes, rest. Everything will be better tomorrow.* Then one thought crashed through her mind like a freight train.

Maya.

With a heavy gasp, she burst through the dazed bubble and sat up. Everything hurt as if she'd been beaten. A line of blood trickled down her forehead and across her right eye. All around her the world had gone mad.

The shock waves had shattered windows, hurled commuting hovercraft out of the sky, and smashed the market like a child's toy. Booths had collapsed, and the injured roamed about in a panic, searching for loved ones.

Gritting her teeth, she climbed to her feet.

"Maya?" she called. Then louder. Then again, turning frantically. "Maya!"

Her cries were drowned out as a high-pitched roar echoed across the massive metropolis. She looked skyward and stumbled back a step.

Ships. Black and sleek, with edges that glowed red like bloody knives slicing through the sky. With another *boom* and shock wave, a rift opened overhead and spat out more.

Then, all at once, they struck.

Fiery destruction lanced from the ships—beams that cut and burned through everything in their path. Skyscrapers toppled. Hovercrafts took to the air as roads collapsed, only to be vaporized. Debris crashed to the ground, scattering the screaming crowds.

Fighting against the tide of people running to escape, she plunged back into the market, shouting Maya's name until her throat burned. So much to search through. How would she—

"Mommy!"

Brown curls and big brown eyes came into view. Maya was crying and her cheek was scraped, but they'd found each other. The shock wave had separated them, but now she could see her little girl and there was only a hundred feet between them.

A burst of wind shoved her back. From high up, the wind hit the ground and blasted out in all directions to clear a wide, circular space. In its wake, a ship plummeted from the dark sky and landed. This one was bigger than the others.

It blocked her way to Maya, who stared at her with pleading eyes. Holding out a staying hand, she silently begged her daughter to wait. With one eye on the terrifying ship, she began to pick her way around the edge of the circle.

A ramp extended from the ship. With an ominous *hiss* the hatch opened. Bright red light poured out, revealing the backlit outlines of two figures.

A man and a woman, wearing armor unlike anything she'd ever seen. Side by side they marched down the ramp. They surveyed the destruction, their faces bent in cruel satisfaction.

As their feet touched the ground, a drone floated out from the ship to hover a few meters in front of them. A light on its undercarriage blinked on.

A whine rang in her ears. Every device that could broadcast video switched on. Two cruel faces filled the screens—not only across the city, but across the world. One by one, a panicked populace saw those faces and stood still. What could possibly be happening?

"You were warned, Regent," the man said.

"We offered you friendship," the woman said.

"And what did you do?"

"Rejected us."

"*Rejected* us!"

"Rejected everything we could have done together."

She kept moving, darting between piles of wreckage. Whoever those two were, they would not keep her from her daughter.

"We warned you," the man said again. "And now, your world—"

"Your *Time*—"

"Must burn."

Her eyes widened at those last words. Forgetting about

stealth, she broke into a run, her vision filled with Maya. Only fifty feet away!

Then forty.

The attackers lifted their hands. The air around them distorted, crackling with energy. For an instant they held still.

Twenty feet. She stretched out her hand as Maya stretched out hers. Almost—

Lighting struck the ground nearby. With a yelp, she dropped to her knees as a wave of fire passed overhead. A massive ice spike whistled through the air, barely missing her.

The attackers weren't aiming for her. They weren't even *looking* at her. Waves of destruction poured from them in every direction.

"Mommy!"

Maya appeared through the smoke, small enough to have slipped between the attacks.

"Maya!"

As they reached for each other, a beam of distortions cut between them, forcing them apart again. The man was pointing at a building a hundred yards beyond them. The distortion lanced toward the building, turning the ground beneath it to dust.

The building shuddered, distortions racing across its surface and sinking in deeper, like an acid spiderweb. The building shook harder but refused to fall.

She looked back at the armored man, waiting for him to give up and move on. Waiting for the moment she could finally take Maya in her arms. No way could one man destroy a skyscraper.

But then he snarled and his outstretched hand clenched into a fist. The air trembled. In that instant she realized what was about to happen, and life seemed to move in slow motion.

"Maya, run!"

The armored man unleashed his full power. The distortion beam grew, and as it did, the destruction around it spread wider.

Maya stared at her, wide-eyed and frozen in place. She screamed again for the girl to run, standing her ground until the growing beam began to disintegrate her clothes and peel away her top layers of skin. Finally, she was forced to back away.

"Maya, baby girl, please just run. Run!"

Maya, so sweet and innocent, not knowing even the concept of destruction, just reached out to her mother, her eyes pleading for comfort, for safety.

In the space of a heartbeat, Maya disintegrated.

Gone.

She screamed Maya's name. Fell to her knees. Grabbed fistfuls of her own hair and yanked. Turned inside out while her vision blurred and her throat caught fire. Screamed. Fell to the ground screaming over and over and over again.

All around her, the world was ending.

Good.

She wanted it to.

"The war raged on after that," Callie said. "The Regent had peacekeepers, but not a real army, so everyone banded together to build one. I spent the next six months at the bottom of a bottle. Since I survived when Maya didn't, I figured I'd just let alcohol kill me. Couldn't save my own daughter, so what else was I good for?"

Valentine had never heard a heavier silence. Callie paused to regather herself.

"That's when the Regent found me. He pulled me out of

the gutter, showed me the truth about what happened. Gave me a purpose."

"What truth?" Valentine asked. "What did he say?"

"About a month before that day, there was a disturbance inside Eldurfall—the capital city, where I lived—and the Regent intervened. He moved whatever it was out of the city, fought it, and won. No one knew then, but it was the same man and woman. They were Time travelers from our ancient past, and they wanted a piece of the future. The Regent saw their hunger for power, and when he refused a partnership, they attacked. So, he threw them out of our century. That should have been the end."

Trembling now, she gripped the edge of the table to steady herself.

"Instead they stole our technology, used it to weaponize the people of their century, and then invaded ours. They wanted vengeance. We were their first victims."

Fred rubbed his hands wearily across his face. "A war between Time periods. This world just keeps getting crazier."

Asha spoke next, her voice unusually soft. "This Regent offered you a mission?"

Callie nodded. "Project Rectify."

Valentine's eyes flicked to Callie's wrist, where a small tattoo hid under the silver bracelet. A tattoo that said RECTIFY. Callie caught the motion and they shared a knowing look. Two years ago, she had explained the tattoo as a personal mantra. Now Valentine understood.

"It was a chance to use the Timeline against them," Callie continued. "If we could track down their point of origin, we could stop the war before it began. We could save everyone, and I'd get what the Regent knew I wanted . . . needed . . . all along."

"Which is?" Neil asked.

"To find the ones who killed my baby girl, and take them down with me."

Neil leaned back in his chair, staring at her as if she were a stranger.

"The Regent brought me back to life," she said. "Taught me how to fight, how to manipulate. My bones are laced with a material you don't know about yet. Some of my muscle strands are synthetic, making me faster and stronger. My blood carries more oxygen. I can run flat out for miles before I need to rest. And there's more. All to make me a better assassin."

"How much better?" Malcolm said.

Callie reached across the table, picked up a screwdriver, and flicked her wrist. It sank into the wall with a solid *clang*.

Malcolm's eyebrows climbed. "Ah."

"So, why are you here, my dear?" Oma Grace said.

Callie studied the floor with an expression Valentine couldn't decipher. She tried to speak, but then just shook her head.

"Callie."

Neil's voice was quiet, but it cracked like a whip. Callie flinched, met his eyes, and forced herself to stand straighter.

"There were three stages to Project Rectify. First, find our enemy at an early point in their lives. Second, send an agent to neutralize them before they become a threat. Third, if that doesn't prevent their corruption of the Timeline, send an army to stop them on a large scale."

"Conquer the past to save the future," John said.

"Yes. When the Regent found their origin, he showed me their faces again. He told me their true names, where and when to find them, and sent me back to save my people. So, to answer your question," she faced Oma Grace, "I'm here because the two faces I saw—the ones that took Maya from me—belonged to Malcolm and Valentine Gilbert."

CHAPTER 8

She came here to kill us.
Valentine gripped the sides of her chair, feeling as if the air had been sucked from the room. *It can't be. It can't!* Her eyes narrowed at Callie. *How much of the last two years has been manipulation?*

No one in the room seemed to know what to say. Except one.

"That's messed up," Fred said. "But ain't no way these two are mass murderers."

Callie's lips trembled and her eyes glistened. As if now that all had been revealed, her armor was stripped away. "I saw their faces, Fred. Heard their voices. What was I supposed to think?"

Fred exploded from his chair. "Say my friends are killers again. *Say it!*"

"Fred," Valentine said. "Thank you, but that won't accomplish anything."

"She's right," Malcolm said. "I'm upset, believe me, but fighting won't tell us what really happened."

"They could have been imposters," John said. "Holograms, even."

"Non-corporeal holograms would be possible," Callie admitted. "But even in my century, hard light projections that sophisticated are just as much magic as they are now. These people destroyed things. Please, I'm not saying this to upset you. I only want you to understand."

"I understand," Neil said. "You came here to murder my children."

He brimmed with cold rage. Even Callie seemed intimidated as Neil stood, staring her down.

"Meeting us. Pretending to love us. All so you could get close enough to hurt them. Am I right?"

Callie looked down.

"Am I right?"

"Yes."

His eyes seemed to catch fire. "What was the plan? Stab my kids in their sleep so they can't fight back? When were you planning to do it?"

Callie, the trained killer, began to cry. As Valentine watched the woman, a surprising realization hit her. She believed those tears.

Neil stepped toward her. "When, Callie?"

Malcolm grasped his shoulder. "Dad, wait."

"When?"

"I was already supposed to do it," Callie burst out. "Two years ago."

"Then why did you wait?" Neil demanded. "To learn about my kids? What hurts them? That's what assassins do, isn't it?"

Anguish twisted Callie's expression.

"For two years, I've sent false reports." She choked back fresh tears. "I told the Regent the twins were running and I was tracking them. I sold him a lie until I could find a way to protect the twins *and* save my people. But he must know I betrayed him. That's why they're all coming now."

"You think that makes it okay?" Neil said. "You think—?"

Valentine stood now. "Dad, please."

Seeing the look in her eye, he stopped. Valentine turned to Callie.

"Why?"

Callie closed her eyes. "Because I fell in love. With your father, with both of you. I deceived you at first, but then . . ." Her eyes opened. "I looked at you and Malcolm—really looked—and I didn't see a trace of the monsters who killed my little girl."

She turned to Neil.

"I looked at you and saw not a father of warlords, but a man trying his best. I waited for that darkness to appear, but it never did. Every day I saw who you all truly were, and I fell more in love. Then one day I just knew. The Regent had to be wrong. There had to be another explanation."

"And what was it?" Asha asked.

"I don't know. All I do know is these two amazing kids are not murderers, and I don't think they ever will be. Neil—"

"Get out," Neil said.

Callie flinched as if he'd struck her. "What do you—"

"Don't ask. You know what I mean. I mean get out. Get. Out."

The venom in his voice stunned them all. Tears fell from Neil's eyes as he began to shout.

"Get out!"

"Dad," Malcolm said. "She has information we need."

Neil couldn't hear them. He stormed toward Callie while she backed away from him and toward the door.

"You don't deserve to be here, you never did, and you never will. Get out!"

Callie's back hit the door. She stared at him, choking back

sobs, trying so hard to be strong. Scrubbing at her cheeks, she looked past him to Oma Grace.

"I'm so sorry."

With that, she opened the door and left. Neil slammed the door behind her and sagged against it. Eyes shut, he rested his forehead on the cold steel.

Valentine looked to her companions, feeling lost. *What on earth do we do now?*

CHAPTER 9

Valentine couldn't get comfortable.

The others had long since fallen sleep. The enemy knew where everyone lived, so they all bunked together in the close quarters of John's workshop, sleeping where they fell.

Resting on the couch, wrapped in John's embrace and surrounded by those closest to her, she should feel safe. But . . . *We're less ready than ever.*

Callie had not returned and wouldn't answer her phone. The twins' dad had spent the rest of the evening brooding with a bottle of wine.

We still have no clue what we're facing. Is the Regent our enemy, or has he just been deceived? What's he hiding behind that wall of fire?

Stop.

She willed herself to relax, snuggling deeper into her boyfriend's tender grasp. In his arms, she didn't have to be so strong.

But no sleep would come. *How does Mal do it? How does he relax in the face of disaster?* Valentine glanced toward his spot on the floor, then sat bolt upright. *Where is he?*

"Valentine?" John whispered groggily, reaching for her.

Okay, calm down. Just use your head.

She forced herself to slow down. If anyone could locate Malcolm, she could. Eyes closed, she absorbed a trickle of Time and gave it a gentle flick.

A wave radiated from her. Expanding like a radar signal, it passed through everything in the immediate area. Living things, inanimate objects, even tracing the currents of the Timeline.

A familiar signature *pinged* back. She blew out a relieved breath.

"It's okay," she whispered. "I'll be back."

Outside, the cloudless night shimmered with starlight. Valentine took a few steps into the yard and stopped between a row of old vehicles, where Malcolm was gazing up.

"Never saw this many in Chicago," she said.

Malcolm gave a wistful smile. "Remember the day we found out we were moving here?"

"It felt like a death sentence."

"All I could think about was leaving. Now I can't bear to lose it."

Valentine looped her arm around his. "This is home now. Everyone we love is here. We'll find a way to protect it."

"You're right. It's not the first time we've been clueless and outmatched."

"What makes you think we're outmatched?" she said.

"We're two teenagers waiting for an army of killer machines as it burns through Time with the sole purpose of hunting us down."

"Oh, right, that."

It was so absurd, they couldn't help laughing.

"And we're facing them without the Chrona," Valentine added. "So if you've got any new tricks up your sleeve, now's the time to share."

At that, the memory flared to life in her head. The one she had filed away, knowing it was imperative for him to see.

"Actually, I think I have something," she said. "But you'll really have to trust me."

Time pulsed inside her like a living thing, eager to be wielded. Valentine held it close, waiting until her brother was ready. His face pinched in concentration.

"Can you make some kind of isolating bubble?" she had asked. "Something to protect everything else from us?"

As it turned out, he could. Palms out, Malcolm exerted his will on the Timeline immediately surrounding them. Valentine felt a temporal *shift* as he gripped it, and somehow it began to fold around them.

She couldn't think of another way to describe the feeling. It was like Malcolm had taken the fabric of the universe and folded that solidified energy over itself, wrapping it around them like a protective sphere.

Trembling with exertion, he sealed the folds together. With a last gasp of effort, he relaxed and the sphere held on its own—like their own little pocket hidden inside the Timeline.

"There," he said. "Whatever happens, it should just bounce around in here with us. Your turn?"

"Right. Might want to step back. I did this by accident the first time, and it almost got away from me."

"What is it?"

"No clue. But I remember how it happened." Suddenly nervous, she cracked her knuckles and shook out her hands. *This was a bad idea. But he has to see.*

"Okay," she said, bracing herself. "Here we go."

Valentine beckoned and Time poured into her, light and vitality racing through every atom. Deep inside she felt the thrum of the universe, and she savored the sensation as a piece of it bent to her will.

A discarded engine block sat between them. John had said it was beyond repair, so Valentine hoped he wouldn't mind.

Concentrating, she conjured a bubble of fast Time above the engine. She pushed it faster. Then faster, driven by the immense power flowing through her, until finally it transformed.

The bubble collapsed into a pinpoint of light, then turned the truest black—a dark deeper than Valentine had ever seen. Gauzy waves of blackness swirled around it, lifting and cresting and falling back into the orb. It grew to grapefruit size.

The engine sprang from the ground and collided with it, and instantly the iron began to warp as if some unseen force were pulling it apart molecule by molecule. Fingers of distorted metal curled upward, touched the orb, and disappeared into the black.

Valentine spared a glance for Malcolm and saw him staring wide-eyed. He reached for it out of sheer wonder, but pulled back when she called his name.

"What do you feel?" she asked.

He shook his head. "Nothing. But, like, an infinite nothing."

The orb was growing more quickly now, as if it had acquired a taste for consuming whatever came near. Valentine felt a breeze as the air began swirling toward it. Her clothes ruffled and her necklace floated in its direction.

"Uh, Val?"

Malcolm's expression had morphed from wonder to trepidation. Only then did Valentine realize how big the orb was getting. It was the size of a basketball now, and the wind was starting to howl.

"Whoa, okay!"

Forming a secondary Time bubble around the orb, she repeated the suppression method she had used before. Once again, as she poured a tremendous flow of Time into the bubble, the concentrated energy exerted pressure on the blackness. Almost reluctantly, the orb shrank until it winked out of existence.

Malcolm sent a pulse of Time into his protective bubble. The folds unraveled, and the universe straightened out again as his creation dissipated into the Timeline.

The twins exchanged relieved glances.

"Sorry," Valentine said. "I just really want to figure out what this thing is. Maybe there's a way to use it."

"We'd have to learn how to control it," Malcolm said. "You saw how it swallowed that engine. What would happen if it got out of control?"

"You're right. We have to be careful."

Malcolm grinned. "It was pretty cool, though. Did you get kind of a black hole vibe?"

"Sort of, but different."

"Maybe the Chrona knows. Let's ask her." He looked up, pretending to search.

Valentine giggled. "Somehow, I get the feeling she won't hear you." She studied her feet, embarrassed at her next admission. "In my head, I've been calling it the Night Blossom."

Malcolm eyed her.

"Those dark waves that swirl around it, how it all moved. It reminded me of flower petals." She shrugged. "It doesn't really make sense."

Malcolm tapped his chin. "Well, even if we don't figure out what it is, at least we got to name it."

The twins fell quiet. Valentine's eyes wandered back up

to drink in the starlight. Her trick had been enough of a drain that she could probably sleep now, but something inside her wasn't ready.

"I should sleep," Malcolm said before she could. "But I keep thinking, what if this is our last quiet night?" He pointed at the stars. "What if we won't be able to stop and look at them?"

Valentine nodded. "And if this doesn't go our way—"

"—will we ever look at them again?"

"Or will there be even fewer of us there to share it?" She rubbed her arms, suddenly chilled. "Are we crazy for trying to make plans when there's no telling what'll happen tomorrow?"

"No," Malcolm insisted. "You want John and science and discovery in your life. No matter what happens here, you're always going to want that." He rested his hand on her arm. "Don't let that go, Val. Not ever. When things get crazy, it'll tether you to something real. Something beyond all this."

Gratefully she squeezed his hand. "In that case, what about you? Any clues yet?"

"Not one. I want to make a difference, and I want to make Asha happy, and right now I want to protect my family. Until this is over, that'll have to be enough." His grin returned. "And hey, maybe I'll stumble onto some way to fix this broken old universe."

Valentine laughed. "One thing at a time, okay?"

"Yeah, you're probably right."

A deep yawn cut off her reply. "Okay, that's a sign. We really should try to sleep."

Malcolm nodded. Together they turned toward John's lab.

As they retreated, a shadow stirred behind their backs. Little more than a dark blur, it moved silently between cars and stopped at a spot facing the door, the same spot the blur had occupied before the Gilbert twins had emerged.

Settling in for a long night, the blur watched and waited for the right moment to act.

CHAPTER 10

"All the usual toys." John handed Fred and Asha their new gear belts. "Time grenades, accelerator rings, personal shield, skippers, shadow controller. It's all upgraded, plus some surprises."

Fred and Asha unfurled their belts. The twins watched in amusement as they searched the compartments like children who'd been told a present was hidden inside.

In short order, they discovered three new compartments, tiny and arranged side by side. But when each opened, instead of revealing a new gadget, it revealed a button.

"What do these do?" Asha said.

John pointed at the white button. "Gravity nullifier."

"Dude, we can fly?" Fred exclaimed.

"The effect lasts ten seconds, and it's better suited to, say, climbing a wall." He pointed to the blue button. "Phase shifter. Lasts the same length of time. If you ever wanted to walk through a wall, now you can. Lucius Carmichael's pocket watch did something similar."

Asha nodded in appreciation. "Useful. And this red button?"

John grew serious. "Self-destruct."

Fred snorted. "Ain't plannin' to blow myself up."

"Every system needs a fail-safe," John said. "This button also functions as a dial. You can choose up to a thirty-second delay, which means you don't have to be wearing it."

"Clever, babe," Valentine said, brushing his arm.

John's cheeks colored. Malcolm resisted the urge to tease them. It was sweet how they could still do that to each other.

"A'ight. My turn, I guess." Fred retrieved a duffel bag.

The twins exchanged bemused glances.

"Your turn for what?" Malcolm asked.

Fred moved toward the bathroom. "Y'all ain't the only ones with surprises. Fred's got a few, too."

"Is one of them that Fred speaks in third person now?" Valentine teased.

He shook his head. "No faith at all."

The bathroom door clicked shut. Two minutes later, it opened to reveal a figure that had ceased to be Fred and somehow become . . .

"Whoa," Malcolm said.

Fred had mentioned it in passing. Just one offhanded comment about doing more in his travels than learning to fight. Something about acquiring rare equipment.

When you're Fred Marshall, all the world's a store and there's no credit limit, Malcolm thought.

They had assumed Fred was talking about his katana, with its folding diamond-coated blade. Now, though, he stood before them in body armor that looked as if it had fallen out of a comic book. Sleek black with small accents of dark green, it moved with him as if it were molded to his skin. Hundreds of small yet pliable armor segments covered his body, joined together by a flexible not-quite-fabric.

A thin visor wrapped around his eyes, like a miniaturized

version of the tactical goggles Malcolm had seen Special Forces wear. Standing there with his new physique and exotic gear, Fred looked a million miles away from the rich party boy they had met a few years ago.

"Okay, no kidding around," Valentine said. "Are you actually Batman?"

Fred smirked. "Told ya. Come on, check it out!"

They gathered around, peppering him with questions. The armor was feather-light because the plates contained a highly advanced non-Newtonian fluid. Only when struck would they harden. Vital organs were protected by thin sheets of super-ceramic. Titanium and carbon fiber strands wove through the fabric covering his joints and holding the armor plates together.

Donning the silver spectacles, John scanned his friend and found even more to admire. The armor had been wired with sensors that tracked Fred's vitals as well as scores of environmental data points. They fed into his visor, which offered fun options for visual augmentation.

"Truly impressive, Fred," John said. "Where did you find it?"

"The dark corners of the world," Fred said. "Tracked down some tech, had other pieces custom built. Scientists, armor-smiths, warlords, assassins. One of 'em even made me become an ordained minister before he'd sell me anything. Some people who deal in this stuff are crazy-town, but it's worth it if I can help."

Touched, Malcolm gripped Fred's shoulder. "The enemy won't know what hit them."

Poking at the armor, Asha nodded her approval. "It appears we're as prepared as we can be."

"Actually," John said, "there's one more thing."

Approaching the wall of sealed containers where he kept

in-progress gadgets, he retrieved a box and set it before the twins with a smile.

Valentine's eyebrows climbed. "For us?"

He nodded. "Just for you two."

Malcolm glanced at Asha, who was trying and failing to keep her expression neutral. Whatever this was, she knew about it. He narrowed his eyes at her, and she replied with an innocent look that she had never truly mastered.

Finally, Malcolm could stand the suspense no more. At the touch of his thumb on the print reader, the box folded open to reveal two smaller boxes, one for each of them.

Malcolm ripped the cardboard top without ceremony. Inside was a swathe of black fabric, neatly folded, which he picked up and shook out.

"Oooooh," Valentine said, her eyes dancing. "It's perfect."

Malcolm held the gift up, at a loss for words. *A jacket. A totally awesome jacket.* Strong but silky smooth, the fabric was subtly shiny. He slipped it on and fastened the zipper halfway.

It was form-fitting across the torso, with long sleeves. At his waist the fabric flared, reaching down to mid-thigh. Though mostly black, the high collar and bottom hem were edged with royal blue. The left side of the chest bore silver embroidery in the shape of his old pocket watch.

The cut of Valentine's jacket was identical, except for where it accommodated her more feminine form. Where Malcolm's was accented with blue, hers was a rich crimson, and the embroidery on her chest displayed her old caduceus.

Malcolm beheld his sister in awe. Standing proudly, she looked like a hero out of legend. The way she gazed back at him made him think that just maybe the same was true for him. Twisting and turning, he tested out the feel of it.

"What's this fabric? It's amazing"

Valentine bent and stretched. "Feels strong, but it stretches with me."

"It, uh, doesn't actually have a name yet," John said. "One of my contacts has friends in the textile world, so he did me a favor. Technically, it's still untested."

"The weave is fire, friction, and impact resistant," Asha said. "Not armor, but still added protection."

John agreed. "Think of them less like armor and more like uniforms."

"So the enemy will know who they're dealing with," Asha said.

Malcolm felt pinpricks of heat behind his eyes. Blinking, he gathered Asha and John into a tight embrace. Valentine joined in.

"Thank you," he said. "It's perfect."

Asha planted a kiss on his lips. "You look like a warrior king, my love."

It was the highest compliment Malcolm had heard Asha give anyone. He kissed back just before the group hug dispersed.

"Thank you," Valentine said. "All of you."

"For everything," Malcolm added. "We couldn't ask for better—"

A *boom* shook the ground. The walls rattled. Even the air around them vibrated.

"Is that . . . ?" Valentine said.

"I don't know," Malcolm said. "How could—"

"—they get here so fast—"

"—without us noticing?"

Malcolm turned to warn the others and tell them to run. But instead of fear, their expressions showed puzzlement.

"Are you all right?" John said. "Why don't you sit down?"

His voice faded, drowned out by a wave of pressure and static like the crackling sound of an empty radio channel. It grew louder and heavier and closer. Malcolm swayed, the static racing through his nerves and into his brain.

"Wha—?"

The last thing he felt was the floor. Then there was only static. Then nothing at all.

CHAPTER 11

One.

Static, loud as a jet.

Flames, hot as a star.

Pressure, like a vise around his head.

One.

Pressure heavier than a mountain.

Malcolm groaned.

One.

Too much.

Can't take it or

Boom

Six.

With a sharp gasp, Malcolm sat up. Seconds later, Valentine came to with her own gasp, and her vision cast about wildly until her eyes settled on him.

"Welcome back," their father said.

Everyone knelt around them. Neil's eyes were squinting and strained, as if he'd been holding back tears.

As that static faded, Malcolm's awareness returned. Asha's hand clutched his. When he locked eyes with her, she pulled him into a fierce embrace. He clutched her like an anchor.

"How long?" he asked her.

"Half an hour," she said.

"What happened?" John said, in a similar embrace with Valentine. "Why were you both saying numbers?"

"Numbers?" Valentine said.

"The number one, over and over," Oma Grace said. "Then, just once, you said *six*."

"More like yelled it," Fred added. "That was freaky."

"Do you know why?" Asha said.

The twins shared a look. Malcolm had assumed it was some kind of fever dream, but hearing that Valentine had experienced the same, he knew it was real. Judging by the tension on her face, she knew it, too.

"Turn on the news," she said.

They moved to John's largest display. The moment he turned to a 24-hour news station, it was there.

"*. . . just like the other three that have appeared around the world,*" the reporter yelled, his jacket flapping in blustering winds. "*This one, in Shenzhen, China, appeared with no warning, and no one can explain how such a phenomenon might occur.*"

"*Can you zoom in?*" the anchor asked from her desk. "*We'd like to give the viewers the best possible look.*"

The reporter moved out of frame and the camera zoomed. As the lens refocused, it came into view. Malcolm's insides went cold.

A tower of fire.

It must have been a hundred stories tall and wider than a football field.

"Merciful Lord," Oma Grace breathed.

"Its effect is so intense that buildings around it are warping," the reporter continued. *"No attempts to scan or even approach it have been successful."*

Malcolm opened his hand. Without looking, Asha slid her hand into his. They served as anchors for each other.

"Is there any way to get closer, or . . . We are receiving word that another occurrence has been spotted." The camera switched back to the anchorwoman. *"That's five—repeat, five—so far. Hamilton, New Zealand. Casablanca, Morocco. Norilsk, Siberia. Shenzhen, China. And now Villa la Angostura, Argentina. With no working theories available, who knows if and where another may appear?"*

The twins locked eyes. *This is it,* Malcolm thought with sinking dread. *It's happening.*

"Kids, please," their dad pleaded. "What is this?"

Malcolm had to take a deep breath before he could speak. "That static—the pressure that knocked us out—it was from a shock wave in the Timeline."

"And the numbers," Valentine said. "This whole time, there's been one giant wall of fire. The shock wave happened because it split into six smaller ones and they spread out. Like a final approach, I think."

"These are what's been coming?" Fred asked. "Why a bunch of fire? What's that accomplish?"

"Only five have appeared," John said. "So, where would the sixth . . . ?"

Though he trailed off, everyone knew.

"Ladder," John commanded. With an acknowledging chime,

a ladder unfolded from the ceiling and a hatch opened to the roof. "We'll need a better vantage point."

The lab was tall enough to look over most buildings in the immediate area. One by one, they scrambled onto the roof.

Valentine turned a continuous circle, as if trying to peer everywhere at once. "I'd tell everyone to be ready . . ."

Malcolm studied the opposite directions. "But we don't even know what to be ready f—aaah!"

He crumpled to his knees, clutching his head. An intense burning sensation swept through him, followed by waves of nausea and white-hot agony. Pressure slammed down on him with a vengeance. Valentine fell next to him, hands to her temples.

"To the west!" Asha cried.

Malcolm forced his eyes open. Stumbling forward, he clung to the roof's parapet and pulled himself up just enough to look westward.

"I don't see anything," Neil said.

Malcolm did.

Near the center of town, a column of Time distorted, bending and twisting back on itself, as if trying to contain a force that was slowly breaking through.

"Oh, God," Valentine said, stumbling against the parapet next to him. "Here it comes."

What Malcolm felt next wasn't a *shift*. The Timeline split open with a thunderous *crack*. A blazing rift replaced the distortions, at least a hundred stories tall. Howling wind swept from the wound in the Timeline, hot and angry. The twins cried out as the universe screamed in their minds, its fabric shredding.

Their family gasped and stumbled back.

"No. Way," Fred said.

Time shuddered and the rift widened. A thousand secondary rips spread out from it.

Then fire burst from the rift. *So much fire.*

It seemed to fill the western sky. Like an endless maelstrom, not seeping or flowing through the rift, but shoving and forcing—a monster determined to break through and devour them.

Malcolm could hear tires screeching, glass breaking, and panicked cries. The people of Emmett's Bluff had dealt with enough Time-traveling invaders to know what it meant.

"Run," he whispered, begging each of the thirty thousand people. "Please, just run."

Because this time, he truly didn't know how to save them.

Then again, where could they run? This wasn't just about their town anymore. Across the world, six towers now burned, and right now all he could do was watch.

An earsplitting *snap* echoed across Emmett's Bluff. With a *whoosh*, the flames began to dissipate. Starting at ground level, they wavered and then disappeared. As the effect rose higher, what was hiding underneath began to appear.

"What in Eternity?" Asha said.

Finally, all but the topmost flames disappeared. The rift in Time closed. What remained was the furthest thing from what Malcolm had expected.

If he hadn't known the invaders were from the future before, this would have removed all doubt. And it was . . .

"Beautiful," Oma Grace said, confused and conflicted and terrified. "How can it be so beautiful?"

As the flames and the rift receded, the agony faded as well. Gripping the parapet with one hand and Valentine with the other, Malcolm stood to face this thing.

A new skyscraper now dominated an entire block of

downtown Emmett's Bluff. Not a crude fortress, nor a dark and brooding lair. It glittered in the sunlight, a hundred-story work of art.

Like a grand yet delicate sculpture, it reached toward the sky with swathes of glass and chrome and sparkling white stone. Waves of them swept over each other, weaving in and out and joining together seamlessly before separating again. At the top, a flame still burned, as if it were a giant torch.

It was breathtaking. And it had come there to kill them.

"Kids," Neil said. "What do we do now?"

To his shame, Malcolm had nothing.

Valentine hugged herself, haunted. "How many people do you think were downtown when that arrived?"

He shook his head, not wanting to think about it.

"We just have to hope they got out in time," he said, not believing his own words.

"We'll make sure they take no one else," Asha said, her voice like steel.

"Dude," Fred said, tapping his visor. "I can't spot any breaks in that thing. Not a joint or a seam. Like it's all one big piece, or . . . Hold up a sec."

Malcolm felt their group collectively tense, waiting as Fred studied the skyscraper, head cocked in apparent confusion. Finally, he removed the visor and offered it to the twins.

"Y'all should see this. Not sure what it means."

Valentine nudged it toward Malcolm. "You first."

Malcolm donned the device and took a moment to adjust to the magnification. He tried to focus, doing his best to ignore the data streaming on either side of his vision.

"Ground level," Fred said. "Look at the base. See it?"

Malcolm nodded. The skyscraper's wide base was roughly oval-shaped. Along the curve of that oval, not far above ground level, three separate doors were opening. One faced southeast, another northeast, and the third true east. Which meant that one pointed in the direction of John's shop.

"Hey," Asha said, coming closer. "What do you see?"

"Three doors are opening. Big ones—maybe thirty feet across."

"Can you see inside?" Valentine asked.

"Just shadows so far and . . . Wait, something's coming."

Platforms emerged from the doors, each carrying a ring at least twenty feet wide. Malcolm couldn't tell if they were stone or frosted glass or some future metal, but as the rings began to spin he knew exactly what they were for.

An array of shimmering metallic coils surrounded each ring. Malcolm's attention pulled to the ring facing southeast, and he noted that the coils pointed southeast as well. As the ring spun faster, waves of energy concentrated around the coils.

Valentine shook his arm. "Mal, what's going on? I feel something."

He felt the stirring in his chest, too. Whipping off the visor, he handed it over and she quickly donned it. After taking a second to zoom, she gasped.

"Rings like the Empyrean Bridge," Malcolm said to Asha. Her eyes widened as he turned to explain to the others. "They've got three rings, and each one is spinning up, probably to open a portal. I can feel Time responding."

"Are you saying more is coming, Malcolm?" Oma Grace asked.

"Maybe, but I couldn't tell you what or—"

He cut off as a spike of agony pierced his temples.

Fire lanced from the southeast ring array. Like a laser beam, it struck southeast across town, reducing anything in its path to cinders. Streets, cars, houses, shops—all became ash as the flames burned through Emmett's Bluff.

Whoever was inside that thing, they had just declared war.

CHAPTER 12

"N o!" Valentine cried.

In less than a minute, the beam of fire burned through miles of Emmett's Bluff. Somewhere on the south side of town, it stopped and a gush of flames burst upward. Then the fire dissipated, leaving a scorched furrow across the town.

Where the fire had moved upward, in its place now stood a ten-story replica of the skyscraper, right down to the glass and steel and the torch-like flame on top.

"Okay, what is going on?" Fred demanded, trembling. "What are they doing?"

Malcolm felt Asha grip his shoulder.

"People are dying out there, Mal," she said. "How do we fight this?"

He rested his hands on the parapet, a support to help him stay on his feet. Even now the pressure in his head was building again.

"The southeast ring's gone dark." Valentine tapped the visor. "But another one is powering up."

"Which one?" Malcolm asked.

"Northeast ring."

Swaying, she gave the visor back to Fred. John offered a supportive arm. She steadied against him and her eyes locked with Malcolm's.

An entire conversation passed between them. They were unprepared. Overwhelmed. Wracked with pain. But it was still time to go to work.

"Would you take a few steps back?" he said to everyone.

"More than a few," Valentine added.

"Yeah. Far side of the roof would be better."

As they retreated, the ring's presence grew in Malcolm's mind. Already the burning sensation was resurging. They didn't have long.

They faced the skyscraper, no longer needing Fred's visor. The northeast ring burned like a bonfire in their Chronauri perceptions.

"Whoa." Malcolm touched his temple. "Whatever power source they're using, I've never felt anything so big."

"That temporal signature," Valentine replied. "I can feel it echoing over decades."

Steeling himself, Malcolm gave a weak salute, which she mirrored back.

"Ready?" he said.

"Ready. Count it down."

"Three . . ."

Malcolm beckoned to Time. Energy rushed in like a raging torrent, and his corona shined silvery white. He gasped, fighting through fiery pain to keep control. With a *shift*, Valentine glowed like a star as the universe bathed her in its radiance.

"Two . . ."

The twins lifted their hands, holding their power at the

edge of release. In the distance, the ring spun up to full speed and the coils hummed to life.

"One!"

Malcolm conjured a bubble of slowed Time around the array: platform, ring, and coils. As his hand clenched into a fist, he filled the bubble with millions of microscopic bubbles, each slowing Time at the molecular level. It was a deeper, quicker freeze that would plummet the array toward absolute zero, leaving it dangerously brittle.

Just in time for Valentine. Thunder boomed overhead. From a cloudless sky, bolts of lightning rained down on the array.

Filled with Time, the twins' perceptions raced far beyond normal. It let them watch in satisfaction as frost spread over the array, then whoop in triumph as lightning struck home.

Then watch in horror as everything went wrong.

The frost melted, the bubbles burst. Malcolm felt a sharp yank as Time was ripped from his control, only to be absorbed by the coils.

Mere inches from obliterating the ring, Valentine's lightning unraveled. With a gasp, she rocked back. Malcolm felt the coils seize her Time, too, and soak it up like a sponge.

Agony stabbed through them like burning spikes, breaking their grip on Time.

"What was that?" Valentine said.

"Those coils absorbed our power!" Malcolm recoiled, instinctively trying to back away from the pain. "I can feel it, Val. The ring . . ."

"It didn't just take the power. It's using it."

"We just made it stronger."

Malcolm's heart sank out of his chest and into the ground below. He could only watch in helpless despair as the ring array fired. Once more, flames cut a burning swathe through Emmett's Bluff.

The destruction blazed northeast, ancillary explosions erupting as it leveled a gas station and then a power relay. It burned through town and up into the foothills. When the flames reached a point high on a rocky ledge, they spiked upward and another ten-story tower appeared.

The ring array powered down and the fire dispersed. The twins collapsed, breathing hard.

"Mal," Valentine said desperately, tears streaking her face. "I don't know what to do."

He pulled her close, choking back his own tears. *We're failing everyone. Whatever happens, it's because we couldn't stop it.*

As if on cue, the third ring array bloomed in his perception, powering up to fire eastward. If the flames didn't tear right through John's lab, they would come awfully close. The twins had only one card left to play.

"The rift itself," Malcolm said. "If attacking the ring doesn't work, let's shut down their effect."

Valentine dragged herself to her feet. Malcolm followed, leaning heavily on the parapet again. Without it he would've ended up back on his knees.

"This is going to hurt," she said.

"I know."

They opened themselves to Time. Malcolm's insides cried out in protest. He kept going.

"I'll redirect," he said. "You close."

"Got it."

Valentine released an audible groan as her corona flared. Temporal waves emanated from the twins, sending ripples through the Time stream.

The ring array fired. The universe screamed as threads of reality ripped and burned. The rift aimed straight for them.

In unison, the twins unleashed a storm of Time.

Wielding the power as if it were his own hands, Malcolm grabbed the spreading rift and shoved. Up . . . up . . . up he pushed with all his might, striving to redirect it skyward.

Valentine tightened her will around the rift. Reaching through the relentless flames, she worked to weave the damage back together.

Slowly the rift's trajectory began to turn upward. Its advance faltered, the flames weakened, and a burst of elation filled Malcolm. For a moment, they were succeeding.

Then the power behind the flames drew back, as if regathering itself, and struck with renewed ferocity. Like a thunderclap it hit the twins, shredding their tenuous grip and throwing them back like rag dolls.

Malcolm's head rattled. Hands gripped the twins and helped them to their feet. As the stars cleared from his vision, he saw his family's fear. They couldn't have followed everything that happened, but the twins' defeat was obvious.

He beheld the flames as they grew larger, burning inexorably toward him and everyone he loved. His heart like lead, he faced his family.

"I'm sorry," he said. "But you've got to run."

Asha gripped his arm tighter. "And you're coming with us."

"I believe the time to run is past, my dears." Oma Grace gave a sad smile. "I love you all."

She was right. They had known from the beginning what the cost of staying might be. Now here they were.

Clutching each other, facing the oncoming flames. Less than thirty seconds away now, and already Malcolm could feel the heat on his skin. Holding Asha, he breathed in her scent one more time.

"I love you," he whispered.

"I love you," Asha said, punctuating her words with a last kiss. "To the end."

Bracing himself, Malcolm focused on her ice-blue eyes and waited for the flames.

CHAPTER 13

Flames loomed in Malcolm's peripheral vision, growing until he could feel nothing but the heat and Asha's hands in his.

Something in the rift's path exploded. Someone out there screamed. The ground began to tremble.

So hot . . .

> *. . . I'm sorry, I'm so sorry we couldn't . . .*
>
> *Wait.*
>
> *Is that . . . ?*

Agape, Malcolm whirled to face east. With the advancing fire at his back, he pumped his fist in the air and cheered at the top of his lungs. A split second later, Valentine's expression burst with elation and she joined him in cheering. For a heartbeat, their family watched them as if they might be insane.

"Mal!" Asha tugged on his arm. "What's going on?"

"They're here!"

"Who?"

On the eastern edge of town, a red vortex burst open; the most massive he'd ever seen, at least fifty stories tall. The approaching Time signature grew stronger and stronger, leaving no doubt now. The vortex twisted and warped, as if it were pliable fabric stretching to fit the shape of something underneath.

"Val, what is this?" John shouted.

She beamed back at him. "Hope."

With a thunderous *boom*, the Eon Palace appeared. Not just the palace, but its walled grounds and a grove of trees, between which sat the powerful Empyrean Bridge. The Time machine's signature blazed in Malcolm's perceptions.

Lights glowed across the surface of the palace. They pulsed brighter once, twice, and on the third pulse a deep *thrum* passed through the town. A near-transparent energy dome emanated from the structure. In a blink it extended over the eastern third of Emmett's Bluff, passing through Malcolm and his family.

Everything trembled as the dome collided with the oncoming flames. Both slammed to a halt, stalemated against each other. Malcolm gritted his teeth, feeling the twist and pull where two monumental forces struggled for dominance.

The palace lights pulsed again, and with a final push the dome extended. Malcolm felt the skyscraper's power twist back on itself. Something inside the ring array *snapped*, and the ring vaporized in a ball of its own energy.

The flames died, the rift closed, and for a moment all was silent.

Then everyone was cheering. The twins, their family, their town. Suddenly they weren't so alone.

"Kids, what is that?" Neil said.

"Home! My people have come." Drawing one *qama*, Asha saluted them. "The Eon Palace has never *shifted* like this before. My parents are holding nothing back."

"Then this must be as bad as we thought," Malcolm said.

Valentine agreed. "Let's get to the palace. We need to plan our next move quickly."

"Yo, hold up." Facing west, Fred donned his visor again. "That third ring's toast, but another door opened. Take a look."

He passed the visor to Malcolm, who zoomed in and went stiff. "Cyonics, the humanoid ones."

"How many?" Asha said.

"Maybe a hundred."

He heard a metallic rasp as she drew her second blade.

"Advance guard," she said. "They'll attack the dome shield, test it for weaknesses."

"Are you sure?" Valentine said.

"Not completely, but it is a very old war tactic."

"If so," Fred said, "seems like something we should have a problem with. Right, y'all?"

Turning, Malcolm zoomed the visor toward the Eon Palace and its grounds. Though they looked like ants, he could see armored people making preparations.

"They're getting ready, but we're closer," he said.

As he removed the visor, their group shared a look with each other. A moment of quiet, each of them understanding and accepting what they needed to do.

"I'll run overwatch," John said. Giving Valentine a quick kiss, he headed for the roof hatch. "Just catch them before they reach the shield."

Neil and Oma Grace volunteered to help John. They followed him through the hatch, leaving the twins on the roof with Asha and Fred.

Removing their phones and any valuables, they tossed them down the hatch for safekeeping. The twins zipped up their new jackets, closing them from waist to neck.

"Do we need a plan?" Valentine said, tugging at her sleeves.

"Yeah," Fred said, drawing his katana. "Break stuff."

Asha laughed and slapped his shoulder in agreement. "Confront them at the shield. Send them home."

"We can't just wait at the shield," Malcolm said. "Who knows what they'll do to people who get in their way?"

"Then we take the fight to them," Valentine said.

Malcolm nodded, extending a bubble of fast Time around them all. The world outside slowed to a crawl. "Wherever they are now, that's where they fall."

Asha gave a wicked grin. With a small *shift*, her signature burned bright. Sizzling red energy washed over her blades and armor.

Fred pumped his fist. "Let's bring the pain!"

Adrenaline surged through Malcolm—a focused eagerness. For too long they'd lived in fear, waiting for another enemy to threaten their people. Now they could do something.

"Okay." He squared his shoulders. "Here we go."

As one they stepped forward, and the world blurred around them.

At one heartbeat, they arrived at the shield and passed through it. At two heartbeats, miles flew by under their feet. At three, they came to a stop.

Right in the middle of the Cyonic force.

They stood in the center of an intersection, where people were abandoning gridlocked cars and fleeing. Deadly machines surrounded their group, moving in slow motion.

They were divided into squads of ten. Sleek masterpieces of technology, white and chrome with serene human faces as if designed to match the artistry of the skyscraper. But if Charlotte

Corday had taught Malcolm anything, it was that even something beautiful could kill.

"Ready?" Malcolm called. Receiving three quick affirmations, he set his jaw. "Okay. Let's make it rain."

The Time bubble dropped.

Malcolm loosed a fireball that melted a hole clean through the nearest Cyonic's chest. As the machine fell, he sent a spray of ice spikes to impale the two behind it.

The Cyonics stumbled back and raised their plasma rifles. Before they could take aim, he wrapped their heads in fast Time bubbles and spun them. Internal circuitry melted and dripped down their shoulders.

Pointing at two more, Malcolm targeted the power sources under their armor. Spinning up two more fast Time bubbles, he forced the batteries to work faster and faster until they overloaded and the Cyonics blew to pieces.

After two-point-four seconds, half the squad was down. Turning a dark smile on the other half, Malcolm unleashed havoc.

Fred donned two accelerator rings and targeted a squadron that had their backs to him. Which let him use one of his favorite tactics: Cheat to win.

Fred dashed up behind the nearest Cyonic, rammed his sword through its back and twisted until he saw sparks. The machine lurched. Fred reached around it with his free hand, grabbed its gun hand and pulled the trigger.

Plasma fire ripped through the squad. Holding the impaled Cyonic like a shield, Fred raked the weapon across the machine ranks, reducing half a dozen to smoking debris.

The remaining three returned fire. Sizzling blasts impacted his Cyonic shield, tearing away chunks of armor. A flash of green smashed into his right flank, knocking him down to one knee. His armor held, but *holy crap did that hurt*.

Refocusing, he stood and—

Motion over his left shoulder. Too late, he realized a Cyonic had managed to flank him. Too slowly, he swung around to—

"Fred, drop!"

Asha. Fred fell to his knees and ducked as a shadow flew overhead.

Asha spun on her toes, her *qamas* windmilling. The blades deflected one plasma bolt, and then another, sending them back at the machines that had fired them.

A mechanical whirring came from over her shoulder. Without looking, she flicked her wrist backward. Her blade bit into something metal, and sparks showered her neck.

Asha grinned, spun to make sure the machine was dead, and stiffened. A Cyonic had circled behind Fred and taken aim at the base of his skull.

"Fred, drop!" she shouted.

Her friend crouched. Asha pumped more power to her leg armor and took a flying leap.

Midflight, she flung a *qama* and skewered Fred's Cyonic through the eye. With a fierce cry, she landed in front of another and cleaved it from head to torso. As the machine split into halves, she burst through its sparking frame and charged toward the next squad.

"Thanks, girl!" Fred called.

The *qama* she'd thrown now flew back into her hand. The

next squad moved to surround her, trying to isolate her from her friends. She gave a vicious laugh and become a blazing steel whirlwind.

Green bolts glanced off her armor, the concussive force knocking her back but never piercing. The machines wouldn't know this metal had been designed to channel energy. Asha spun, using one blade to deflect the blasts while the other relieved the machines of their heads.

Something struck her chest with the force of Thor's hammer. Asha's fleet flew out from under her. She smacked onto the pavement with a gasp.

Breathless, she rolled and searched for her attacker, intent on extracting vengeance.

Until she saw who it was.

Valentine leapt into a front handspring, fire whip twirling and snapping. Cyonic armor shattered with every snap-explosion. Smooth like a dancer, she landed back on her feet and spun on pointed toes, radiating beautiful destruction.

Grinding to a halt, she drank in energy and threw a wave of super-fast Time. The last three Cyonics burst into ash.

Valentine searched for the next threat. She found it—but it wasn't a threat to her. Eyes wide, she reached toward Asha.

With the pop of a thousand microscopic, ultra-fast Time bubbles, a burst of gravity slammed into Asha's chest. She crashed to the ground.

Eighty yards away, a Cyonic perched on a rooftop with a sniper rifle. One-sixteenth of a second after Asha fell, a blazing green bolt sliced through the air where her head had been.

The sniper fired next at Valentine. Filled with Time, she

watched it approach at a snail's pace. *Plasma bolt. Energy and superheated gas, sheathed in a magnetic field.* She cracked her neck. *Try this on for size.*

Valentine wrapped the plasma bolt in hyper-slowed Time. The superheated gas flashed into a spike of ice.

Robbed of its energy, the bolt's forward momentum halted and its magnetic sheath unraveled. Valentine flicked it with her will and reversed its path. Flying back the way it had come, the ice hit the sniper between the eyes. Its head exploded in a shower of frozen clockwork.

Valentine offered Asha a helping hand. As her friend stood, an ice wall appeared beside them just in time to block a barrage of plasma fire.

She sensed Malcolm's Time signature as he sent Entropy Blades spinning through the squad that had fired on them. Half the squad shredded to ribbons.

Malcolm appeared at her side. "You good?"

Valentine clenched her fist and lightning bolts fell among the remains of the squad, blasting them into debris.

"I am now. Thanks."

"Nice move with the sniper."

She grinned. "By the way, let's 'make it rain?'"

Malcolm shrugged. "Hey, it felt right at the time."

Chuckling, he searched for his next target—they still had about thirty Cyonics to dispatch. Then he realized no one was shooting at them.

"I didn't think machines would be programmed to retreat."

"They're regrouping." Fred tapped his visor. "More are coming. A lot more."

"Destroyers, too?" Asha said.

"And a third type, kinda like Cyonics but twice as big."

A moment later the mechanical army came into view, marching straight for them.

Malcolm's heart pounded. *You're a Sixth-sev Chronauri. They should be scared of you.* But years of pre-Chronauri instinct didn't just disappear. For a moment, he was a teenage geek facing down an army of killer machines from the future.

Swallowing hard, he forced himself to look at the beautiful fortress that brushed the clouds, and the destructive mechanical horde it had released onto his town. Whoever the Regent was, whatever his reasons for doing this, they couldn't give him an inch or falter for a moment. The world depended on it.

Only a hundred yards away now. Mere seconds.

To the machines' right, the walls of an office building exploded outward. Shattered bricks and smoke flew into the street.

Ember Guard poured through, silver-gray armor blazing as they rained sudden carnage down on the machine army's flank. Malcolm's jaw dropped.

To the machines' left, the ground swelled up like a bubble, rising until the pavement split open. A horde of Watchers poured from an underground tunnel.

Upgrades, Malcolm thought, the first real word that rang through his shock. While the Ember Guard looked as he remembered, the Watchers now wore mechanized armor that looked like what Iron Man would have built if he'd been from the Middle Ages.

For a moment, Malcolm and his companions stood dumbfounded. Two wildly different armies had traversed centuries of Time to do battle here, on the streets of Emmett's Bluff.

Fred summed it up perfectly. "Holy. Crap."

Asha whirled her *qamas* eagerly. "Anyone notice they left the middle for us?"

She was right. While the army's flanks were busy, the forwardmost forces had not yet been engaged. One by one, they broke into wide grins.

"How about we meet them in the middle?" Malcolm said.

With that, they shouted raucous battle cries and charged.

The twins, their friends, and the forces of Everwatch fell over the machines like crashing waves. Malcolm waded into the thick of the fight with pure destruction blazing from his hands. Waves of Cyonics fell before him.

The battle passed like a fever dream. Before Malcolm knew it, half of the machine army was retreating. Finally able to catch his breath, he surveyed the scene proudly. An hour ago, they had been facing certain death. *Look at us now.*

One by one, their battle group came back together. He and Valentine exchanged a knowing smile. Asha slid her arms around his waist. Fred appeared with the visor hanging from his neck and a Cyonic head hanging from his belt.

"Really, Fred?" Valentine said.

"Battle trophy, dawg. You know you want one, don't even hate."

Valentine peered past the group, head tilted. "Hey, you guys notice how everyone keeps looking at us but they're staying away?"

"Yeah, I caught that." Malcolm looked to Asha. "We do something wrong?"

"Nothing wrong," a deep, accented voice said behind them. "You intimidate them."

The group turned. A tall, dark-skinned man stood before them, the red glow fading from his massive iron war hammer.

Malcolm smiled. "Captain Armel!"

With a wide smile of his own, the commander of the Ember

Guard greeted them. Malcolm, Valentine, and Fred received hearty handshakes, while Asha leapt into his arms.

"My princess," Armel said. "What a treasure it is to see you again."

"Your timing was perfect, as always," Asha said, beaming at the man who'd protected her family since before she was born.

The captain set her back to her feet. "I expect a full report soon, soldier," he said, his tone much softer than his words.

Asha gave a salute. "Of course, sir."

"My instructions are to escort you all to the Eon Palace," Armel said. "The king and queen are eager to see you, and there is much to discuss. This fight is far from over."

"What about everyone in town?" Valentine asked. "Can we get them under the shield?"

The captain pursed his lips. "I'm uncertain if we have the time or resources. There is a whole world to consider."

"Captain," Malcolm said, "we're grateful for your help, but this isn't negotiable. There's a lot of terrified people out there, and we've lost enough of them already."

After a moment, Armel nodded. "Of course, you're right. We will find a way."

"A'ight then," Fred said. "Let's get moving."

But the captain didn't move. Instead he glanced at Malcolm with a coy smile.

Malcolm's eyebrows raised. "Something wrong, captain?"

"There's someone in our ranks who wanted to meet you," Armel said, gesturing past Malcolm. "One of our new Watchers."

Malcolm turned to see a Watcher approaching. With whirs and clanks, the armored form came within arm's reach and stood there studying him. He shifted uncomfortably.

The Watcher set down his giant sword. His gauntlets clicked

open and folded into his bracers. Finally, he reached up and pressed a button on the inside of his helmet.

As it folded away to reveal steely eyes and grey hair, Malcolm's knees turned to water.

"Walter."

CHAPTER 14

Valentine hadn't seen her brother this happy since his first kiss with Asha. Only now it was happiness of a different kind. He'd gotten his friend back—one they all thought was gone forever.

Though Malcolm was closer to Walter than Valentine was, she still admired the man. He'd held ready to fight his enemy for more than a century, and in the end, Emmett's Bluff still existed because of his sacrifice.

But the clock was ticking, and the king and queen were eager to meet with them. So they moved the reunion onto the Sled, the Ember Guard's hovering shuttle.

On the way, they had stopped at John's lab, where Valentine witnessed part two of the reunion. John had heard the news about Walter over the comms and rushed out to meet his old friend as soon as they touched down.

On catching sight of him, Oma Grace had dropped a glass and pulled Walter into a tearful embrace. The old soldier hugged her back, doing his best to endure the outpouring of affection.

Valentine sat back now, relaxing next to Asha against one of the Sled's padded seats. With a contented smile, she watched as her brother, grandmother, and boyfriend all clustered around Walter Crane.

"I was worried you and Lucius killed each other," Malcolm said. "He must have been furious."

"Oh, he was, and he tried," Walter said. "Little punk attacked me as soon as we fell through the portal. I knocked him flat on his back. Told him if he ever misbehaved, I'd find him and feed him to the biggest carnivore I could find."

"You separated?" Oma Grace said.

Walter nodded. "Tracked him down every six months or so. Made sure he wasn't trying to cause trouble, that he knew I was watching. But without his toys, he was finished. Spent most of his time hiding in caves, painting on the walls."

"How long were you there before Everwatch found you?" John said.

"A few years, maybe. Not so bad. It was quiet and I got to travel as far as my feet could take me." He grinned. "You should've seen Carmichael's face when they came for me. Right after I tracked him down again, a portal opened and the Ember Guard came through. His eyes lit up like it was Christmas morning. Fool thought he was going home."

Armel chuckled. "We made it clear that he was going nowhere. We had come for the man who saved Emmett's Bluff."

"Boy pouted like his dog had run away," Walter said, chuckling. "Anyway, they invited me to live in Everwatch, said I could do whatever job I wanted. But soon as I saw the Watchers, nothing else would do."

"Somehow that's not surprising, old friend," John said.

"Indeed." Oma Grace laid her hand on his arm. "I'm so glad you found happiness."

The Sled gave a gentle lurch and settled down with a thump.

"We have arrived," Armel said. "Please follow me to the Command Deck."

"Command Deck?" Valentine asked. The Eon Palace was huge, but she didn't recall seeing anything called the Command Deck before.

Armel began to speak, then hesitated. "You will see."

The lift rose silently, carrying them up through the central structure of the Eon Palace. Valentine allowed herself a moment of pure joy at being back inside this amazing place. John squeezed her hand, giving her a knowing smile.

"That dome shield, Captain," John said. "I'm very curious how it works."

"Dual-layer energy barrier," Captain Armel replied. "The outer layer is a repulsing field of harnessed kinetic force. The second layer uses temporal harmonics generated by the Empyrean Bridge. It blocks anything with a Time signature from your future."

"So, those machines shouldn't be able to pierce it," Asha said.

"For as long as it holds."

"That's the bomb diggity, bro," Fred said. "They didn't know what hit 'em."

Captain Armel furrowed his brow.

"That means he's impressed," Valentine explained. "And he's glad you're helping."

"True that."

"Empyrean Bridge?" Neil asked.

"Their Time machine, I believe, dear," Oma Grace said.

While the discussion continued, Valentine found her attention wandering. This was the first calm moment she'd had all day, the first chance to be still and think. As she soaked in her surroundings, a few key details began to register.

The lift was different. Its motion was even smoother and quieter, and the control panel had greeted the twins as if it remembered them.

Walter's armor reflected the ancient-meets-future mentality of Everwatch. It had the same dark blues and greys of the Eon Palace, the same subtly shifting lights. From a distance, it resembled the work of a master armorsmith from the Middle Ages.

Up close, though, the plates flowed together with laser precision. As Walter moved, it emitted subtle whirring sounds, suggesting advanced clockwork hidden inside. When the twins visited Everwatch two years ago, the Watchers had possessed nothing even close to this.

The shield Armel had described was a scientific wonder— not only for the knowledge it would have taken to create, but for the immense power required to generate it.

Then there was Armel himself. Though his captain's eyes bore the same inner kindness, they crinkled at the edges. His ebony skin bore scars Valentine hadn't seen before. His hair and goatee had gone from black to salt-and-pepper.

Valentine peered up at him intently enough that he noticed. "Do you need something, Miss Gilbert?"

"How long has it been, captain? For Everwatch, I mean. From our point of view, we haven't seen you for two years, but, well, that doesn't mean it was two years for you."

Captain Armel's eyes twinkled, but his expression closed tight. "Perhaps I should let my king and queen answer that."

"Playing coy, captain?" Malcolm teased. "That's not really your style."

He chuckled. "Only among friends, Malcolm."

A few stories shy of the Eon Palace's peak, the lift stopped and the doors opened with a *hiss*. They followed Captain Armel down a curved hallway.

Valentine heard another *hiss* and looked behind them. A lift door had opened, but no one stepped out. Weird.

The hallway terminated at a massive pair of armored doors, another thing she hadn't seen in the Palace before. She filed that away as a wide, yellow beam washed over them all.

"Armel and guests," the captain said.

The doors trilled a series of tones, and with a heavy internal *clunk*, split open and slid into the walls. As they strolled through, Valentine's jaw dropped.

They stood at a far end of the Command Center, oval-shaped and nearly a hundred feet across. At least fifty Watcher support staff were hard at work.

To the left were dozens of workstations, each an open circle with a uniformed man or woman sitting in the center, tapping commands into curved glass panels. Valentine noted that as the operators swiveled, their workstations spun with them.

Three tables dominated the center: a giant oval one that mimicked the shape of the room, flanked by two smaller circular tables. The curved edges of each table boasted a wide array of controls. Three-dimensional holographic displays hovered above each, showing everything from international news feeds to a topographical breakdown of Emmett's Bluff.

On Valentine's right, the entire wall was a curved sheet of glass looking out on the town. Lines of information scrolled across the glass, fed by two multi-station computer banks. Valentine even noticed glowing outlines around various buildings with data popping up beside them.

She exchanged an astonished glance with Malcolm. "This was—"

"—not here last time," he finished. "I knew Everwatch had tech, but they used to keep it hidden. More—"

"—underneath everything," Valentine said. "Looks like they've stopped hiding it."

"That's for sure."

"One moment. I'll retrieve the king. Please wait here and do not touch anything." Armel narrowed his eyes at Fred. "Especially you."

"Aw, now that's just cold," Fred protested as the captain walked away.

The group chuckled and watched as Captain Armel crossed the Command Center. He made his way to the glass viewport, where an observation platform sat between the two computer banks. Only then did Valentine notice a man standing on the platform, facing out.

Valentine saw long, black hair shot through with gray, adorned with a silver circlet. *King Jerrik is here.* Which meant the queen couldn't be far. Asha would be thrilled to see her parents. Curiously, Jerrik was flanked by two children, a boy and a girl. Trainees, maybe.

Captain Armel spoke briefly. With a nod, King Jerrik turned.

Only, it wasn't King Jerrik.

"Whoa," John said.

"Hey," Neil began. "Isn't that—?"

"Thorn!" Valentine said.

Behind them all, Walter laughed quietly to himself. He'd known all along.

King Tyrathorn Corvonian broke into a wide grin. With a

gleeful laugh, he practically threw himself across the room and gathered as many of them as he could into a hug.

"My friends, what a joy it is to see you," he said. "It has been far too long. Where is—"

He cut off with an *oof* as Asha flew into his arms. His smile melted into something deeper. A happy tear fell from his eye.

"Oh, Ashandara," he said, voice thick with emotion. "Look what a beautiful woman you have become. So many days gone by."

Pulling back, she stared hard at him. "Never so long again. Promise me, brother."

"I swear it. We will have many more days together, you and I."

"And our parents?"

"Safe back in Everwatch. When they chose to retire, the people insisted that I accept the crown. These years, I have done my best to justify their faith."

"A pleasure to see you, dear boy," Oma Grace said. "Thank you for coming to help us."

"How could we not?" Tyrathorn replied. "My friends were in danger, and the Timeline with them."

Oh, right. We're all in mortal danger. For a moment, Valentine had forgotten.

As she studied the Command Center, a corner of the viewport blurred for an instant and returned to normal. Something about that should have stuck in her mind, but the next surprise chased away all other thoughts.

The children that had flanked Tyrathorn at the viewport now approached. He beckoned the girl and boy forward. Valentine guessed they might be fourteen and ten, respectively.

"My friends," Tyrathorn said, swelling with pride. "Meet my daughter Meilyn, and my son Xander."

Valentine gasped along with everyone else. The children gave formal bows.

"Welcome to the Eon Palace," Meilyn said, every bit the young princess.

"We are honored by your presence," Xander followed. His eyes fell on Oma Grace and grew big as saucers. "Are you one of the Ancients?"

Her eyes glittered with amusement. "A lesser woman would take offense at that, young man."

"Excuse him, please," Tyrathorn said. "All in Everwatch know of the great warriors who spent a century defending their people. You, your allies," he nodded at Walter and John, "and the one who sacrificed all."

"Clive," Walter said, looking solemn. "Would've been nice to say goodbye."

"They know us here?" Oma Grace said, her cheeks reddening.

"They know you all. Here, my friends, you are legends."

"Thorn," Valentine said, finally finding her voice, "how long has it been? Who's their mother? What else . . ."

She trailed off as Fred approached Tyrathorn's children and sank to his knees. As if he couldn't help himself, he reached out to touch their faces.

"Their eyes," he said, almost whispering.

Valentine noticed them now: ice blue like their father's, though with a much different shape. Yet they seemed familiar.

"Xander. Alexander, my middle name . . ." Fred looked to Tyrathorn, full of hope. "Where is she?"

A throat cleared behind them. "Gotta say, in all my years, I never saw a sorrier group of heroes."

Valentine turned, and her insides leapt. An Asian woman leaned against the wall, wearing her trademark smirk. She wore the silver circlet of the queen.

"My friends," Tyrathorn said, "I believe you know my wife."

CHAPTER 15

Winter hugged Fred first, then worked her way around the rest of the group. Then she found Fred again. They stood in the middle of the Command Center, clutched in a tight embrace.

"You missed all sorts o' cool stuff, girl," Fred said, voice muffled with his face pressed against her shoulder. "When did you get taller?"

"When did you get muscles?" she returned.

"Like I said, cool stuff. You gonna explain all this?"

Still holding Fred, she turned a warm gaze on Tyrathorn. "About five years after I got here, it just . . . happened. I woke up one day and couldn't live without him."

"Nor I her," Tyrathorn said, radiating love in her direction.

"So, you've been happy?" Fred asked.

"So happy. But every day I missed you all." Winter's eyes welled with tears. "It's been so long."

Fred pulled out of their embrace. "How long?"

Winter hesitated.

"I'm thirty-eight years old, Fred. For us it's been over twenty years. Much of it, we've spent preparing for this war."

Valentine's mind reeled. *Twenty years?*

Winter braced herself for Fred's reaction. She stared up at him with veiled fear in her eyes. How would he react?

Fred burst into laughter, pointing a finger at her face. "You're an old lady now! What, d'you forget your walker next to your pill box?"

Relaxing, Winter pointed right back at him. "Whatever, idiot. You were crying a minute ago. I heard you."

"Screw you. Those were ninja tears. Fight me, bro."

"I've got moves you've never seen. I will *spank* you, son."

"Children," Tyrathorn muttered to Meilyn and Xander, "leave us to catch up with the . . . legendary heroes, please."

As the children slipped away, Tyrathorn cleared his throat. Then again, louder. Winter and Fred turned to him with innocent expressions.

Valentine couldn't contain her own laugher anymore. The rest soon joined her, releasing oceans of pent-up tension, savoring the joy of being reunited and safe with the people they loved. Even if it was just for a moment.

Winter moved to her husband's side and slid an arm around his waist. "Sorry, babe. Just felt like old times."

Tyrathorn caressed her cheek. "Never apologize for that, my love."

Valentine's heart swelled for her friend. Winter had come through tragedy before finding her way here. Whatever danger had brought them all together again, at least they got to see her happy.

John grasped Valentine's hand, gazing at her with the same love she saw in Winter and Tyrathorn. Bursting with feeling, she leaned up and placed a soft kiss on his lips.

"Could that be us someday?" she whispered.

"There is no other life I want," John said. "We'll come through this, Valentine. Then we'll have our life together."

She leaned against him, a warm glow filling her. From the corner of her eye, she saw Asha and Malcolm in much the same embrace. *One more reason to get through this alive. We have to win, whatever it takes.*

As if reading her thoughts, Tyrathorn took charge. "My friends, though it pains me to say it, there is work to be done. Shall we?"

Beckoning, he stepped over to the large oval table. The rest followed, taking places around the table. Valentine hoped Everwatch had arrived with a plan.

"We know nothing about this enemy," Tyrathorn said. "Their purpose and their full capabilities remain a mystery."

Valentine's heart sank.

"Well, that's disappointing," Malcolm said.

Tyrathorn held up his hands. "That said, we are not completely in the dark." He typed a series of commands on the table. "Here is what we *do* know."

The floating hologram changed to a translucent model of the earth, with six spots around the globe pulsing red.

"That's where the skyscrapers are?" Valentine asked.

"Yes. But yours is different than the other five."

Tyrathorn reached for the projection and spread his hands. In response, the projection zoomed in on one location. The picture reoriented to show a bird's-eye view of the Chinese city of Shenzhen.

Entire blocks were in flames, buildings toppled, roads destroyed, and holographic people still fleeing. A skyscraper loomed over the carnage, identical to the one in Emmett's Bluff with one key difference. Three mini-towers had appeared with it, as opposed to the two here.

"No one was able to stop that third tower from appearing," Malcolm said.

"No one even came close," Winter said. "And because of that, look what's happening."

She tapped more commands. Multiple screens appeared in the air to hover beside Shenzhen. While some showed Chinese news coverage, others played cell phone videos and social media streams.

Valentine's insides went cold. Her hands went to her mouth.

"Dude," Fred said in a haunted voice. "What's happening?"

In Emmett's Bluff, fires burned atop the skyscraper and its supporting towers. In Shenzhen, they had become beams of fire that connected the invading structures to each other. A network of flames joined them together.

For miles around, the city warped as if Valentine was seeing it through a funhouse mirror. The buildings, even the ground. And now that she saw it, she could *feel* it.

"Time, space," she said, breathless. "They're being twisted."

"Why ain't the same thing happening here?" Fred said.

"The third tower," Malcolm said. "They must not be able to do this unless all the towers get through."

John tapped his chin. "Like a closed-loop system. Maybe it's cycling power, using its own feedback to build that power more and more. But it only works if the system is complete. Just a guess."

Valentine nodded. "But it makes sense."

"Their military must have tried something," Walter said, his gravelly voice tense.

"They did," Tyrathorn replied.

A few more keystrokes and one screen enlarged. From a rooftop miles away, a cell phone captured fighter jets racing toward the invasion zone. Voices spoke in Mandarin, growing more excited as the jets launched a volley of missiles.

Valentine unconsciously held her breath. *Please work. Please be that simple.*

But no. The instant those missiles crossed the horizon of warped Time and space, they went haywire. Some collided together, some detonated, and others just dropped out of the sky.

The jets circled back for another try. As they turned, the fire atop the skyscraper flared. Like a giant laser it lanced out to burn them from the sky. Reduced to ash, they disintegrated before ever hitting the ground.

Videos showed other forces trying: tanks, ground troops, anything they could throw at the skyscraper and its support towers. All with identical results.

"In this century, I do not believe there is a military that can stand up to them," Tyrathorn said. "Whatever can be done, it will have to be done by us."

"What about here?" Neil said. "Is the army trying anything?"

Malcolm pointed at a smaller projection beside the others. "This says they're considering options, but they've seen all those videos from other places. I don't think they know what to do."

"At least they haven't dropped a nuke," Fred observed.

"Let's make sure they don't have to," Walter said.

"Which means pressing our advantage," Winter replied. Swiping at the main hologram, she spun through images until they came to Emmett's Bluff. "When their ring array blew, we detected all sorts of feedback and power surges. We figure they're busy trying to fix it—for now, anyway."

Valentine studied the glowing outline of her town, her

stomach roiling at the thought of seeing it twisting like the others. *We stopped Lucius Carmichael. We stopped Charlotte Corday. There must be a way to—*

Wait a minute.

As Valentine's thoughts drifted to the past, an old image in her memories combined with this new one in front of her. She stepped closer to the table.

"May I?"

At a nod from Tyrathorn, her fingers flew across the keys, calling up a second projection of Emmett's Bluff. Twelve points on the image began to glow red, arranged in a circle like the numbers on a clock. A circle that cut right through the town.

"Anyone remember this?"

"Lucius's energy beams," Malcolm said. "That's where they punched through the ground."

"Exactly. Watch this."

Aligning both projections of Emmett's Bluff, Valentine pushed them together until the two images merged into one. Now it displayed Lucius' twelve energy beam vents, the skyscraper, and its two support towers.

"Notice anything interesting?" Valentine asked the group.

Their stunned expressions were all the confirmation she needed.

"What the . . . ?" Malcolm said. "I mean, why?"

The skyscraper sat exactly where Lucius's westernmost energy beam had torn through the town. The two support towers sat exactly where the northernmost and southernmost beams had struck. As Valentine keyed one last entry, another spot pulsed brighter. If the third tower had appeared, it would have materialized exactly where Lucius' house with no doors had stood.

That spot was now protected inside the Eon Palace's shield.

"Oh, merciful Lord," Oma Grace gasped. "Please, no. Not him again."

Asha asked, "Are you saying your old enemy is doing this?"

Winter shook her head. "We keep Carmichael under surveillance. Believe me, he's busy enough trying to survive prehistoric times without all his gadgets."

"Why, then?" Valentine said. "This can't be an accident."

Malcolm shook his head. "Yet another mystery."

"We do know one truth," Tyrathorn said. "Their plan relies on these tower configurations, and across the world, only one has failed to complete."

Valentine understood. "So, whatever they're trying, we're the one thing standing in their way. For the entire world, the last stand will happen here."

"Which means they'll try everything to bring down our shield," Winter said.

"So they can do . . . whatever they're trying to do," Neil said.

"And we still have no clue what that is," Malcolm added.

Valentine turned, intending to respond, when her line of vision slipped over Malcolm's shoulder. Near the back wall, the faintest blur drifted past a workstation. This time her mind caught it, connecting it with the half-dozen other times she had noticed and dismissed it.

"Keep talking," she whispered. "Something's up."

By the subtle change in Malcolm's expression, she knew he'd caught her meaning and was now serving as a distraction.

"There's something else," he said. "The Empyrean Bridge, my pocket watch, even Lucius's master Time machine—they all essentially do the same thing."

Pushing away sight and sound, Valentine left the physical

behind and sank into the temporal. Her Chronauri perceptions sharpened, becoming her sole vision of the world around her.

Instead of air, she saw the currents of Time flowing through the Command Center. She felt the table's imperceptibly slow breakdown as the energy streamed around it.

"They slice through the Timeline, make a tunnel to a day and location," Malcolm continued. "It's surgical, trying for as little resistance as possible. Lucius did it because it required less power, and Everwatch does it because it's less destructive to the Timeline."

All around Valentine, Watchers pulsed with the faint glows of their internal Time batteries. Though John's Time pulsed like anyone else's, Valentine always felt his signature first.

Tyrathorn's signature was unique—she could see the scars of his former Chronauri power, like a broken blade. Asha also stood out, sustained by pulses from two batteries: the one she'd been born with, and the one Malcolm had created. Malcolm himself blazed, an open conduit to universal power.

"But the skyscraper did the opposite," he said. "It *ripped* its way into the past, burning Time as it moved. Whoever's controlling this, it's like they wanted to damage as much of the Timeline as possible. Why would they do that?"

Valentine catalogued them all. One by one, she matched temporal signatures to what her eyes had observed when they arrived, until she found it.

One extra signature pulsed in her perceptions. Someone else was here. They stood near the back wall, the faintest blur among shadows.

Not for long.

Valentine sheathed herself in fast Time and moved. In a blink, she closed the distance and reached into the shadows.

Her hands gripped something solid that tried to squirm away. Valentine shoved hard, and the invisible spy smashed against the wall.

The cloaking device sputtered and died to reveal a slender, armored figure. Conjuring long spikes of fire, Valentine held them at the spy's throat.

"I know it's you. Might as well stop hiding."

Hands raised in surrender. The helmet peeled back and long, dark hair spilled out.

Valentine nodded. "Hello, Callie."

CHAPTER 16

"Our shield should have blocked you," Tyrathorn said. He and Winter had been shocked, to say the least, on learning the truth of Callie's origins. Now he regarded her with untrusting eyes. "How did you get past it?"

"I snuck onto your hovercraft," Callie replied. "You all may hate me, but you *need* me. I know how this army fights, and I can help you uncover the Regent's plan."

"I thought you knew his plan," Malcolm challenged.

Callie grimaced. "Apparently, only one version. But I know how to find the truth, and where to get more information about the Pyre—that's what everyone calls the skyscraper. The main one is back in Eldurfall."

"Elder-what?" Fred scoffed.

"Eldurfall. It's my home, our capital city. After we were invaded, the Regent said he had a plan to save us, but it would take the whole world's support." She pointed at the image of Shenzhen. "The first part was building his mechanical army. The second was building five copies of the Pyre around the world. No one knew why, but he'd always been right before, so we trusted him."

"You said you can get information," Winter said. "How do you plan to do that?"

Now Callie looked uncertain. "I have a contact in Eldurfall, but it means you'll have to send me back where I came from."

Asha smirked. "Back into the arms of your waiting master?"

"I think not," Tyrathorn said. "Surely you understand your position here."

"Why not jump back with whatever device brought you here?" Walter asked.

Callie shook her head. "I don't have a device. The Regent did . . . something. I'm not sure what, but it sent me here."

"Then how were you supposed to get back home?" Valentine said. She and Callie shared a look, and in that moment she knew. "You weren't supposed to get home, were you? This was a one-way trip."

Callie nodded. "I left everything behind for this."

Valentine rocked back. The shock she felt seemed to waft through the room as all the implications sank in. That was how important Callie's mission had been to her. For the chance to avenge her daughter, she had left her whole world behind, knowing she would never see it again.

Valentine felt a glimmer of admiration. She knew now what had to happen.

"Then I'm going with you."

Her words met with protest. What if this was a trap? As she stared into Callie's eyes, though, Valentine knew the truth.

"It's not a trap," she said. "And it may be our only chance at survival."

"She's right," Malcolm said, quieting the objections. "Look at us. We're clueless, and sitting here staring at screens isn't going to change that. We need to do something the enemy won't expect. We're going."

Valentine smiled. "We?"

"You think I'd let you see the future without me? We'll take Ember Guard beacons and be back only a few minutes after we left."

"Are you certain?" Oma Grace said, brow furrowed.

"I'm tired of being afraid," Valentine said. "It's time we fought back."

Malcolm turned to Tyrathorn. "If you're willing, when can we use the Bridge?"

Tyrathorn shot a questioning look at one of his Watchers, who gave a curt nod.

"How about in two hours?"

"We'll take it," Valentine said. "Thank you, Thorn."

He clapped a hand on her shoulder. "Bring us good intel, my friend. That's all the thanks I'll need." He faced the rest of the group. "Anyone without an assignment, follow me. There is much to be done."

As everyone scattered, Callie stood rooted in place. Valentine saw that she and Neil had finally looked each other in the eye.

"Neil," Callie said, one hand pressed unconsciously to her stomach.

He walked past Callie as he beckoned to the twins. "Come on, kids. Let's get you ready."

The shower had been a welcome relief. Feeling renewed, Valentine donned her new jacket. She couldn't help feeling stronger wearing it. *Maybe that's why people wear uniforms. Huh.*

She shook out her damp hair and joined her family on the balcony. Malcolm and her dad stood against the balustrade while Oma Grace rested in a chair. As a family, they shared a quiet moment, not knowing when another one would come.

Eventually, Valentine cleared her throat. "So, not going to try talking us out of this?"

Oma Grace chuckled. "After the shenanigans I got up to at your age, my girl, it would be hypocritical." Her laughter faded. "Of course, I will worry. This man commands terrifying power. But someone must stand against evil, and once again, there's only us."

"Not only us," Malcolm said. "Not this time. We may be outmatched, but we have friends at our back. People we can trust."

Valentine looked to their dad next. He considered, and then shook his head.

"You two still take my breath away. I mean, the things you can do . . ." His voice fell, almost to a whisper. "How could I ask you not to go? How could I put our family above anyone else's? If we get a chance to help, we have to take it. So go. Do what you have to do, and maybe save the world if you can."

With a grateful smile, Valentine rested her hand on his. He squeezed back.

"You should write that speech down," Malcolm said. "Use it in your next book."

They shared a laugh. Valentine embraced a surge of emotion within her: love and gratitude and the audacity to hope that it would last. That they would survive to feel this again.

A soft knock sounded from the front door.

"I'll get it." Oma Grace rose from her chair and stepped inside. When she returned, her demeanor had gone stiff. "We have a guest."

She moved to sit, revealing Callie, who stood in the doorway.

Valentine turned toward her, as did Malcolm. Neil pressed his hands against the balustrade and stayed facing away, as if he sensed Callie's presence.

"Hello," she said. Her voice was hesitant, so much different than the self-assured warrior they had seen earlier. Brimming with quiet desperation, she looked toward her husband. "Neil?"

Their dad glanced over his shoulder, but did not turn. "What do you want?"

"To tell you the truth. About everything."

Neil said nothing.

"You see, I . . ." Callie hesitated. "I didn't come here looking for a family. I had one before, and it was taken from me. For years, I thought I knew exactly who was responsible, but now I'm as lost as when it first happened."

Her shoulders heaved. She clamped down on the emotion, reigning herself in.

"I still see Maya's face sometimes. Still hear her call my name. Every time I turn to look for her, I see it again, the moment I lost her. Sometimes when I close my eyes, I can't sleep because it's all I see."

She breathed in hard, blinking back tears.

"For so long, I hated everything. All I wanted was for it to end, because what did I have to live for? Then a great and powerful man offered me a chance to *do* something." She shook her head ruefully. "I never even questioned him. Not once. He told me who took my little girl, then forged me into a weapon and threw me at them. And I wanted so badly to be that weapon, Neil. I came here ready to kill them. Ready to die doing it."

Valentine could see Callie's strong exterior cracking. She lay exposed before them as never before.

"Then I met a beautiful man and his beautiful family, and I . . . I started to question. Was I given the whole truth? Or was I chosen because vengeance would blind me?"

Taking a step toward him, Callie reached out.

"I'm broken, Neil. I lived with that hate until it was the only thing keeping me alive. I wanted to hate you, too. It would have been so much easier. But you were all so . . . bright. I started to remember how it felt to love, to be loved. And then I started to hope. It was a dream, but somehow you made it real."

The floodgates opened, and tears streamed down Callie's face. "For so long, all I wanted was revenge. Now all I want is to hear that you love me."

Valentine's heart ached for the woman. She saw desperate hope in her eyes, silently pleading that her husband would turn and embrace her and tell her everything would be okay.

But he didn't, and the hope in Callie's eyes slowly died. She struggled to pull her armor back on. Sniffling, she squared her shoulders.

"You saved me, Neil. So now, whether you love me or not, whether you ever want me again or not, I will live my last breath trying to save you." As she backed away, she leaned her hand against the door frame for support. "I love you, Neil Gilbert. Always."

When the front door clicked shut, Neil sagged. Valentine saw him trembling.

"Dad," she said softly. "You still love her. Go get her."

He shook his head vehemently. "She betrayed us. For God's sake, Valentine, she tried to kill you."

"No." Valentine pressed. "That's why she came here, but she never did it."

"And she had plenty of chances," Malcolm said.

Neil's chest heaved. "Why are you defending her? Why aren't you angry?"

"Because I think I understand her," Valentine said. "And I feel sorry for her."

"The past two years, a lot of people have tried to kill us," Malcolm said. "*Really* tried, and some nearly succeeded. Compared to that, someone coming to kill us but then choosing to be our friend instead? It's actually kind of sweet."

"They're right, you know," Oma Grace said.

Neil half-turned to her. "*Et tu*, Mom?"

"My son." She gave him a sympathetic smile. "You're working this hard to hate her because you feel like it's what you should do. But you love Callie, and so do we. Take it from someone who's seen a lot of Time. Don't waste any of it being miserable when you could be happy."

He turned fully to face them, looking lost. "I just don't know."

Valentine rested a hand on his chest. "We forgive her, Dad. It's okay for you to forgive her, too."

Neil clutched her hand, then reached out with his other arm to pull Malcolm in close. "You two are pretty great."

CHAPTER 17

The Empyrean Bridge was powering up. Malcolm could feel the *shift* of temporal energies around it.

Exiting the Eon Palace with his family, he turned and followed a footpath across the palace grounds. The path led them to a copse of trees.

"I thought something was blocking travel to the future," Oma Grace said as they walked. "Isn't that what Winter's message said?"

"Now that the Pyre is here, they think the way is open again," Malcolm replied.

Neil shook his head, incredulous. "You're both braver than I ever was. Everything you're willing to do. I just wish Emily were here to see this. She'd be so proud."

Malcolm's insides warmed. It felt good to imagine their mother seeing what they were trying to become. Even now, he could see her smile, the sparkle in her eye.

Neil chuckled. "Too bad you can't use this machine, pop back and say hi, or even . . ."

He drifted off, looking as if someone had sucker-punched him. A sinking dread fell over Malcolm. He exchanged a heavy look with Valentine. They had known this conversation might happen. Now here it was, at the most inconvenient time.

"You don't think . . ." Neil said. "But, I mean, could you?"

"Dad." Malcolm stopped and faced his father. "We can't."

Oma Grace glanced between them. "Can't what, dear?"

"We can't go back and save Mom, or even warn her she's going to get sick. Believe me, we've talked about it." Malcolm took a deep breath, his heart aching. "But there are bigger things at stake here, and trying that could ruin everything."

For an instant, anger washed over Neil's face. He seemed to bury it. "Why?"

Malcolm tried to speak, but the words lodged in his chest.

"Think about it, Dad," Valentine said, her voice tinged with sadness. "If mom hadn't died, what would have happened? We'd have stayed in Chicago. That means never moving here, never stopping Lucius. We would have just seen Emmett's Bluff on the news, a smoking crater, and Oma gone with it."

Swallowing hard, Malcolm found his voice again. "Imagine if we never discovered what we are. If Charlotte Corday had been able to destroy Everwatch."

"Thousands dead, and a corrupted Timeline," Valentine said. "If we're going to keep it all safe, it means . . ."

She was unable to say the words.

"It means letting our own loss stay that way," Malcolm finished. "Sacrificing Mom to save the world."

Neil's eyes glistened. Sniffling, he pulled the twins into a tight hug. Oma Grace joined the embrace. Malcolm savored the feeling and stored it away, promising himself there would be more moments like this.

"You both have so much of her," their dad said. Releasing

them, he gave a gentle push toward the end of the path. "What are you waiting for? Go be her heroes."

One of the Empyrean Bridge's three rings spun on its axis, faster and faster until it became a blur. With a *boom* that rattled the trees, it transformed into a massive, red vortex.

Standing on the Bridge's wide stone platform, Malcolm noticed the light peripherally, his senses registering a tunnel as it sliced deftly through the Timeline. But in this moment, he focused on only one thing.

Asha clasped her hands around his neck. His senses filled up with her blue eyes, the faint scent of cinnamon, and the press of her skin against his. Her gaze drank him in hungrily.

"Go find a way to beat them," she said. "Then you'd better make it back to me."

"What if I get lost?" he teased.

"Then I'll cut through the universe and find you." Her gaze softened. "I love you, Malcolm. Be careful. We know nothing about this enemy."

Malcolm caressed her cheek. "I really wish I could think of something romantic to say right now."

She pulled him closer. "Then shut up."

Before he knew it, they were kissing. Fire raced through his veins as they clutched each other, saying goodbye in a way that hurt less than actually saying it. When they parted, Asha rested her forehead against his.

"Just stay alive," she whispered. "For me."

"It is time," Tyrathorn called.

"Ha! Time travel pun, nice," Fred said, then noticed no one

else was laughing. He began to grumble. "End of the world, everyone's gotta act all serious."

Malcolm gave Asha one last squeeze. A dozen feet away, Valentine finished her goodbyes with John. Together the twins approached the vortex. Callie waited for them at its horizon.

"Safe journey, my friends," Tyrathorn said.

Winter grinned. "See you in a few minutes."

"Bring me back a souvenir," Fred added.

Winter elbowed him. "You do know we're trying to save the world, right?"

"Chill, girl, it can be small."

The twins laughed, grateful for the tension relief.

"Thank you, Fred," Valentine said. "Just the send-off we needed."

Malcolm agreed, then grew serious again as they lined up next to Callie. This close to the vortex, he felt a vague sense of vertigo, as if standing at the edge of a high cliff.

"Okay." Setting his jaw, he stepped forward. "Here we go."

Light burst around the trio, stretching into radiant lines as they rocketed through Time and space. Malcolm could feel the universe part around them as the tunnel flung them forward.

Sights and sounds over a thousand years flashed by, glimpses of a world changing in rapid blinks. When they fled to Everwatch two years ago, the terror of the moment had left no room to enjoy the journey. Now he drank it in, allowing himself to savor the thrill.

All too soon, it ended. The tunnel shrank and he could feel them slowing for arrival. As the walls of light constricted around them, Valentine and Callie moved closer until they were within reach of each other.

Finally, in the near distance, a red vortex bloomed open. One by one, they slowed until they could calmly step through.

"Malcolm, Valentine," Callie said. "Welcome to 3094."

Malcolm pursed his lips. "Looks like an alley."

Callie gave a tight laugh. "Couldn't very well pop out in public."

Winding through dark alleys, she brought them to the edge of a major street. Malcolm saw what looked like a street market.

Callie held up a hand. "Wait here."

Then she was gone, diving into the crowd. Malcolm studied what little he could see of the market, fidgeting and anxious to move.

"I don't like just sitting here," he said.

"Yeah. Especially when she's our guide."

He raised an eyebrow. "I thought we'd forgiven her."

"We have, but Callie's home now. Who knows how that could play with her head?"

He hadn't thought of that. "Just have to stay alert, I guess."

After a moment of quiet, Valentine's lips quirked up in a mischievous smile. "I know we're trying to save everything, but is it wrong that I'm really excited to see what's out there?"

"If so, we're wrong together. Whatever they're cooking smells amazing."

A Time signature appeared behind them. The twins whipped around but saw no one. Still the presence pulsed. As they prepared to defend, the darkness rippled and Callie appeared.

"Whoa," she said, hands raised. "It's just me."

She tossed each of them a red cube that fit in their palm,

then leaned heavily against the wall and stared at the ground. The twins exchanged a puzzled look before examining the cubes.

They felt like some kind of plastic-fabric hybrid. All sides were perfectly smooth, betraying no extra folds or creases or anything to indicate their purpose.

"Uh, Callie?" Malcolm said.

"Slap it against your chest," she said without looking up.

With a shrug they complied, and then gasped as the cubes unfolded into clothing. The material stretched and wrapped around them to form sweater-like pullovers.

"Sweet," Malcolm said, staring down at himself. "Hey, what's this do?"

The left cuff bore a round dot like a button. Malcolm pressed it and the sweater changed from red to blue. "Ha!"

"Right side of your collar," Callie said, still staring down.

He found another button there. Valentine pressed hers first, then yelped as the garment sprouted a hood around her head. Then a half-mask formed diagonally across her face. Malcolm's did the same, except his mask covered from forehead to cheekbones.

"Does everyone wear masks these days?" he said.

"Sometimes." Callie shrugged. "It's in style."

Valentine adjusted hers. "It's pretty comfortable."

"And it'll work to our advantage. I'm guessing everyone in the city hates our faces." Malcolm turned to Callie. "Right?"

"No."

"Oh. I thought—"

"Everyone in the world."

His insides soured. "Oh."

Valentine brushed his shoulder. "There's only so many battles we can fight at once."

She was right, and they had far more at stake than reputation. "So, what's next?"

Callie didn't respond, and she still didn't look at them. Was she having second thoughts?

"Hey," Valentine said, resting a hand on her arm. "What's wrong?"

Callie looked up, tears streaming down her face. Malcolm could see she was shaking.

"This is the first—" her voice cracked. She swallowed hard. "Um, the first time I've been in that market since . . ."

The memory crashed into Malcolm: Callie trying to keep a lid on her anguish as she recounted the attack. The death of her daughter.

"You were shopping at this market?"

She nodded. "Never thought I'd see it again."

Valentine wrapped her arm around the woman's shoulders and pulled her close. Callie let herself be held, and for a moment she cried quietly into Valentine's neck. Then, with a last sob, she pulled herself together faster than anyone Malcolm had ever seen.

"Okay, let's go." She headed for the mouth of the alley. "My armor's passive countermeasures should keep surveillance from identifying you, but keep those masks on."

With that, they walked into the future city of Eldurfall.

Malcolm gaped at the gleaming city. This part was situated on a series of high hills. In the distance, the terrain flattened into a vast plain, which was covered by the rest of the great city, spreading as far as he could see.

Layers, Malcolm thought. Eldurfall wasn't just a flat grid of streets with buildings between them. They were all built atop and across and between each other, a web constantly pulsing with light and activity, machines flying between it all. Highways of light snaked through the air. Malcolm saw one change direction to let traffic flow another way.

The ground on which they walked was a pattern of repeating hexagons, something synthetic and sleek that still provided enough friction to be traveled on.

Valentine stomped lightly on one of the hexagons. "Are these solar panels?"

Callie glanced over her shoulder. "Solar, geothermal, electromagnetic, even the friction of foot traffic. They collect enough to power the whole city."

They crossed a city square, which allowed them to see a variety of buildings at once. While some designs were familiar, others could never have existed in the twenty-first century. They rose in impossible shapes, twisty and strange, elegant and beautiful, in configurations that wouldn't be possible in the twins' world.

One building was the color of sand, with a sparkling, blue waterfall pouring over the side of the roof. Halfway down the building, the water faded and disappeared. Another was tall and square, with each individual floor slowly spinning at different speeds.

Yet the buildings weren't half as interesting as the people. Malcolm's first surprise had been that many still walked, even with whatever future transportation they had. It let him observe streams of people as they flowed by.

The popular style seemed a mix of dramatic and utilitarian, as if a high-fashion designer had decided to make clothes for construction workers. There were few neutral statements when it came to hairstyles, either. Hair was either dark, cropped close, and slicked down, or long and loud with bright, unnatural colors.

Then there were synthetic varieties, like a woman with hair that wasn't hair, but something like fiber optics streaming with light. Observing tattoos, Malcolm realized that ink was not just ink in the thirty-first century. It moved, changing colors and configurations. Then there was . . .

"Stop," Callie whispered. "You both look like tourists. We're trying to blend in."

"Sorry," Valentine murmured.

Right. We're among the enemy now, technically. Malcolm schooled his expression.

In among the wonders, he could also see the scars. Bumping his sister, he nodded toward a corner of the square, where charred black furrows cut across three adjacent buildings—two of which had lost their top floors.

"Courtesy of our imposters?" he whispered.

She grimaced. "I forgot they've been fighting a war here, too."

Leaving the square behind, they crisscrossed a series of smaller streets. Foot traffic lessened, and this new neighborhood felt quieter. Malcolm guessed these were office buildings and warehouses, more likely to be deserted at night.

"Where are you taking us?" he asked.

"Being a spy means knowing people who know things they shouldn't. Early on, I met one of the biggest black-market dealers on the planet."

"What does he deal?" Valentine asked.

"Information, mainly, but also talent. If you need something done, he knows people who'll get it done for you. His base of operations is right here in my city."

"Makes sense, this being the capital," Malcolm said. "Where there's government, there's dirty secrets."

"How alert do we have to be?" Valentine said. "Is he dangerous?"

Callie smirked. "He's a jock. We'll be fine."

"Jock?" Malcolm said. "Like, he's into sports?"

"Sorry, I forgot. Here, jocks are the hardcore computer geeks. Athletes aren't a big deal these days."

Malcolm chuckled at the irony, then stopped short as they rounded a corner.

"Whoa."

"Oh, wow," Valentine said.

Nestled between buildings was a little park unlike anything they had ever seen.

Callie grinned. "Cybernetic botany. They're hybrids, equal parts organic and synthetic."

Malcolm stared, at a loss for words. The trees weren't wood, but they weren't plastic or metal. Their leaves rustled in the breeze, translucent and glowing a soft blue.

Birds sang among them, fluttering between blooms that glowed in yellows and pinks and oranges. Studying a bird as it zoomed by, Malcolm realized it was mechanical.

"You know, Callie," Valentine said, her eyes sparkling, "your world is pretty awesome."

"I really did love it here." Callie sighed. Then she shook herself and started off again.

Around the other side of the park, a warehouse-type building sat dark and quiet, the perfect kind of place for a black-market gangster. At least that hadn't changed over a millennium.

Callie stopped near a set of double doors and faced the twins. "You don't speak until I say. You don't touch anything or look anyone in the eye for too long. And for God's sake, keep those masks on. Deal?"

Malcolm exchanged a wary glance with Valentine and nodded.

"Deal," they said in unison.

Callie stared hard for a moment longer. "Okay. Get ready."

Callie approached a black panel to the left of the doors and made a tiny hand gesture. Before Malcolm could puzzle over that, the doors opened inward and he got his first glimpse inside.

"You have got to be kidding me."

CHAPTER 18

A mountain of a man stood facing them. Like an anthropomorphic pile of muscles, he stomped forward until he filled the doorway. Valentine noticed his left arm was mechanical, as was his left eye. The mountain studied the twins, measuring their threat level.

Then his eyes landed on Callie. His stern expression morphed into one of respect.

"Calypso," he said, his voice rumbling like a rock slide. "Thought you'd gone somewhere exotic."

Callie's manner turned sultry. "You know I can't bear to leave you alone, Vasily."

He inclined his chin toward the twins. "And the runts?"

"Fresh recruits, just along for the ride."

"They look fragile." Vasily studied them. "Are you fragile?"

Valentine felt a surge of annoyance. "Come take a swing and find out."

Callie glanced at her, a subtle warning. She chastised herself. *Nice going, Val.*

Vasily only chuckled.

"Qubit here tonight?" Callie asked.

He nodded, hooking a thumb over his shoulder. "You remember where to go?"

"If I get lost, I'll be sure to whistle," she cooed.

He pointed at the silver bracelet adorning Callie's wrist. "Long as I don't see any armor, we're grundy."

He stepped aside, and the twins followed Callie into the strangest night club Valentine had ever seen.

Black floor, black walls, and a high black ceiling. Only basic lighting. A thousand people filled the huge space, doing what people normally did in clubs. They lounged on couches and milled around with exotic drinks in their hands.

Most packed onto the dance floor. The crowd danced with abandon, swaying and undulating to . . . nothing. No thumping bass, no electronic beat. No music at all.

Yet the nonexistent beat was the *same* for everyone. As the trio picked their way through the crowd, Valentine saw eyes darting to and fro, synchronized as if they beheld the same unseen vision. Even Callie's eyes followed theirs. Every so often, the crowd cheered at nothing.

Valentine thought she understood.

"You all have cybernetic implants, don't you?" she said. "While we walked, I didn't see one screen. Not even a billboard. Now there's music we can't hear."

"Huh," Malcolm said. "You think all their computing is internal now?"

"I'll bet they project images onto the retina, so you don't actually need a screen. Even sound signals could bypass the ears and go right to the brain."

Callie looked impressed. "Organic computing's been around a long time. Now we're given the biohardware while still in the womb, and it grows with us from the day we're born."

Valentine's eyebrows climbed. "Wow. In the future, everyone's a cyborg."

Callie pursed her lips. "That's a primitive term, but you get the idea."

Malcolm shook his head. "Wow. We must seem like cavemen to you."

Callie gave a reluctant nod. "My implants are basically useless in your century. At first, I missed being able to interface with everything. It's like you traveling to the Middle Ages and asking for the Wi-Fi password."

Malcolm looked to Valentine. "They'd burn you at the stake for being a witch."

"And what about you?" she returned.

"I'm pretty sure they'd make me king."

"Oh, sure. You know you're never going to own a castle, right?"

"Hey, do I try to spoil *your* dreams?"

They arrived at the back of the club, where metal stairs led to a doorway high up on the wall. To either side of the door, the wall became wide stretches of black glass. Callie stopped with her hands on the rail, her attention turned inward.

"By the way," Malcolm said. "Grundy?"

"Slang," she replied mechanically. "It basically means 'all good.'"

"Ah."

She gave the twins a last look before ascending the stairs, and Valentine almost stepped back in alarm. Callie had ceased to be the femme fatale who flirted with the bouncer and slinked sensually through a throng of revelers. Now, by changing a hundred subtle cues, she had become the steel-eyed assassin.

Metal clinked beneath their feet as they followed Callie

up the stairs. When they reached the door, she didn't move or speak. Valentine guessed she was waiting for confirmation they wouldn't be able to perceive.

Callie stepped through the door. Valentine gaped, then forced her expression back to neutral. Callie hadn't waited for the door to open and then stepped through. She had literally stepped *through* the door.

Exchanging an uncertain glance with Malcolm, she followed.

They passed through the door as if it were air. *Was it always a hologram, or did it change for us?*

The room was sleek and solid white, except for the wall of smoky glass that looked out on the dance floor. The only thing in it besides bare walls was a wide, curved desk. White, of course.

A man sat behind the desk, wearing a crimson suit with a crimson shirt and tie. Valentine stared, taken aback. This was a world-class information broker? He looked like the sniveling weasel from old gangster movies.

Callie stopped on the other side of the desk. Scrubbing his fingers through his thinning brown hair, the man leaned back and eyed her.

"Well hello, dollface," he said with a smirk. His voice was high-pitched yet raspy, like how a smoker might sound. Now that Valentine thought about it, though, she hadn't seen anyone smoking.

"Qubit." Callie stared him down. "We have business."

Qubit's smirk fell into disappointment. "Why don't you ever pretend to flirt with me? How come my bouncer always has the fun and I get the assassin?"

"Because if I ever come to kill you, I want you to see it coming."

Qubit laughed as if it was the best joke he'd heard all day. "All right, fine, Calypso. Have a seat, you and your kiddies there."

As he gestured across the desk, three tiles floated up from the floor and stretched into vaguely chair-like shapes. Callie chose the left seat while Malcolm chose the middle, leaving the far right for Valentine.

She settled onto the smooth white surface, pleasantly surprised at how its contours supported her. Then she realized it was morphing subtly into a shape that complemented her. *The future's not so bad. When its people aren't trying to kill us.*

Qubit lounged back in his chair. "So, tell me what I can do for the illustrious Regent today."

For an instant, Callie sat still as a statue. She appeared to be gathering her courage. *Not surprising*, Valentine mused. *Once she tells him, she's officially a traitor and there's no going back.*

Then her uncertainty evaporated. "The Regent lied. To all of us."

Qubit's eyebrows raised, but he said nothing.

"You know my mission. I *know* you know because you know everything. Well, I got within seconds of doing it. But, then . . ."

"You couldn't?" Qubit said, incredulous. "*You?* I thought you lived for the kill."

"No," she snapped. "I lived for the Regent. I thought I owed him everything. But I only lived for two kills."

"And yet, here you are, without the Gilbert twins' heads."

"They weren't what we've been told, Q," Callie insisted.

He gestured dismissively. "Regent always said they were clever snakes."

"It was more than that. The twins I met, they could never be monsters. I knew there had to be something else going on. But before I could figure it out, the Regent invaded." She leaned forward, desperate. "Q, people in that century are dying. Innocent people. I need to stop it, but I don't know the Regent's full plan. I don't even know how the Pyre works or why he sent six of them. I need the best intel in the world." She gripped the edge of his desk. "Please. Help me save them."

Qubit stared at her, as if trying to decide if this was another mask of the fearsome Calypso, or the real woman asking for real help. Then he stared into space, jaw working as if he were chewing on her words. Finally, he gave a resigned sigh.

"How am I supposed to know, dollface? How am I supposed to believe you enough to turn traitor with you?"

Callie didn't answer. Instead she glanced at the twins and nodded. Bracing herself, Valentine slid back the mask and hood. As her wavy, red hair spilled out over her shoulders, Qubit stared in curiosity. Then she saw the light switch on behind his eyes.

Exploding out of his chair, Qubit stumbled backward until he smacked into the wall.

"Defend me!" he shouted.

Over his shoulder, two compartments opened and gun turrets appeared. Peripherally, Valentine wondered if their targeting was linked to Qubit's eyes, since they immediately aimed at her and Malcolm.

Outwardly, she waved her hand toward the cannon taking aim at her. A bubble of super-fast Time reduced the weapon to a pool of molten metal. Malcolm unleashed a wave of Entropy Blades and sliced his cannon to ribbons.

They stared calmly at the data gangster, waiting for him to either attack again or relax. Despite his appearance, though, Qubit was smart. It showed as he processed what the twins had just done, the power it suggested, and the fact that they hadn't turned that power on him. Hesitantly, he stepped away from the wall and sat down.

"Why am I not dead?" he asked.

Valentine glanced at Callie. "Because she's right. All we want is to protect our people."

"That's why we need to know what's so special about those towers," Malcolm added. "Help us. Please."

Qubit looked as if the walls were crashing down around him but he didn't want to believe it. He scrubbed his fingers through his hair again before shooting a look at Callie.

"If anyone but you had come with this . . ." He trailed off, but the meaning was clear. He pointed at the twins. "If you aren't attacking us, who *is*? Why do they look like you?"

Valentine held up her hands. "I'm sorry; we're as lost as you."

"But when we find them," Malcolm said, his expression grim, "we'll have a few questions for them."

With a resigned sigh, Qubit reached inside a desk drawer while looking to Callie. "Your implants still work?"

She nodded as he withdrew a black box the size of his palm. Flipping open the lid, he revealed devices the size and shape of gelcap pills. Half metal and half glass, they blinked with subtle patterns of light.

Qubit plucked one from the box, then twisted and separated it into two halves. He set the flat end of each against his temples, where they gently latched on.

"These will let you see and hear what we can," he said. "Every so often, someone's allergic to the implants, so they have to use these."

Qubit removed them and slid them toward Valentine, then offered another pair to Malcolm. Valentine worked to hide her excitement, while Malcolm followed a bit more reluctantly.

As soon as the devices latched onto her temples, Valentine gasped. *Whoa.* She couldn't help herself. It was like seeing color after spending her life color-blind. Not just seeing color, but hearing it, too.

Streams of data scrolled over the walls, the ceiling, the desk. At various places there were virtual screens showing video feeds: some looked like news channels, while others were clearly secret feeds from covert locations that Qubit probably shouldn't know existed. When Valentine focused on a screen, its audio feed streamed into her ears.

"Whoa," Malcolm breathed.

"Hey, I think they like it," Qubit said, a twinkle in his eye.

"Is this how everything is here?" Valentine said.

Qubit gestured behind her. "See for yourself."

Turning, she caught a glimpse through the windows and nearly fell over. Before she knew it, she was up and pressed against the glass. On the other side, the monochrome night club had become a different world.

Lights of every color streamed from ceiling to floor. The black floor had disappeared. Instead it changed periodically, looking like ocean waves and then like clouds, then the surface of a comet hurtling through a star field, and more.

The dancers had their own tricks. Valentine spotted one man, tall and dark and dressed in a fine suit, who suddenly seemed to catch fire. Then the "fire" disappeared and left him wearing a different suit.

A curvy, blonde woman swayed with the music, then leapt to the side while a digital copy of herself kept dancing in the same place. She did it again, and then there were three identical versions of her dancing together.

Then there was the music. Even in Qubit's office, she could

feel the rhythmic thumping of a bass beat. Not just hear it, but *feel* it through her feet, as if it were real and not a projection into her mind.

It made her wonder what she'd missed as they'd walked the city streets. Nearly everything here was a virtual projection, yet it looked, sounded, and felt as real as anything she'd ever experienced.

Malcolm appeared next to her. "Can you imagine the vertigo, dancing on a cloud?"

She shook her head, astounded. "How?"

Qubit chuckled. "Once you know exactly how the brain works, convincing it something is real becomes child's play."

"Valentine, Malcolm," Callie said, gesturing at her seat.

Oh, right. For a moment, she'd forgotten why they were here. She peeled herself away from the window and took her seat. Malcolm followed, putting on his serious face.

"We're not looking to hurt anyone," she said. "We just want to stop the invasion. But whatever's powering those Pyres is too strong."

"And we don't even know what they're for," Malcolm added. "What can you tell us?"

"Plenty," Qubit said, fingers flying across a virtual keyboard filled with symbols Valentine didn't recognize. "Have a look at this. It'll feel weird at first, but just bear with me."

Virtual screens popped open. Hovering in front of their faces, they displayed wire-frame outlines of the Pyre's superstructure.

Valentine waited for facts and figures—the secrets they'd come here to get. Then, as she leaned closer, she saw there was far more to those glowing lines.

"Now grab the image and do this," Qubit said, pinching his fingers and then throwing his arms out wide.

The twins and Callie complied. Once again, Valentine was amazed that it felt tangible in her hands. Spreading her arms, she gaped as the projection grew into a full three-dimensional hologram. Her chair now sat in the center of the Pyre's image, as if she was sitting inside the building.

What she thought she had seen before now came into sharp focus. The virtual lines were actually streams of data offering up details on the Pyre's construction.

As Valentine studied, soaking in as much data as possible, those lines began to pulse brighter. The data moved faster, changing until facts and figures mingled with code that Valentine couldn't decipher.

The data fed faster through the device at her temples. Faster, always faster, pulsing as the code sank deeper into her mind. The white lines flashed, then turned red. *Something's wrong.* Then, in a burst of awareness, Valentine realized.

It's a trap.

Fighting down panic, she reached for the device affixed to her temples, and found that her arms couldn't move.

CHAPTER 19

The red wire frame collapsed, constricting against Valentine and trapping her in place. Her companions twisted in vain against their virtual bonds.

Callie glared venom at Qubit. "What do you think you're doing?"

Qubit's superior smirk returned. "Oh, just uploading a little biovirus while the pretty lights distracted you. Had to find some way to keep you here for the Regent."

"The Regent's not even in this century," Callie spat.

"No, but when his people collect you, I'm sure they'll let him know our mortal enemies have been captured. Along with a traitor, of course."

"You know these won't hold us forever," Valentine warned.

"Good thing I alerted them right when you got here," Qubit retorted. "I'd say you have maybe two minutes."

"You have no idea who you're betraying, Q," Callie said.

Qubit's smirk turned dark. Rising from his chair, he came around the desk to face her.

"Who do you think helped the Regent plan his invasion? Build his Pyres? Certainly not you, the blindly loyal weapon who thought she was an insider but never really had a clue."

Callie seethed. "What are you talking about?"

"Are you that naive? The invasion was always going to happen, and on a much grander scale than anyone knows. History is about to get a major rewrite."

Returning to his chair, Qubit called up another screen.

"Wow. They're sending Praetorian Suppressors. Not taking any chances." He flashed a fake grin at the twins. "Our esteemed guests seem confused, Calypso. Care to explain?"

Callie looked as if she'd rather rip his head off. Instead she turned to the twins. "Praetorians are the secret ultra-elite guard. Only a few of them exist."

"Want to know why, kiddies?" Qubit tapped out another command and data streamed into the twins' virtual interfaces. "Because a few are all they need."

Technical readouts for the Praetorians downloaded into Valentine's brain. Dread filled the pit of her stomach like hot coals.

Praetorians were the size of Cyonics, but they made the Cyonics look like windup toys. Praetorian Berserkers were unstoppable implements of destruction. Praetorian Infiltrators were assassin killers with unparalleled stealth, speed, and agility.

Then there were Praetorian Suppressors, which were built to kill Chronauri.

While the outer shell was a phalanx of weaponry, the heart was an engine that fed on Time. No, it *consumed* Time. The files showed footage of a Suppressor powering up, then venting flames as Time burned and died inside it.

The flames reminded her of those she'd felt burning a swathe across the Timeline. The agony had disoriented the twins so badly that they could barely wield their own power.

Oh, no, she thought. *What if we can't fight them?*

The Suppressors had to have a weakness. There *had* to be more data buried in the Regent's files. If only there was a way to search.

Wait.

A desperate idea began taking shape. Could her mind survive it? As she took stock of her situation, she decided it hardly seemed to matter. *Either die here, or die a prisoner.* She'd rather go down fighting.

Malcolm's head cocked to the side, curious. He'd seen her expression change. *Follow my lead,* she shouted mentally, hoping their twin bond would give him at least the general idea.

Valentine shoved her panic into a dark corner. Then, with a *shift*, she closed her eyes and allowed Time to flow into her.

The trick was to pull this off without appearing to move faster or change in any way. Which meant Valentine couldn't wrap her whole body in fast Time. Her body had to keep moving at normal speed.

So, instead, she formed the bubble around her brain.

Qubit began to speak. "After all this, it was me that took down the—"

Inside the bubble, she pushed Time to move faster. Faster. *Faster.* Compared with the outside world, her thoughts raced beyond description. Still she pushed harder.

Her heart beat like drum once. *Thump!*

Twice. *Thump!*

The third heartbeat . . . didn't come. At least, not yet. In the space between them, Valentine's mind went to work.

Qubit called it a biovirus. That's how he hijacked our bodies. There's no way to punch a virus. So, she had to beat it on its own terms.

The device on her temples let her brain interface with the

computerized world of this century. Which meant she could do more than just download information. She could send commands.

Valentine went on the offensive, using her connection to tunnel into Qubit's systems. In relative nanoseconds, she'd mapped his network and found its connections to the global meshworks. Her consciousness rode the digital wave, melting through Qubit's firewall and spreading across the globe in less than a blink.

People in Valentine's century loved to broadcast their knowledge online, everything from the philosophy of cat videos to instructions on slinging computer code. Betting on the continuity of human nature, she guessed the same would be true now.

And . . . there they are.

In an imperceptible flash, she located network nodes boasting thousands of free university-level training programs. In the time it took for Valentine's neurons to fire, she absorbed a mountain of technical knowledge. Suddenly she knew how the computers of the future worked, from quantum computing and beyond.

Now she needed the raw knowledge to take shape. That meant turning to darker corners of the meshworks—learning the skills of hackers and cyber-criminals. Pushing her mind faster, Valentine found secret code books and tutorials, even first- and secondhand accounts of legendary hacks . . .

. . . until she knew enough to build three computer programs.

As she created a virtual work terminal, a strong *shift* hit her senses and a text box bloomed open in her vision.

>FOUND YOU.

Malcolm.

Oceans of data streamed by as he absorbed what she'd collected, then prepared his own work terminal.

>WHAT CAN I DO?

In the time it took for him to message her, Valentine had already completed one of her programs and unleashed it. Wordlessly, she split the workload and passed him the framework for one of the remaining two programs.

>NICE :-D

They set to work, slamming out code so quickly that she could feel the planetary meshworks struggling to keep up. Lines of code flashed onto the virtual screen faster than any eye could follow. It would have taken elite programmers weeks, if not months, to build what she and Malcolm were building in the space between moments.

For this to work, it would have to happen in the right phases. Phase One had already begun. Valentine worked feverishly on Phase Three. Just as she placed the last flourishes on her code, Malcolm delivered Phase Two back to her terminal.

They were almost ready. When the meshworks next cycled, Phase Two would begin. For a human brain perceiving at normal speed, a computer cycle was so impossibly fast that it didn't register in conscious thought. For the twins now, it felt like an unbearable stretch of minutes.

Just before it happened, she felt it coming. The meshworks cycled.

Valentine's worm returned, completing Phase One. Her little program had just scraped all the data from Qubit's private network, packaged it, and delivered the huge file to the device at her temples. She saved it to local memory and sent a copy to Malcolm.

Phase Two began. Malcolm's first task had been to learn how

Qubit's biovirus was built, which he had done by comparing the code against black-hat hacker databases. Then he'd studied the training materials collected by Valentine, learning how to code the perfect antivirus.

Which he now deployed.

Qubit's biovirus began to break down under the onslaught of Malcolm's antivirus. With deadly precision, his code crawled inside Qubit's and ripped it to shreds.

Wearing a grim smile, Valentine launched Phase Three: the nastiest virus she could design, using every vicious trick she'd learned in those dark corners of the meshworks. Then she dropped her bubble of super-fast Time. As her thoughts screeched back to normal speed, everything happened at once.

The biovirus failed.

Their bonds disappeared.

Qubit's network melted.

Data ceased to stream across his office. The music died. Outside the windows, his club became just a warehouse painted black.

Clutching his head, Qubit screamed. Not a scream of physical pain, but one of loss. After the twins had taken all his data, they'd erased his copies and all backups. Decades' worth of black-market intelligence—the beating heart of his power—gone.

"What have you done!"

Slowly, the twins rose from their chairs and approached the desk, Callie at their side. Through tears, Qubit glared up at them.

"You think you've changed anything? The Praetorians are still coming, and you still didn't get everything I have. Good luck facing the Regent without it, you prehistoric trash."

Valentine looked to Malcolm. "Did we miss something?"

His gaze turned inward as he scanned the files they'd

collected. He gave a tight-lipped nod. "We have a lot, but not all. It's like someone hid the key jigsaw pieces."

Valentine turned a hard stare on Qubit. The gangster radiated defiant satisfaction.

"I may be ruined," he said, "but so are you."

Shaking her head, Valentine pressed her palm down on his desk. "Not if you hand over the data now."

Radiating fast Time from her palm, Valentine *pushed* and the desk's molecules unraveled. It burst into dust. She stepped through the cloud, coming straight for Qubit.

He fell out of his chair and scrambled back toward the wall. Valentine reached for him just as a tone sounded.

On the far wall to her right, a hidden door slid open. Two Praetorian Suppressors appeared.

One look at the machines and their true purpose was clear. Gone were the soothing white and chrome exteriors, the calm voices and serene faces of the Cyonics.

In their place were sharp edges, blood-red armor, and savage weapons. Their faces were a flat metal plate with one angry, red eye in the center and a tiny slit for a mouth. The slit was angled like a downward *V*, giving them a permanent scowl.

"Heh, good luck." Qubit slapped his palm against the wall and melted through it.

Valentine whipped back and forth between the machines and the spot where Qubit had disappeared. *We need his data, and every second we fight, he'll get farther away!*

Yet, a fight was inevitable. The Praetorians were already advancing as their Time-destroying hearts spun to life. Valentine gritted her teeth against the pain.

Qubit's wall imploded in flames to reveal a hidden passage. Facing it, Callie brandished a cannon on her left forearm. Her bracelet unfolded fully now, encasing her head-to-toe in armor scales.

The Suppressors stalked forward with the slow confidence of predators. Callie placed herself between the machines and the twins. She turned back to them just as the armor closed over her face.

"Go get him," she said.

Malcolm shook his head. "There's no way you can—"

"Malcolm," Callie pleaded. "Let me protect you. Go now!"

What other option did they have? Muttering a silent prayer for Callie, Valentine grabbed her brother and dove through the wall.

As they turned to chase their enemy down, she caught a last glimpse of Callie squaring off against the machines.

CHAPTER 20

Callie had seen Suppressors take down a Chronauri once. It hadn't been pretty.

This was going to hurt.

"The Gilbert twins are under my protection," she said.

"Irrelevant. The Chronauri will fall."

"Well, I know something you don't. The Regent never fully trusted A.I. to win his battles."

Callie entered a secret code into her HUD, unlocking the Last Resort protocol. Triple power surged through her armor. Magnetic shielding protected her vital organs. Every enhancement in her body kicked into overdrive.

"And you're not getting past me."

Power Level 94%, her HUD showed. She would have to keep an eye on that.

The edges of her HUD flashed—the Praetorians had target lock. Each carried a heavy plasma cannon on its left shoulder.

She locked onto them as well, labeling them Scrap and Shamble. In this last moment of calm, it was all she could do.

Okay, then.

Callie charged.

Closing the distance, she slipped between the machines.

This forced them to turn toward her, which meant they now faced each other. There were so few Praetorians, their makers wouldn't risk them accidentally destroying each other in battle. A subroutine activated, and their cannons pointed down at the floor.

Shamble adapted and swung its fist, but Callie was already moving.

Dodging the blow, she hooked her arm around the machine's, fired her boosters, and sent them both flying. They crunched into the ceiling, half-burying in the once-pristine surface.

Callie gritted her teeth as plasma fire from Scrap burst against her back. The magnetic shielding held, but at heavy cost to her power core. Spinning, she rocketed back toward the floor and used Shamble as a battering ram. They plowed through layers of plasticrete to burst into the storage room below.

Callie took half an instant to catch her breath, and Shamble grabbed her by the faceplate. The Praetorian flung her through stacks of wooden crates until she smashed into the wall. Halfway to her feet, plasma fire raked across her torso.

As Callie rocked back, she took quick aim with her cutting laser. Power surged down her arm, and red light blasted across the room. Shamble's left arm fell away. She cursed to herself. *Missed the cannon.*

Power Level 68%

Scrap dropped through the ceiling, scanning for her. Thanks to the weapons fire, all cover was gone. To her surprise, though, the Praetorians stepped back.

Why would—?

Her insides went cold. Shamble's abdomen peeled open to reveal four Taipan missiles. Callie's armor was tough, but it wasn't built for this. *Have to change the game.* With a silent apology to her armor, she issued a command.

"Parthian logic bomb."

Her HUD flashed red. She ignored it.

"Build."

A high-pitched whine filled her helmet. Her armor's three processor cores pushed to their limits, building a virtual bomb out of computer code.

Everything happened at once. One processor core burned out with a staticky *pop*. Her HUD flashed as Shamble's missiles locked on. A chime signaled that her weapon was ready.

"Deploy."

Her systems wailed in protest. The Praetorians shuddered and ground to a halt. Shamble's missile dropped to the floor. The machines stood stiff, overloaded by a burst of unfriendly data.

Callie shoved off the wall and charged. A half dozen steps away, she leapt.

Legs forward, she fired her boosters at Scrap's face. The machine flew back and embedded in the wall with a crunch.

As she landed, Callie fired a grappler from her forearm. Trailing monofilament line, it latched onto Shamble's shoulder cannon.

Too close now for missiles, Shamble fired the cannon. Callie yanked the grappler line and snapped the weapon to the side. The plasma bolt went wide.

Shamble swung its remaining arm. Callie dodged, wrapped the line around the arm, and pulled. Shamble swung again, while simultaneously firing its cannon.

Still sluggish from the logic bomb, the Praetorian hadn't compensated for Callie's grappler. Or the fact that swinging its arm had yanked the line and reoriented the cannon.

Plasma bolts blasted through its own head. Belching smoke, it toppled with a *clank*.

Wasting no time, Callie yanked a missile from Shamble's torso and faced Scrap. The machine struggled to extricate itself from the wall.

Callie gave a humorless smile. "Here, let me help."

Holding the missile, she sent the command to fire. A bright flash, a boom, a wave of heat. Half the wall disintegrated, while Scrap flew a dozen yards and clattered onto the dance floor.

The room filled with panicked screams. As Callie stepped through the hole, club patrons scattered for the exits. She moved between them, focused on Scrap.

Approaching, she deployed her plasma blade. One flick of her wrist and Scrap's cannon went skittering. Another flick and its head cleaved in two.

Power level 38%

She had cut it close. But the Suppressors wouldn't be harming her family today. She reached for her comm.

Before she could, there was a ripping sound. Then a burning pain, starting from her back and radiating through her left flank. Suddenly cold and confused, Callie peered down.

The tip of a blade protruded from her abdomen, matte black and coated with her blood.

In shock, she realized what it was, and where it had come from.

Oh, no.

CHAPTER 21

Malcolm kept a steady pace, like a hunter waiting for his prey to tire out.

Qubit took a corner too fast. At the end of the darkened hallway, he tripped and rolled. Clutching his ribs, he looked back down the hallway. His eyes widened like saucers.

Malcolm traced his fingers along the wall, leaving a wake of crackling ice to spread across the wall and onto the floor and ceiling. Valentine traced the opposite wall to create an expanding wake of fire. Overhead and underfoot, they met and *hissed* into steam.

"Stay away. I'm warning you!" Qubit said, fleeing down the next hallway.

"Is it wrong that I'm enjoying this?" Malcolm said.

"After what he tried back there, I sure am."

As they rounded the corner, he spotted Qubit fleeing up a flight of stairs, toward the roof.

Malcolm started to climb. "I thought people only ran upstairs in bad horror movies."

"Everyone here does think we're murderers. Maybe to him, he's the hero."

"Or maybe he's got an escape plan."

They came to the last door, a heavy one. Without pausing, Malcolm kicked it open and the twins stepped onto the roof.

Sure enough, Qubit stood on the ledge with his back to them, looking skyward. At the sound of the door, he whipped around and flashed a gloating grin.

"Really not your day, is it?" he said.

Arms wide, he flicked his wrist in a practiced manner. Smoke puffed from his red suit as patches of the fabric burned away, revealing boosters. They flared, lifting him off the roof.

"I'm sure the Regent will enjoy hearing—"

Malcolm felt a *shift*. Valentine's corona glowed as her bubble of slowed Time enveloped the gangster. Now a minute for them would be a hundred for him.

"God, I hate the ones who talk too much," she said.

"We do need him to talk a little," Malcolm replied. "Sorry."

Sighing, Valentine curled her fingers and the bubble floated closer. The twins relieved Qubit of his ugly suit and its hidden surprises until he was down to his undershirt and boxers. To make sure he didn't panic and jump off the roof, they placed him with his back to a utility shed.

They stood within arm's reach. Malcolm put on his best annoyed face.

"Ready?" Valentine said.

He nodded, and she dropped the bubble.

"—everything I saw today . . ." He stopped short, taking in his situation. "Aw, that was my favorite suit."

Valentine scoffed. "Don't act like you don't have a closet full of those."

"Yeah," Malcolm said. "Red suits with repulser tech aren't exactly an impulse buy."

Qubit huffed, pouting. "Fine, whatever. Just get on with it and kill me."

Malcolm exchanged a glance with his sister. Whatever evidence there was against them, it was strong enough that a world-class information broker believed it. *What's really going on here?*

"We don't want your life; we want information," he said. "You helped the Regent build the Pyres?"

Qubit rolled his eyes. "I told you, I don't get my hands dirty. I just know things."

"Like what the Pyres are built for," Valentine said. "You gave us schematics, but they only showed us the shell, not what's inside."

"Who do you think I'm more afraid of, you or the Regent?" Qubit sneered. "Melt my brain all you want. I'm not giving you a thing."

Something clicked in Malcolm's mind. "Everything you have . . ."

"What?" Valentine said.

"Yeah, what?" Qubit echoed.

"Back in the office, when we scoured your network." Malcolm pointed a finger at Qubit. "You said we didn't get everything you have. If you were talking about your memory, you would say we didn't get everything you *know*."

Qubit tried to look confident, but Malcolm saw uncertainty behind that oily bravado. Valentine must have spotted it, too.

"You've got a private server," she said, fire dancing between her fingers. "Where is it?"

"Bet I can guess." Malcolm gestured at the device affixed to her temples. "Can I borrow those?"

Valentine handed them over, and Malcolm placed them on Qubit's head.

"Hey!" He jerked back.

"Play nice," Malcolm warned.

Qubit grumbled but stopped resisting. The devices gave off a glow as they latched on. Reactivating his own, Malcolm called up their networking functions and connected to Qubit's.

"I wondered why you would keep these around," Malcolm said. "I mean, why would someone as connected as you need these? They're old tech, right?"

Malcolm logged into Qubit's devices as a remote administrator. Taking control, he broadcast a signal query. His little network advertised an open connection and searched for ping-back responses.

"Then you said that one thing, and it got me thinking," he continued. "If Qubit has a private server, where's the one place he could be sure it stays secret? And how would he access it?"

His query received a response. He grinned, and Qubit's sarcastic shell crumbled. Projected onto Malcolm's vision, a lockbox glowed in the center of Qubit's brain.

"After that, it just made sense. Implant a digital safe in your own head—"

"—and lock it down so only primitive tech can access it," Valentine finished.

With the network established, Malcolm didn't need the physical connection anymore. Removing the devices from Qubit's temples, he affixed them back onto Valentine's.

"It's encrypted," he told her.

She grinned. "Give me ten seconds."

Qubit huffed. "This is *so* not grundy."

"You could always try to run," Malcolm said.

The look in Qubit's eyes said he knew how that would go.

"A-ha!" Valentine said.

The lockbox opened and a list of files appeared—hundreds of them. *How many secrets are walking around in this guy's head?*

They shared the connection to Qubit's secret server. Together the twins scrolled through the files, noting a few interesting code names.

-*Verticore*

-*Dynamite Mercy*

-*The Chaos Merchant*

-*Dracona Fraction*

Halfway down the list, they saw one file name and screeched to a halt.

-*Project Rectify*

They shared a look.

"Could it be so simple?" Valentine said.

"I doubt they ever thought we'd find this, so yeah," Malcolm said. "Only one way to know."

With a hand pressed to her stomach, Valentine nodded. "Do it."

At his command, the file opened to reveal a list of subfolders. Malcolm found the folder labeled PYRE. Heart pounding in his ears, he prepared to open it.

"Mal, wait," Valentine said.

Her selector hovered over a different file—VITIATE. It meant "to corrupt." More importantly, it was a direct antonym of RECTIFY. Could it relate to how all this began?

He steeled himself. "Okay, do it."

Valentine opened the folder, and out poured thousands of video files. Before their eyes, the twins saw a horror that had previously only been described to them.

Black ships poured through portals. Energy beams raked

Eldurfall. Buildings toppled, streets crumbled. People ran. Screamed. Died. So much fire.

Each file came from a different camera across the city. A different view of the carnage. As he made himself watch, Malcolm realized he was trembling. Valentine's hand grasped his.

Then one video appeared and Malcolm saw a familiar face. His heart lurched into his throat as Callie stumbled through the ruins of a street market, yelling, searching.

"Maya!" Valentine gasped.

Malcolm saw her then. Further down the street, she cried out for her mother, tears staining her cheeks.

Then a ship landed between them. A ramp extended, separating mother from child. Two figures appeared.

All Malcolm's insides dropped to the ground. "Oh, God, no."

Malcolm and Valentine Gilbert descended from the ship, scowling and heavily armored.

"It's a lie," Valentine whispered. "A trick. It has to be."

Then their doppelgängers unleashed waves of destruction. Valentine choked back sobs as Maya disintegrated. As Callie screamed.

Swallowing his own tears, Malcolm looked to Qubit. "This isn't us."

The gangster stared at them with a new expression now. One of hatred.

"My brother died that night. The Regent showed me everything. One day you'll take your own century by force. You'll twist it, pervert it, and use your people to kill us. So the only way to save our time is to cut yours loose."

Malcolm faltered. "What does that mean?"

Qubit stood straighter, as if their despair was feeding him strength. He raised his left arm for the twins to examine.

"Imagine I'm stuck out in the woods in your century. I get injured, then get one of your dark-age infections. Gangrene, I guess. Stretching from here to here."

With his other hand, he pointed between his fingers and elbow.

"Whole forearm eaten up by disease. Now, say I want to live, and I want to keep the rest of my arm. What can I do?"

"Amputate," Valentine said.

"Right." He pointed at his elbow again. "I'd amputate here. Now, if I used a knife and just started hacking away, I'd bleed out. So, what can I do?"

The answer came to Malcolm, and it filled him with dread. Suddenly he thought he saw where Qubit was going.

"You can cauterize it," he said.

"Right again. And how can I do that?"

"Fire," Valentine said, and her mouth fell open. "No. Please tell me he's not . . ."

Qubit smiled darkly. "All that weird fire the Regent uses? It's not just for show. It's what happens when you destroy Time itself. Burn enough of it and you open a wound in the universe. Keep burning it, and the wound becomes a scar."

Throat dry, Malcolm swallowed. "So, the Regent plans to burn all our Time?"

Qubit thumped Malcolm's forehead. "What do you think the Pyres are for, genius? Once all six of them network, they'll incinerate so much Time that your whole century becomes cosmic scar tissue. All the years up until your point of history— they'll be cut loose. Then all the Regent needs to do is seal the scar. The Timeline will keep going from there, and our people will be safe. From *you*."

"But . . . but . . . he's breaking the Timeline, and billions will die!" Valentine stammered. "How can he do that? How can your people let him?"

Qubit laughed in her face. "You think they know? They don't want to know. This perfect little world the Regent built for them—they want it back so badly, they'll believe anything he says."

"When they realize what he's done, they won't stand for it," Malcolm said. "Not the good ones. They'll fight back."

Qubit's expression turned pitying. He shook his head. "Oh, kiddies. Afterward, they won't even remember there was a war. You'll be erased. The Regent will tell the people he fixed some random anomaly, and they'll swallow it and move on with their vapid little lives."

He poked Malcolm in the chest.

"Those of us who do know? We'll let it happen. We'll know you got what you deserved." He laughed. "You've already lost, and you don't even know it."

Malcolm's anger blazed. He reached for the gangster, but Valentine got there first. She slammed him back against the shed.

"How do we stop it? Tell me!"

"Not my department, sweetheart. Even if I did know, you think I'd breathe a word to you? I've seen the things you two end up doing. Far as I'm concerned, you can all burn."

This was pointless. Qubit would happily die if it meant getting vengeance. Whatever they managed to pull from his secret server, it would have to be enough.

Malcolm laid a hand on Valentine's shoulder. With a deep breath, she let go.

Swallowing his own rage, he scanned the PYRE folder enough to see that it had complete schematics. He downloaded every scrap of data, launched a nasty virus into the server, and closed the connection. In minutes, the last of Qubit's information empire would be dust.

It was time to go. But as the twins turned to leave, Malcolm couldn't stop himself from one parting word.

"If we're so evil, if we're such cold-blooded killers," he said, "why are we leaving you alive?"

He had to say it, for himself. He never expected the question to penetrate. Never expected to see Qubit pause, mentally step back, maybe ask what he had never allowed himself to ask.

But it did. And Qubit did. Malcolm could see it in his eyes, like lightning from a clear blue sky. Doubt.

Taking the victory, Malcolm turned with Valentine and headed back toward the door.

Before they could reach it, the door flew off its hinges.

CHAPTER 22

The steel door flew a dozen feet before crashing down. Two figures tumbled through the doorway and rolled to a stop.

Callie sat on top of a strange machine. Smaller than her, it was sheathed in matte black armor that seemed to drink in the shadows. Its only facial feature—a tiny slit where its eyes should be—glowed red.

Her armor sparked and whined, and a few pieces were clearly missing. Valentine noticed the machine was missing an arm. Then she saw it hanging from Callie's shoulder. Its blade had skewered her.

On its back, the machine fired a beam from its eye, right at Callie's face. She dodged, barely quick enough, and the beam carved a furrow on the side of her helmet.

"Just," Callie raised her arm, "die!"

She struck, her armor shearing away as her blade plunged into the machine's eye. The beam sputtered and died.

Twisting, Callie cut through the top of its skull, spewing a shower of sparks and hardware. The machine gave a final shudder and died.

Sitting atop its husk, Callie worked to catch her breath.

"Holy *ta-mahdey*," Qubit said. "She just killed an Infiltrator."

Valentine had forgotten he was there. The twins shot him matching glares. He wilted under their ire and scuttled back through the doorway.

"A third Praetorian came?" Malcolm said when he'd gone.

Callie nodded. *Praetorian Infiltrator. A machine built to kill assassins*, Valentine thought she remembered. *Built to kill Callie.*

Approaching, Valentine sank to her knees. She reached for the blade protruding from Callie's shoulder, still attached to the severed arm.

"Are you okay?" Valentine said.

Callie gave a faint gasp as the blade slid free. "I heal pretty fast, and the armor kept me going. Just need rest."

"What happened to the Suppressors?" Malcolm said.

"Dead."

With a labored grinding noise, her helmet retracted. Valentine stifled a gasp. Callie's nose was crooked and bloody, her bottom lip split, and the skin around her left eye swollen and purple. A burn mark traced the left side of her head.

Valentine felt her eyes glisten. A lump rose in her throat.

"You fought three killing machines by yourself. To save us." Before she knew it, she was hugging her stepmother. "Thank you."

Malcolm joined in. Callie groaned under the affection assault, laughed as they apologized for squeezing her, and then pulled them back in again.

"So . . . you don't hate me?"

"We never hated you," Malcolm said. "But if anyone questions what side you're on now, we'll set them straight."

Valentine pulled back enough to look Callie in the eye. "Dad doesn't really hate you either. Don't give up on him."

Now it was Callie's turn to almost cry. Swallowing tears, she gave a brave nod. "I'm not so easy to get rid of."

Malcolm nudged the Infiltrator's skull. "I think that's an understatement."

They shared a quiet laugh, one full of relief. Callie plucked gently at Valentine's sleeve.

"I like these," she said, referring their uniforms. "You look like proper . . . I was going to say soldiers, but that's not right, is it? You're both so special, and I don't mean the Time powers. I'm glad everyone can see it now."

Smiling, Valentine gave her hand an affectionate squeeze.

"Hate to ruin the moment," Malcolm said, "but we should get out of here. We got what we needed. Do you need new armor?"

Callie shook her head. "It's organic ceramic, kind of like hyper-advanced abalone shell. It'll heal itself. Did you find Qubit's data cache?"

Valentine gave an involuntary sigh. Momentarily forgotten, the heaviness of their discovery now returned. Callie glanced between them, and her expression clouded over.

"Is it bad?"

"Worse than we imagined," Valentine said.

Quickly as she could, she outlined the terrible truths that Qubit had revealed. Callie's head dipped low. Jaw clenched, she glared down at the Praetorian.

"I trusted that man. Gave him everything. All along, he was using me." She squared her shoulders. "Not anymore."

Callie braced herself and stood, then swayed and fell back to her knees. Accepting the twins' support, she stood and clung to them.

"I might need a day to get back in fighting shape."

"Everwatch must have doctors," Malcolm said, pulling out the Everwatch Beacon. "And they'll need these files."

Looking at the device, Valentine felt a stab of loss. Clive had designed the prototype. What would he say to them now, with the whole of the Timeline at risk?

At that, a new thought sparked in her head. Valentine couldn't know if it's what Clive would have said, but even the memory of their friend was helping. Malcolm's finger hovered over the button, ready to—

"Stop," she said. "We're missing something."

"We got everything Qubit had," Malcolm replied.

"Yes. Including the exact time and location when 'we' first attacked. What could we learn from seeing it ourselves?"

Horror painted Callie's face. "Please don't make me go there again. I can't."

But Valentine knew the look in Malcolm's eye. He'd picked up her thread, and she could see him unraveling it in his mind.

"Whether it's a trick, or whether it really is future us, there's no better way to see the truth." He gave Callie a sympathetic look. "I'm sorry, but we have to."

A tear fell down Callie's cheek. She wiped it away and stood straighter. The agony was still there, but now she visibly donned mental armor.

"How?" she said. "The Beacon will only take us home."

"We're Sixth-*sev* Chronauri. We should act like it," Malcolm said. "I have an idea."

Light streamed by in a constant rush. Valentine's stomach jumped with the sensation of speed as they plunged backward through the Timeline. Beyond the lights, she could see the world outside racing by.

They traveled side by side, Callie clutched tightly between the twins. Working in unison with Malcolm, Valentine exerted her will on the portal until their direction of travel changed.

Slowly they drifted away from the center, until they could touch the radiant temporal wall as it flew by. Valentine brushed it, marveling as a stream of light parted around her hand like rushing water.

"Tell me when," Malcolm called.

Valentine nodded. Keeping gentle contact with the wall, she extended her Chronauri senses until they bumped up against the light. Then she pushed a little harder, until her perceptions passed beyond the wall and into the physical world.

She gasped. Instead of just seeing the years pass by, she could *feel* them now. And not just years, but days, hours, seconds, and beyond.

Time's journey across the millennia bloomed in Valentine's consciousness. Turning forward and backward, she could cast her attention in either direction and feel it flow through moment after moment.

The sense was just there, suddenly a part of her, as if she'd opened a door she never knew was a door in the first place. *This is what it means to be Sixth-sev, she realized. A glimmer of it, anyway. When we hit our full potential, what else will we be able to see?*

"Whoa," Malcolm breathed. "What did you do?"

"You feel that?"

"Oh, yeah," he said, eyes wide. "I feel it all."

Before Valentine could respond, the moment they'd been searching for bloomed in her awareness, approaching fast.

"Get ready," she called.

"I see it."

Valentine counted down. Months passed, then weeks . . . days . . . hours . . . minutes . . .

"Now!"

Gathering Time at the tips of his fingers, Malcolm jabbed hard at the wall. With a *boom* and a spray of light like sparks, his hand broke through. Where light had scattered from Valentine's fingers, the entire wall parted around Malcolm's hand.

One hand locked tight on Callie, Valentine reached out with the other. Calling Time, she grabbed the edge of the opening and pulled. The tear in Time widened, vibrating under her grip like a beehive. Their descent through the Timeline slowed, then stopped altogether.

"We're here," Malcolm called.

Valentine sent Callie through first. Once she was safely on the other side, the twins followed. Like stepping from one room into another, they exited their portal and reentered the real world.

They stood on the roof of a squat building. All around them, Eldurfall buzzed with activity. Millions went about their lives, blissfully unaware that the peace they took for granted was about to be shattered.

"Only a few minutes away," Valentine said.

"I can feel it." Full of wonder, Malcolm gazed at Valentine. "I don't know what you did, but it's like . . . like I can feel Time differently now."

"Like the Timeline's a calendar in your head, and you can flip to any day you want?"

He brightened. "That's it!"

"So, you can see the future now?" Callie said, her face showing trepidation.

"No," Valentine said. "It's more like an awareness of Time's flow across the ages. I can just feel it now."

"It's how we knew when to stop here," Malcolm said. "We knew the date and time, and I just felt it coming."

Valentine shrugged. "I don't know if I'd call it a power by itself, but—"

"—what if it's a foundation for the real stuff Sixth-*sev* can do?" Malcolm finished.

"Yeah."

"What about that?" Callie gestured at the tear they'd come through.

Valentine peered back through the oval-shaped opening. She could still see light racing by on the other side. "I'm guessing it'll stay open until we close it."

"Guessing?"

"It's not like we've done this before."

Callie kept eyeing the portal, her jaw muscles working overtime. Her breaths were shorter now, and her eyes had a barely masked desperation.

Valentine touched her arm. "Do you want to stay near it? If it starts closing, let us know."

Callie released a breath and nodded. With a grateful look, she returned to the opening. With her back turned to the twins—and the rest of Eldurfall—she folded her legs and sat. Valentine guessed she would be working hard to ignore what was about to happen.

Valentine joined Malcolm at the far edge of the roof. Kneeling, she leaned against the short parapet and peered over the side. Below, a bustling street market stretched for blocks.

"Someone's cooking down there," Malcolm said. "Smells good. Think we have time for a snack?"

They shared a tense laugh, and then grew serious. Valentine hugged herself. It was a warm night, but she felt like shivering.

"Is this what the Chrona feels all the time?" she said. "Standing in a moment, knowing what's about to happen?"

"Knowing that you can never save everyone." Malcolm blew out a breath. "How do you tell someone that protecting the Timeline means letting them die? How do you keep it from driving you crazy? It's a—"

"—burden no one in their right mind would want."

"If we ever meet her, maybe we can ask how she copes."

"That'd be nice. Though I won't hold my breath."

Valentine cut off as Time began to *shift*. In the sky, distortions rippled through the Timeline. Something was approaching from the past.

Just as Valentine had hoped, they got their first clue. "Mal."

"I know."

"You feel where they're coming from?"

"Yeah. How does that make sense?"

"It doesn't."

They shared a significant look. Seconds later, portals opened and black ships came screaming through.

Valentine gripped the parapet until her knuckles turned white. *You're just here to observe*, she reminded herself. *What you learn can save lives.*

In seconds, Eldurfall descended into chaos. Being here for real, feeling their building tremble, hearing the screams of terror and pain, Valentine understood even more why Callie had done what she did.

Burying her feelings as much as possible, she focused

externally, forcing herself to watch for anything that might help her understand. Nothing presented itself until she reached out to a passing ship and swept through it with her Chronauri senses.

She rocked back. "Whoa. Mal, take a reading on a ship."

"But I'm looking for—"

"Please do it."

Malcolm complied, and once again they shared a look.

"That's doesn't make sense either," he said.

"No."

"I mean, what the Regent told people . . . what Qubit told us . . ."

"I know. None of it adds up," she said. "Unless this goes deeper than we thought."

The twins had only a moment to absorb their discoveries. Then Malcolm's eye slipped over her shoulder, and his expression turned dark.

"Val," he said. "They're here."

Cold dread gripped Valentine. She turned to see a new ship approaching, different from the others.

She focused on her breathing, keeping it steady, even as the ship landed, as "they" came down the ramp and laid waste to everything they saw, as little Maya vanished from existence.

Right then, Valentine discovered the lie. Or part of it, anyway. She trembled as she fought to keep all her senses trained on their doppelgängers to make sure of what she sensed.

Malcolm's voice rose above the din, seething with rage. "Lies. I *knew* it. All lies, and for what? What does this accomplish?"

It was all the confirmation she needed. "You feel it, too."

"I feel it." He glared down at their enemy. "Whoever that is, they're going to be sorry."

Valentine agreed, but they couldn't get carried away yet. "We still have to figure out who they actually are."

The "twins" destroying the city stopped short. In unison, they whipped around and glared upward, right at the roof Valentine and Malcolm knelt on.

"Oh—" Valentine began.

"—crap," Malcolm finished as they pushed away from the edge. "Time to go."

They raced across the rooftop, collected Callie without slowing, and aimed for their escape hatch.

"What happened?" Callie asked.

"Just run!" Valentine said.

With a flying leap, they disappeared back through Time.

CHAPTER 23

"She needs a doctor," Malcolm called as they appeared through the portal.

"Whoa," Fred said, eyeing Callie's wounds. "Ouch, girl."

"I'll take her to the Medica," Winter said, accepting support of Callie's weight. They aimed for the Sled, which hovered beside the platform.

"Thanks," Callie said. "I just need patching up."

The twins' dad approached and pulled them into a relieved hug. "You're okay?"

"A little shaken, that's all," Malcolm said. "But—"

"—determined," Valentine finished. "Thorn!"

Across the platform, Eternal King Tyrathorn Corvonian turned. Stepping away from the Ember Guard he'd been conversing with, he aimed for the twins.

"What happened to her?" Neil said.

To Malcolm's surprise, he was covertly watching Callie. She moved slowly, but was almost at the Sled's rear hatch.

"She saved our lives," Malcolm said.

Neil nodded, chewing on his bottom lip. Which meant he was debating with himself.

"Plenty of room on that Sled," Malcolm said. "She nearly died for us back there."

They shared a look, and Malcolm saw the first hints of softness returning to his father's eyes. Neil nodded slowly, hesitant. Then, squeezing Malcolm's shoulder in thanks, he turned to follow his wife.

As the Sled whooshed away, the twins made for the platform steps at a fast pace. Tyrathorn joined them.

"What news?" he said.

Valentine handed him the device she had worn on her temples. "Technical readouts for the Pyre and a lot more."

They descended to the stone walkway leading to the Eon Palace.

"My technicians will analyze it." Tyrathorn shot them an approving grin. "Most impressive. How was the future?"

"Shiny," Malcolm said.

He glanced back at the Empyrean Bridge as the portal closed. Despite the danger, he couldn't help wondering if they would see Eldurfall again. Maybe if they survived. If they could go there without looking over their shoulders.

We will survive, he repeated to himself. *We'll save our century and theirs, too.*

Just then, a presence bloomed in his consciousness, a temporal signature barreling toward him like a rocket. Before Malcolm could react, Asha's arms and legs were wrapped around him. Her lips sought his with urgency. When his mind caught up, he returned the sentiment in full.

When they finally parted, Malcolm laughed while trying to take in a full breath. He felt his cheeks heat. "I missed you, too."

Asha betrayed not even a shred of embarrassment. Her

eyes seemed only to hold him. "Any longer and I'd have dived in after you."

"Weren't we only gone five minutes?"

She clutched his hand. "That's four minutes too long."

"Aside from technical data," Tyrathorn said, "did you discover anything else?"

"Hah," Malcolm said, exchanging a significant look with his sister. "You could say that."

"Good. We will take any advantage." Tyrathorn hefted the tiny computer in his palm. "This requires time to analyze, and I am sure you want to refresh yourselves. We shall reconvene in two hours."

"You're healing remarkably quickly," the physician said.

Lying on the examination table in the Medica, Callie shrugged. "It's how they built me."

The doctor nodded as if she heard that on a regular basis. "Even without our help, you'd be functional in a few days. I suspect you'd like to get back out there sooner, though?"

"Yes," Callie said. "This war won't last a few days."

There was an unexpected movement over the doctor's shoulder. Callie glanced toward it and froze, as if the air had been sucked from her lungs.

"Neil."

Her husband just looked at her, his face an unreadable mask. He didn't move from the doorway.

Glancing back and forth between them, the doctor seemed to catch the sudden change in mood. With a few keystrokes on her console, a clockwork arm extended over the bed, bearing lasers and other tools Callie didn't recognize, and went to work mending her flank.

"Call if you need anything," the doctor said before excusing herself.

Then they were alone, staring at each other, and Neil still hadn't moved. Callie couldn't remember the last time she felt so unsure of herself.

"Hi," she said.

"Is it true what Malcolm said? Did you risk yourself to save them?"

"There were machines. Special ones built to kill people like them. I did my best to hold them off."

His stare seemed to dig into her. "You came to kill them, and now you're willing to die for them?"

Callie forced herself to stop, to think before answering. For so long, her life had been built on deception. A foundation of lies big and small. *I can't do that anymore. I won't, especially not with him.* She had to be completely honest, not even slanting the truth to her advantage.

"In my century, few knew I existed. The ones who did—they feared me. I was this . . . phantom. All rage and vengeance. A walking nightmare." She paused to take a shaky breath. "Then I met all of you, and it was like I woke up to a dream. You made me believe again."

Neil stepped into the room. "Believe in what?"

"Anything. A real life. Maybe, if I was lucky, even love." She swallowed a wave of emotion, determined to say it all. "Even if it's over now, it was everything to me, and it came from all of you. So yes, I would die for them. A thousand times over."

Neil approached the foot of her bed. He stopped there. To Callie's dismay, he looked down and grimaced.

"I want so much to hate you. To see you as a liar and a monster. I've tried to stop loving you."

Every word drove a dagger into Callie's heart. She struggled to keep her mental armor strong, and failed.

"Every time I try," Neil said, "I see the way you treat my kids and my mom. I see how much they love you. I see the way you look at me. I remember how I feel whenever you walk into the room."

He paused, not knowing how every word dangled Callie over a chasm. She clung to each one. He stepped to the side of her bed, and she fought to quell the hope rising within. Life didn't work out that way for her.

"My family learned why you came here, and within a day they forgave you. I think, way faster than I could, they saw who you were underneath all the pain. All your tragedy." Finally, he looked into her eyes. "I'm still angry. We have a lot to talk about. But . . ."

Suddenly he was beside her. Leaning over the bed, he took her face in his hands and kissed her.

Callie's insides burst like fireworks. Reaching around the machine at her side, she pulled him into as tight an embrace as she could. With every kiss, a little piece of her knit back together.

When the kiss ended, Neil stayed close, leaning his forehead against hers. Callie realized then that she was crying. As she held the man she loved again, his happy tears mingled with hers.

Malcolm stood with Valentine, gazing through the forward window of the Command Center. Nearly two hours after returning, they drank in Emmett's Bluff, and the beautiful skyscraper that was trying to burn it to ash.

How much longer before the Pyre is repaired? Will we be ready when it counts?

As he traced the contours of the town, from southern plains to northern hills, something else struck him.

"Val," he said. "Anything about Eldurfall seem familiar to you?"

"What do you mean?"

"I don't mean all the skyscrapers. More like—"

He cut off as the main doors opened. The appointed hour for the debriefing approached, and the first to arrive were Neil and Callie.

They were holding hands.

"Well, look at that," Malcolm said.

Valentine sighed with relief. "Good."

Neil and Callie joined them at the window, where happy hugs were shared. A moment of peace before the storm. To Malcolm's pleasant surprise, Callie's wounds were noticeably improved.

"Back in the fight tomorrow?" he asked.

Callie gave an eager grin. "Back in now. I'm not missing any of this."

Malcolm glanced around the Command Center. No one else was close enough to hear.

"I'm curious," he said. "Where is Eldurfall? Geographically, I mean."

She paused. "Why do you ask?"

"I noticed the land followed a certain contour."

"You're right," Valentine said, resting a finger on her chin. "I remember now. Half was high up, then there was a slope, and the rest of the city spread out below."

With a knowing grin, Callie shook her head. "How did I

think you wouldn't notice? Sorry. I didn't know how you'd react, so I kept it myself."

Malcolm blew out an astonished breath. "Wow."

Their dad looked back and forth between them. "What am I missing?"

"Eldurfall," Valentine said, "is Emmett's Bluff a thousand years from now."

Eyes wide, Neil looked to Callie. She nodded.

"Coincidence?" he asked. "Or something more?"

"I wish I knew," she said.

Tyrathorn arrived with the rest of their party. Waving a greeting to them, he stood at the largest table and waited for everyone to gather around.

Malcolm took a slow, calming breath. He felt like they were standing at the edge of a waterfall, half weightless as they leaned forward and prepared to dive, not knowing what they would find under the water, only that they had to leap.

"Hey," Valentine whispered. "You okay?"

"Yeah. It's just . . . what if this is the last time we're all together?"

Malcolm watched the question hit her and sink in. Then, with effort, she mentally pushed through. He could see it: she was choosing to hope. He would have to do the same.

She nodded toward the table. "Come on."

The twins stood by Tyrathorn, waiting as everyone took positions. Neil. Callie. Oma Grace. Asha. Winter. Fred. Walter. Captain Armel. Last to arrive was John, who squeezed in next to Valentine and snuck a kiss, then whispered in her ear until she blushed.

Malcolm squared his shoulders. *Now we leap.*

"You're doing what we asked?" he said to Tyrathorn.

"My agents are deployed as we speak. Many of your people have fled, but we are locating those that stayed and bringing them here."

"Thank you." Malcolm faced everyone else. "There are still mysteries, but we found answers, too. We have schematics for the Pyre, and there's more data that Thorn's people are tearing apart."

"Then there's the Regent," Valentine said. "He lied to his own people. We suspected it before, but now we have proof. Starting with these."

Her fingers flew across the controls. A hologram appeared above the table's center, a black ship shaped like a jagged blade.

"These are the ships that attacked Eldurfall. The Regent told everyone that we stole his tech, corrupted it, and then corrupted the people of our century and invaded. Well, we jumped back and watched this attack for ourselves."

A shocked murmur rose from the group.

"Yo, are you serious?" Fred said.

"That seems foolhardy, kid," Walter said.

"We had to see for ourselves," Malcolm said. "Everyone's Time energy is unique, like a fingerprint. So, first we scanned those ships for signatures, and we discovered something. They had none."

"Meaning no pilots," Valentine explained. "Unmanned drones. The Regent told everyone we sent people to attack, but the only things attacking were machines."

"Also, they invaded through Time portals, and we traced them back to their point of origin," Malcolm continued. "The Regent told his people that we invaded from our century. But the drones traveled from a date only weeks before the attack."

"Then there's our doppelgängers," Valentine said. "We can

sense anyone's temporal signature, but it's easier with Chronauri because they shine so much brighter. So when they attacked, we knew right away that something was wrong."

"So," Captain Armel said hesitantly, "it wasn't actually you?"

Valentine shook her head.

Palpable relief rippled through their friends and family. A tension that Malcolm hadn't even noticed was now fading, everyone relaxing and sharing nervous grins.

"That's very good news, my boy," Oma Grace said.

The twins exchanged a look.

"Wait," Malcolm said. "You really thought it might be us?"

"Don't take it personally," Winter said. "We had to be prepared for anything."

Valentine gaped. "Seriously?"

"Power corrupts, kid," Walter said. "You've seen that."

There was a moment of tense silence while the twins pondered this.

"I guess you're right," Valentine said. She looked at Tyrathorn. "I mean, it's not like you planned to go dark when you started. Right? It just happened."

Tyrathorn gave a solemn nod. "Oh, yes. And despite the decades of good to follow, my regret for those early mistakes has never faded."

They were right. If Malcolm was close to someone with cosmic power at their fingertips, he might have moments of doubt, too. The people here loved him and Valentine, he knew that. Swallowing his pride, he pushed through the initial hurt.

"So, what did you sense?" Asha said. "What was wrong with your imposters?"

"Their temporal signatures were identical to each other,"

Malcolm said. "That's not possible. Whoever they really are, their power comes from a single source."

"And it's a source we've felt before," Valentine added. "When the Pyre first arrived, we felt a huge signature broadcasting from it. There was one power source—one person—driving everything, and it's the same signature we felt from the imposters."

"Whoa," Fred said. "You're saying the Regent faked an attack on the future, just so he could build a toaster army and start a war here?"

"Someone did," Valentine said. "Based on what Callie's told us, who could it be but the Regent?"

"But, why?" Oma Grace asked. "Callie, you said he was a good leader, didn't you? A peaceful man."

"Yes," Callie said. "Everyone loved him. So when he presented all his evidence and asked the world to help, no one hesitated."

"Then what does all this destruction gain him?" Oma Grace said.

No one had an answer. What made it even worse for Malcolm was knowing everything else. They hadn't even revealed yet what the Pyres were built for.

He hesitated, the terrible truth lodging in his throat. *They have a right to know the stakes*, he reminded himself.

So he told them everything. The Pyres had been built to burn their century until it became a permanent scar, cutting the Timeline in two. Billions dead, and a future infinitely corrupted.

The stunned silence was overwhelming.

John cleared his throat. His voice came out subdued. "I understand how one man could conceive this. But how could a world of decent people tolerate it?"

"Only a handful know the Regent's real plan," Valentine said. "The rest of the world thinks their savior is going to fix everything."

"And if he succeeds," Malcolm said, "he destroys us and writes his own history. In that corrupted Timeline, no one will remember there was ever a war. Because none of us will have existed."

"And we still do not know the reason," Tyrathorn said. "All the deception, all the destruction, for what?"

Another helpless silence. As Tyrathorn prepared to speak again, a piercing alert rang from the holotable. He checked his display and then whipped his head toward another workstation.

"Katerina?" he called.

"Yes, sir," a technician said. "I believe I've found it."

"A moment, please," Tyrathorn said.

He and Winter moved to study Katerina's display, while she pointed and whispered explanations. The conversation lasted mere minutes, but to Malcolm it stretched on. Waiting for answers felt like waiting under a gallows. When his friends came back, would they have news of salvation or doom?

He snapped from his reverie as the king and queen returned, looking serious.

"Our people have made some discoveries," Winter said.

"Yes," Tyrathorn said. "Thanks to the intelligence you provided, we know how the Pyre works."

Tyrathorn paused, holding their hopes in his hand. Then his heavy expression became a smile.

"And we know how to get inside."

The plan wasn't perfect.

They had spent the next hour poring over the findings, debating and strategizing, proposing a dozen plans and then discarding them. When they finished, golden late-afternoon sunlight bathed the Command Center.

The plan was aggressive, dangerous, and more than a little crazy, but Malcolm thought it could work.

Still, it wasn't perfect.

"Our force is too small," Walter said. "We'll have to make smarter choices than the enemy."

"Agreed," Tyrathorn said. "We brought as many Ember Guard and Watchers as we could, but even the Empyrean Bridge has limitations."

"We'll make do," Captain Armel said. "Few battle plans are ever ideal, and few armies in history have had what they needed."

"We got a reason to win," Fred said. "That'll make the difference."

"It'll have to," Winter said. "We can't hold back for a second if—"

She was interrupted by a young girl in an Eon Palace uniform who approached.

"Apologies, Queen Winter, but they said it was urgent."

"Who?" Winter said.

"Local refugees are outside the throne room. They're demanding an audience."

"How many?" Tyrathorn asked.

"Um, all of them, I think."

The king and queen exchanged a look.

Tyrathorn shrugged. "They are your people, my love. Whatever you think is best."

She gave him a smile and turned to the aide. "Let them know we're coming, please."

"Mal and I are coming, too," Valentine said.

"Of course." Tyrathorn addressed the others. "We all have our tasks. Let us be at them. When night falls, we strike."

The team broke into groups, the twins following Winter and Tyrathorn toward the main doors. When he crossed paths with Captain Armel, though, Malcolm stopped him.

"Captain, I know your role in this isn't what you wanted," he said. "I did suggest it, but still. I'm sorry."

The old soldier nodded his thanks. "You're correct. I don't like it. But I do understand it. Much as I would like to be the point of our spear . . ."

"I suggested you because we need someone we trust completely. It's necessary, if we're going to give it all we've got."

"You're a good man, Malcolm, and Tyrathorn is my oldest friend. Do not worry. I'm a soldier; I know how to follow orders. Especially when they're from people I hold in such high esteem."

He offered his hand. Relieved, Malcolm took it.

"Thank you, captain."

"Let's save the world together."

Feeling brighter, Malcolm met the others at the lift. Together they descended to ground level and took a hidden passage into the throne room. Across the grand hall, the giant double doors were closed and heavily fortified. Malcolm recalled their last visit to Everwatch.

"Worried about invaders, Thorn?" he teased.

Tyrathorn grinned. "Have I told you about my friends' first visit here, long ago? Friends who blew these doors to pieces?"

"Yeah, this is why we can't have nice things," Winter said.

"I'm sure they had their reasons," Valentine replied.

They shared a quiet laugh. Tyrathorn's hands rested on the massive door handles. Even through the reinforcement, the murmur of voices could be heard beyond. He glanced over his shoulder.

"Ready?"

Without waiting for a response, he pulled and the double doors swung open with a *whoosh*. Malcolm peered over his friend's shoulder and gaped.

There must have been a thousand people crowding around the doorway. At their head was a familiar face.

"You in charge here?" said Coach Boomer, their old gym teacher.

"We are. How can we help you, sir?" Tyrathorn said.

"I'll tell you how you can help me. Word is—"

Coach Boomer's eyes landed on Malcolm and Valentine. He paused, eyebrows raised.

"Gilbert twins. You're mixed up in this?"

"Um," Malcolm said. *Talk about worlds colliding.*

"For a while now," Valentine replied.

"Hm. Heard rumors about twin kids a couple years ago, when the French teacher went crazy. That was you?"

Malcolm found his voice. With something this big happening, what was the point of hiding anymore? "Yes, it was."

Coach Boomer studied them, chewing the inside of his cheek. Eventually he nodded.

"Well, you two were always weird."

He turned back on Tyrathorn.

"Word on the street is you're planning something." He nodded in the direction of the Pyre. "That right?"

"You are correct, sir. However, we cannot divulge—"

"Good," Boomer interrupted. "We're helping."

"Excuse me?" Winter said.

The coach looked to her, his eyes narrowed. "I know you

from somewhere. You look like . . . never mind. Whatever you're planning, we're in."

"Are you sure?" Valentine said.

"Make no mistake, sir," Tyrathorn said. "This is a real war."

"And this is a real gun."

Reaching into his jacket, Boomer pulled out a silver .50 caliber Desert Eagle. Behind him, dozens more drew guns and knives and swords. Malcolm thought he even saw a pitchfork.

"First lightning storms, then ice monsters, and now these guys? We're all sick of it. So, give us whatever spare gear you've got," Coach Boomer said. "This is our town. They think they can waltz in and take it? They've got another thing coming."

They exchanged bemused looks. Was this really happening? As the crowd awaited a response, Valentine spoke in a low voice.

"Thorn, you know that part of the plan we didn't like? The one we didn't have enough people for? Well . . ."

The king barked a laugh, then extended his hand to the coach. "It would be my honor, sir. Please, all of you, follow me to the armory. Tonight, we fight!"

A cheer went up from the crowd as they followed. Watching them stream by, Malcolm shook his head in disbelief.

"Did you ever think this would happen?" he asked his sister.

"Never. But one thing I know, now more than ever." She looked to Malcolm with an eager glint in her eye. "The Regent's not going to know what hit him."

CHAPTER 24

John stood before the massive, curved window of the Command Center. Night had fallen and their forces held ready, waiting for his direction. Once more he would be their overwatch.

To either side of him, a half dozen technicians sat at computer consoles, tasked only with carrying out his orders. All wore multi-channel long-range comm units modeled after his own. All had memorized Valentine's stolen data.

John closed his eyes and took thirty seconds to steady himself. He pictured his own fear as if it were steam, rising out of his body and evaporating into thin air. In the absence of fear came clarity. Stillness.

When his internal clock struck thirty, he opened his eyes and went to work.

"Confirm Tower Squads One and Two are in place and ready," he commanded. "Acquire visual confirmation and toss to my display."

He raised his hands like an orchestra conductor. On each finger he wore a black ring set with a blue jewel. At his motion, the jewels glowed. The window onto Emmett's Bluff flickered in response, and waves of data flowed down the glass in the same glowing blue.

"Tower Squad One confirms."

"Tower Squad Two confirms."

Two camera feeds appeared on the glass, sent by the squad leaders. Tower Squad One waited in the shadows fifty yards from the southern mini-tower. Pointing at the squad's camera feed, John "grabbed" it and slid it across the glass until it hovered next to the actual mini-tower. The structure's flaming top was visible in the distance.

Tower Squad Two had taken a similar position within sight of the northern mini-tower. John performed the same action with its camera feed.

"Activate their transponders," John called.

Dots appeared on the glass to north and south. John had only to point at any dot and he could access live data for the soldier it belonged to. Twenty dots clustered near each target: six light green for Ember Guard, fourteen dark green for Watchers.

"Apply intel extrapolation to mini-towers. Highlight ingress points."

A grid overlaid the structures, highlighting vulnerabilities identified by the data files from Eldurfall. A red square pulsed at the point of entry they had chosen.

"The scalpels are in place." John cracked his knuckles. "Now for the hammer. Paint a circle around the Verge."

In the abandoned building that directly faced the front doors of the Pyre, a large, blinking circle appeared on the display. John opened a comm channel.

"Commander Shah, please confirm the Verge is ready to deploy."

"Charging now, General. We await your order."

John paused. After his next words, the war wouldn't stop until somebody lost. He drank in the sight of his home, wanting to remember it just as it was. Just for one moment.

He squared his shoulders. "Order given, Commander. Let's ring the bell."

Battalion Commander Shah gazed up at the machine they had constructed, sneaking it piece by piece into the building. It was the size of a cement truck, but it kicked like something much bigger. This would be highly satisfying.

"Go order!" he called. "Charge to full."

His soldiers swarmed the device. A deep hum filled the building as the Verge powered up, its spherical core spinning furiously. Shah stepped behind the line drawn on the floor, keeping well away from the tangle of tubes and coils that made up the emitter.

"Charged and ready, Commander," his chief technician called.

"Fire."

The hum became a deep, gut-churning *thrum*. The building's western wall blasted to dust. Shah looked out upon the night, his view dominated by the chrome-and-white behemoth threatening this place.

A smile crossed his weathered face. "Light them up."

The Verge fired again. A missile of concentrated sound burst against the Pyre's shiny surface, shaking it from roof to foundation. A shallow dent appeared in the skyscraper's exterior, but it held strong.

"Again. Keep firing."

Once more the Pyre trembled. The dent deepened.

As the third sonic missile struck, the Pyre's ground-level doors opened. Waves of Cyonics poured into the night.

Shah keyed his comm. "General Carter, we have their attention."

"Well done, Commander. Don't let up." John addressed his team. "Paint the enemy red."

The technicians complied. What looked like a glowing, red river poured from the Pyre, streaming toward Commander Shah and the Verge. John tensed. *More than we expected.*

"ETA?" he said.

"Cyonics are fifty seconds out from the Verge."

John stood still, every cell in his body vibrating as he forced himself to wait. *We planned it this way for a reason,* he reminded himself.

"Sir?" a technician said, hesitant. "Commander Shah's force is very small."

"Hold," John said.

"Thirty seconds, sir."

"Hold!"

Red light swarmed John's display, almost on top of Shah. *Please let this work.*

"Sir!"

John opened his comm. "Tower Squad leaders, *now.*"

To the north and south, massive gouts of flame jetted from the mini-towers.

"Towers breached," a technician said.

"Tower Squads, attack," John ordered. "Find a way to bring them down."

Video feeds showed the squads charging inside. Returning

his attention to the Pyre, John saw exactly what he'd hoped to see. With two new threats revealed, the mechanical army had experienced a moment caught between objectives.

Time to spring the trap.

"Activate transponders for all Pyrefighter Battalions," John ordered. "Give me feeds from all battalion commanders."

All around the Pyre, transponder dots glowed to life. Dozens, then hundreds, and when the dots stopped appearing they numbered nearly three thousand. Light green for Ember Guard, dark green for Watchers, gold for volunteers from Emmett's Bluff.

Divided into ten battle groups, they hid in surrounding buildings, awaiting his order.

John gave a grim nod. "All Pyrefighter Battalions, attack."

Three thousand pinpoints of light flooded the street. Seconds later they smashed into the machines, cutting off their charge toward Commander Shah and the Verge.

To John's relief, the timing had worked. He had deployed the battalions soon enough to intercept the advance guard, but late enough that the enemy was committed and could not retreat.

As seconds ticked into minutes, he soaked up the symphony of battle moving across his display. His mind absorbed the notes being played, and he set about fine-tuning the song.

Battle line bowing, right flank. John reached out and "grabbed" a cluster of light green dots. With a wave, he re-tasked them to support the line of gold dots that were falling back.

Epsilon Battalion's video feed. John grabbed the video and rewound it ten seconds. There it was. That Destroyer charging them was only a distraction.

"Warn Commander Abishai he's about to be flanked by Praetorians. Send fast-Time Ember Guard against the Berserkers, Watchers against the Suppressors."

"Yes, sir."

John allowed himself a flash of pride. This plan was holding together. When dawn came, the world might just be safe again.

But first, the *real* plan had to begin.

John stepped over to a side workstation, calling up the data they would need for the most dangerous assignment. Unlike the battle on the street, this one had zero margin for error.

John switched his comm to a new channel. "Malcolm, Valentine, we're ready."

CHAPTER 25

The twins had puzzled over why the Regent's structures were placed in line with the craters Lucius Carmichael had created. Was it a symbol that their old enemy had returned?

Boom.

Then the stolen files revealed the truth. The Regent hadn't chosen those spots for symbolism, but for stability. By placing the Pyre and the mini-towers there, they could easily root the foundations deep within the earth.

Malcolm found himself strangely grateful for their old enemy. If he hadn't done what he did, they wouldn't be in his westernmost tunnel now. They wouldn't be standing at the spot where it ended.

At the outer wall of the Pyre's foundation.

Boom.

The greatest danger, they had known, would be detection. If a small force cut its way inside, the enemy might notice the vibrations and send machines in overwhelming numbers. Unless a separate force attacked, drawing the mechanical hordes onto the street. The Regent would still have forces inside as guards, Malcolm was sure of that. But every little bit helped.

Boom.

The Verge struck the Pyre again. The earthen tunnel Malcolm stood in trembled, raining dirt on them.

"Feels like it's almost our turn," Valentine said.

Malcolm turned to inspect the rest of their squad. "Everyone good to go?"

"Of course," Asha said.

"Seconded," Tyrathorn said.

"I'm always ready." Fred elbowed Winter. "Ain't that right, girl?"

Winter rolled her eyes. "You still talk like a frat boy and you're not even in college yet."

"Yeah, well, I haven't had fifty extra years to get so boring. What's it like?"

She shook her head, grinning. "*Some* of us are ready, Mal."

Malcolm chuckled. It brought back warm feelings to see his old friends together again—even if it took a Time war to do it.

Boom.

Valentine faced Callie. "Sure you want to do this? These are your people."

Callie's face was stone. "They killed my daughter."

Malcolm didn't ask further. Callie's whole vibe was cold, walking death. She would do her part, even if it killed her.

Last, he turned to the four High Protectors of the Ember Guard. In the lead was Vash, the tall, blonde guardswoman who had escorted them through Everwatch two years ago.

Before he could ask, she nodded. "We know our assignments."

"Good. Then you're up first."

Boom.

"Malcolm, Valentine, we're ready."

"Thanks, love," Valentine replied.

"I'll send you a ping whenever the Verge is about to fire."

"We'll be ready," Malcolm said.

"Form up," Vash commanded her Ember Guard. "Prepare for a Corvonian Cascade. I am the locus."

She drew a broadsword, its blade covered in wavy etchings like Damascus steel, and stood before the wall. The High Protectors formed a single-file line behind her, each with a hand on the shoulder in front of them.

"I haven't heard of that technique," Malcolm said.

"We rarely use it," Vash said. "It's very dangerous. The Chronauri acting as the locus could burn out. Or die."

Malcolm's eyebrows climbed. "Wow. You're risking . . ."

She eyed him, and he thought better of finishing that statement. Vash knew perfectly well what she was risking.

"What if Mal or I do it instead?" Valentine said.

"Out of the question. Use your power now, and you may as well light a signal fire to tell them you're coming. Also, you haven't practiced. This skill is very specific."

She must be afraid. Even a soldier like her would be. But she showed only determination.

Malcolm's admiration grew. "Thank you, Vash."

The soldier gave a tight nod. "It's what we do, Malcolm."

Ping. The small signal tone sounded in everyone's comm.

Boom.

Vash glanced over shoulder. "We'll catch the next one. Begin!"

Malcolm felt a *shift*.

The fourth High Protector in line reached through his nexus and absorbed Time. Then he *pushed* the absorbed power— that was the only way Malcolm could describe the feeling.

Responding to his will, it streamed into the third High Protector as a constant flow.

The third High Protector opened her nexus and did the same, drawing in Time and pushing it forward along with the fourth High Protector's energy. The second in line repeated this, until all the rushing streams of their collective power flowed into Vash.

With the power of four Chronauri in her hands, Vash blazed, her corona a coruscating display of colors. She was shaking, but her jaw was set and her posture was strong.

Pushing hard, she surged all four streams of power into her broadsword. The weapon glowed as brightly as she did.

Ping.

Boom.

With a clang-crack, Vash's blade pierced the Pyre's shell. The squad let out a collective whoop of triumph. The slice was only a foot wide, but it was a start.

Vash's chest heaved. "More."

"Vash," the soldier behind her said warily. "There's no need—"

"More! That's an order."

The man hesitated, then nodded. Malcolm felt the *shift* spike, each High Protector absorbing as much as they could. Vash gritted her teeth as all that power slammed into her.

Ping.

Boom.

Vash loosed a cry and swung.

The wall imploded. Her weapon shattered. A blast wave knocked everyone but the twins onto their backs.

Malcolm had instinctively shielded his face. Now, in the silence that followed, he lowered his arms and peered at the wall. Or what used to be a wall, and was now a gaping six-foot hole. His jaw hung open.

Valentine keyed her comm. "John, start the clock. We're going in."

The lowest levels of the Pyre bore none of its trademark beauty, just dimly lit industrial piping with webs of cabling snaking around it, going who knew where and supporting who knew what high above.

Only two service lifts reached this deep. In a dark corner, the grimy lift doors faced each other across a small platform.

Four Cyonics stood guard. Plasma cannons in hand, they scanned the darkness for threats that would never come this way.

A glass orb flew from the shadows, striking a Cyonic in the chest. The glass shattered, and with a sound like gale-force winds, a storm of red light enveloped the machine.

A long dagger flew from another direction, blazing red, to skewer the next Cyonic through its mechanical eye.

The remaining machines turned as Callie dropped her cloaking field. She spun, blades flashed, and their heads flew into the darkness.

The deepest shadows dissipated, and the squad appeared. Asha yanked her *qama* free of the metal skull.

Malcolm looked over at Callie. "Fast enough?"

She nodded. "None of them sent a distress call."

"We need to move faster, though," Valentine said. "They can't hold out there forever."

She was right. Lives hinged on their success, and the sooner, the better.

"You all know the plan," Malcolm said. "And you have

copies of the Pyre's schematics. We'll break into groups and hit our objective separately."

Each group had been instructed to choose their approach secretly, without telling the others. If any were captured, they couldn't divulge what they didn't know. The only things they all shared were the final rendezvous point and matching clocks to synchronize their arrivals.

"Look after each other," Valentine said. "These machines won't hesitate, so you shouldn't either. Also, thanks to Callie, you know what the Regent looks like. If you see him, run."

Looking at their brave companions, Malcolm felt a swell of pride. "Thank you."

"Yes," Valentine said. "Thanks for doing this. Now, let's go save the world."

They pressed call buttons for the lifts. As they waited, Malcolm felt a warm presence draw near. A hand slid into his and squeezed. He turned to Asha as she pressed against his body and gazed up at him.

"Never forget how much I love you," she whispered. "I'll carry you into battle with me."

His heart swelled. How had something so amazing happened to him? A warrior princess with a heart of fire, and she looked at him as if he were the only thing in this world.

"I will love you, Asha, until the last moment in this universe," he whispered back. "Whatever we face up there, I'll come through it so I can come back to you."

Her loving expression turned desperate, needful. "Malcolm . . ."

They fell into each other. Heat radiated through Malcolm as they kissed, wonderful and agonizing and soul-soothing. Asha's lips, soft yet aggressive, always seeking him.

When infinity had passed, they parted. The world around them came slowly, reluctantly back into focus.

Only then did Malcolm notice the hidden grins. The quiet elbowing, the stifled laughs. Only then did he remember they were sharing a small space with other people.

"Um, how long were we kissing?" he whispered to Asha.

Her entire face was red. "I have no idea."

Malcolm should have guessed who would break the silence first.

"Since we're about to punch death in the face," Fred said, "anyone else wanna make out?"

CHAPTER 26

"On the top floor of the Pyre, there is a chamber," Vash said. "In this chamber lies a device that is the beating heart of the Regent's war. It consumes Time—not simply using it, but destroying it. The stolen schematics have shown us this. When we destroy the device, we will save not only this town, not only this world, but the Timeline itself."

Crouched on the landing of a twenty-fifth-floor stairwell, Vash gazed proudly at her team of High Protectors. This was everything they had trained for, and more.

"So," Charlie said, "we gonna get rolling soon, cap'n? The wife and I got dinner plans."

Vash tried to glare, but couldn't contain her laughter. The rest of the squad broke when she did.

"At least tell me your wife is cooking," Neema said, sticking another explosive to the wall. "If you are, I may just root for the machines."

"That's something we didn't think of," Aziz said, fastening the last of his charges. "Instead of fighting, why not just feed the Regent your famous casserole?"

"Hey, don't be bitter 'cause no one loves you two," Charlie said.

"You know I'm in a committed relationship with chocolate," Neema replied.

Vash keyed her comm. "General Carter, status check."

"The other squads are in place, and the first move is yours. Good hunting."

"Give them a sixty-count and turn them loose. We'll be engaged by then."

"Will do."

When she finished, her squad was all business again. Vash met each of their eyes, not saying a word. Every Ember Guard knew their job well. With a single nod, they moved.

The stairwell glowed as they charged upward, each warrior drinking in Time through their nexus. Weapons appeared, made of fire, ice, and steel.

When they reached the thirtieth floor, Vash palmed her remote and pressed the button. They didn't break stride as, five stories below, the stairwell exploded.

"If that doesn't get their attention . . ." Aziz said.

Three flights above, the stairwell door opened. A horde of Cyonics poured through.

"Charlie, cover us," Vash ordered.

"Got it."

Charlie leapt onto the handrail. Palming two devices, he took aim and heaved them up the stairwell's open center. The first created a kinetic blast that shoved their pursuers back with a *bang*. The second burst into thick smoke, filling the open center for a hundred feet.

That was their cue. Neema and Aziz pressed the anti-grav button on their gear belts. Leaping onto the wall, they dashed sideways up the stairwell.

Vash grabbed the handrail and launched across the open

center, flying up one flight. She grabbed the handrail again, launched again, and soared higher. When she flipped back onto the stairs, she was right behind the Cyonics.

A sword of flames appeared in each hand. With an aggressive shout, Vash cut into the machine hordes.

Her squad arrived, seeming to attack from every direction, even high up on the walls. The High Protectors closed around the Cyonics like a vise, crushing them until nothing remained.

It was just the beginning. Detonating more explosives behind them, they ascended level after level. Two more Cyonic waves fell before them.

In the heart of enemy territory, this stairwell became their personal war zone.

At the fifty-second floor, Vash held up a staying hand. "Phase Two."

Aziz slapped a squarish device against the door and pressed the center button. With a loud *hiss* the door warped, then folded over on itself, and finally it melted to the floor.

Neema took the lead. "Forty yards to the nearest lift."

They followed her through the twists and turns of the Pyre's glittering, white hallways, leaving chaos in their wake. Bombs of fire, acid, gravity, and pure concussive force assaulted the fifty-second floor as they ran.

They rounded the last corner to a bank of four lifts. Moments later they were rising toward the eighty-sixth floor.

Everyone used the reprieve to catch their breath. The car flew skyward, silent except for the sound of soothing piano music.

Vash caught movement over her shoulder. She turned to see Charlie bobbing his head rhythmically. Her eyebrows raised.

"Don't even pretend you don't like this song," Charlie said. "It's a classic."

Aziz scoffed. "Classic for who?"

Charlie shrugged. "Your mom seemed to like it when I used to visit her."

Neema feigned a shiver. "I'm suddenly glad my mother died when the pyramids were being built."

The lift slowed.

"Form up," Vash commanded. "We keep making noise until we hit the next stairwell, then it's a last climb to the top."

She felt a series of *shifts*—her squad replenishing their Time. With a gentle chime, the lift stopped. The door opened on a large open area, completely empty.

Except for the giant Destroyer standing guard.

Vash grinned. "Finally."

Fred fell back against the wall, a Cyonic's hand locked around his throat. He sent an electric current coursing across his armor. The Cyonic shivered, stunned for an instant.

Fred grabbed the machine, spun, and shoved it against the wall. A steel spike shot from his wrist to pin its weapon arm. He fired another spike through its forehead. Then, just because, he drew his katana and swung. Its skull went flying.

"Yo, heads up!" he called.

Winter ducked, then finished dispatching her last Cyonic. As it fell, she twirled her sword of Goujian and slid it into her scabbard.

"Think we got 'em all," Fred said.

"Ready to go up?" Winter said, her gilded Watcher armor whirring.

"You know it. Lead the way."

Somewhere in the distance, there was another explosion.

Winter grinned. "The High Protectors are embracing their assignment."

"Wouldn't you?" Fred said. "They got the best one."

"Take it up with Carter. It was his idea. Speaking of . . ." Winter keyed her comm. "John, level sixty-two is clear. Where to?"

"Eighty-eight. After that's clear, head up top."

"Got it." Winter turned to Fred. "See? More machines to kill. We're having fun, too."

"I guess."

They arrived at a bank of lifts. Winter pressed the call button.

"By the way, 'heads up'?" she said. "Puns, Fred? Come on, you're better than that."

"Whatever, grandma. Sure you didn't break a hip back there?"

The lift door opened. Winter shoved Fred before stepping inside. He recovered just in time to leap through the door as it slid shut.

"Say grandma again, and I'll make you call me 'my queen.'"

"Try it and I'll tell everyone about that field trip in eighth grade. You blamed it on food poisoning, right?"

"You know I command an entire army, right?"

"Psh, bring 'em on."

They fell quiet. Fred found himself gazing sidelong at Winter, his oldest and best friend, who had endured heart-rending tragedy in Emmett's Bluff, then found solace in the most unlikely of places. Not the twists and turns a small-town teenager expects their life to take. Being friends with Malcolm and Valentine Gilbert had set them both on strange paths. Strange, but better.

"You look happy," he said.

She gave a soft smile. "I really am. When this is over, you should visit Everwatch. Get to know Meilyn and Xander."

Fred smiled. "Just try and stop me."

As the lift door opened, Winter gave Fred's hand a quick squeeze.

"All right, enough sappy crap," she said. "Let's break stuff."

They stepped out into a hallway—one of a seemingly endless labyrinth. Fred consulted the schematics and picked a direction. He held his katana ready at every corner. Just in case.

Winter left her ancient Chinese sword in its scabbard, opting for a weapon that Fred had only encountered once. He thought they called it a *kusarigama*. She held a long chain in her hands. From one end hung a heavy, curved blade. With a flick of her wrist, the blade began to whirl.

"Not far," she said. "A few more."

They rounded a corner and skidded to a halt. This hallway was long and narrow, with no breaks. Just a hundred feet of straight walls.

And twenty Cyonics.

One machine stepped forward.

"Lay down your weapons," it said in that annoyingly calm voice. "Give us locations of all your allies, and the Regent may have mercy on—"

Fred's steel spike smashed between its eyes, spraying clockwork. A chain wrapped around the Cyonic's neck; then Winter pulled and her blade sheared clean through it. The Cyonic collapsed, twitching and sparking.

"That was just a taste." Fred beckoned to the machines. "Who wants dinner?"

The hallway became a storm of plasma and steel.

Fred charged into the fray. *Duck under a blade. Spin and slash.* Two mechanical arms, a leg, and a head went flying. Machines dropped hard.

Fred crouched beside a dead robot. "Can I borrow this?"

It didn't argue, so he took its plasma cannon and raked the next three machines with exploding green bolts. Two of them fell, belching smoke.

With a friendly smile, Fred waved at the third. "Got a present for ya. Catch!"

He squeezed a clear, glass ball three times and hurled it like a baseball. To his delight, the Cyonic caught the object and held it up, studying its red center.

The time grenade burst in its hand, enveloping the machine in a storm of red light. In seconds, super-fast temporal energy aged its gears and armor until they crumbled to dust.

Fred pumped his fist. "Home run!"

Then the Cyonic fell, revealing another right behind it. It's cannon pointed right at Fred.

Before it could attack, a chain and blade hooked around its cannon; then the chain wrapped around its head. Winter sailed by and yanked hard. The chain tightened. The blade sliced through the gun, then the Cyonic's head.

She flashed a grin, then waded back into battle, whirling her kusarigama through machinery like a helicopter blade of death. Fred charged in behind her.

Working in tandem, they plowed through the horde. While Winter's blade spun high, Fred went low, chopping through knees and torsos. Mechanical parts rained down around him as they rolled forward.

Finally, the last Cyonic's head sliced free of its body. With a spin kick, Winter launched it away. As the machine fell, she locked eyes with Fred.

"Heads up."

Fred shook his head. "Way cooler when I say it."

Laughing, Winter gestured down the hall. "Come on. The others will be ahead of us now, and we need to get the timing just right."

CHAPTER 27

The Pyre shuddered.

"I can't tell if that's from the Verge, or our people inside," Asha whispered.

"Either way, it makes our mission easier," Tyrathorn said.

It sounded as if he was grinning. He was cloaked in shadows, though, and she couldn't see his face.

At first, it had felt strange to see him wearing the armor of a Watcher instead of an Ember Guard. Asha had had to remind herself that, from her brother's point of view, he had lived without temporal powers for decades. As they launched their part in this attack, he had quickly demonstrated that he didn't need to be Chronauri to be a threat.

Of the three-pronged invasion plan, they had received the quietest task. The High Protectors were to sow utter chaos and confusion, like turning a volume knob to ten. Fred and Winter brought more focused destruction, like a volume six.

The Corvonians kept to volume two. They had ascended the skyscraper using all stealth, fighting only when patrols or building systems could be dispatched silently.

Now on the ninety-third floor, they stood in a deep alcove

off a main passage. Using shadow-cloak devices, they waited like patient predators.

Footsteps approached. Keying options inside her helmet—upgraded when Everwatch arrived—Asha cycled through visual display modes. When she arrived at the electromagnetic spectrum, the world came into focus. Not its physical form, but the shape and flow of electromagnetic energy. Two humanoid forms were drawing near.

"Winter and Fred," Asha whispered.

New forms appeared on her HUD, moving in from a different direction.

"Cyonics," Tyrathorn said. "Moving to ambush our friends."

"Care to spoil their party, brother?"

"Why, I thought you would never ask, sister."

Asha paused, reflecting.

"I've missed this," she said. "I've missed you."

"Too true, Ashandara. When this war is over, we must not let the years slip by again. You are too important to me."

They fell silent as Winter and Fred passed. The Cyonics hunting them would not be far behind. Asha heard her brother chuckling.

"What is it?"

"Back when we battled the Frost Hammer, you would never have expressed affection so openly," Tyrathorn said. "The boy has softened your heart. I mean that in a good way."

She felt her cheeks warm. "Malcolm showed me there's more to life than fighting until I die. He didn't even do it on purpose—it's just who he is. I feel so peaceful with him."

"Ironic, considering he's . . ."

"Probably one of the most powerful beings in the universe?"

"Yes, that."

"He doesn't even think about it. All that power, Thorn. Others would wear it like a crown. Malcolm wears it like a favorite old sweater. He only cares what it can do for other people." Asha smiled. "I've never met anyone like him."

"You really do love him."

"I always will."

"Then I will return to Everwatch a happy—"

Ten Cyonics marched by in two columns, pursuing Winter and Fred. Asha drew one of her *qamas* and stood poised as the machines passed them, unaware. They rounded the next corner.

The Corvonians dropped the shadows and followed their prey. Swift and quiet as the wind, they dashed up behind the last two Cyonics.

Reaching through her nexus, Asha tapped her own Time just enough to power her weapon. The razor-sharp edge glowed red, multiplying its cutting power.

Three . . . two . . . one.

Asha wrapped her arm around the Cyonic's face and plunged her blade into its back. Like a hot knife through butter, it sliced armor and pierced the main power relay. Beside her, there was a barely audible rasp as Tyrathorn did the same. The machines died without so much as a rattle.

They lowered the darkened shells silently to the floor. For a tense moment they held still, waiting to be detected. The other Cyonics just kept marching.

With a shared look of triumph, they approached the next two machines.

Grab. Slice. Kill. Asha felt a rush of satisfaction as her blade burst through the Cyonic's chest. She laid this one down with the same quiet care. Again Tyrathorn's attacked matched hers.

Only six targets left.

Now four.

As they approached the two lead Cyonics, Asha saw Winter and Fred in the distance. With a tap on Tyrathorn's shoulder, she gestured forward.

He caught sight of their friends, and with a shared grin the siblings communicated everything they needed to. *Now we have a little fun.*

Asha came up behind her target, as she had done before. But instead of a stealth takedown, she raised her *qama* high.

With a fierce cry she cleaved through the Cyonic's head and down into its chest. As she pierced the power core, Asha sent a rush of Time through her blade. The machine blew apart in a dazzling burst of light.

Winter and Fred whirled around, as did the last Cyonic.

Tyrathorn drove his sword under its chin and twisted. With a roar, he ripped the head free and smashed it against the wall. The body clattered to the floor.

"Holy crap," Fred said.

Winter smiled at her husband. "Thanks for the assist."

"I would smash a million machines for you, my love," Tyrathorn said.

Asha shook her head, amused. Sometimes love was weird. "Final objective's a few floors up."

Another explosion rattled the Pyre, this time from somewhere above.

Their comms crackled.

"Would you all mind standing back, please?" John said.

They exchanged confused looks.

"Um, sure?" Fred said. "What's up?"

"How far should we move?" Winter asked.

"You'll see in a second. Thirty feet should be fine."

Still puzzled, they complied. As soon as they had cleared, a *boom* came from above.

"Hey, y'all," Fred said. "John never said if this was a good thing or a bad thing."

Another explosion, this one closer. Asha drew her second *qama* and stood ready.

The ceiling exploded, raining fire and shrapnel where they had just been standing. Asha coiled, ready to strike. If anything came out of that smoke, it was going down hard.

But when the air cleared, the only thing there was rubble.

"Okay, you can approach," John said.

Asha took the lead. Stepping gingerly toward the hole, she craned her neck to look through the ceiling without exposing her body.

She found herself peering up through six floors. At the top, four smiling faces peered down at them.

"What's up, guys?" Charlie said. "We found the thing."

Vash beckoned. "Care to join us?"

"Exactly how many bombs did you bring?" Winter said.

"Uh, all of them, I think," Aziz replied.

"Don't worry. We saved enough for this," Neema said.

They stuck their last explosives to the massive steel doors. The word *RECTIFY* was emblazoned across them. For now, at least.

"Schematics say the power source lies on the other side," Vash said. "We breach on your command."

Winter and Tyrathorn exchanged a glance, then nodded.

"Go," Tyrathorn ordered.

"All right, here comes the boom." Charlie pressed the button.

Once more the building rocked. The doors blasted off their hinges. The walls around them shredded, leaving a jagged hole.

Vash tapped her helmet. "I detect no movement inside."

"Agreed," Winter said. "Let's move."

They passed through the shattered doorway. Beyond it was a chamber that the stolen schematics had identified as the heart of the Pyre.

Inside, they found absolutely nothing.

Asha turned a full circle, agape. The room was dome-shaped, fifty feet wide and just as tall. Dimly lit, though she didn't see actual lights. Except for the hole they had blown in the side, it was an unbroken expanse of sparkling, white quartz.

"Okay, y'all," Fred said. "I'm waiting for the punch line."

"You and me both," Winter said.

"Be alert," Tyrathorn called. "The enemy—"

The ambient light pulsed brighter. A mechanical hum rumbled through the walls. Moving in unison, everyone turned their backs to each other and formed a circle facing outward.

Ten doorways opened in the solid-white surface, each allowing a machine to stomp through. Though identical to each other, they were wildly different than anything the squad had faced.

But Asha knew them. She had studied their schematic.

"Praetorian Berserkers," she breathed.

Eight feet tall, gunmetal armor bristling with spikes, they stalked forward as if they enjoyed trapping their prey. Step by step, the noose tightened around Asha and her allies.

Segments of the Praetorian armor split open, allowing weaponry to unfold: Blades, cannons, flamethrowers, and a few others that hadn't been in the schematics.

"Do not give them an inch," Tyrathorn said.

Halfway to them, the Berserkers stopped. Except for one,

which took another step forward before speaking, a booming mechanical voice that bounced off the walls.

"The Regent congratulates you on making it this far. But you will go no farther."

Tyrathorn confronted the Praetorian, coming within arm's reach. He shook his head. "Falsified schematics. A trail of counterfeit bread crumbs, leading us astray while the real heart of the Pyre lies elsewhere."

"Correct," the machine replied.

"No matter what happens here, our people will keep fighting."

"Incorrect," the machine boomed. "The Regent knows you are the tip of the spear. As you fall, the rest will follow."

"You underestimate them," Tyrathorn said.

Asha tightened her grip on the *qamas*, preparing herself.

"You see, no one is immune to hubris, not even your master," Tyrathorn continued. "How else could he believe that we wouldn't discover his deception?"

To Asha's left, a Praetorian shuddered violently. Sparks flew from its eye sockets, smoke spewed from the seams around its joints. With a mechanical groan, it toppled onto its face.

The air above it shimmered. Callie appeared, standing on the machine's back. Deploying her plasma blade, she sliced its head free and kicked it away.

"The true tip of our spear remains free to challenge the Regent," Tyrathorn said. "Even if we fall, you will not have *them*."

At those words, the machine reexamined its squad. Then it stomped closer, looming threateningly over Tyrathorn.

"Tell us," it demanded. "Where are the Gilbert twins?"

CHAPTER 28

Valentine leaned against the wall and listened to her friends over the comm.

"Finally, something went right," she said.

"Wish I could see them take those Berserkers down," Malcolm said.

Silently Valentine thanked John and the Everwatch technicians. After realizing the schematics were leading them toward a trap, they had devised a way to turn the Regent's deception against him. Which was why they had poured so much effort into attacking the wrong target. Why they'd done it as loudly and visibly as possible.

While their friends drew the spotlight, Valentine and Malcolm had slipped through the skyscraper like shadows. They waited now outside the Pyre's true heart. John had cut through the lies and deduced its real location. Behind a wall that appeared like any other, a small chamber hid between the tenth and eleventh floors.

Unlike the trap room high above, this one had no doors. No way in or out. Unless you knew how to deal with that sort of thing.

They waited for John's word, ready to move. Valentine

noticed she was fidgeting and worked harder to gather her confidence.

"I'm nervous, too," Malcolm said. "Whatever's in that room, it's . . ."

Valentine nodded. "I've never felt so much power."

Even now she could feel that temporal signature radiating through the wall, like the brightest light Valentine had ever seen and the loudest sound she had ever heard. She could have stood a thousand miles away and pointed exactly in its direction.

Despite the tension, she flashed an ironic grin. "Remember when the biggest thing we worried about was our grade point average?"

Malcolm chuckled. "After this, senior year's going to be a snooze. And we still need to pick a college, *and* a major.

"Maybe someplace teaches Surviving Supervillains 101."

"At this point, I'm pretty sure we could teach that class."

They shared a laugh, and Valentine found her thoughts drifting toward the future.

"I keep trying to imagine living two lives for the rest of my life," she said. "Like we've been doing these last couple years. One life with family and school and work, the other with all of this."

"The balance has never been easy," Malcolm said. "But all the things we can do, all the people we've helped—they make this worth it. Right?"

Valentine hesitated. Malcolm turned to examine her in surprise.

"Don't get me wrong, Mal, I love that we've helped people. I wouldn't change that for anything. But would I choose this over a real life? A real family?" She shrugged. "I think about the future a lot, and the things I see clearly are you and Dad and

Oma Grace. I see marrying John, being mad scientists together, maybe having kids. The Chronauri stuff, I see it, too, but it's all so . . . foggy."

Malcolm's eyebrows climbed. "Wow. Guess I assumed . . . Well, I don't know why I'm surprised. We're different in other ways, too."

"How do you see the future?"

"Well," he said, pursing his lips in thought, "I see Asha, you, and our family. I see learning what being Sixth-*sev* really means, using it for good. Maybe figuring out how to fix the Timeline. But college, day jobs, houses and kids, the mundane life stuff? For me, all *that* is foggy."

Valentine glanced at the wall they leaned on. "Right now, I'll consider having any future a victory."

"I guess we'll just have to win. Personally, I'd like to be around for our futures."

"Extra motivation. I'll take it."

Valentine grasped her brother's hand and squeezed. Whatever they were about to face, as always, it brought her comfort to know he would be there beside her.

"*Valentine, Malcolm,*" John's voice crackled through the comm. "*Get ready.*"

The twins stood. Valentine resisted the urge to start stretching, an old habit from years of dance training. She keyed her comm.

"John. How's it going out there?"

"*Thorn and his team are doing well. The battle on the street is fierce, but we're holding our own.*" He seemed to hesitate. "*The Regent is out here, too. Looks just like Callie described him.*"

Valentine stiffened. "What's he doing?"

"Just standing back and commanding. When he appeared, we thought he'd attack us himself, but so far nothing."

Valentine shared a puzzled look with Malcolm.

"What we're feeling in there," her brother tapped the wall, "I just assumed it was from him. But if he's out there—"

"—something else must be in here."

Valentine had thought they were solving the Regent's puzzles. It appeared the mystery went deeper.

"It's time," John said. *"Whatever you find in there, just stay safe. Valentine, I love you."*

A flash of warmth enveloped Valentine. "I love you, John. See you soon."

She forced herself to close the channel. The real fight was about to begin, and she needed every shred of focus.

"Well. Mustn't keep our adoring public waiting." Malcolm turned to Valentine and saluted. "Sergeant."

She saluted back. "Sergeant."

They faced the wall together, each drawing a thumb-sized device from their jacket. They were simple, just a metal tube with a blue button on one end. The twins shared a glance and pressed the buttons.

Their phase shifters went to work. Valentine felt no different, but the device hummed in her hand. She reached out to touch the wall.

Her hand passed through it.

The twins exchanged hopeful smiles and plunged through the wall.

The real chamber was shaped identically to the trap room, but that's where the similarities ended. The room above was smooth and empty. This one had been built for a real purpose.

While the floor was of dull industrial steel, the walls and domed ceiling were more like aged copper. Their surface had been shaped into a honeycomb pattern of repeating nonagons. In the center of each nonagon, an amber jewel the size of Valentine's fist sparkled subtly in the low light.

In the center of the chamber, an eight-foot sphere hovered just above the floor. *No, not exactly a sphere*, Valentine thought. This was a nonagon, too, except three-dimensional. As it spun in place, beams of light pulsed from its surface and were instantly absorbed by the surrounding jewels.

"Whoa," Valentine said. "Those energy pulses—"

"—are channeling more than enough Time to power this thing."

"That temporal signature, it *is* the same one from Eldurfall."

"Without doubt."

"So, is that some kind of battery?"

Malcolm grimaced. "I don't know about you, but I've had just about enough of mysteries."

Valentine felt a *shift* as he absorbed Time. An Entropy Blade shimmered around his outstretched fingers. The twins had yet to find something it couldn't cut through.

Valentine nodded. "Let's get this done."

Together they approached the nonagon. Valentine could see their distorted reflections in the aged copper, or whatever it was. She saw Malcolm take a deep breath.

Then he struck. The nonagon shuddered, while the Entropy Blade penetrated less than inch deep. His arm began to shake.

"It's resisting," he said through gritted teeth.

"Are you okay?"

"Don't worry. I've got this."

Valentine felt him stream more Time into the weapon. With a grunt he pushed harder, and slowly the Entropy Blade sank in. The twins breathed matching sighs of relief. So far, so good.

Blinding light burst from the cut. Valentine cried out and threw an arm over her eyes. There was a strange *sizzle-whoosh* sound.

A wall of pure force tossed her back. She spun around, crashed hard into the wall, and fell to the floor. A half second later, Malcolm dropped beside her.

Valentine opened herself and Time rushed in, bathing her cells in its radiance. The room stopped spinning, her body stopped aching, and once again she could think clearly.

"You okay?" she said as they both stood.

Malcolm cracked his neck, glaring at the nonagon. "Never better."

"Must be a security measure. If we both try cutting it, maybe . . ."

With an echoing *crack*, a glowing seam appeared in the surface of the nonagon. Like an eggshell, the object split open, emitting a burst of light.

When the light faded, a man stood facing them. Valentine's jaw dropped. *No. That's not possible.*

Tall and lean, with dark hair and a pale face with high cheekbones, he wore a black suit, the style of which could have come from any number of centuries. Or none of them. The only surprise was his youth—Valentine thought he looked no older than thirty. Aside from that, there was no mistaking this man's identity.

"John," Valentine whispered through her comm. "Please confirm the Regent is—"

"—is out on the battlefield, commanding his army," the man interrupted, his deep voice rumbling through the chamber. "But how could that be? He's standing right in front of you."

That power radiating from him was *the* power, the overwhelming temporal signature the twins had felt behind everything. Valentine stood stunned, caught between answers and new questions.

"*Valentine*," John said.

The instant she heard his voice, she knew something was wrong. The Regent wore a dark smile while John spoke, as if he knew what John was saying.

"I'm here, John."

"*He's still out here. But thirty seconds ago, he appeared in the mini-towers, too. Both of them at once. Our squads in those towers . . . they're all dead.*" He paused, out of breath. "*Something is very wrong here.*"

"John," Malcolm said, glaring daggers at their enemy. "Tell everyone to evacuate the Pyre."

"*But, Malcolm . . .*"

"Full retreat, John," Valentine echoed. "Now, please."

There was a pause over the line. Valentine could picture John warring within himself, weighing their instincts against his judgment.

"*Okay,*" he said finally. "*I'll get them out.*"

"Thank you. I love you."

Before he could respond, Valentine pulled the comm from her ear and crushed it in her palm. Malcolm mirrored her, and device fragments fell at their feet.

She turned her full attention to the Regent now. Since

revealing himself, he had simply stood and waited. As if there were no rush. As if he had all the Time in the world.

"Malcolm, Valentine. At last we meet." He gave a slight bow and stepped toward them. "Now that we have a moment alone, let us discuss your future."

CHAPTER 29

"*Are you trippin', dude?*" Fred said. "*Full retreat?*"

"I don't have time to argue, Fred," John returned. "That's the order from Valentine and Malcolm. Just get out, okay? I need help with about a thousand things here anyway."

Fred gave an angry huff. "*This is so wrong.*"

"That's an understatement. But we all knew the plan could change."

John closed the channel before Fred could give him more grief. Stealing five seconds, he shut his eyes and ordered his thoughts. Then he dove in once more, working desperately to salvage the defense of his home.

He had hoped to destroy the mini-towers, disrupting the plan to burn their century into a scar on the Timeline. But the Regent controlled them now. If John sent more soldiers, they would die just as quickly as the others.

A good general knew when to abandon a strategy. Pointing at both towers, John waved his hands. The data surrounding them on the glass swiped away. He tapped out new commands.

"Before the battle began," he said to the technicians on either side of him, "I told you to plan some fun surprises we could spring on the enemy. Now we're going to use them."

"Which ones, sir?"

John cracked his knuckles. "All of them. My friends need time to win this war, and we're going to buy it for them."

"You want to discuss our future," Valentine repeated. "You mean, the future you're actively trying to destroy?"

"If you wanted to talk, maybe you should've called instead of invading," Malcolm said.

"A means to an end. When my objective is accomplished, my forces and I will take our leave." The Regent stepped closer, his hawkish stare weighing and measuring them. "Make no mistake; I promised my people protection from the Gilbert twins and their corrupt century, and I am willing to bring fire and death. But that is not the only way to end this."

"You promised to protect your people from a lie," she returned.

"With ships that you built," Malcolm said. "With imposters wearing our faces. What would your people think if they knew who really attacked them?"

"You're right; there *is* another way to end this," Valentine said.

She grabbed a rush of Time and threw the first attack that popped into her mind. A temporal stasis capsule appeared around the Regent's left arm.

Valentine's heart sank. A stasis capsule should work on him, as it had on the twins when they had first dropped into Everwatch. A type of suspended animation that rapid-cycled its prisoner between thousands of individual moments, it was effective against even powerful enemies.

But it had to trap the whole person, and the Regent had somehow resisted Valentine's full power.

A microsecond later, there was a *shift* from Malcolm. Another capsule appeared around the Regent's left leg and half his torso. Staring down at himself, their enemy grunted in apparent surprise.

Elation surged through Valentine. Malcolm had taken her mistake and salvaged it into a strategy. She went for it full force.

Channeling more Time, she closed a stasis capsule around the Regent's right shoulder. Then his right knee. Malcolm leapfrogged over her, placing capsule after capsule in the spaces between Valentine's.

The Regent's alarm and confusion grew. He would be feeling the effects by now. Less than a second after Valentine began, he was trapped within dozens of stasis capsules, only his head remaining free. Glaring at the twins, he clenched his jaw as if preparing to fight back.

Valentine held up a finger. "I wouldn't do that."

"What have you done to me?"

Valentine stole an instant to cast her Chronauri senses out wide, searching for the Regent's temporal signature. She found none in the mini-towers or on the battlefield. Only a single presence, right here in this room.

Whoa, we actually did it! Valentine buried her astonishment and put on a mask of confidence. "Right now, all the parts of your body are cycling through different moments."

"Who knows what moving might do to you?" Malcolm said, wearing a satisfied smile. "Pieces of you might just fly off into different parts of the Timeline."

Valentine closed the distance between them, Malcolm at her side. The Regent's glare grew more venomous with every step. But behind the venom, Valentine thought she caught a hint of fear.

"You almost did it," she said, "almost had everyone fooled. Even I started to wonder if we might attack Eldurfall someday. It wouldn't be the first time good people went bad."

"But then we went there," Malcolm said.

The Regent's eyes widened.

"We saw the first attack you blamed on us." Malcolm pointed in his face. "An attack that came from you."

"Until now, though, we hadn't figured out one thing," Valentine said. "Our imposters. Where they came from. Why they had identical temporal signatures. Today we realized that signature was yours."

"Meaning they used your power to kill your people," Malcolm added.

"But still, there were two of them. Even if you wore some kind of hologram, how could you be in two places at once?" Valentine said. "Minutes ago, we found the answer. You're in here, but you're also outside fighting."

She exchanged a glance with Malcolm. He nodded. They had reached the same conclusion, it seemed.

"The fake twins," she continued, "were *both* you, using whatever crazy trick you're using now."

The Regent lifted his chin arrogantly. "It might be crazy to you. For the Genesis Flame, it is as easy as breathing."

Valentine paused. *The what?* That name was new.

It didn't matter right now. There was still one mystery left to solve.

"I don't get it," Malcolm said. "From what we saw in

Eldurfall, you were a pretty good leader. Your government actually worked. People were happy. They trusted you. An entire world kingdom in palm of your hand. Was that not enough?"

The Regent said nothing. Studying his face, though, Valentine caught the subtle change in his expression. The twist of bitterness. The hunger of greed.

"Oh, my God," she said, truly astounded. "It *wasn't* enough, was it? Then what do you really want?"

He stared hard at her. "Everything."

That shook her. The fire behind his eyes. The insatiable darkness underneath. She worked to maintain her confident mask.

"We'll see how your people feel about that when we take you back," she said. "When we show them what you've done. Then you won't control any century, ours or yours."

That seemed to drain his arrogance. His chin dropped low. Malcolm took his cue and swept in.

"Unless you go back now," he said. "You're losing, Regent. We have you here, and our people are holding off your machines. This war doesn't have to cost more lives in any century. Recall your army. Return to Eldurfall and fix the damage you caused, and leave the Timeline alone. That's the deal. That's your *only* deal."

"Please," Valentine added, hoping he could see her sincerity. "Stop this now. Help us save everyone."

The Regent studied the floor. "So, you're not going to kill me?"

"We don't kill," Valentine said. "There's always another way."

His expression fell. Valentine suspected his whole posture

would have sagged if he could move freely. When he spoke next, his voice was subdued.

"Fire and extinction. That is what I brought to your doorstep. I could see no other way. To achieve my true purpose, I must walk a path paved with bones. That path culminated in your deaths. The annihilation of two Sixth-*sev* Chronauri would surely open the way for my final victory."

How would our deaths do anything to help him? Valentine held onto the question, not wanting to interrupt.

"But then I beheld you with my own eyes, and I . . . I was compelled to study you. If I could measure your quality, find in you what was necessary, I could leave this bloody path behind. I could invite you to join me. To ascend with me. To serve as my right and left hand when I fulfill my purpose. And to my great surprise, you offered me mercy."

The Regent paused, heaving a sigh.

"Mercy." He looked at the twins now. "The language of pretenders. The currency of the frail."

His face twisted. As he spoke, his voice regained its strength and his posture began to change.

"You offer it to me, not because you are righteous, but because you lack the stomach for anything greater. Because while you claim to protect the innocent, you stop short of the action it requires."

The Regent stood straighter. Cold fear lanced through Valentine: he shouldn't have been able to move.

With a dizzying *shift*, the Regent's corona blazed. The stasis capsules swelled and then burst, shredding like paper. A shock wave sent the twins to the floor. When Valentine looked up, she saw their enemy looming above them.

"Such paltry chains?" he said. "You wield the power of a king with all the instincts of a slave."

The Regent extended his right arm and the air above his palm began to warp. Valentine felt an odd pulling in the Timeline, then a collapse. There was a flash of light. She clutched her temples as the universe screamed in protest.

An ornate Templar sword appeared in his hand, glittering like a diamond. Its insides pulsed with radiant energy, as if formed from lightning.

Panic seized Valentine. She could *feel* that weapon. It wasn't made of diamond, or even lightning, but layer on upon layer of temporal energy. As the blade moved, Time and space warped around it.

Even more frightening was the unbridled fervor in the Regent's eyes.

"I have measured your quality and found it lacking. I judge your resistance an act of treason, and in accord with my right, sentence you to death. Your Time ends now."

CHAPTER 30

The luminous sword filled Valentine's vision. She drank in as much Time as she could and prepared to fight back. Holding the blade high, the Regent prepared to strike.

Before he could, the wall to Valentine's right exploded. Shrapnel rocketed across the room on bursts of flame, filling the chamber with noise, dust, and debris.

As the Regent flinched away from the blast, Valentine formed an Entropy Blade and flung it with everything she had. Malcolm's Entropy Blade hit first, slicing clean through the Regent's sword arm. He yelped in pain just as Valentine's attack hit the sword. It flew from his grip.

She expected to see the Regent's arm fall away, or at least go limp. But as the cloth of his suit jacket fell from his arm, she saw there wasn't even a cut on his skin. *He heals better than we do!*

The Regent was Sixth-*sev*. He had to be. *But how is that possible? The only one left besides us is the Chrona.* Shaking her questions away, Valentine leapt up to face him and whatever machines had just arrived to back him up.

Fred and Winter charged through the smoke. Asha

and Tyrathorn came next, followed by the High Protectors. Brandishing weapons, their friends confronted the Regent.

"Yo, it's about time you got outta our century," Fred said.

"Ah, the pawns have arrived." The Regent spread his arms wide. "Come bow to your king."

They rushed in and closed around the Regent, giving the twins a chance to regroup. Like a tornado, they assaulted him from all sides with gale-force ice, fire, and steel.

The Regent flowed between them like a black wind, never slowing. His suit began to tatter from the assault, yet the flesh underneath remained whole.

With a flash of light, two High Protectors, Winter, and Tyrathorn went flying. Others filled the gap and came at him harder.

It was all happening so fast. Valentine stood at a loss, shocked at her friends' appearance and the sudden ferocity of the battle. Had the battle lasted seconds or hours? She felt a hand on her arm and shook herself back to the present.

"I know," Malcolm said. "We can be overwhelmed later. Right now, I was thinking. Remember when we were training, and we took Thorn down for the first time?"

Valentine remembered. "You think it might work?"

Malcolm nodded at the glimmering blade stuck halfway into the floor. "It's worth a shot."

They didn't plan or discuss. They didn't need to. Instead they turned and began their work with twin *shifts*. While Malcolm began to manipulate the atmosphere, Valentine sheathed herself in fast Time and moved.

The room blurred around her. Then her senses adjusted and all became clear, with everyone moving in slow motion in relation to her. She circled to the far side of the battle, directly across from Malcolm, with her friends and the Regent between them.

She could feel Malcolm's power swelling, see the crackle in the air around him. He hovered on the edge, waiting for her.

Just one . . . deep . . . breath. She centered herself, focusing on this task. On this moment.

Let's see how you like these *paltry chains.*

Valentine cast a bubble of super-slowed Time around the Regent. She gave it a twist, and the bubble became a block of hardened ice. The ice began to fracture instantly; the Regent wasted no time getting out of such a simple trap.

"Drop!" Malcolm yelled.

Their friends hit the floor. The block shattered.

Malcolm threw a massive lightning bolt. Ice shards flashed into steam as the bolt leapt through them, following a path straight to its target.

The lightning struck the Regent square in the chest and sent him sailing back into Valentine's waiting arms. She wrapped one arm around his chest and jabbed an Entropy Blade through his heart.

The Regent gasped. It wouldn't kill him—she had seen that much—but it would hurt.

Valentine reached back with her free hand and grabbed his mysterious sword. Immense power rang through her as she pulled it free and swung it around. With his own weapon at his neck, he might . . .

Valentine gaped. The sword was no longer in her hand. The Regent glanced over his shoulder at her, wearing a dangerous smile.

In a flash of light, the sword appeared in his hand. Valentine released him and leapt back, drinking in Time. She pointed toward him, on the cusp of releasing her power.

Quicker than she could follow, the Regent slashed. Pain blazed up her arm, flesh and muscle parting from the impossibly sharp blade. It pulsed brighter as it touched her.

Valentine cried out, then choked off with a gasp. The Time she had absorbed was gone, stolen by the blade like a leech. Breathless, she tried to back away but fell to her knees. Blood streamed from the deep cut on her arm.

For a Chronauri Third-*sev* or higher, Time could be replenished. For anyone else, once their Time was gone, that was it. No Time, no life. That blade would kill a normal person in seconds.

She managed to suck in a breath. "Don't let it touch you!"

The Regent loomed over her kneeling form. She struggled to move, to strike, but only managed to sway. He drew back and aimed for her neck.

Steel spikes peppered his flank and head, sinking in with a crunch. The Regent grunted in pain, then stumbled as Fred followed up with a Time grenade.

The Regent went down on one knee, red light blazing angrily around him.

With visible effort, he stood back up. He waved and the light storm dissipated, the spikes disintegrated. Like Malcolm's Entropy Blade, he had aged the steel until it simply became dust.

The Regent faced Fred with stone-cold murder in his eyes. Even if it was for just an instant, the attack had hurt him.

It also served as a handy distraction. Dashing up behind the Regent, Malcolm super-concentrated Time over his fist until the space around it warped with gravitational force.

His punch shook the walls. The Regent spun from its force, and Malcolm followed with a second punch to the jaw. The

Regent swayed. Valentine practically saw stars flying around his head.

Malcolm grabbed for the sword, but as he reached out, it disappeared. Valentine blinked, and then there were two Regents. The second stood behind Malcolm with sword raised.

"Move!" Valentine shouted.

Malcolm dove away, but not before taking a cut to the shoulder. Like her, he gasped in shock and fell over. The blade pulsed again.

Valentine could feel it siphon her brother's power. She reached for Time and managed to draw in a trickle, but nausea swept through her along with it. She clutched her stomach. It seemed her body would need a minute to recover.

Both Regents disappeared; then only one reappeared. Standing over Malcolm, he made a show of swiping blood away from his lip.

"You will never—"

Behind the Regent, the air rippled and Callie appeared. She leapt onto his back, wrapped her legs around his waist, ignited her plasma blade, and drove it in between his shoulders. The blazing weapon burst through his chest. Eyes wide, the Regent gasped in genuine shock.

The team came at him with everything, like a whirlwind knocking him back and forth. Finally, Asha slithered up behind and sliced through his hamstrings. With a cry, the Regent dropped to his knees.

Grabbing the Regent's hair, Callie yanked his head back so she could look into his eyes. "My daughter sends her greetings."

With a snarl, she twisted the blade. The Regent's face contorted in agony.

The twins looked on in amazement. *They're doing it!*

Valentine struggled to stand, to draw in more Time. It came a little easier now, but still too slowly.

Eyeing Callie with equal venom, the Regent drew in a shaky breath.

"When I killed your daughter," he rasped, "I didn't even notice."

The hatred on Callie's face deepened. But beneath that, Valentine saw her struggling to hold back tears.

"Not until I reviewed the footage to ensure my deception would hold. Then I saw, and I knew. Your grief, your rage—they could be bent to my will."

Sitting straighter, the Regent wrapped both hands around the plasma blade. His skin sizzled and smoked.

"You were destined to be a traitor. Your punishment just came before the crime. And I will make it last forever."

Callie's blade unraveled.

The energy reversed into her armor, shredding plates over her arm and knocking her back. She hit the floor and rolled to her feet, clutching the injured arm. Her baleful glare could have set someone on fire.

In the seconds it took for the Regent to stand, his wounds healed. The remains of his shirt and jacket fell away, revealing a lean frame corded with muscles. He eyed them all with disdain.

"I would say I'm disappointed," he said, "but it would imply that I expected better."

Valentine's pain was dissipating. Beside her, Malcolm sat up and gave her a nod. He was still hurting but getting ready to fight again.

As the shock of that impossible weapon faded, the glow of Time brushed her senses again. The twins helped each other to their feet, wounds slowly closing.

RYANDALTON

"We hurt you once," Asha spat. Her *qamas* flared brighter. "We can do it ag—"

The Regent rolled his eyes. With a wave of his hand, Asha's words cut off and she stood like a statue.

"I believe the pawns have had their say," he said to the twins. "Wouldn't you agree?"

Malcolm practically growled. Valentine expected their friends to react in anger. They didn't react all. Like Asha, they appeared to be frozen in Time.

"What did you do to them?" Valentine demanded.

The Regent shook his head in derision. "If you need to ask, you have not earned the answer."

Valentine would never admit it to the Regent, but he might have been right. She hadn't even felt a *shift*, hadn't felt his power stirring at all. He had simply gestured, and the flow of Time within their friends had stopped. *He's doing things we've never even thought of.*

"Asha was right," Malcolm said. "You're not the first to come here and pick a fight, thinking you've already won."

"But I will be the last."

"As long as one of us breathes, we'll never stop fighting you," Valentine said. "Not for a second."

Annoyance flashed across his face. "Well, then, let's walk through the next sequence of events logically, shall we? First, I will neutralize your power, returning you to the children you truly are."

The Regent pressed his palms together, then drew them slowly apart. The twins gasped.

Valentine suddenly felt empty. She reached out for Time's warm light . . . and found nothing. If the Timeline flowed like a river, the Regent had just parted the waters, forcing it to flow around the twins but beyond their reach.

They were utterly defenseless. She fought back a wave of panic.

"Next, I will expand the charge of treason to your allies and resume carrying out the sentence."

A second Regent appeared next to Charlie, one of the High Protectors. Casually, that Regent placed his hand on the soldier's arm. Before her eyes, Charlie aged, then withered, then crumbled into dust.

"No!" Malcolm cried.

"With each sentence I carry out," the Regent continued.

A third Regent appeared next to Neema. She became dust next. Valentine's eyes burned with tears.

"I cut more of the head off your meager resistance."

A fourth Regent appeared. Aziz fell.

A fifth Regent appeared behind Vash.

Valentine reached toward their friend. "Please, don't!"

The Regent drove his glowing sword through her back. The blade sliced through armor and flesh alike, pulsing as it stole her Time. Valentine gave a desperate sob.

The weapon drained Vash. But even when her Time was empty, the Regent didn't stop. Instead the sword dove deeper, clawing its way to the very center of her being until it found the spark, the source of her Chronauri power. The weapon stole that, too, ripping it away from Vash as she blew into dust.

Valentine choked back a scream. As hot tears streamed down her face, the Regent closed his eyes. He gave a satisfied sigh as Vash's power merged with his. How was that possible?

"I will deliver justice from highest commander to lowliest soldier. Until, inevitably, your resistance becomes dust as well."

The copies of the Regent disappeared, leaving only the man in front of them. He stepped closer, cold menace in his eyes.

"You mistook me for the usual Time-traveling vagabonds who vie for scraps of power. I was and am a king. This is my birthright, and I will walk over your bones to claim it."

He turned, fixing attention on his next target. Valentine followed his eye and black dread filled her.

"Today," the Regent said, "even royalty shall fall."

Valentine blinked and suddenly he had moved. He stood before Asha now, blade in hand.

The air split with Malcolm's cry. Charging in, he shoved Asha away just as the Regent's blow hit home.

The blade sank in between his ribs. Malcolm lurched; then his eyes seemed to catch fire. Glaring in defiance, he grabbed the blade with one hand and their enemy's throat with the other.

Valentine felt the weapon clawing at her brother's insides, seeking to steal his power. In seconds, there would be nothing left of him.

Then she was moving. As if flying through a dream, she retrieved two objects from Asha's gear belt and came up behind the Regent.

Pumping her fists three times, Valentine smashed the time grenades against either side of his head. They burst, unleashing temporal storms.

As the Regent lurched in surprise, she dove past and grabbed his blade with both hands. It sliced deep into her palms as she pulled. It ravaged her insides, trying to take her power, too. She didn't care. With a shout, she pulled it free of her brother.

The twins toppled to the floor arm in arm, bleeding and utterly spent.

"Thanks," Malcolm whispered hoarsely.

Footsteps approached. Straining, Valentine rolled over and faced their enemy. Once again, they had hurt him just enough to stoke his rage. He breathed hard, clutching his weapon.

Valentine searched for a last burst of power. All she found were tears.

"Why?" she pleaded. "Why are you doing this? What do you really want?"

The Regent had been preparing a death blow. Now he seemed taken aback.

"After so many centuries, so many failed attempts, I came to realize what it would require. Killing Sixth-*sev* Chronauri. Damaging the Timeline enough to break it. Threatening the very fabric of the universe." He thumped a fist against his chest. "I accepted that burden because it was necessary. Because it was the only way."

Valentine felt her last strength failing, her consciousness slipping away. She clung to it as hard as she could. "The only way to what?"

"The only way to make her face me."

She? Who?

Valentine's Chronauri senses roared to life. Something huge was out there, and it was hurtling toward them. All of Time vibrated around her, as if someone had grabbed the Timeline and plucked it like a guitar string.

Suddenly she knew.

So did the Regent. Euphoric relief crossed his face. He breathed in deeply, as if savoring the sensation.

"Finally."

The vibration stopped. The approaching presence disappeared. They hovered in the moment as nothing happened. The Regent cast around the room, growing outraged.

"Coward!" he spat. "Come to me."

Time lurched in a way Valentine had never felt. Behind the Regent, the Timeline folded, then folded again, then unfolded.

A woman stepped through. Old and small of frame, with gray hair and long, flowing robes, she appeared the antithesis of their enemy.

The Regent whipped around to face her. "At last you—"

The woman stretched an open palm toward him. The Regent flew back and smashed against the wall, hovering above the floor. A cacophony of sensations hit Valentine, so many, so fast, so strong that she couldn't begin to follow them.

The aged copper warped and buckled under the impact. As the woman stepped closer, the Regent sank farther into the metal.

His effects unraveled. Time crashed back into Valentine, and she felt her friends' signatures pulsing. She gasped in agony and relief. Malcolm stirred but didn't fully wake.

While she fought to stay conscious, her dying body began to knit itself slowly back together. Above the pain and bone-deep exhaustion, though, Valentine burned with a hope she hadn't dared to feel.

The Chrona had arrived.

The diminutive woman fixed the Regent with a glare, hard as stone.

"Arsinoë," the Regent said. "Eternity has not been kind to you."

"And you, Helios, still have much to learn," the Chrona replied. "All of this to draw me out, and still you are unprepared."

The Chrona and the Regent already know each other? Valentine's head swam with questions.

"Feel my wrath," the Chrona said. "And remember who you trifle with."

Something in Time twisted. Valentine heard the Regent scream—a real scream of actual pain. She saw him drop to the floor, struggle to stand, then fall. He didn't move again.

Mercifully, unconsciousness wrapped around Valentine. As she sank into warm oblivion, the last thing she felt was her body being lifted from the floor.

"Rest now," the Chrona said. "You have much yet to do."

CHAPTER 31

Asha felt the Regent's hold on her evaporate.

He was down. She didn't dare believe he was dead, though. This war wouldn't end so easily.

She sought out Malcolm. When she found him sprawled next to Valentine, her insides went cold. *Oh, no.* Sprinting to his side, she fell to her knees.

He was bleeding—*really* bleeding. Asha hadn't realized until now that she'd never seen him bleed like this. Time had always healed him.

"Mal," she said, an urgent whisper. "Mal, wake up. Please!"

She clamped a hand over the wound in his side. He was sweating, his forehead cold and clammy, but mercifully he groaned and stirred.

He looked up at her through heavy-lidded eyes. "Double cheeseburger, please."

Well, at least he was awake.

He groaned again. "My sister?"

Asha eyed Valentine. "She's alive. Don't worry; we'll fix her."

Malcolm sighed and relaxed.

"Can you walk?" she asked. "We need—"

She cut off as a strong presence drew close.

"Girl," a woman's voice said softly.

"Whoever you are, can you help us?"

"Asha." The voice was stronger now. "Look at me."

Asha felt herself stand. At her full height, she towered over the old woman. But when she gazed into her eyes, what she saw was endless.

The woman let her look for a moment. "You know who I am?"

Agape, she nodded. She could never have explained how, but yes, she knew. *The Chrona knows my name.*

"Good. Then carry Malcolm. We must leave this place." The Chrona faced the others. "Tyrathorn, carry Valentine. Fred, tell John to activate your contingency."

Fred's brow furrowed. "Uh, just who in the—"

"Fred," Winter cut in. "I'm guessing this is the Chrona. You know? The ultimate authority over the Timeline?"

Fred beheld the woman, wide-eyed, stunned silent. *A small miracle,* Asha thought.

"Uh, sure, whatever you need." He turned away to speak into his comm.

"Winter," the Chrona said, "lead the way."

Asha bent toward Malcolm. She paused to drink in his face, to thank Eternity that her love had survived. Then she scooped him up and followed.

As Asha passed through the hole they had blown in the wall, she cast a last glance back into the mysterious chamber. They didn't want to leave anything important behind. That's when it dawned on her.

"Wait!" she called, halting. "The other High Protectors; where are they?"

Realization crossed the others' faces. Something wasn't right.

The Chrona's face showed regret. "I am sorry, child."

"No!" Tyrathorn gasped. "They cannot be. I have known Vash since I was a child. She always . . ."

Swallowing hard, Asha pushed back her tears and squared her shoulders. "We will mourn them later. First, we survive."

They pushed on, avoiding roving machines this time, taking the stairs down a dozen floors, crossing toward the front of the skyscraper that faced the Eon Palace. They traveled down a long, straight hallway, then turned down a much shorter one that terminated in double doors.

"Your emergency escape?" the Chrona said.

Winter nodded. "Just through those doors."

"Wait, escape?" Asha said.

Everything had happened so fast. Asha had been so grateful to find Malcolm alive, what they were doing hadn't fully registered. Now, though, her mind came back to her fully.

She moved up to face the Chrona. "Why are we running?"

The old woman met her gaze. But for a moment, what looked back at Asha was not the Chrona.

The infinity behind her eyes clouded over, her expression betraying the fact that she had no idea who Asha was. Slowly she looked up and down, side to side, like a lost child trying to remember where she was.

Then, as quickly as the moment had come, it disappeared. The old eyes blinked and the clouds faded. Her face showed recognition again.

"Asha. Repeat the question, please."

"The Regent is down. We should strike while he's weak and finish this."

"Girl has a point," Fred said.

"Agreed," Winter said.

The Chrona studied them, emotions flashing across her face, too quick for Asha to decipher. Eventually the woman looked down at the floor, seeming embarrassed and somehow older.

"If only we could," she said. "But I . . ."

"But you cannot," Tyrathorn finished. "Can you?"

The Chrona hesitated, then shook her head.

Asha glanced at her brother. He hadn't agreed with her as Winter and Fred had.

"I can feel it in you," he said. "What you did to the Regent, it took almost everything you had. The rest was a brave front."

Wide-eyed, Asha turned on the Chrona. All her life, she had been raised believing this woman was practically a god. Nearly all-powerful.

"What happened to you?" she asked.

The Chrona looked up at her. "Time happened."

What did that even mean?

The Chrona shook herself and straightened. "Right now, it doesn't matter. I have bought us a window to escape, and we must take it."

She resumed walking. All they could do was follow.

"The injury I inflicted on Helios—on the Regent—will keep him unconscious for hours. When he wakes, he will not be at full strength for several days. This will give your forces a chance to regroup, while I take Valentine and Malcolm with me."

"Why take them?" Asha said.

"And where?" Winter said.

They stopped outside the double doors.

"For the Timeline to have a chance of surviving this man's wrath, the Gilbert twins must learn what they truly are. I will teach them all that I can." The Chrona gestured at the doors. "Winter, if you please."

Winter cracked her knuckles and stepped forward. As she approached the doors, the skyscraper vibrated.

"The Verge is still working," Tyrathorn said, sounding relieved.

"Good thing," Winter said. Drawing back armored fists, she gave a shout and punched the doors right off their frame. "Otherwise we'd be stuck in here."

They filed into the large, open room, and then Asha understood. The far wall had buckled inward horribly, as if the fist of a giant had repeatedly punched the Pyre's outer surface. Just then, the building shook again and the wall caved in farther.

The sonic attacks from the Verge had covered their invasion, but its purpose had been twofold. Hammering repeatedly at the skyscraper, it had slowly softened the outer shell in one spot: the room they now stood in.

"*Stand clear of the wall*," John said over the comm.

Asha backed away and the wall blew apart like tissue paper. The Sled, Everwatch's flying transport, flew into the room and stopped with a gust of wind.

Thrusters roaring, it spun until its nose faced outward and hovered in place. The rear hatch bloomed open and a ramp extended. Then Asha caught sight of their rescuer.

"Captain!" she cried.

Captain Armel saluted her. "My friends, your chariot awaits."

So, this was the special duty John had kept the captain in reserve for. Asha understood now. A contingency this important couldn't have been entrusted to just anyone.

"Not a moment to waste!" he called over the roar of the thrusters. "Please climb in."

Asha's comm crackled.

"*Everyone be alert,*" John said. "*The Sled's sensors are picking up a strange presence. Almost like—*"

A Praetorian Infiltrator appeared next to Captain Armel.

Kicking him out of the way, the machine dove to the floor and crawled beneath the Sled. No one had reacted quickly enough to stop it. The vehicle whined in protest and rocked violently as bashing sounds of metal on metal erupted from beneath.

A thruster exploded. The Sled dropped to the floor, smashing the Praetorian beneath it, then leapt back into the air and lurched to the side. They barely dodged as the vehicle crashed into the left wall.

The Sled spun, port side dragging the floor and sending up sparks. The extended ramp clipped the wall and sheared off. As the Sled careened toward the right wall, Captain Armel leapt through the rear hatch and clung on.

He shook like a rag doll as its nose buried into the right wall. Fighting his way to the cockpit, he managed to take the controls. With a mechanical groan, the Sled settled to the floor.

Asha rushed toward the rear hatch, allies on her heels. They gathered around the smoking vehicle and peered inside.

"Captain?" she called.

"Alive and well, princess." Armel walked shakily toward the hatch and leaned against the open door. His scalp bore a nasty cut. "Blasted clever machines."

Asha keyed her comm. "John. Praetorian Infiltrator damaged the Sled, but no casualties."

"*Thank God. See you all soon.*"

Climbing aboard, Winter retrieved a first aid kit and went to work bandaging Armel.

"Do not be so sure, John," Captain Armel said.

"Is the damage that bad?" Tyrathorn asked.

"Two of five thrusters are destroyed. It's possible to fly with three, but difficult. I will need to rig some modifications."

"How long will it take?" Winter said.

Captain Armel winced. "Five minutes, maybe ten. And I'll need help."

Fred brightened. "That ain't so bad."

"*Guys*," John said.

Fred's face fell. "Let me guess. It's bad?"

"*You have Cyonics approaching. Not sure how many, but I recommend getting into the Sled and sealing it. Fix the problem from the inside.*"

"Impossible, general," Captain Armel said. "Modifications to the frame and the thrusters themselves will be necessary."

"Then we shall stand and fight!" Tyrathorn said.

"There is far more at stake here than killing a few machines, young man," the Chrona said. "You're all wounded, and the survival of the Gilbert twins is paramount."

"Too bad we ain't got someone super powerful on our side," Fred said.

The Chrona glared until his sarcasm melted.

"I need as many hands as possible," Captain Armel added. "Or we're never getting out of here."

Winter huffed. "Then what other options . . . ?"

Protect the Timeline. Protect the world. It's all that matters. The words echoed in Asha's mind. In this war, saving everyone meant protecting Malcolm and Valentine at all costs.

While the others scrambled for a plan, she gazed down at Malcolm, her sweet boy who loved history books and old movies. Who still blushed when they kissed. She held him now, unconscious and helpless, but still radiant.

The Timeline needed the Gilbert twins. That was why

she had volunteered to stay in Emmett's Bluff two years ago. She had wanted to stay, of course—by then she had already fallen hopelessly in love. But above all, a soldier did her duty. As soon as the twins had ascended to Sixth-*sev*, Asha's purpose had been clear.

She was their shield. If anyone wanted to hurt them, they would have to go through her.

"Someone needs to buy us time," she said, cutting through the chatter. "I'll do it."

The others fell quiet and looked to her. She laid Malcolm gently on a bench, then turned back to them.

"I haven't gotten to kill nearly enough machines today, so I claim the right of battle for myself."

"Ashandara," Tyrathorn said, "you do not have to—"

"This is war, Thorn," she interrupted. "Risk is part of the game."

Her brother studied her, then nodded. "Right. Carry on. Captain, tell us what you need."

While the others sprang into action, Asha knelt beside Malcolm for just a moment longer. Just one more gaze at him. She brushed his face with the back of her hand.

His eyes fluttered open and found her. Though dreamy and half-awake, they brightened as he smiled. "Hey."

"How are you feeling?"

"Oh, never better."

Asha grinned. "Liar."

"Wow."

"What?"

Shakily, he brought up his hand to brush her cheek. "You are so pretty."

Warmth flooded Asha. She gave herself a moment to savor it. To savor him.

"I need to go for a little while," she said.

"Why?"

"It's my turn to help save the world."

"Oh," Malcolm said, struggling to keep his eyes open. His words came slower. "I'll bet you could save it by yourself."

"I'm going to try."

"Asha—"

She stopped his words with a kiss, drinking in his warmth and his scent and his lips, the essence of the boy she loved. The memory would go with her into battle.

After an eternity, she pulled away. "I love you, Malcolm."

He gave another dreamy smile before drifting away. "I love you back, Asha."

Then he was asleep. Squeezing his hand one last time, Asha stood and faced the hatch.

Don't look back.

She stepped through, dropped to the floor, and left the Sled and her family behind.

Don't look back.

Aiming for the broken doorway, she keyed her comm. "John, point me at the Cyonics."

"*Just you?*"

"I can handle a few walking toasters. Just get me there."

"*Got it. Tracking now.*"

When she reached the long hallway they had escaped through, Asha picked up the pace. The warm butterflies of a love-struck girl evaporated as she walked, leaving a steel warrior in their place.

The Cyonics threatened the world, and they had come after Asha's family. It would be their last mistake.

CHAPTER 32

A sha turned down the next hallway. This one curved until the other end was out of sight.

"*Around the curve, you'll intersect with another hallway,*" John said in her ear. "*A squad is there, about to turn your way.*"

"Got it."

Reaching through her nexus, she seized her own Time and channeled it outward. The air around her sizzled and popped. Her armor glowed with cascading waves of red light, like an ember at the heart of a raging fire. She drew her *qamas*. They blazed angrily, carving ionized trails through the air as she moved.

Every cell in her body sang with power. At the apex of the curve, she broke into a sprint. The hallway flew by in a blur. As she neared the end, she saw the shadow of the first machine approach the corner.

Asha got there first.

Pouring on a burst of speed, she leapt across the Cyonics' path. Before their processors could load a defensive program, she kicked off the opposite wall, spun around, and chopped the head off the lead machine.

Midflight, she sized up her enemy. *Squad of ten . . . nine now. Two-column formation. Guns ready. Okay.* By the time her feet touched the floor she knew her strategy, and without breaking stride she attacked.

Crouch and spin.

Throw left-hand *qama* through Cyonic 2's chest.

Slice through Cyonic 3's knees with right-hand *qama*.

Stab through Cyonic 3's back as it falls, puncturing power core.

Asha pulled her blade free and somersaulted forward, using the momentum to fling a time grenade. Cyonics 4 and 5 turned to dust in a storm of angry, red light.

She retrieved her blade from Cyonic 2's chest and barreled forward as dead machines fell behind her.

Dodge plasma bolt. Deflect another.

Chop through Cyonic 6's cannon.

Spin. Elbow strike to face.

Asha's armored elbow smashed through Cyonic 6's face and out the back of its skull, spewing clockwork like raindrops.

Let Cyonic 7 take aim. Kick cannon as it fires.

Grin as plasma blasts a hole through Cyonic 8.

Drive *qama* under Cyonic 7's chin, up through its skull. Twist.

Throw time grenade at Cyonics 9 and 10. Miss on purpose. Wait for them to dodge.

Relieve them of their heads.

Skidding to a halt, Asha savored the moment as Cyonics 7 through 10 clattered to the ground behind her. *Let's see Captain Armel beat that.*

She got the space of a breath to enjoy the victory. Then more sounds of mechanical marching drew near.

Standing at the intersection of two hallways, she watched

as a full squad approached from the hallway to her left, another full squad from her right. Weapons forward, they fanned out to cut off retreat from all sides.

A Cyonic with an extra stripe down its synthetic torso—the mark of a higher rank, possibly—stepped from the horde.

"Stand down," it said in its artificially soothing voice. "You are surrounded."

With a mirthless laugh, Asha flourished her blades. They blazed brighter.

"All I am surrounded by," she said, "is scrap metal."

Shouting, Asha leapt.

"Captain, what's your status?" John said.

"*It won't be pretty, but a few more minutes and we can fly out of here.*"

"Valentine and Malcolm?"

"*Wounded and resting. Winter is guarding them. What of Asha?*"

John consulted the feeds. His eyebrows raised.

"Currently making two Cyonic squads regret the day they rolled off the assembly line."

Armel gave a tight laugh. "*I expected nothing less.*"

"I'll direct her back to you now."

"*Perhaps you should let her finish. Asha gets cranky if her battles are cut short.*"

John grinned. "A sound strategy. Contact me when you're ready."

"*Will do. Armel out.*"

John went back to directing their forces, but reserved some

attention for Asha. She was nearly finished working out her rage on the enemy. Soon they could all come back home.

On her knees, Asha slammed her remaining *qama* through the last Cyonic's eye. The machine gave a last sparking rattle and lay still.

Breathing hard, she laughed darkly at the sea of robot corpses around her. She bled from a dozen cuts, ached from the burn of a half-dozen plasma bolts. Her armor was scorched and pocked. Shakily, she came to her feet with the gleam of victory in her eyes.

She raised her left hand. The second *qama* whirled back into her grip, and she returned both weapons to the sheaths on her back.

"*Are you injured?*" John asked.

"No more than usual."

"*Well done. Armel is calling you back,*" John said. "*Unless you plan to tear the skyscraper down, too.*"

Asha grinned. "Don't tempt me."

Keying off her comm, Asha turned back the way she had come. Then a new sound echoed down the hallway behind her. Drawing weapons, she whirled to face whatever enemy dared to sneak up on her. She froze, going pale.

Only in a handful of moments in her life had Asha experienced true, bone-deep fear. This one eclipsed them all.

The Regent stood at the far end of the hall.

He eyed her as he stood as if staying upright was a struggle. His chest heaved as if he'd been running for miles. He squinted like someone with a splitting headache.

No. The Chrona said he'd be down for hours!

The Chrona had diminished him. As he stalked toward her, Asha could see it in the way he moved. But the woman hadn't disabled him as much as she'd thought.

"Ah, the princess," the Regent said disdainfully. He glanced over her shoulder, in the Sled's direction. "You stand between me and my prey, little one."

If she ran, he would be right on her heels. There would be no time for the Sled to retreat. In their state, the twins and the Chrona couldn't stand against even a wounded Regent.

Which left only one option. With a deep breath, Asha grabbed hold of her terror and swept it away. She squared off with the Regent, blocking his path.

"Don't be a fool," he said. "Drop your weapons and you may live to serve me."

Asha's weapon blazed as she pointed it toward the Regent. "Come and take them."

His expression darkened. Shaking his head as if to chastise her, the Regent stepped forward again.

"*Sled's ready,*" John said. "*Armel says you've got to move.*"

He didn't know the Regent was there. She could hear it in his voice—the lack of fear.

"Tell them to leave," she said. "I'll be fine."

"*What do you mean . . . oh. Oh, dear God. Asha, run! Just run. You can make it before—*"

"I'm right where I'm supposed to be."

"*Please, Asha, don't—*"

She didn't hear the rest. The Regent came close, and she could see he intended to breeze right by, swatting her aside like a fly.

She reached inside herself, far deeper than ever before, to the power that was uniquely hers. She had two Time batteries:

the one she had been born with, and the one Malcolm had given her. He had saved Asha's life that day. Now she would return the favor.

With a furious roar, she charged.

John's heart sat like a stone. This couldn't be happening. He was supposed to keep them safe.

He could only watch as Asha flung herself against the Regent again and again and again. Every time, he cast her off and kept moving toward the Sled, and every time, she came back.

In this terrible moment, John understood the full weight of command. The price of not even victory, but merely survival. With a soul heavier than he had ever known, he keyed the comm.

"C-Captain Armel," he said, tripping over the words. "Go order. Take off now. Get back behind the shield while you still can."

"*Negative, General. Asha has not returned.*"

"Captain . . . the Regent is awake, and he's coming for you. Asha is the only thing slowing him down. She's giving you a chance."

A heavy pause hung over the connection.

"*I will assist her. Direct me to—*"

"Captain." John hated himself for his next words. "The Gilbert twins and the Chrona must survive. You have to go *now*."

Armel cursed. John heard him unbuckling from his seat.

"*I will not hear this madness, John. Either all of us leave, or none.*"

Armel had watched Asha grow up, treated her like the daughter he never had. John couldn't expect him to think tactically in this terrible moment.

But someone had to.

Choking back tears, John tapped his own controls.

"Captain," he said, "I am so sorry."

Taking remote command of the Sled, John closed the rear hatch and locked it. Armel cried out in rage.

John's vision blurred, tears streaking down his face. "I'm sorry. I'm so sorry."

The Sled lifted, then sputtered and lurched and dropped back down. Armel was fighting, using tricks of his own to wrest control back from John. A glance at the other feeds and John's insides froze all over again. Asha was still fighting, and amazingly she was slowing the Regent down, but still he drew closer.

John fought through sobs, through rage at himself, his fingers flying across the keys. If he didn't win this battle with Armel, everyone would lose.

Malcolm fought the heavy fog wrapped around him, struggling toward consciousness. Something was wrong; he could feel it. People were shouting, the Sled lurched up and down, and a dark presence approached.

Asha. He felt her, too. In his Chronauri senses, she blazed brighter than he had ever seen. Her power intertwined with the power he'd given her, and she was using every shred of it.

That wasn't right. She should be conserving her Time between fights. What was happening? He tried to sit up and failed. He tried to call for her, but managed only an incoherent groan.

Asha . . .

She was lying in the long hallway, head swimming, struggling for breath. The Regent stalked ahead after tossing her through the ceiling. He had struck her armored chest plate enough to shatter it. Along with a few ribs, she suspected. Falling back to this level hadn't helped.

One more turn and he would find them. Asha could hear the Sled's engines echoing down the hall. *Why haven't they left?*

She shook her head. Fine, then. She would keep going until doomsday if she had to.

Picking through the shards of her armor, she twisted her nexus free and slapped it against her chest. It clung to her fine chainmail, and once again the power of Time flowed from her.

Asha burst from the floor and raced around the Regent like a tornado, raining cuts and kicks on him from every direction. He grunted, stumbling as she sliced his throat and then his Achilles tendon. Giving a frustrated huff, he lashed out with a thunderous punch.

Asha burst clear through the left wall and tumbled to the floor in the next room. *Get up get up get up!* Forcing herself to her feet, she shook away the nausea. The Regent was still walking.

Two can play that game. Releasing an animal growl, Asha sprinted down the room on her side of the wall.

At the end of the room, she activated the phase shifter on her gear belt. With a leap, she passed through the wall as if it wasn't there. The Regent whipped around to stare at her in shock.

Asha deactivated the phase shifter and collided with the Regent, smashing him halfway through the right wall. Before he could respond, she danced back and hit him with a Time grenade, then another, and another.

When the swirling red storm cleared, the Regent was on his hands and knees, chest heaving. He glared up at her.

"You're no Second-*sev*," he said.

"No. I'm something new." Asha raised her blades. "And I'm not moving."

The Regent shook his head in resignation. "So be it."

He began to stand. Asha leapt closer and swung both *qamas* at his neck.

The Regent moved like a snake. His right fist struck her thigh. She cried out as her femur snapped, and she toppled hard to the floor.

Without another word, the Regent left her behind. She had hurt him, but not enough. He stalked forward now with a noticeable limp, intent on destroying everything.

Only three steps left. Then two. Then one. Asha saw the Regent turn and face the broken doorway that led to their escape room. Blue light bathed him—the light from the Sled's thrusters—and murderous hunger twisted his face. The end was here.

No, it's not.

Jaw clenched, Asha shunted massive flows of energy to her thigh armor. The armor constricted, holding her bone and muscle tissue together. The metal moved with her will, helping her leg work when it should have given out.

Stifling a scream of agony, Asha forced herself to her feet. *My heart, my sword will ever blaze.* Step. Step. Step. Sheer will drove her forward, vision tunneling down until all she could see was the Regent. Step. Step. Step. *For all of time, for all my days.*

The Regent reached an open palm toward the Sled, body tensed as he gathered his power to strike.

"Curse your mother, curse your father, curse your house to the tenth generation!" Armel spat.

John accepted the hatred. He deserved it. As Armel shouted his final protest, John won their digital tug of war.

"I'm so sorry," he said, sure that he would be saying it for the rest of his life.

He sent the command to fly.

Asha landed on the Regent's back and clung tightly. With a growl, he tried to shake her off, but she would not be moved. The Sled's thrusters flared. Only a few more seconds!

The Regent threw back his head and cracked against her nose. Asha accepted the pain. Nothing would stop her now. She had been born for this moment.

"You will not have them!" she cried in his ear. "Not today. Not ever."

Asha couldn't kill him. She didn't know if anything could. But Malcolm and Valentine didn't need her to kill him; all they needed was Time. And she was about to give it to them.

The Sled lifted and turned toward the sky. Frantic, the Regent reached out again, trembling as he summoned enough power to burn it from existence.

Asha locked her legs around the Regent's waist, leaving her hands free. With a twist of the dial on her gear belt, she set its self-destruct for ten seconds. She called to her *qamas* and they spun eagerly into her grip.

Summoning all she had, Asha reached around the Regent and drove both *qamas* through his chest. He gasped in shock. Flailing, he struggled futilely to strike her.

She was far from finished. Whatever the future held for the Regent, she knew for certain that he would remember this moment.

With a heave, she drove the entirety of her *qamas* through the Regent's chest. They cut clear through him, appearing between his shoulder blades.

She kept going, driving the blades into her own chest. Deeper and deeper, until she felt the steel tips reach the very center of her. She envisioned the twin Time batteries beating there like temporal hearts. Hearts made of pure energy.

Channeling all the Time she had left, she fed it through her blades and back into herself, then back through the blades and into herself again. Driving every shred of power with her will, Asha created a cascading feedback loop that built and built, growing more powerful yet more unstable with every microsecond.

"Live," she whispered. "Everyone live. For me."

With a final cry, she pushed the feedback loop past its breaking point. At the very instant her gear belt exploded, Asha transformed into the most powerful Time bomb ever created.

The last thing she heard was the Regent's cry of agony and loss. The last thing she saw was the Sled escaping into the sky.

With the contentment of a warrior who had conquered all, Asha embraced Eternity.

CHAPTER 33

Malcolm floated in a black void.

Opposing sensations crashed over him like waves. Bone-deep ache followed by numbness, numbness chased away by agony, agony drowned by loss.

He struggled toward the surface, toward muted light and muffled sounds. Inch by torturous inch, he pulled himself up, and finally he broke the surface to wake in his body.

He wished he hadn't.

A cacophony of misery assaulted him. The Eon Palace infirmary had devolved into a scene out of some tragic play. It couldn't be real.

Tyrathorn clung to Winter, sobbing into her shoulder. Winter herself shed tears but struggled to keep them quiet and be strong for her husband.

John leaned against the wall as if he couldn't support his own weight. Red-eyed, he stared into the middle distance. Bellowing in helpless rage, Armel grabbed his shirt and punched him hard in the face, then drew back again.

"It's okay," John said, wiping away tears. "I deserve it."

So Armel punched him again, then again, screaming curses

until John slid to the floor. Only then did Armel crumple next to John, a puddle of his own grief.

Fred sat cross-legged on the floor, his head in his hands. His weapons and armor had been flung across the room.

Malcolm lay on a medical bed. Though he was awake, the void was still near. It almost had physical weight, like the bone-crushing gravity that the Frost Hammer had wielded.

On the right side of his bed, Dad and Callie watched him with deep concern. On the left, Valentine clung to his hand with both of hers. Her cheeks were wet.

"Oh, God, Mal," she said. "I'm so sorry."

What did she mean? "For what?"

Before he could finish, it hit him like a freight train. The void, the loss, the grief hovering on the edge of memory.

For two years, on waking every morning, Malcolm had extended his Chronauri senses until he could feel his family, his friends. He found their temporal signatures, little pulses of energy in the stream of Time. It told him they were okay.

Every single morning, the brightest pulse, the most beautiful, warmed him inside. It brought him life and joy and hope. Except now, where Asha's signature was once a bright star, there was a black void.

Malcolm's heart shattered.

"No!"

He exploded from the bed, desperate to search for her, certain he could find her. If only he looked hard enough. If only he were strong enough.

The world blurred around him. More shouting, maybe from himself. The room became a whirl, until he slammed against the back wall of the infirmary.

His legs failed. Collapsing into a heap, he swam once again

through the void, regretting that he had ever fought it. He hoped that it would take him down and never let him back up.

Arms encircled him, pulled him in close. He felt long hair brush his neck.

"It's okay," Valentine whispered. "Just let go. It's okay; I'm here. I'm not leaving."

Malcolm's chest heaved, his screams devolving into sobs. The void opened underneath him. A gaping maw, drinking the sorrow that gushed from him, never filling up. He would never cry enough, he would never hurt enough, to make it go away.

"Let it out. It's okay," Valentine said. "Don't worry. I'm here. I'll protect you."

She clung tighter, sharing his tears, holding his body together while his insides fell apart. Until he was certain he would disappear.

Good. He wanted to. What was the point of anything anymore?

For an eternity he lay there, helpless in Valentine's arms. True to her word, she never moved.

At some point, in a space between endless waves of grief, the infirmary door slid open. Soft footsteps approached, and a gentle *whoosh* of robes.

"Girl," a soft voice said, "can he move? Our moment has come, and we must leave."

Malcolm looked up. The Chrona stood overhead with her hands held out to them. He saw determination in her eyes.

"Asha's sacrifice will not be for nothing, Malcolm," she said. "I will teach you how to ensure it. If you want to learn, come with me now."

A glimmer of hope in the void. Faint, wavering, and fragile. But for Asha . . .

Malcolm reached up and grasped the Chrona's hand. A moment later, Valentine followed.

Like rushing winds, temporal sensations swirled around them. The Chrona played Time like it was a piano and she a virtuoso, until finally she hit the last breathtaking notes.

A doorway opened in the universe. The moment stopped, then pulled and stretched, becoming a tunnel of light. The doorway reached out and embraced them.

Malcolm felt the universe fall away.

They were gone in a flash of light.

John had been able to exchange one parting glance with Valentine. A look that held love and comfort, that promised she would return and everything would be okay, even if it took everything she had left. His heart went with her.

When the moment passed, the burdens of command sat heavy on his shoulders once more. They still had work to do, and it wouldn't wait for them to grieve.

"A heart bright and strong and pure has left this world today," Armel said. He cast a dark look on John. "Because of you."

That wasn't true. John was no stranger to grief, though. He knew sometimes you just needed to blame something. So, for the moment, he accepted his friend's hatred.

But then Fred stirred. "Dude. That's a load of crap. You think anyone could force Asha Corvonian to do anything? Girl was fearless like I'd never seen." He took a deep breath to choke back tears. "She saved us all today."

Armel's eyes flashed. His hand crept unconsciously toward his giant war hammer.

"It's okay, Fred," John said quickly. "I had command today, and we lost. Maybe if I had found a better way, Asha would . . ."

He couldn't finish the sentence. A wave of misery welled up, choking off his words.

"My sister is ten times the hero I will ever be," Tyrathorn whispered. "She always was. If she could have written her own end, it would have been something like this."

A truer statement had never been spoken. It solidified in John's mind what he needed to do. With tremendous effort, he pushed against the wall and stood.

As one they all peered up at him. He could see their wounds, both physical and emotional. John knew their quality. They would stand and fight again, but right now, someone had to lead them forward.

"She was the best of us," he said. "So, let's honor her by surviving. The Regent is down, but he's going to recover, which means we're not finished. Not until this war is won."

"What can we do?" Callie said. "We've retreated, and the Regent's army is in the Pyre."

"Two armies back within their fortresses, licking their wounds," Tyrathorn said. "This reprieve will not last."

"Didn't the shield stop him before?" Neil asked.

"He was playing a long game to draw out the Chrona," Winter said. "Once he recovers, I doubt he'll be so patient."

"For a moment, I felt that man's true power," Tyrathorn said. "It was . . . daunting. The shield may not be enough."

"Another attack *is* coming." John turned to Armel and extended his hand. "Whatever our personal feelings, there's a world counting on us."

For a long moment, the captain considered his hand. John

could see the gears turning behind his eyes. Finally, he stood and grasped it.

"Then, until the twins return, it's a game of survival," Captain Armel said. "While I draw breath, I vow this world shall be safe."

Relieved, John gave him a grateful nod. Somehow, he had a feeling they would need the captain before the end.

"So, just to recap," Winter said sardonically, "we don't know when the Regent will recover, or what he'll do when he does. We don't know how or when he'll deploy his army. And we don't know when the twins are coming back, which means we don't know how long we need to survive. That about it?"

"Unbeatable odds." Fred stood, hefting his katana. "Girl, don't you know that's just another Thursday for us?"

Despite himself, John smiled. "We'll have a few surprises waiting. As for Valentine and Malcolm, the Chrona told me how long they'll be gone."

"That's something, at least," Callie said. "How long?"

Just then, John's comm chimed. He keyed it to his command channel, on broadcast so all in the room could hear.

"Yes?"

"*Forgive the interruption, general,*" one of his technicians said, "*but the Cyonic army is redeploying.*"

John's heart dropped into his stomach. "What?"

"*They march for the Eon Palace.*"

"You gotta be kidding me," Fred said.

"Doesn't this guy take a break?" Winter said, exasperated.

"We'll be there shortly," John said. Closing the channel, he faced his friends. "I had hoped this war would be a sprint. Turns out it will be a marathon."

"John," Captain Armel said, radiating tension. "How long until the Gilbert twins return?"

"Forty-six hours?" Valentine said.

Malcolm lay on something hard. *Where am I?* His sister's voice sounded so far away. Even through the mental fog, though, he could hear the fear in it.

"We're leaving them alone against the Regent for *two days*? Why?" She demanded. "He'll tear them apart!"

"The Timeline is damaged, you know this," the Chrona said. "The cracks are spreading, nowhere more so than in Emmett's Bluff in the twenty-first century. Press too hard, too often, and it will shatter beyond repair. Time must pass before returning."

"Even for you?" Valentine said, incredulous. "Aren't you supposed to be, like, in charge of all this?"

"There is much you don't understand."

"Then explain it to me."

Their voices brought Malcolm back. Now awake, though, he found he cared nothing for their argument. Only one thing mattered. Weak and wounded, he stumbled to his feet and confronted the Chrona.

"Bring her back."

"I beg your pardon?"

"I know you can do it. Go back before she died and pull her out." He pointed accusingly. "You're supposed to be this all-powerful protector? Then prove it. Bring her back."

"Mal," Valentine said, gently grasping his arm. "You know she can't. Even if she could, we swore not to tamper with our own Timelines."

"I don't care. I don't care!" he said, laughing for some reason, knowing he looked and sounded unhinged but not caring about that either. "How much will this universe take from us, Val, before we take something back? Huh?"

By the look on her face, she had no answer. Malcolm knew what he would say next wasn't fair.

"What if it had been John?"

Valentine stiffened.

"What would you do to get him back?"

She looked down at her feet.

"Exactly what you're doing now."

Squaring her shoulders, Valentine looked him hard in the eye.

"And you would say exactly what I'm saying. I would hate it, but I would know you're right. Just like you know I'm right."

He pointed at his sister, mouth open, ready to attack. At the last instant, though, all the desperate arguments died on his lips. Of course she was right. Even through the storm of mind-scrambling grief, Malcolm knew he wasn't rational. Someone with his power, with his responsibilities, couldn't afford to be irrational.

He would have to rely on Valentine, then. Until he got his mind right, she would have to be his compass. Because if it were up to him, he might just blow up the world trying to bring Asha back.

"Promise me this isn't the end," he said, trembling. "That he'll answer for Asha, for Callie's daughter, for everything. Promise me!"

Valentine pulled him into an embrace. He clung to her like a lifeline, felt her tears run down his neck.

"I promise," she said. "Asha saved us, and we're going to save everyone else."

If Malcolm was lost at sea, Valentine's voice was the

lighthouse that guided him home. He sagged until she was practically holding him up.

"I'm scared, Val," he confessed.

"I'm here," she said. "Don't worry. I'll protect you."

With monumental effort, Malcolm imagined sewing the shards of himself back together, at least long enough to learn from the Chrona. Long enough to finish this war.

It was only then that his surroundings came into focus. Looking past his sister, Malcolm saw where they stood and his jaw fell open.

"Where are we?"

Valentine gave an ironic laugh. "I haven't had time to ask."

They turned to the Chrona, expectant. But for a moment, the person they saw wasn't the Chrona.

The deep windows of her eyes had clouded over. She stared at them blankly as if they were strangers. She took in their surroundings, looking lost, as if someone else had brought her there. Behind the confusion, Malcolm thought he saw fear.

"Um, Chrona?" He waved, trying to recall what the Regent had called her. "Arsinoë?"

Flinching, the Chrona blinked and the clouds dispersed from her eyes.

"Where were we, now?" she asked.

The twins exchanged a look.

Valentine gestured at their surroundings. "That's what we'd like to know. Is this where you live?"

It was a sunny, warm afternoon. They stood on the roof of a white building, among many other white buildings along a rocky coastline. Below them was a sparkling, blue sea.

Gazing out, the Chrona breathed in deeply and seemed to relax. "Santorini, the way I like to remember it."

"Greece," Malcolm said. "That makes sense."

His sister eyed him. "Why?"

"Because if her real name is Arsinoë, and the Regent's real name is Helios, then I think I know who they are."

CHAPTER 34

"Everwatch thinks the original three Chrona were all siblings," Malcolm said. "But that's not true, is it?" The Chrona shook her head, eyes twinkling with mischief.

"Mal," Valentine said. "Care to clue me in?"

"Valentine," Malcolm said. "Meet Arsinoë, daughter of Ptolemy XII, and youngest sister of Cleopatra."

Her eyebrows shot up. "You mean, like *the* Cleopatra?"

"Don't sound so impressed," the Chrona said. "She was an awful person. Tried to have me killed more than once."

"And everyone thinks she succeeded," Malcolm said. "History says Cleopatra had her murdered so she couldn't be a political rival. Arsinoë died on the steps of the Temple of Artemis. Except, she didn't, did she?"

"My killer took pity on me, and helped me escape into hiding."

"Wow," Valentine said. "Every history book is wrong."

"Who do you think wrote the histories?" the Chrona said. "I lived peacefully for some time. Then, when I learned of my dreadful sister and her dreadful husbands' deaths, I took it upon myself to salvage our family line."

Malcolm thought he had all the pieces now. "That's when you found the twins, isn't it?"

"Very good, Malcolm."

"Twins?" Valentine asked.

"Cleopatra Selene the Second, and Alexander Helios," Malcolm said. "Fraternal twins, the children of Cleopatra. Which would make them Arsinoë's niece and nephew."

"I masqueraded as a tutor. Managed to insert myself into their lives as a governess of sorts." The Chrona shook her head, wistful. "Our blood had greatness in it. I thought if I could teach them well enough, maybe they could bring something good into this world. Something lasting. That was my hope."

"But, here we are, in this mess," Valentine said. "Which means something went wrong, didn't it? What happened to you?"

The Chrona stared into the distance as if she were seeing some ancient memory. After a moment, her gaze returned to the present.

"A story for another day," she said. "The tale of my life is not nearly as important as your training. We must begin at once."

"Not to sound ungrateful," Malcolm said, "but how will forty-six hours be enough to learn what we need?"

The Chrona paused, studying him. He felt as if his insides were being evaluated.

"You both still think like them," she said eventually. "Like normal people. It is one of many challenges you must overcome."

"What does that mean?" Valentine said.

"It means you must begin thinking like someone unbound by clocks and calendars. Like true Sixth-*sev* Chronauri. I said you would return to Emmett's Bluff in forty-six hours. Did you honestly believe that means forty-six hours for *us*?"

Malcolm rocked back on his heels. *How had I not thought of that? It's Time Travel 101.* A glance at Valentine showed similar astonishment on her face.

"In this place," the Chrona said, "Time is what we make it."

As if to punctuate her statement, she waved her hand and the picturesque Greek landscape disappeared. They stood somewhere strange, beautiful, and almost alien, yet somehow familiar.

The ground was a vast plane of something prismatic and translucent, like faceted diamond or crystal. A current of energy flowed beneath the surface, constant and powerful, an endless river all the way to the horizon and beyond. Arcs like lightning flashed here and there under the surface.

Malcolm's eyes followed it to the horizon, then lifted to behold the sky, only to find that there *was* no sky. Not like Earth's, anyway. Was it gray or white or light blue? Was it a solid surface or a swirling layer of thick, cloudlike cover? His eyes couldn't focus on it.

Valentine found her voice first. "Whoa. Where *are* we?"

"You're in my home. Without this place, there would be no Chrona." Smiling, she held her arms open. "Welcome to the Aegis."

It was all too overwhelming to pick a good question out of the thousands Malcolm wanted to ask. He picked the simplest one.

"How long can we train here?"

"That, boy, is entirely up to you." The Chrona grew serious. "Now, shall we begin?"

"They appear to be testing the shield," John's technician said. "Probing it for weaknesses."

"They are even digging underground," another technician

added. "Using the old Carmichael tunnels to approach us that way. It's how they discovered the shield was actually a sphere, not a dome."

John nodded. While he hid in his fortress, recovering, Cyonics came at the Eon Palace with every tactic, weapon, and trick in their arsenal, searching for some way to get through the shield.

So far, every effort had failed, one of the few real victories for the good guys. But victories didn't always last.

"Deploy squads to mirror the Cyonics within the shield," John said. "If any get through, we'll need an immediate response. Follow this pattern."

He called up an image of the Eon Palace and traced a defensive plan around their perimeter. His technicians went to work relaying orders to the Ember Guard and Watchers.

He suppressed a weary sigh. "Okay, next objective. Display a statistical breakdown of our assets, prebattle and postbattle."

Two streams of data cascaded down the glass side by side: the army he had taken into battle versus the army that had returned from battle. He grimaced.

"One-third of our forces down. Not ideal when the real battle is ahead."

"Most are only injuries," a technician offered. "Some may be well enough to fight when the time comes."

John considered, then shook his head. "That would be nice, but we can't count on it."

There was another set of data he needed to examine, and it filled him with dread. He braced himself.

"The data we pirated from the Pyre. Display it next to ours."

A third stream of information appeared. John and his team had managed to hack the Regent's surveillance and piggyback onto its data streams. Their pirate signal had been detected and shut down eventually, but not before revealing details about the enemy.

John had been too afraid to see the machines' postbattle numbers. Now he forced himself to look.

He found himself smiling from ear to ear. The mission inside the Pyre had been an abject failure, but as for their battle on the streets . . .

"We *won?*" a technician said.

"Two-thirds," John breathed, astonished. "They lost two-thirds of their forces."

He gazed between his technicians, relishing their shock and relief. In the face of devastating losses, this was the burst of hope they desperately needed. Excitedly, John began to package the data into graphical form to share with his friends.

"Only forty hours to go," he said. "We're going to win this."

No one disagreed.

He wasn't healing quickly enough. Whenever he wielded Time, the wounds stabbed him like a hot knife. He cursed Arsinoë's name, and whatever name belonged to that so-called princess.

They fancied themselves clever. His aunt's attack had struck deep, damaging the source of his power. That girl's relentless assault had resulted in . . . well, he wasn't quite sure. The stab wounds in his chest hadn't fully closed as they should have. What had she done to him?

Hiding a grimace, the Regent lowered himself gingerly into his chair at the far end of the Pyre's control center. At least the peasants hadn't found this room. From here he could survey his minions' preparations.

He may have suffered a setback, but this war would not end until he claimed what was rightfully his. Not if he had to shred the universe to do it.

Again he envisioned the Gilbert twins melting in the flames as he burned this century to a smoldering scar on the Timeline. If Arsinoë failed to return and face him, if she failed to answer for her betrayal, she would be forced to watch it happen.

Or once he defeated her and claimed his birthright, he might just burn the Timeline anyway. A dark smile crossed his face.

Lost armies didn't matter. Damage to his Pyre didn't matter. They were the cost of war. He wondered, though, how much loss the Gilbert twins were prepared to endure. Though they didn't know it, their limits would soon be tested.

When he unleashed Leviathan.

Then he would show them the true meaning of loss.

CHAPTER 35

Valentine kept pace with her brother as he walked. Side by side, they followed the flow of the powerful energy current beneath their feet

Malcolm was in agony. Valentine could see it in the dark circles under his eyes, feel it in the cloud over his head. He was trying, but even the smallest effort taxed him.

He caught her looking. Turning quickly, she refocused on the crystalline surface.

"I think I'm starting to see it now," she said, "movement in the Time stream."

Malcolm nodded. "Yeah. The more I look, the more I'm able to see. Like my eyes are starting to adjust."

"Not your eyes, boy," the Chrona said from several paces back. "Your mind. Your heart. Everything in you that is Chronauri."

It made sense in a crazy, cosmic sort of way. When the Chrona first began teaching them about this place—the Aegis, she called it—it had been difficult to process at first. Yet here they were now, learning how to use it.

Pay attention! Valentine forced her mind to stop wandering.

The sooner they became real Sixth-*sev*, the sooner they could help their friends.

She stopped short and stared down between her feet. "Whoa."

Malcolm followed her gaze. "What is it?"

"Mal, I see it," she breathed. "I see it all!"

It had just happened, like flipping a switch in her brain. One second, she saw the prismatic floor and energy current beneath it. The next, they parted like clouds and she could see past them.

Down into the universe. Into the Timeline, which the Aegis hovered above. Focusing harder, Valentine found the day and the place directly beneath her.

"Rome in 2024," she said, astonished.

Malcolm came beside her and looked down. "Hm. I'll take your word for it."

She grabbed his arm and pointed. "You're not seeing this?"

"Not yet. Haven't found the trick, I guess."

"It's not a trick. It's . . . I don't know. I just focused and it happened."

"Focus on that place and step forward," the Chrona said. "Watch and feel the Timeline shift beneath you."

Holding her breath, Valentine complied. Three steps later, Rome had advanced another century. The ancient ruins contrasted even more sharply with the shiny future surrounding them.

To her amazement, she could pick individual people out of the crowd. One dark-haired woman was strolling toward an office building, going to work for the day. Valentine moved forward a fraction of an inch and watched the same woman leaving her office that same evening.

"You really meant it," she said, breathless.

"I really did," the Chrona said.

When the Chrona had begun this lesson, it called a memory back to Valentine's mind. Their conflict with the Frost Hammer was beginning, and Asha had just arrived in Emmett's Bluff. In those early days, she had taught them truths about the universe.

Valentine remembered her using a paper towel roll to illustrate. Within it, Asha had said, was the whole universe. Particles floating inside that cardboard tube represented galaxies, star systems, planets, the people on them—everything.

Then she had gently blown into one end. That rush of air, the current that propelled all those particles forward, was like Time. Time was the energy that drove the universe.

If that current was Time, then the cardboard tube itself was the Aegis. When the mission to protect the Timeline first began, Arsinoë built it with the help of Helios and Selene, and the three of them together became the Chrona. From this position above the Timeline, they could look down upon every moment in the universe.

Given its sterile appearance, they also gave it the ability to reflect copies of favorite places. Which was how the Chrona had made it appear to be Santorini.

As she stared through the universe, Valentine couldn't pull her gaze away. It was too beautiful for words.

"Malcolm?" she heard the Chrona say.

"I'm sure I'll get it eventually."

"We both know the reason you lag, boy."

The conversation faded into background noise. Valentine's attention fell further downward, focusing on future Rome's bustling sidewalk. Smells of garlic, tomato, and wine wafted from curbside trattorias. In a nearby piazza, someone was playing the harp while a wandering vendor hawked pashmina scarves.

She wavered with something like vertigo, as if she were staring over the edge of a tall building. Her head began to swim, and before she knew it, the Aegis's crystalline surface disappeared.

She was falling, reality blurring around her. With a *whoosh*, air raced by in a burst and her insides lurched.

The universe reverted to a normal pace. Valentine's thoughts and vision cleared, and she realized where she was.

A sidewalk beneath her feet. Warm, breezy air thick with mouthwatering scents. The dark-haired woman walking by, on the way from her office to meet friends for dinner.

Did I just . . . ?

She had allowed her thoughts to stray. For an instant she had wanted desperately to be here for real.

Before she could take another step, a storm of temporal sensations burst around her. A hand reached through the maelstrom and clamped onto her shoulder. The universe blurred again, and in the next blink she was back beside Malcolm.

"Holy . . . Mal, I just went down there!" she said.

"I figured," he replied. Smirking, he gestured at the Chrona. "You disappeared. Then she said some really creative curses and disappeared, too. How was it?"

"Amazing. I've never felt . . ."

She met the Chrona's eyes and trailed off. The woman's glare could have melted iron.

"Sorry. How did I do that?"

The Chrona stared as if she couldn't measure the stupidity of the question. "How do you suppose I move from place to place, girl? This is not just an observatory; it is how I safeguard the Timeline. It even allows me to place limits on the use of Time."

She paused, seeming to run out of steam. Valentine used the

moment to process. These were truths about the nature of the universe, and about the Chrona, that not even Everwatch knew.

More important, it made something else plain to Valentine. "That's why the Regent was baiting you. He doesn't care about the war. What he really wants is this place."

The Chrona nodded. "Helios is determined to destroy me, for reasons you will learn eventually. But, ultimately, yes. What he really wants is control of the Aegis. Royalty is in our blood, and he believes ultimate rulership to be his birthright."

"Hypothetically," Valentine said, "what would happen if he got what he wants?"

The Chrona's posture drooped. "Attacking your century, threatening to burn a scar into the Timeline—it is the barest fraction of what he could do with the Aegis. Across the universe, from the beginning of Time to the end, all would be vulnerable to his whims. This is why we fight him, not just to save the world, but to save everything."

"Whoa," Valentine said, her voice barely a whisper.

She swayed, suddenly dizzy, wishing deeply that this place had chairs handy. Something changed beside her, and she turned to see an overstuffed armchair waiting. With an ironic chuckle, she sat.

"That's a lot to process," Malcolm said. After observing her, he moved to sit and a chair appeared beneath him.

"You see now, even more, why we must prevail," the Chrona said.

Malcolm's eyes narrowed at the Chrona. "Yeah. But there's more to this place, isn't there? Something you're not showing us."

The sudden suspicion in his voice puzzled Valentine. What did he see that she didn't?

He gestured at the prismatic floor. "You've already shown

us the illusions this place can create, and I think you've still got one going."

The Chrona's expression hardened. "Careful, boy."

"The days of being careful are over. You said it yourself—we need to learn everything. So, why don't you show us what this place *really* looks like?"

The old woman glared, but Malcolm didn't budge. Valentine glanced back and forth between them, unsure which way to fall. In the end, she didn't have to choose.

The Chrona sighed. "I intended to reveal it when you were ready, because you will never un-see it. However, since you insist."

She closed her eyes, concentrated, and the Aegis . . . changed.

Overhead, the not-sky darkened. Something like thunder rumbled. The air around them—if it was even really air—grew noticeably colder.

Then Valentine looked down and gasped. She shot to her feet. "What happened?"

The floor's prismatic quality was waning. Spiderwebs of black cracks were spreading across Time, covering untold millennia. Where new cracks formed, gouts of flames spewed forth as Time burned.

As Valentine studied the patterns, she found one place that seemed to be the epicenter of destruction to the Timeline, where layer upon layer of damage spanned years. A place of shadow and flame, so broken and fragile that the Aegis might just shatter around it.

Valentine didn't have to look closer to know. Deep inside, she had been feeling it.

The epicenter was Emmett's Bluff in the twenty-first century.

"Oh, God," she said. "Mal."

"I know," he said. "I can see it."

Her breaths heaved as she fought off a wave of panic. "Even if we beat the Regent, this damage is already done. The Timeline could still break. If, if we can't fix this . . ."

"We'll find a way, Val." He reached out, and they clung to each other. "We have to, or everything ends."

CHAPTER 36

"**W**here are we going?"

Valentine glanced over her shoulder. "Now, why would I ruin the surprise?"

Malcolm tried to look stern, but he couldn't hide a smile. "At least tell me where we are. And when."

"A city in Egypt. And, um, a *while* ago."

"Oh, that narrows it down some. Thanks."

"Just enjoy the walk. Have I ever steered you wrong?"

"Well, you did buy me that orange paisley shirt once."

"That was seventh grade. Let it go."

The twins wound through a maze of smaller stone streets before turning onto a massive thoroughfare. Malcolm, ever the history geek, slowed to gawk at the city. Valentine dropped back to walk by his side, enjoying his wonder.

The avenue bustled with activity. To their left, between rows of buildings, Valentine glimpsed a blue sea and a busy port. In all other directions the ancient city sprawled, a breathtaking expanse of carved stone.

Malcolm's torment, always hiding under the surface, seemed just a little muted. Maybe this field trip would help the way Valentine had hoped.

It was one of a dozen excursions the twins had taken. Between exhaustive training sessions, the Chrona had ordered them to "indulge themselves" by going on walks through places both historical and futuristic. No real objectives, just go see them, so long as they only observed.

The Chrona hadn't given a reason, but Valentine thought she could guess. It was a constant reminder of what they were protecting.

As a bonus, they were getting to practice with the Aegis, learning how to work with it. According to the Chrona, the twins should eventually be able to travel through Time with their own ability. But that required extremely high levels of skill and power, and they weren't there yet.

Valentine had asked when they would learn about the Aegis's most important function: setting rules and limitations over Time. The Chrona had just stared at her, then moved on to a different subject. Which probably meant *never*. Valentine couldn't blame her. They weren't the Chrona, after all.

"Wherever we are, it's really old." Malcolm's eyes never stopped roving, drinking in all the details. "The art style, the stonework, kinda reminds me of . . ."

Peering to the left, he trailed off. Between two buildings, they now had a clear view of the port, and a building standing tall among the waters.

"The lighthouse," Malcolm said, astonished. "We're in Alexandria!"

"Got it even faster than I thought you would."

"Does that mean . . . ?"

Valentine flashed a knowing smile. "It's not far. Follow me."

Minutes later they rounded a corner, and there it was. Malcolm gawked up at the Library of Alexandria, sparkling and new, filled with treasures of knowledge that the people of the twins' century could only theorize about.

"I never dreamed . . ." he said, his voice hushed. "Thank you for this."

Valentine's heart warmed. "This job should come with a few perks, right?"

He nodded, but didn't seem to really hear her.

"So. Ready to go inside?"

He looked like a child standing at the gates of Disneyland, incredulous that this was actually happening. All he could do was nod.

They started toward the main entrance. As they walked, Valentine found her own thoughts wandering back home. Back to John's side, to his warm embrace. He would love to see this, too.

Her heart ached for his presence, his stillness. As much as Valentine loved what she could do, the Aegis would never be home to her. Wherever John was, whatever life they would have—that was home.

Hopefully, someday Malcolm would find that. He deserved to be happy.

"Fun fact," he said. "The library became what it was because of the Chrona's family."

"Seriously?"

"Yep. Early Ptolemaic dynasty, they were patrons long before she was born. It grew a lot because of them."

Mere steps from the library doors, the twins stopped in their tracks. A kind of "window" opened in front of them, hovering like a TV screen that had magically popped into existence.

The Chrona stood on the other side. She looked weary today.

A subtle difference, but the twins had spent long enough in the Aegis to learn about her, too.

"We have an alteration to prevent."

Valentine's heart sank. Malcolm was just starting to enjoy himself. "Can you give us an hour? Then we'll come back."

"No need to return here, girl. I will *shift* your position myself."

"But if we could—"

The world blurred into racing lines of light as the Chrona plucked them from ancient Egypt. Valentine had just enough time to feel annoyed before their journey came to an abrupt halt.

Most of their missions happened this way. The Chrona seemed to like catching them unawares and throwing them into the center of conflicts. In between the dozen or so walking explorations, they had faced down twice as many threats to the Timeline in various centuries. Maybe it was how the Chrona was forcing them to grow.

Now they stood between stone buildings again, on the edge of another ancient city. This one sat by the sea, with a tall mountain situated nearby. The surroundings were beautiful, almost luxurious. Like an ancient resort town.

"Another bad guy to smack down?" Malcolm asked.

"Not today, Malcolm," the Chrona said. Though her window was gone, they could still hear her voice. "A misguided soul, well-intentioned but dangerous nonetheless. She seeks to change a pivotal event."

It was morning, and there was a chill in the air. Valentine turned, wracking her brain for any historical tidbits Malcolm had shared in the past, searching for something to give her a foothold on where or when they were.

Wait. She could figure this out. She just had to remember all the ways their power was growing. Closing her eyes, Valentine cast her Chronauri senses along the Timeline. She felt the flow of years around them, searching for their place in the context of history.

Smiling, she opened her eyes. "November 23, A.D. 79"

"Hm," Malcolm said.

Valentine's heart sank. His heaviness had returned. Throughout their training it had plagued him, slowing his progress, draining his joy.

If he was going to grow as a Chronauri the way they both needed to, something would have to change. Something in his heart. But what, and how? What more could Valentine do to help him?

Malcolm focused on the mountain in the distance. He snapped his fingers. "We're in Pompeii. The Mount Vesuvius eruption?"

"The day it *should* erupt," the Chrona replied. "If a young lady has her way, that will never happen. She has traveled from the future with a machine built to suppress seismic events."

"Would that be so bad?" Valentine asked. "Won't a lot of people die otherwise?"

"Thousands," Malcolm replied.

"Think on it, Valentine," the Chrona said. "History is marked by death. Would you attempt to save everyone? That leads down a path to the very violations we prevent."

"But what if saving these people works out better?" Valentine pressed.

The Chrona sighed. "Our Time here is short, girl. Do not think I am unfeeling, or that I don't understand. I do. So I ask for your trust. When you return, I will explain. Are we agreed?"

Inside Valentine, it was a battle between immediate

compassion and long-term logic. Which would be wiser? She looked to Malcolm.

"She's the Chrona," he said simply. "I'd say she's earned our trust. If she's wrong, we'll find a way to come back and fix it. Okay?"

She nodded, relieved to at least have a direction. Malcolm was right. And since this was part of their training, maybe there would be something else to learn.

"Okay. Where's our target?"

"You must find her, then find how to stop her," the Chrona said. "Alert me when you have finished."

Then she was gone.

"She does seem to enjoy the *throw them in the deep end* style of training," Valentine said.

"Imagine being her at the start," Malcolm said. "You're suddenly this powerful new thing in the universe, and there's literally no one to teach you."

Valentine considered. "I hadn't thought of it like that. I'd probably feel like a caveman trying to build a cell phone."

"Yeah. Then you'd build the phone and have no one to call. There's the real tragedy."

They shared a laugh, turning their attention back to the challenge at hand.

"First, let's find her," Valentine said. "Once we see what she's got, we can figure out how to shut it down."

"I'll check the Timeline for any damage. If she tunneled here, it must have left a mark."

"I'll scan for temporal signatures that don't match the natives."

Valentine felt a *shift* as Malcolm went to work. Closing her eyes again, she cast her Chronauri perceptions along the flows and eddies of the Timeline, finding all the little pulses that indicated life.

When she found the one that pulsed differently, there was no question that it didn't belong here. Like strumming a guitar chord with one string out of tune.

Of course, it had to be in the most troublesome place possible. Valentine opened her eyes at the same moment her brother did. They emitted twin sighs.

"Figures," Malcolm said.

"If it was easy, it wouldn't be fun. Right?"

"Keep telling yourself that."

"How are we going to get there?"

"Well, we can't fly there. Yet."

Valentine eyed him. "Yet. Uh-huh."

"Come on. You still don't think we'll be able to fly?"

"Have you seen the Chrona fly?"

Malcolm shrugged. "Maybe she doesn't want to."

"Or maybe she doesn't live in a fantasy world."

"Says the girl who can control Time with her mind."

Valentine stopped short. "That . . . is actually hard to argue with."

"I know," he said, oozing satisfaction.

"But I'll believe we can fly when I see your feet leave the ground." Drinking in more energy, Valentine wrapped herself in a sheath of fast Time. "Right now, we've got to run."

She didn't get out of breath anymore. Not running at any speed or for any length. The more Valentine channeled Time, the more she lived with it as part of who she was, the more it soaked into her cells. Even the damage she had taken from the Regent was gone.

Most days, it happened so gradually that she didn't notice. Today it was hard *not* to notice as she and Malcolm raced up the side of a mountain like gale-force winds.

If Mount Vesuvius had looked giant from Pompeii, it felt monstrous under their feet. Running up a volcano: another thing to add to the growing list of things Valentine never imagined she would do.

The twins skidded to a halt just short of the peak. Only a few more steps and they would be able to peer inside.

With a roar, the ground trembled. Wide-eyed, Valentine clung to a rocky outcropping to keep from sliding back down the hill. Malcolm latched onto deep-rooted scrub brush.

"Maybe she failed," he said.

Then a high-pitched, mechanical whine echoed inside the crater. As the sound grew in power, the mountain's roar began to subside. The tremors died.

"Whoa," Valentine said. "In our day, people would kill for whatever tech she has."

"Almost a shame we have to destroy it."

Valentine couldn't help agreeing. *The Chrona better have a solid explanation for this.* Despite her doubts, it was time to go to work.

Valentine sprinted the remaining distance to the peak, Malcolm on her heels. Gingerly, she peered over the side.

A beam of golden energy sizzled through the air, inches from her head.

With a yelp, Valentine fell back into her brother, nearly sending them both on a crash course down the slope. They scrambled for purchase as Vesuvius roared and shook again. And again, mechanical sounds suppressed it.

"Stay away!" a woman shouted from inside the crater.

"We're not going to hurt you!" Valentine called.

A golden blast shattered a rocky outcropping overhead.

"I don't think she believes you," Malcolm said.

"I noticed."

"We need to get a look at her machine."

"Yeah. Can you distract her?"

"I could. Or . . ."

Malcolm held up his hand, wearing a look of faraway concentration. His corona glowed as Time *shifted* inside the crater.

". . . we could just slow her down."

Side by side, the twins moved up to stand on the peak. Sure enough, Malcolm's bubble of super-slowed Time had enveloped the lanky, blonde woman and her machine. Whatever it was.

"Nicely done," Valentine said.

"Thanks. Wow, I hadn't expected something so elaborate."

Whoever this woman was, she had come prepared. Her suppression machine wasn't some crudely rigged box of tech. Like a mechanical spiderweb, it stretched across the crater's mouth, multiple support legs anchored into the rock face. A cylindrical mass hung at the center, pointing down inside the mountain.

Vesuvius rumbled. With an earsplitting roar, it shook as if it was trying to cast off the intruders. Even knowing little about volcanos, Valentine could feel the pressure. It was building toward an eruption.

To her shock, the suppression machine whined to life. "Wait, how is it—?"

Malcolm's bubble shattered. The machine raced back to normal speed and suppressed the eruption once again.

This time, though, Valentine felt the machine working and realized their miscalculation. She exchanged an incredulous look with Malcolm.

"That thing is—"

A dozen golden beams shot toward them. Again Malcolm gestured, and with a series of small *shifts*, each beam slowed to a crawl. The air around them sizzled like eggs in a skillet as the beams advanced inch by inch.

Valentine spotted an automated turret on the far side of the crater. Channeling fast Time, she pushed the weapon's inner workings until they overheated and melted to slag.

Two more turrets unfolded and opened fire.

Valentine dove back beneath the crest of the mountain while cannon fire burst overhead. Malcolm joined her a split second later.

"I felt it," he said. "From the noise, I thought the machine was using sound waves, but—"

"—it's trying to open a vortex in the mountain."

"Literally trying to rewind it to some year when it wasn't about to blow."

"I can think of a dozen reasons that'll end badly."

"At least."

"I'm saving thousands!" the woman shouted. "A lost civilization!"

Valentine considered, and then called back. "No, you're twisting the Timeline."

"How much more would you change?" Malcolm added. "Where do you draw the line?"

"Typical excuses to do *nothing*! If you try to stop me, you will be murderers."

Her turrets spewed their fire into the air, working nonstop to hold the twins at bay.

Valentine shook her head in frustration. "If that were a normal machine, this would be easy. But the way it's twisting the Timeline . . ."

"Yeah," Malcolm said. "Hard to know how to shut it down safely."

"Maybe that's the point of this. Giving us something strange, making us figure it out."

Vesuvius roared and shook, only to be suppressed again. As Valentine felt the odd machine do its work, a new thought occurred to her.

"What if, in trying to rewind it, she ends up causing it to erupt when it shouldn't?"

Malcolm blew out a breath. "If it wipes out the wrong civilization, who knows how it could impact the Timeline?"

That sealed it for Valentine. No more playing it soft, and no more trying to debate with the woman. Like so many the twins had faced before, she was beyond reason.

But how could they shut down such a crazy variety of Time machine without harming the Timeline? Desperate for a solution, Valentine grabbed the first idea her instincts threw at her.

"Okay, I'm going to try something," she said. "But it's, um, technically impossible."

Malcolm arched an eyebrow.

"But I think I can make it work!" Suddenly nervous, she swallowed hard. "Just be ready. If it works, you'll know, and I'll need you to get her out of there."

She could see Malcolm wanting to protest. Only his trust in her held him back. Still, he examined her for a long moment before answering.

"Okay," he said slowly. "But I'll be watching. If things go badly, I'm pulling the plug and getting you out first. Deal?"

"Deal. Maybe back up a little. I need to concentrate, so can you do something about those cannons?"

"Gladly."

They were still firing a constant barrage. As Malcolm stepped back, Valentine felt him absorb a huge rush of Time and redirect it. Raising both hands overhead, he tensed and then swung them down toward the earth.

The air crackled. The hairs on Valentine's arms stood on end. With a deafening *boom*, twin lightning bolts lanced out of the clear sky and blew the turrets to pieces.

"Nice." Valentine gave an approving nod. "You didn't even have to look at them."

He gave a wistful smile. "Guess even I'm improving a little."

The sadness in his eyes dropped a lead ball in the pit of her stomach. He was trying so hard, but his heart still lived in the past with Asha. Once again, Valentine promised herself she would find a way to help. With effort, she turned toward their work.

"Be ready," she said.

She closed her eyes and stretched her Chronauri senses. The machine vibrated in Time, an unnatural presence. Valentine followed the path of the temporal energy drilling down into the mountain. She traced the resulting distortions deep inside the earth.

Her senses spread until they beheld Mount Vesuvius and everything within a mile radius. That was where the machine's effects faded. Valentine marked the border in her mind.

Now for the real trick.

Opening her being, she drank in a tidal wave of Time. With

a controlled push, she willed the energy to rush out and fill the Timeline around the mountain. Her bubble of power expanded to the mile radius, until she held everything affected by the machine in her grasp.

Valentine took a moment to quell her uncertainty, to focus on wielding her power like a Sixth-*sev* Chronauri should. Then, with a centering breath, she flexed her will as hard as she could.

All around her, Time stopped.

CHAPTER 37

It was ironic that Valentine had learned this trick from the Regent. The twins had learned from every villain who'd come to Emmett's Bluff looking for trouble, but this felt different. More significant.

Holding the bubble of stopped Time with her will, she parted the flows of the Timeline around it. Just as the Regent had done to cut the twins off from their power, Valentine isolated Mount Vesuvius from the rest of Time. Now whatever happened here wouldn't spill over and damage anything else.

Her insides buzzed with equal parts elation and terror. *I just stopped Time!* A feat the twins and Everwatch had believed to be impossible. As it turned out, stopping Time *was* impossible . . . unless you had the right combination of skill, power, and knowledge of how the Timeline works.

Slowly, the true significance of the twins' potential was revealing itself. Valentine couldn't help wondering—if she could stop Time at such a young age, what might she be able to do decades from now?

She forced her thoughts back on task. Their job wasn't finished yet.

Holding the bubble steady while keeping the flows of Time

at bay took everything she had. Which meant the rest was up to Malcolm. She gave him a significant look. *I'm ready.*

Though he lagged behind her progress, he still had tricks up his sleeve. As Time stopped around them, he stepped inside his own bubble and filled it with his own flows of Time. The counterpressure protected him, allowing him to move as he normally did while everything else stopped.

Now he disappeared over the edge of the mountain. Though Valentine couldn't see him work, she sensed every *shift*, every burst of Time as he tore the machine to pieces. She felt the blonde woman's temporal pulse resume as Malcolm scooped her up and took her with him.

Valentine trembled with exertion. The Time around Vesuvius wanted to flow; that was its nature. Every second she held it back felt like carrying the mountain on her shoulders. She grinned in relief as Malcolm reappeared, their foe tossed over his shoulder.

Grabbing Valentine's outstretched hand, he pulled her into his bubble. In a flash, they were outside the mile radius around Vesuvius.

With an exhausted sigh, she let go. There was a shudder as the Timeline righted itself, and then Time flowed normally.

The mountain tremored as if angry to have been suppressed by the machine. Malcolm kept running, putting miles between them. His other passenger had recovered and was now raining punches on his neck and shoulders.

He dashed to the crest of a distant hill, released his bubble, and skidded to halt. They turned around just as it happened.

With a bone-shaking roar, Mount Vesuvius erupted.

Valentine had never heard a sound fill the sky like that. A compression wave passed over them, carrying an acrid smell.

The twins had just preserved history, protecting the Timeline. A victory in every sense. Still, she couldn't help a twinge of regret.

The blonde woman watched with angry tears. "You monsters! Do you have any idea what you just destroyed?"

Malcolm rolled his eyes. "Last I checked, Vesuvius destroyed it."

"No! Those deaths are on your—"

Valentine's anger blazed. Stalking toward the woman, she pointed right in her face.

"Shut up. You have no idea who we are, or what we've sacrificed to keep the Timeline safe." She kept walking, forcing the woman to back away. "Now, stop acting like a child. Sit down and listen!"

On the last word, Valentine clenched her fist and a lightning bolt struck the ground behind her. Wide-eyed, the woman sank down to sit on the grassy slope.

Malcolm appeared at Valentine's side. He gave her arm a reassuring squeeze and then stepped forward.

"You seem to have good intentions," he told the woman. "But on that scale, Time manipulation has a cost. Anticipating all the side effects is very difficult, even for us."

Though the woman wasn't shouting, she seemed far from satisfied. She aimed narrowed, suspicious eyes up at them.

"I'm a temporal physicist. What gives you the right to tell me anything? And how did you do . . . whatever you did? Tell me now. I deserve to know!"

"Who we are isn't important," Valentine said. "But our message is. The Chrona sees what you're doing, and she says to stop it. Stop *all* of it yourself, or she'll stop it for you."

That broke through. The woman's face went slack, and all

her demands seemed to evaporate. Hugging her knees to her chest, she stared at the grass.

"Are we going to hear from you again?" Malcolm asked.

The woman hesitated, then shook her head.

"You can get back to your year?" Valentine asked.

"Yes."

"Good," Malcolm said.

The twins turned to leave, but then Malcolm stopped and went back. Kneeling, he looked the woman in the eye.

"Just because this is over, it doesn't mean you can't make a difference. You're motivated, and you've got skills. If anyone can find another way to help the world, it's you. Okay?"

To Valentine's surprise, the woman smiled. Wiping away tears, she pulled Malcolm into a hug.

"Thank you," she whispered.

The twins walked until the woman was out of sight, then flashed the intricate temporal code that signaled the Aegis to open, like a combination lock on an invisible door. Leaving the universe behind, they ascended.

The view had changed dramatically. The Chrona cycled between hundreds of illusions, using whatever fit her mood. Everything from jungles to glaciers, from the moon to distant planets.

Today, they returned to a Tuscan villa at sunset. The house sat atop a rolling hill, high enough to give a breathtaking view of the vibrant Italian countryside.

Stopping on the front steps, Valentine turned and drank in the sights and smells. The estate kept a vineyard and an olive grove. Rationally, she knew it was just a convincing illusion, but right now it didn't matter. This was nice.

Malcolm stood at her side. She glanced over and saw him grinning.

"Big day for you," he said. "You found a new power *and* got in that woman's face."

She gave a weak smile. "After you were so nice to her, I kinda feel guilty about that."

"She needed both. Tough love."

"Good Time-cop, bad Time-cop?"

"Yeah, we should remember that. Maybe it'll work again." Malcolm grew more sober. "Seriously, I'm proud of you. What you did back there, there's no way I could have done it. Not yet."

Her smile warmed. "Thanks. It did feel amazing. And I know you'll get there."

He shrugged casually, but she saw the truth underneath. He was worried. Sorrow chained his heart to the past. What could fix that?

Though she tried to hide it, Valentine's concern was growing, too. How long had they been training? Maybe a month. Maybe two. It was hard to tell in this place.

She understood her brother's grief, but sooner or later, the cost of that grief would be too heavy to bear. If they faced the Regent unprepared, the Timeline would pay the price.

There had to be something she could do. Some way to help Malcolm break free, or at least set aside his pain long enough to save everything. Everyone.

You did think of something. The thought came unbidden, and she pushed it away. It came back instantly, as if tired of being ignored. One idea had occurred to her a recently, and she had been debating with herself ever since.

It might work. It also might backfire and make him worse. It might even affect *her* badly. Could she afford to take that risk?

These were desperate days. The Timeline teetered on the edge of a knife, with only the Gilbert twins between it and oblivion. If there was any moment to take a chance, it was now.

No more second-guesses.

"Hey, I have an idea. Come on." Valentine plucked at Malcolm's sleeve and began walking down the hill.

"Huh? Where?"

"Field trip!" she called over her shoulder, not breaking stride.

Footsteps approached, and he appeared beside her. "We just finished a mission. The Chrona's going to want a report."

"It took years for her to contact us. She can wait an hour."

"Are you taking me to the Battle of Thermopylae? I've been saving that for a special occasion."

"You'll just have to trust me." She fixed him with a serious eye. "Can you do that?"

He gave an equally serious nod. "You know I can."

"Good."

Taking Malcolm's hand, she pointed the palm of her free hand forward. The motion didn't actually do anything, but it helped her visualize.

At her command, the Aegis opened.

"Okay," she said. "Here we go."

CHAPTER 38

Malcolm examined their new surroundings with a dubious eye. He had expected something a little more exotic.

"You brought me to a high school."

Valentine nodded. "We're in the past."

"Yeah, I felt that. About a decade before we're born." He raised an eyebrow. "But why?"

"Didn't I ask you to trust me?"

She strolled down the empty hallway. With a helpless shrug, Malcolm followed.

It was quiet for now. If his senses were right, it was midafternoon. Soon the last bell would ring and the empty hallway would clog with teens eager to leave.

Maybe something important happens here? Malcolm couldn't make a guess that felt right. Finally, he just surrendered and followed.

Valentine turned down the next hallway. More rows of lockers, more closed classroom doors. Halfway down, she stopped abruptly and leaned back against the lockers.

With a casual air, she folded her hands together. Her gaze

roved idly up and down the hallway, and her fingers tapped out an aimless beat. As if she was waiting for something.

"Relax, Mal," she said. "You look like you expect an attack. It's really just a high school. I promise."

Adopting an exaggerated lazy posture, Malcolm leaned against the lockers beside her.

"Hey, I'm totally chill. Just another day hanging out in someone else's school. That's where I always go to relax: school."

Valentine laughed. "We don't get a lot of quiet moments. Maybe we should enjoy it a little."

She had a point. Since they had sensed the Regent coming . . . no, long before that, since Malcolm first saw someone inside an old house with no doors, life had come at the twins at breakneck speed. Maybe a little idleness now wouldn't hurt.

He tried relaxing for real. He embraced the quiet, empty space with his sister while they could. No one threatening what they loved. Just being. He let slip a sigh, decompressing.

"That's more like it," Valentine said with a grin. "Welcome to the moment."

The final bell rang.

Classroom doors burst open, and students poured out. In seconds, the hallway teemed with them. Silence gave way to loud conversation and squeaks of sneakers on linoleum. The air crackled with excitement as everyone visited their lockers for the final time that day.

"Should I even bother asking what happens next?" Malcolm said.

"You tell me," Valentine replied.

He glanced at her, expecting to see mischief. But it was gone from her eyes. In its place was something with more weight. More significance.

She gripped his hand and nodded forward. "Mal. Look."

He followed her gaze through the students streaming by to the lockers on the opposite wall. Try as he might, though, Malcolm couldn't spot anything. *Though, it's not like I know what I'm—*

There. A lithe, pale-skinned girl with long, red hair, maybe sixteen. Her back was toward the twins as she dug in her locker.

Closing it now, she turned and knelt beside her bag, ready to stuff her books inside. The motion twirled her light-blue sundress and swished her hair aside. Malcolm got his first clear view of her face, and everything inside him stopped.

"Oh, God," he gasped. "Why?"

"Just watch," Valentine whispered, squeezing his hand. She wore an almost-smile now, and there was a hint of tears in her eyes.

Malcolm refocused just as a random guy brushed roughly by the redhead. Weaving far too quickly through the crowd, he didn't stop to notice when he sent her books spilling to the floor.

The girl sighed. "Thanks," she said to the guy's disappearing back, and turned to regather her things.

Another pair of hands was already there, scooping them into a neat stack. The redhead stopped short, looking pleasantly surprised but wary. The hands belonged to a boy about her age, with short, brown hair and a loose flannel shirt.

Malcolm had thought this might be coming. But thinking hadn't prepared him to see it.

When the books were all arranged, the boy met the girl's eyes. Hesitant and sheepish, he offered them back to her.

"Um, thanks," she said.

"He's not a bad guy, really," the boy said as she packed the books away.

"Who?"

"The one who did that. He's got a good heart, just a bad home life."

"Oh," the redhead said. "That's too bad."

"Yeah."

With the books put away, she slung the bag over her shoulder. On the verge of saying goodbye, she stopped short.

"Hey, I know you, right? Fourth period English?"

The boy glanced at the floor. "Oh, um, yes. Miss Weber's class."

"Yeah. You sit in the back, scribbling stories all the time. You really take it seriously."

He brightened, a little less sheepish now. She actually did remember him.

"I've noticed you, too," he said. "Front row, always answering questions. You're quicker than most."

Now the girl seemed sheepish. "Honestly, I just hope participation helps my grade. It's not my best subject. I'm sure that's obvious."

"Oh, not at all. I always like your answers."

They both looked surprised that he'd said that. Clearing his throat, he gestured at her bag.

"Your books. Did I see *Pride and Prejudice* in there?"

"I just started it."

"It's one of my favorites. You're going to love it."

"Already am. I can hardly put it down."

"It only gets better."

The conversation faded there, but the moment didn't. They held each other's gaze, smiling but unsure, as if each of them wondered whether the other felt what was happening. It had come out of nowhere, out of nothing, but suddenly there was . . . something.

Just a glimmer. But it was there.

The girl moved first, holding out her hand. "I'm Emily Clare."

The boy's smile grew as he accepted it. "Neil Gilbert. Nice to meet you."

"Likewise." Her smile grew with his, then turned shy. "Um, I really should get home. See you in class tomorrow?"

"I'll be there."

"Good." Emily turned to leave, then stopped and half-turned back. "Maybe I'll sit a little farther back tomorrow. You know, see what it's like."

The moment *had* been real. Neil knew it now, Malcolm could see it in his eyes.

"Maybe I'll sit a little farther forward," he said. "See what it's like."

Emily's eyes sparkled. With a last little wave, she turned and melted into the crowd.

Neil stared after her for a moment longer. Then, with a laugh of pleasant surprise, he turned and joined the crowd moving the opposite way.

Malcolm's heart felt as if it could explode. Though tears streamed down his cheeks, he wore a smile that burst with joy. These weren't tears of sorrow or loss, but of happiness at having seen a moment no one ever got to see.

The moment his parents met. The very first moment of all the happy years Neil and Emily would spend together. Already Malcolm could see the seeds of how much they would grow to love each other.

What a gift Valentine had given him. A moment of pure goodness and light.

Malcolm couldn't help thinking forward. Knowing what was to come made this day more precious. Knowing the darkness that would cover them all when Emily Gilbert's light went out.

He thought of his father's grief. The memories of those bleak years were still vivid. Secretly Malcolm had resented Neil for falling as he did. For tumbling down into sorrow without knowing the way out. Now he understood that loss, and the black chasm it tore open in the soul.

Still, there was hope, wasn't there? Their dad had eventually climbed his way out and found the strength to heal, to keep loving the memory of Emily Gilbert while also letting her go, so he could live a whole life again.

With that realization, Malcolm knew why Valentine had brought him here. Really, he had known since the day they left with the Chrona. His heart just hadn't been ready to face it.

He still didn't feel ready, but that mattered little. The world was counting on the Gilbert twins, and Time was running out. So, he would just have to find a way.

He stared down at the floor, gathering the strength to say it.

"I have to let Asha go, don't I?"

Valentine hesitated. "Yeah."

He shook his head, momentarily bitter. "Of course we wouldn't get to mourn like normal people. Not when the world needs saving."

"I'm sorry, Mal."

This was really happening. Just as he had done with his mother, Malcolm had to choose to move on. Not because he was ready, but because the world needed him to.

So, he would gather all his memories of her. Every moment,

every feeling, every touch and kiss and smile and whispered sweet nothing. Every quick look that conveyed a lifetime of love. He would collect them, put them in a book that would be cherished forever.

Then he would put that book on a shelf. When he was feeling strong enough, he would take it down and flip through its pages. He would remember the warmth of Asha's embrace. The eager gleam in her eye when she drew her blades. The ferocity with which she loved him.

He was trembling now. Before he could say anything else, Valentine pulled him into a tight embrace. Only then did the tears fall freely.

"I'm scared, Val," he confessed. "What if I can't let go?"

She squeezed him tighter. "Don't worry. I'm here. I'll protect you. What are sisters for, if not this? We'll find the strength together."

Somehow, he believed her.

CHAPTER 39

Winter watched with grim pleasure as the Ember Guard swarmed the Destroyer.

The battle tank went down, its cockpit hatch shattering with a satisfying crunch. Winter caught a flash as the pilot fell away through a portal.

Beside her, Tyrathorn stared darkly at the Destroyer. The Ember Guard turned in his direction, and he nodded his approval.

"Well done."

Winter and Tyrathorn had taken great pleasure in joining the fight with this squad. Captain Armel had objected, of course. Protecting them was his primary responsibility. When Winter had suggested leading a covert attack squad to pick off stray machines, his displeasure had been plain.

The king and queen should be leading their people, he had said. Without precisely saying the word "irresponsible," he had skillfully implied it.

Winter couldn't bring herself to care. Not while her husband had that look in his eye, a storm of grief, guilt, and helpless rage.

Asha's death was shredding Tyrathorn inside. To have any

chance of coping, he needed action. He needed to *do*. So here they were, striking with Ember Guard and elite Watchers at their backs.

Squeezing his hand, she inclined her head toward the Destroyer. "Care to collect our trophy?"

Tyrathorn gave a wan smile. "Of course, my love."

He was spent, she could see it. But this would be worth the effort. Their soldiers needed it, and even if he couldn't admit it, the king needed it, too.

They approached the hulking machine, then climbed toward the cockpit. Inside, there would be an insignia that marked this Destroyer's battle group. Even Cyonics had small ones inside their armor. That crest would be leaving with them now.

When Winter had learned about the insignias, she had turned their hunt into a collect-the-whole-set game. Now, peering through the shattered armor, she spotted their objective and pointed.

"There. It's closer to you."

Tyrathorn reached into the cockpit. Just short of touching their trophy, he stopped cold. Alarmed, he stared up at her.

"Did you look at this insignia?"

"Yeah. Different battle group. We can start a whole new set with that one."

He stared harder now, a look with significance. When he spoke next, his voice had lowered so only she could hear.

"Winter, have you ever seen this one before? On *any* machine?"

Winter looked closer, wracking her brain for a matching memory. When she realized that she couldn't, she understood the dread in Tyrathorn's voice.

"Oh, no," she said. "We have to get back to the Command Center *now*."

Twenty-seven hours.

John closed his sore and bleary eyes, pinching the bridge of his nose. *Please, just let me keep them safe for one more day.*

"A new insignia," he repeated. "The Destroyer could be from a reserve force."

"Unlikely," Tyrathorn said. "We engaged many machines inside the Pyre, and collected every unique insignia we found. None were like this."

John huffed, frustrated that he wasn't connecting the dots. "Are they making more units in the Pyre? I didn't see evidence of a factory."

"There's a chance it doesn't mean anything," Winter replied. "But we couldn't ignore it this late in the game."

"Agreed," Walter said, looking grim but tough in his Watcher armor. "At the very least, now we know."

"And knowing is half the battle," Fred intoned.

John moved to respond, but stopped short. *Wait a minute.*

There might be an explanation. As John turned it over in his mind and examined it from every angle, it began to feel more like a probability. And the more right it felt, the more he hoped it was wrong.

"Give me a minute," he said.

John stepped back to the viewport. The technicians on either side straightened, shaking away stiffness as they prepared to execute his orders. These were six new technicians—apparently, he'd worn out the original set.

"News crews are still filming the other five Pyres?" he asked.

"From a distance, but yes," a technician to his right replied.

"Find the three clearest feeds for each Pyre and pass them to my display, please. Starting eighteen hours ago."

His people went to work. Slow footsteps approached from behind, and a presence appeared at his side.

"You look like a predator who's caught his prey, but doesn't like how it tastes," Captain Armel said quietly. "What are you not saying?"

John resisted the urge to flinch. The captain's fist had hit even harder than expected, and the memory was still vivid—as were the bruises on his face. Armel had apologized, but it was plain how frayed everyone had become.

"Only a theory," John muttered. "A bad one, I pray."

Videos began popping up on the glass. Each began with a time stamp eighteen hours old, not long after the first battle in Emmett's Bluff had concluded.

"Please watch, captain," John said. "A second set of eyes would be helpful."

"What am I looking for?"

"I have feeling you'll know."

If he was right, it would happen gradually. Too gradually for the casual observer to notice in the moment. There were advantages, however, to watching after the fact.

"Synchronize all time stamps, then play at ten times speed."

The pictures adjusted as his people matched the videos' time stamps to each other. Now they would watch events unfold simultaneously across the world, eighteen hours ago. When each feed was in line with the others, they began to play.

At ten times speed, everything moved with unnatural speed and sharpness. While vaguely uncomfortable to watch, it helped John isolate what he needed.

Around each skyscraper, a large radius had been cleared of anything except the Regent's army. No people, no cars; sometimes even trees and buildings were taken down. Which meant the only consistently moving objects in view were the machines themselves.

John watched them patrol, tracing out overlapping patterns. At ten times speed it was easy to see the complex pattern unfold.

Cyonics, Destroyers, and even an occasional Praetorian made an appearance. John soaked in the feeds, translating what he saw into usable data. After ten minutes, he reached a preliminary conclusion.

"Each Pyre has an army of roughly identical size to the one we fought here," he told Armel. "Would you agree?"

"I have only observed one location so far." The captain eyed him. "Were you watching all five at once? And tabulating numbers?"

Oh. John had assumed they all were. He shrugged.

Armel shook his head in disbelief, but moved on. "For the New Zealand location, I agree, and defer to your judgement about the others."

"Okay." John steeled himself for this next part. "Advance all feeds five hours, twenty times viewing speed."

The technicians complied. John's eyes flitted frantically back and forth now, consuming every bit of data racing across the screens while his mind crunched them into figures.

"Advance five more hours. Increase to thirty times speed."

All other sights and sounds faded away. John's existence focused down to machine placements and patrol patterns and deployment numbers, until finally he was able to lock them together and see the pattern he'd been afraid to see all along.

"You devil," he muttered, thinking of the Regent.

"What?" Winter said. "What do you see?"

The discovery sat like a brick in his stomach. Slowly he turned to face his allies, who watched him worriedly. They were right to feel that way.

"Over these hours, each Pyre has deployed fewer machines to patrol," he said. "They rearrange the patrol patterns to hide the reduction in numbers. But every hour, more machines rotate back inside the Pyre and never reemerge."

He gestured at a technician. "Advance the feeds until they're live."

The videos leapt forward, and now even his friends could spot it. John saw the truth reflected on their faces.

"Help me out here," Neil Gilbert said. "What does all this mean?"

"Based on this, and on what Winter and Tyrathorn discovered," John paused to gather his courage to say it, "I believe those armies are being transferred to Emmett's Bluff. I suspect the Regent is hiding most of them inside the Pyre until he chooses to strike."

"So, you're sayin' next time we fight 'em," Fred said, "we're gonna face an army five times bigger than the last one?"

"I believe so."

Heavy silence filled the Command Center. John searched for something encouraging to say, something to soften the blow. He came up empty.

Then Tyrathorn stepped forward, standing tall. "Take heart, my friends. We still have many things the enemy does not, and wars are not won with numbers alone."

"Doesn't matter what they throw at us," Walter said. "We'll hold the line. We have to."

Brave words from both warriors. But more than ever, even

their fatigue was showing. Their hearts had already been broken. *Can we even last another day?* John wondered.

Tyrathorn leaned on Winter as if she were the only thing keeping him upright. Grace had shed plenty of tears for Asha and Malcolm, and looked ready to shed more. Neil floated between everyone, unsure what he should be doing. Callie was like a sphinx, any inner pain kept under a thick layer of assassin training. On the outside, she was a coiled snake ready to strike at the enemy.

For a split second, habit moved John to scan the room for Asha, and for his old friend Clive. His thoughts stumbled when they weren't there. More than ever, he felt the gaping maw of their absence. Before that emptiness could swallow him, he turned back to his job.

"We need strategies, and I'm open to suggestions." He tried hard to keep the desperation from his voice, only half-succeeding. "Bold moves, crazy ideas. Anything to keep the Timeline in one piece for twenty-seven hours."

He met a sea of hollow gazes, until finally someone answered with something suitably crazy.

"The Pendulum," Walter said. "How many are we holding there?"

Captain Armel stiffened. "Crane, you cannot be suggesting what I think you are."

"Desperate times, captain," Walter said.

"What is the Pendulum?" Callie asked.

"A prison below the Eon Palace," Winter said. "Highly advanced."

"Yo, seriously, we're sitting on a prison?" Fred said. "How advanced?"

"Advanced enough to hold rogue Chronauri. People who threatened the Timeline enough to be hunted down by the Ember Guard."

"Yes," Captain Armel said. "They are prisoners for good reason."

"And if we fail, they die like the rest of us," Walter said. "This is war, captain. Even the worst criminals would fight to save themselves."

"Out of the question!"

"Stop me if I'm wrong," Grace said. "But don't the machine numbers only matter if they get past the shield?"

Fred snorted quietly to himself, then noticed everyone looking in his direction. He put on an innocent face, tried and failed to turn the snort into a cough.

"Well?" Winter demanded.

"Well, what?"

"Why don't you share with the class?"

Fred shook his head. "Naw, girl. It ain't a helpful thought."

"Fred," Tyrathorn said wearily, "given what we face, honesty should be the least of our fears. We are friends. Please say what you think."

He really didn't want to. John could see that much. Wherever Fred had traveled these past two years, whatever his experiences in training so strenuously, he really had grown. There was actually a filter, now, between his brain and his mouth. Even if it was a small one.

"Well," he began, but stopped himself. Then all at once he barreled ahead. "We're gettin' our butts kicked up and down the street. A few wins, yeah, but mainly we're just surviving.

As badly as the Regent's been servin' us, do y'all really expect him *not* to get past the shield?"

Two hours later, John stood outside the door to Winter and Tyrathorn's stateroom, wondering if he should knock or just turn and leave.

After agreeing on a few possible plans, everyone had gone to grab what moments of rest they could. John had elected to stay in the Command Center, reviewing footage he'd grabbed from the Pyre.

Which led to him finding . . . what he found. Which led to him standing there with a memory stick burning a hole in his pocket. John tried to put himself in Tyrathorn's place. Would this bolster him or destroy him?

You are neither warrior nor king, he reminded himself. Any prediction would be no better than a guess. However, some instinct had moved him this far. Maybe he should follow it a little farther.

He knocked on the door.

Winter appeared, looking ready for bed. "Whatever it is, can it wait?"

He held up his hands. "I only need a minute, then I'll leave you to rest."

Winter beckoned him inside and he followed her to a sitting area. She called for Tyrathorn, and a moment later he arrived, still toweling off from a shower. Despite being in his forties now, the king kept himself in impressive fighting shape. Muscles rippled as he sat next to his wife.

"Welcome, John," he said. "What can we do for you?"

John fiddled with the memory stick, uncertain again. *Stop. You're already here; just do it.*

"I found something," he forced out. "You may want to see it, or hate me for showing you. But given who you are, Thorn, and given who *she* was, something told me it would be important."

He set the memory stick on the table between them.

"We knew Asha threw herself into battle to protect your retreat. We knew she was a key reason you escaped. But until now, we had no idea how much we all owe her."

Winter gestured at the object. "What's on that?"

"The Pyre has cameras everywhere. I stole as much as I could. I would have shown you before now, but I didn't realize I had this."

"Please," Tyrathorn said, desperate. "Just tell us."

John steeled himself. "It's Asha's last fight. It shows how she saved you. How she saved *everything*. Thorn, she didn't just face Cyonics, and she didn't just slow the Regent down. She fought like I've never seen to keep him from getting to the Sled. In her last moments, she hurt him—*really* hurt him. It was the most amazing thing I've ever seen."

His friends sat frozen, eyeing the memory stick as if it were a snake.

"So, watch the file or just burn it. I wasn't sure what you'd want, but I knew I had to tell you. Asha died a hero. Everyone should know it."

With the bombshell dropped, John excused himself and left the couple alone.

CHAPTER 40

Swirling lights faded as the twins stepped back into the Aegis. The temporal doorway sealed shut behind them. Its appearance had changed from the Italian countryside to Dunnottar Castle. Not the ruins in the twins' century, but Dunnottar Castle in its prime. Situated at the peak of a green and rocky hill, it overlooked the waters of the northeastern Scottish coast.

Malcolm noted the gray skies and chill winds. Today of all days, that suited him. An appropriate setting for a funeral.

"Give me a few minutes?" he said.

Valentine nodded. "I'll see you inside."

Leaving him to his task, she went inside the castle and shut the heavy oak door. Alone, Malcolm turned to search for the right spot.

After a half hour of wandering, he found it. At the forefront of the castle grounds, a raised earthen outcropping looked out over the sea. Standing there, casting his gaze outward, all Malcolm could see were the waves below and the scuttling, gray clouds above.

A place to say goodbye.

He settled onto the grass, unsure where to start. What to

say. All he knew was that speaking into the wind didn't feel right. Asha deserved more, and he was in a unique position to give it to her.

With a gesture, Malcolm opened a window like the Chrona had used. Like a two-way mirror, he formed it in such a way that he could see through it without anyone knowing it was there.

But which moment to choose? Which Asha to speak to?

Malcolm unfocused his thoughts, filling his mind with memories of her: every smile, every brush of her hand, even the look of intense satisfaction as her blades glowed red. All that was Asha filled Malcolm.

Full of her memory, he cast his will across the Timeline. Using the window like a search light, he wandered across the ages in search of Asha, memories and echoes of the girl he loved more than life.

His thoughts found Everwatch. In the near future, he glimpsed the vigil they would hold for her. A quarter million people filled the streets, holding torches high and singing to the legacy of their warrior princess.

King Tyrathorn had decided to share publicly the footage of Asha's final battle, so that all would see what she had done. Through their eyes, Malcolm watched her stand before the Regent, a mortal facing down godlike power, unwavering.

Asha Doomslayer, they called her, for she had opposed a force of pure destruction and come out victorious. Malcolm's love and admiration soared to new heights.

"Live," she had said. "Everyone live. For me."

He nearly lost himself at those words. *I can't do it. I can't let go; how can I?*

No. Asha would never have tolerated him wallowing forever.

She would have been the first to kick him back up to his feet. To tell him to put his armor on and finish this war.

He pressed further into the future, to a day soon after the vigil. As the sun rose, its rays met something new in the center of Meridian Square. A statue had appeared there overnight, its origins a mystery. The Eon Palace had not commissioned it, and no one ever claimed credit. But somewhere in Everwatch a citizen had chosen their own way to honor her.

The artist must have been a master of the highest order. The statue stood eight feet tall, depicting Asha in the finest detail, perfectly matching even the way she stood. Wearing an expression of defiance, she stared at some unseen enemy with *qamas* held high. The blades glowed with inner light, coruscating shades of red.

At her feet, a plaque was embedded in the base.

ASHANDARA CORVONIAN
PRINCESS OF EVERWATCH
DOOMSLAYER
"I'M NOT MOVING."

Malcolm hadn't realized how much he needed this. Knowing that Asha would be remembered—not just by those who loved her, but by those who owed her their survival—made what he had to do just a little less agonizing.

Now only one thing remained. The window changed. Leaving the future of Everwatch behind, he dove instead into the past.

The years reversed until the window opened on Regeneration Day; one of many, but the only one the Gilbert twins had been present for.

Malcolm's window flew to the top of the Eon Palace. It

found an atrium, a wide courtyard of stones surrounded by trees. Raindrops fell through the open roof and into a temporal bubble.

Inside the bubble, Malcolm and Asha shared their first kiss, the kiss that broke everything open between them. The kiss that promised a thousand kisses to follow.

Until Asha battled her way into his life, Malcolm had believed he would spend it alone. Somehow, he just knew that his path would curve in other directions. Love and companionship were the destiny of others, like his sister.

Asha had changed everything. Whatever Malcolm's future had in store, nothing could take away the years he had spent loving her.

Talk to her. Say what you need to say.

On the other side of the window, Asha held him in a tight embrace. Malcolm focused on her ice-blue eyes—that gaze that never failed to pull him in—and spoke.

"You're not gone," he said. "Not really. I've learned that when someone dies young, they give their Time back to the universe. So your Time, your energy, it's still out there. It's part of the flow, helping to power the Timeline. I can *feel* it."

His chest was tightening. He took a deep breath and pushed on.

"But you were so much more. Others will remember how you fought, but . . . I'll remember how you fit in my arms. How you kissed me like I was the only thing you wanted in the world. Every breath, every look, every moment, I'll carry them with me. Forever."

Malcolm choked back his tears.

"But you're part of the universe now, so . . . I have to give you back to it. *That* Malcolm," he gestured through the window, "you're his forever. But I have to let you go, so I can save everyone else. I have to say goodbye."

Reaching out, Malcolm brushed his fingers across the window. Ripples wafted out from his touch. Asha's faced hovered seemingly inches away, wearing a look of pure contentment.

"I love you, Asha."

Through the window, Asha looked up suddenly and glanced around, as if searching.

"What is it?" past Malcolm asked.

After a moment, she relaxed. "Nothing. I thought someone called my name."

Agape, Malcolm drew back, hands covering his mouth. *I remember that!* He recalled the moment as if it was yesterday. A moment enraptured, with the girl of his dreams in his arms at last, and it seemed her ears had played tricks on her.

Only they hadn't. Malcolm himself had called to her across Time.

Though he expected the realization to hurt, somehow it did the opposite. Now more than ever he knew the truth. No matter what the future held, somewhere in Time, there was a moment when Malcolm and Asha would always be together.

With that truth came peace. Malcolm tucked it away in a corner of his heart, wrapped around his memories of Asha. There they would live, a quiet part of him for the rest of his days.

Gazing through the window, Malcolm allowed himself one last moment.

"Goodbye, Asha."

He released his hold. Slowly the window unraveled, and the vision on the other side faded away. Wiping away tears, Malcolm stood and walked with renewed purpose back to Castle Dunnottar.

He couldn't let anything hold him back now. The universe's survival depended on it.

Valentine met him at the front door. Her face was pinched with worry.

"Val?"

"It's happening again," she said. "Worse than ever."

"Mother?" The Chrona's voice echoed through the castle, desperate and fearful. "Mother, please. I'm scared! Where are you?"

Hot on Valentine's heels, Malcolm entered the dining hall. In the corner, next to a blazing fireplace, the Chrona sat huddled in shadows. She cringed when she saw the twins approach. Valentine stopped short and held out her arm to halt Malcolm.

"Slowly, or she'll run."

"How long?" Malcolm asked.

"I found her this way when we got back. But I didn't want to interrupt you."

"Thanks."

"Please don't hurt her," the Chrona pleaded. "Let me see her? I'll be good!"

Valentine was right. This was worse than the other times. Now, instead of momentarily going blank, the master of all Time seemed to be regressing back to childhood.

Malcolm sighed. "Even here, we're running out of Time. We've got to help her hold it together."

"How?"

"No idea." Malcolm took a tentative step forward. "Let's just start with bringing her back."

Together they advanced toward the Chrona, slow step after

slow step, careful not to make sudden movements. Hands up in a placating gesture, Malcolm tried to speak calmly.

"Arsinoë? We're your friends. We just want to help."

"I don't know you!" The old woman raked at the wall behind her. "I don't!"

Valentine gestured at the castle. "This might be part of the problem. I hadn't thought of that before."

She had a point. With a wave of his hand, Malcolm instructed the Aegis to revert to its natural appearance. The castle and surrounding country faded away.

With a cry, the Chrona tried to back away, not a spark of recognition in her eyes. Malcolm caught her hand. Locating the flow of Time around her heart, he slowed it down ever so slightly.

Next, he dipped his will into the Timeline below and absorbed a small amount of Time. With a flick, he sent a cool wave of slowed Time through the Chrona. As it passed, Malcolm hoped it would help her calm down.

The Chrona stopped struggling. Blinking, she stared at her surroundings in every direction, and finally down at Malcolm's hand grasping hers.

"Do you intend to ask me to dance, Malcolm?"

With a relieved smile, Malcolm let go and stood. "Welcome back."

"Nice trick," Valentine said. "When did you figure that out?"

"Just now," he chuckled. He turned a grateful eye on her. "You were right. I . . . needed to do that. Thanks."

She squeezed his arm. "Of course."

"How long this time?" The Chrona asked, climbing to her feet.

Valentine winced. "Longer."

"Cracks in my own mind." The Chrona grimaced. "As if

cracks in the Timeline weren't enough. Going mad is decidedly annoying."

Conversation continued between the two women, but for Malcolm their voices faded. His attention fell into the crystalline floor of the Aegis. He could see Emmett's Bluff in the hours following the twins' departure.

The Chrona had forbidden them from looking in on those forty-six hours. Whatever struggles their friends were facing, it would help nothing for them to abandon training early to help. In fact, going back too soon might shatter the dangerously fragile fabric of the universe there.

Malcolm had heeded the warning, not focusing closely enough to see individual moments or people. Even from this vantage point, though, it was impossible to miss the spreading cracks, like fiery spiderwebs. They multiplied even as he watched.

Then it struck him like a lightning bolt. "They're connected!"

The conversation halted. Valentine and the Chrona turned.

"Context, Malcolm," the Chrona said.

"Oh, right. The damage to the Timeline and your brain thing—I'll bet they're connected. You and the others built this place with your own power, right? You've also lived here for . . . how many years?"

The Chrona's eyes unfocused. "I can scarcely remember. Has it been billions? More?"

"That's a good point," Valentine said. "We know the damage to the Timeline has accelerated because of the Regent. I'd actually be surprised if it didn't affect you."

"Which means if we can fix the Timeline somehow, that might just fix you."

The Chrona pondered this, her face changing from resistance to fear, then to curiosity, then cautious hope.

"I never considered that." She gestured down at her aged body. "As my mind has splintered, my bond with Time has also been slipping, which accounts for my physically aging while Helios still appears young. Even in my thoughts, I have begun to feel old. If you are right, though, it's a glimmer of hope I've not had in a long while. I would very much like to return to my prime. To protect the Timeline properly once again."

"Another reason to win," Valentine said.

"Not a moment to lose, then," the Chrona said. "Back to work?"

The twins eagerly agreed. With a gesture, she conjured projections of three seats arranged facing each other. They all sat.

"Your mission at Vesuvius," she said, all business again. "What did you learn?"

"How to stop Time," Valentine said proudly. "I thought it was impossible."

"For any less than Sixth-*sev*, it would be, but you also found the secret. Not even I could stop the whole Timeline. One might as well command Victoria Falls to freeze with but a look. But . . ."

Valentine picked up the thread. "If you separate a smaller area from the whole Timeline, you can stop that piece."

"Correct, and well done. Malcolm, you also developed a new skill, moving through Valentine's stopped Time unaffected. That was clever work."

Malcolm beamed. "Thanks."

"Now, what else did you two learn?"

On the verge of responding, Malcolm stopped short. His sister looked equally puzzled.

"You mean, like a life lesson or something?" Valentine said.

"In a way. This responsibility we have, what did you learn about it? What new challenge did Cosima make you face?"

"Cosima? Oh, the volcano woman?" Valentine said.

The Chrona nodded. "I warned her before not to follow through with her plan. That's how she knew my name. As you see, though, some people simply will not listen."

Valentine went back to looking puzzled. Malcolm reviewed every moment of their encounter. Even as non-Chronauri, she had posed a formidable challenge, not to mention . . .

That was it.

"She wasn't doing something evil," he said. "She was trying to save lives."

Realization bloomed on Valentine's face. "Yes."

"It all happened so fast," Malcolm offered. "I'll admit, even I wondered if we should just let her do it."

"And therein lies the lesson," the Chrona said. "Your compassion is admirable. However, sometimes we must make choices that seem harsh in the moment but serve a greater purpose. Tragedies happen, and not only can we not prevent them all, we *should* not. The Timeline is too important to be bent to one, or two, or three people's will. For Cosima, the distortions in the Timeline from that one change would have been immeasurable."

"And who knows if saving that one city might result in greater evil later," Valentine said.

"Perhaps. Yet, there is an even greater application." The Chrona leaned forward. "If we defeat Helios, our task will not stop there. For thousands of years, he has slowly corrupted the course of world events, working behind the scenes until finally he could position himself as world leader. Now, think of how he is viewed in Callie's century."

"Everyone loves him," Malcolm said.

"Yes. This could not have happened if he didn't do positive things for them. Yet they were for evil ends, and they resulted in a history corrupted by one man's obsession. To return order to the Timeline, we must right his wrongs, even if they seem good in the short term."

Sitting back, Malcolm blew out a breath. He understood the reasoning and the necessity, but the thought of undoing more events that seemed positive would never be easy.

"Too bad we can't just, I don't know, *remodel* the Aegis," he said. "Tear out what's not working, put in new and improved rules. Maybe that could help the Timeline heal."

The Chrona frowned. "What do you mean, what's not working?"

She really hadn't thought about this? Malcolm furrowed his brow.

"I know you did the best you could, but even you have to see the problems. The Aegis, the rules you put in place, they're not really working."

"Mal," Valentine warned.

He waved away her objection. They needed real talk.

The Chrona bristled. "Have you seen the universe break apart anytime recently?"

"Ask me in a few days," he returned more hotly than he'd intended. He took a slow breath and regrouped. "You did what no one else could have. I know that. But you built the Aegis as if we live in a perfect world, and we don't. Time travel damages the Aegis because your goal was to keep people from doing it. But of course they were going to, so why not build a way to do it safely? Something like . . . Timeways, special roads with more enforceable rules."

"Timeways?" Valentine smirked.

Despite himself, Malcolm laughed. "Fine, you can pick the name. The point is, the Aegis would be easier to protect this way. Allow for Time travel under certain conditions. Allow minor adjustments to events as long as they don't impact the Timeline as a whole. I'm sure Everwatch would help you monitor it. People are going to try whether you allow them to or not, so why not adapt? It's like an earthquake-proof building. They survive because they're flexible."

He stopped, having said more than he had intended. He wasn't sure if his ideas were possible. All he knew was the old ways were no longer working, and something had to change. Malcolm hoped the Chrona could see his good intentions.

For a long moment, the old woman stared at the floor, eyes unfocused as she processed Malcolm's words. What was she seeing?

"I had forgotten what it feels like," she finally said. "Humility. Accepting instruction. Perhaps I have lived up here for too long. Heard only my own thoughts for too long."

As she looked up at Malcolm, her expression softened.

"There is much for you to learn. Still, perhaps the seed of your idea is valid. I cannot remake the Aegis. But there may be ways to improve it. As you grow, we will talk more on this."

She studied Malcolm more closely now.

"I sense a change in you. How do you feel?"

He cast another grateful look at his sister. "I feel . . . ready."

The Chrona nodded, looking pleased.

"Good. Then we shall step up your training."

Without warning she struck, Time warping around her. As if in slow motion, Malcolm watched her attack fly at them.

The twins leapt to their feet and prepared to defend.

CHAPTER 41

While seconds ticked by in Emmett's Bluff, days passed in the Aegis. Valentine hoped her friends were holding on.

Today the twins were trapped in a literal maze, a fun house of death for anyone less than a high-level Chronauri. Now that Malcolm had dealt with his grief and caught up with Valentine, the Chrona had stopped holding back.

Coming around a blind corner, Valentine gasped and dropped to the ground. Some kind of Time tornado flew overhead, moving sideways as if it had been shot from a rifle. Valentine's insides roiled in sympathy with the way the tornado twisted Time, weaponizing it.

"No, girl!" the Chrona's voice echoed off the stone-and-steel walls. "You still behave like your old self."

Kicking off the ground, Valentine flipped back to her feet and kept moving.

"Your first instinct is to act physically, not temporally," the Chrona continued. "You must come to see Time as your heartbeat, your muscles, a seamless extension of yourself. If you cannot, the universe contains clever rogues who will gladly take you down."

In the distance, there was a small explosion. Valentine heard her brother's startled yelp.

"You, Malcolm, think *too* hard about what you're doing," the Chrona said. "Creative solutions have their place, but you must also learn that brute force is a viable tool. Let instinct decide for you in the moment."

Since Malcolm's breakthrough, their days had become an exhausting blur. Training, then listening for hours as the Chrona lectured on the nature of Time and its place in the universe, which informed their own place in it.

Then combat training, as they were doing now. The Chrona liked to grin and call it "aggressive survival."

With the Aegis at her fingertips, she could create any conditions she wanted to throw at them. Unlike when she had rescued them from the Regent, the Chrona's power here seemed inexhaustible.

Valentine felt a subtle *shift* beneath her feet. She began to leap out of the way, but then stopped herself. *No, think temporally. My Time is far more powerful than my body.*

Casting a wave of slowed Time down through the ground, she felt whatever was approaching slow to a crawl. At a leisurely pace now, she moved twenty feet away and prepared her response.

A giant drill burst through the ground where she had stood. Inside the spiraled tip, Valentine sensed a warhead of compressed temporal energy like John's grenades.

Weapons like this no longer worried her. Absorbing Time, Valentine shaped it into a spike and flung it. As it pierced the warhead, she willed it to burst into razor-sharp shards of Time. The warhead shredded, energy dissipating.

"Better," the Chrona said. "Keep pushing. You are not axial yet."

That word again. *Axial*. The Chrona kept saying it but wouldn't fully explain what she meant. Only that it was something the twins had not yet achieved, something important that she was pushing them toward.

Tyrathorn had talked about the Axial Shift, the moment when the Chrona, the Regent, and his sister Selene had first achieved Chronauri power. Did this relate to that?

Valentine pushed aside the questions. With a smirk, she nodded. "I'll keep that in mind."

The smirk wasn't a reaction to her teacher. It was a moment of triumph. Finally, she had traced the source of that warhead's power. *Here's some brute force for you.*

Valentine turned to face a stone wall. Drinking in Time, she willed a selection of atoms to move faster, and faster, until they were vibrating violently against the atoms moving at normal speed.

A grinding sound. Then a shudder. The stones tore themselves apart in bursts of light.

On the other side, the Chrona waited in a secret chamber. *Capture me before I take you down*, she had challenged. Now she looked at Valentine with surprise.

Behind the old woman, the stones in the far wall began to glow. Waves of heat emanated as they grew to bright orange, then sank into a molten pool. Standing on the other side, Malcolm pumped his fist in triumph.

Valentine laughed. When she looked back at their teacher, though, the Chrona's expression had changed from surprise to something devious.

She waved a hand at Valentine, and a vortex opened

between them. An earsplitting horn blared, and a locomotive burst through the portal, barreling toward her.

Valentine fell back with a cry. Acting on instinct, she enveloped the nose of the locomotive in super-fast Time. She had aged objects into disintegration this way before.

Survive. Her instinct shut out all other thoughts. Valentine poured all her power into the bubble, then opened her being like a conduit and channeled more, forcing Time inside it to spin faster and faster and faster until the *shift.*

A Night Blossom!

The bubble collapsed into a pinpoint of light, then darkened into an orb of impossibly deep black. Inky shadows wafted from it in waves, cresting over each other and then collapsing back into the orb.

It started the size of a marble. Then the locomotive began to warp with a metallic screech, and the orb inflated to the size of a beach ball.

The locomotive's nose crumpled and disappeared into the orb. Again the blackness grew, and again a sound of rending metal filled the air. As if it were being eaten by a shadow monster, the great machine collapsed into Night Blossom and disappeared.

The blackness kept growing. Valentine had seen this before. Night Blossoms never faded on their own, only grew more ravenous until they were shut down.

Surrounding the orb in a temporal bubble, she infused a constant rush of Time. The pressure would force the Night Blossom closed. But this one had grown larger than the others, and Valentine felt it resist her.

She felt a flash of cold fear. Then the Chrona's signature wrested control of the bubble from her. Commanding an astonishing amount of Time, she collapsed the orb and unraveled the bubble.

With a relieved sigh, Valentine rested her hands on her knees and worked to catch her breath.

"Night Blossom," Malcolm called. "Nice one."

Shaking her head, she straightened. "Scary but effective, I guess. First time I've had a train thrown at me, so . . ."

The Chrona stepped up and smacked her hard across the face. Dazed, Valentine grabbed at her stinging cheek. The old woman had put some of her power behind that strike.

"Whoa!" Malcolm said, sprinting toward them.

Valentine met the Chrona's glare with her own. "Hey, what the?"

"*Never* that, girl. Not ever! Do you realize what you might have done?"

Malcolm arrived then and must have noted the dangerous look in Valentine's eye. He gripped her shoulder.

"Let it go. Like steam, remember?" He turned to the Chrona. "But that was not cool."

"Night Blossom," the Chrona spat. "Giving it a name does not make it less foolish."

Valentine closed her eyes as they spoke. She had to come down from this, or it would just keep building inside her. Gathering the fear, the stress, and the anger, she imagined them rising from her body like steam and evaporating.

"Well, maybe you should have warned us how dangerous it is," Malcolm said.

"I did not believe you powerful enough to do it," the Chrona explained. "Not yet."

"Then who really failed here?" Malcolm returned. "The student or the teacher?"

In the ensuing silence, Valentine opened her eyes to see the Chrona regarding her. The old woman's expression had softened.

"My apologies, Valentine. In this case, you deserve better instruction. I allowed fear to govern my actions, and that will never do. It will not happen again, you have my word."

Calmer now, Valentine offered a conciliatory smile. "It's okay. We're all stressed."

"I must remind myself that you two are not Helios and Selene. You do not possess the dark ambition that drove them. Still, I am trying to teach you responsibility from the beginning."

"And we're grateful," Malcolm said. "Maybe we should take a break. I feel like we've been going for days."

With a gesture, he summoned plush chairs arranged in a circle, as they had so many times before. Valentine sank into hers with an involuntary sigh.

"I've forgotten what an actual day feels like," she said.

"The Aegis will do that," the Chrona said. "When you exist above the flow of Time, your perception changes."

Valentine understood that now. The longer they stayed, the harder it was to gauge exactly how many weeks had passed. She couldn't imagine the Chrona's feeling after countless years.

Despite the endless lessons, she still felt woefully under-educated about Time and the universe. So much to learn, and despite what the Aegis did with Time, there wasn't any to waste.

"Would you tell me more about the Night Blossom?" she asked. "Is it like a black hole?"

"It is far more dangerous. What you call a Night Blossom is, in truth, a tear in the universe so deep that it goes beyond reality itself. Essentially, Valentine, you cut through Time, space, and the universe until you reached the black oblivion that lies beyond all things. An infinite expanse of nothingness that even I do not fully comprehend.

"Wow," Malcolm said. "Is there anything beyond it?"

"I truly do not know. Perhaps beyond the black there is another reality, another universe, or perhaps merely an endless void. Either way, whatever touches your sphere cannot escape. It falls out of reality and into eternal nothingness. In the truest sense, it ceases to exist forever."

Valentine shivered. "Glad I never got curious and touched it."

"If you had, you would not be here with us. I doubt even I could withstand it. Once it has you, it does not let go until you are consumed, and then its hunger only increases. That is the real danger—if a Night Blossom escaped your control, it could grow until it consumes the universe itself. Even a Sixth-*sev* has her limits."

"Good thing no one else can do it," Malcolm said. "Someone would try to make it a weapon."

The Chrona winced. "Someone did, boy. Before Selene died, she tried to defeat me with one. Only with great effort was I able to close it before it did real damage."

With that information, questions came back into Valentine's mind. Questions she had decided not to ask before, as the Chrona didn't appear ready to speak of it. Now, though, they couldn't hold anything back.

"What happened to you three?" she asked. "How did you become this?"

"And what really happened when you fought?" Malcolm asked, looking excited that they finally got to talk about this.

The Chrona leaned back in her chair, her eyes unfocused as if she were staring into a memory. For minutes, she made no reply. Valentine began to wonder if she would answer at all. But then . . .

"Assassins found us," she began. "Cleopatra had hired very famous and very feared assassins to find and kill me. When I faked my death and went into hiding, they believed their job finished. However, years later, while I masqueraded as the twins' governess, one of them recognized me. That night, a great lightning storm descended on our city. I had been at the market with Helios and Selene, and I cut through back alleys to rush them home. That is where they fell upon us."

Shuddering, she drew in a slow breath, as if preparing to relive the moment.

"It happened so quickly. A flash of knives in the dark. I saw the children fall, and before I could even cry out, a blade plunged into my heart. As I fell, lightning flashed and thunder shook the ground. Then, as blackness closed around me, I saw a light that was brighter than all others. I could see it *and* feel it. With my dying breath, I reached out and somehow grabbed the light. It filled me like nothing I had ever felt. Then it burst from me, a wave like the fire of creation. When I returned to my senses, the assassins were little more than ash, and the twins still lived. I felt that same light pulsing inside them. From that moment, we were forever changed."

It was surreal, Valentine reflected, learning the exact point when all of this started. After years of mystery, so many rare truths were being revealed.

"So, you three were the first Chronauri," she said. "And the most powerful."

The Chrona nodded. "I had always felt the Ptolemy bloodline carried something special. But in truth, if we had not done this, eventually someone else would have. We spent years believing we were the only ones, but then new sensations began to reach us. Echoes of power from across this ocean of energy we called Time. It was then that we realized we had caused an awakening that spread across the Timeline. Everwatch called it the Axial Shift."

"It must have been scary to realize that," Malcolm said. "Like it was spinning out of control."

She nodded. "That is exactly how it felt. As the phenomenon spread, people began to flail about with these new abilities and cause all manner of disruptions. If they had continued unchecked, the damage to the universe would have been catastrophic. We realized then that, just like any other great power, this one must be governed. Helios had taken to calling us the Genesis Flame—the origin point for a fire that had spread into infinity. Therefore, we agreed it was our duty to bring order to chaos. Together, the three of us built the Aegis and established limitations. The *sev* system of power levels, the limitation of drawing power through a nexus. Selene even conceived a barrier to block others from achieving Sixth-*sev*. It held strong until the two of you came along."

Valentine blew out a breath, overwhelmed. She had wondered about that, but to have an absolute answer. . . well, it changed things. It made their actions that much more important.

"So, we really are two of only five *ever*," she said.

"You are."

"Jeez," Malcolm said. "No pressure, right? Save the universe, and try not to turn evil while we do it."

The Chrona gave them a sympathetic look. "I meant my words before. You are not my niece and nephew. As your power grows, you still think only of helping others. Looking back, I should have seen the signs." She paused, as if reliving a memory she would rather not. "The more we worked with Time, the more it became an inseparable part of us. It was the blood in our veins. Our power increased without ceasing, and we realized that our growth might be limitless. Eventually, Helios and Selene forgot that we were still human. The more they believed we were gods, the more they chafed under the limitations we placed on ourselves."

"What did they really want?" Valentine said.

"Everything. We were the first and most powerful Chronauri, and by lineage we were genuine royalty. In their minds, it was not our responsibility to watch and protect the Timeline, it was our birthright to be its rulers. They wanted to reshape history, and humanity, to their vision."

"And that's when things went bad," Malcolm said.

The Chrona nodded sadly. "I tried for so long to reason with them. Eventually I could no longer sit by and hope they would come to their senses. I intervened, and that is when they attacked. The battle grew so fierce that we nearly broke the Timeline ourselves. But I knew I could not give an inch."

"You were all so strong," Valentine said. "How did you stand against two of them?"

The Chrona gave a wistful smile. "I was always the strongest. Though extremely difficult, I fought them both to a stalemate. We were hurt and exhausted, and I begged them to let that be the end. I hoped they might see reason. But . . ."

She drifted off, overwhelmed with emotion. Valentine's heart went out to the woman. She likely hadn't had to relive these memories for a very long while, but she was doing it for them. With effort, she regained her composure.

"As I pleaded with them, I saw something in Selene's eyes, something like the innocent young girl I once knew. A few minutes more and I could have brought her back. But then Helios did something very much like a Ptolemy. Something that would have made his mother proud. Even I did not know it was possible." Fresh tears fell and she wiped them away. "That internal spark all Chronauri have, that special place inside that gives us our power? I know you have felt it. While Selene was distracted, Helios turned on her and ripped that spark from inside her. He joined it with his own and his power multiplied."

The twins' jaws dropped.

"How is that possible?" Malcolm said.

"Even now, I do not know."

"He killed his own sister in cold blood?" Valentine said, horrified. "He's worse than I thought."

"Selene lived," the Chrona replied. "For a moment, at least. We both were shocked to our bones at what he'd done, and in that moment Helios killed her to ensure she could never take her power back. Again, his mother would have applauded the tactic. But I was forced to watch helpless while the niece I had loved was murdered."

Valentine sat thunderstruck. Just when she thought they were getting a handle on the universe, on what was possible, something new came along.

"How did you survive after that?" she asked.

The Chrona looked down, ashamed. "Helios experienced a moment of disorientation. I would like to say I used it to reason with him, but Selene's death enraged me. I struck with such force that I believe it inflicted the first cracks upon the Aegis. Before my eyes he appeared to disintegrate, and for millennia I believed him dead. Unfortunately, I underestimated his devious nature."

"You really thought he was dead until now?" Valentine asked, incredulous.

"He managed to hide from me, quietly scheming and subtly corrupting history to suit his aims. When the Regent finally appeared, and then revealed his own power, I realized to my own horror that I had failed to protect the Timeline all along."

She looked up.

"Now it falls to both of you to help me fix it. For that I am truly sorry. But in truth, my dears, there are no two people I would rather have at my side. I believe you will both do great things, and the Timeline will flow true once again."

"All these things you're telling us," Valentine said. "And inside, I still feel like a high school kid."

"Same," Malcolm admitted. "The things you've done, even what Helios and Selene did . . . you really believe we'll be able to match you?"

The Chrona smiled—the first truly hopeful smile they had seen in a long while.

"No, Malcolm. I believe that, when you're both ready, you will surpass us all."

CHAPTER 42

The Regent studied the main viewscreen. Across Emmett's Bluff the Eon Palace stood, small and weak, yet managing to mock him from behind its inscrutable shield.

Soon, though, Everwatch would know true defeat. This Pyre would network with the others, and the Chrona would no longer be able to hide in the Aegis.

That's when he would have her. When he would finally get what he'd really come for.

After Selene's death, he had tried to reclaim his birthright less directly, by sneaking back into the Aegis—which he had helped build—hoping to catch Arsinoë unawares and assassinate her. Then, as the only living Sixth-*sev*, he would take control of the Aegis and assume command over Time.

Except, Arsinoë had found a way to change the Aegis. Where before he could enter it with a thought, now he tried and was rebuffed. It was as if she had replaced an open doorway with a locked vault.

The offense had burrowed under his skin. How dare she block him from claiming his birthright?

Very soon, he would be healed. Which meant that, very

soon, Arsinoë would have to intervene. When he killed her, when he took her power for himself, the Aegis would recognize her temporal signature and open for him.

By right of blood, it belonged to him anyway. This was justice.

A servant approached gingerly. "Sir, Leviathan is ready."

A thrill washed over the Regent.

"Begin Cyonic deployment," he commanded. "And hail the Eon Palace. I wish to speak with their general."

The servant bowed and backed away. The Regent stood before the viewscreen and adopted his most commanding posture. They fancied themselves heroes? Fine.

He would make it their downfall.

Keep it together for seven more hours. Just seven.

Scrubbing sleep from his eyes, John hastily buttoned his shirt. The alert had kicked him out of a deep slumber.

Something was happening to the Pyre. Even stranger, the Regent wanted to speak with him. Barreling down the hallway, John burst into the Command Center.

"Report."

"The machines are marching for us," Captain Armel said.

"Lots more than before," Walter Crane added.

"The Regent awaits an audience with you," a technician added. Looking thunderstruck, she gestured at the forward viewing glass. "Also, the Pyre is . . . I don't know, sir."

John peered through the glass and stopped short. "What in—?"

The Pyre's white and chrome outer shell had split into four sections and spread wider. Inside it, the superstructure appeared to be rebuilding into a new form. Huge mechanized pieces were even bursting through the ground around the Pyre and joining . . . whatever this was.

John heard the main doors open behind him.

"You have got to be kidding me," Winter said.

"Tell me this is that fool's last trick," Fred said.

"Any theories?" Tyrathorn asked.

Quickly donning the black rings with the glowing blue jewels, John flicked his fingers at the glass and called up his data streams.

"They're pulling extreme amounts of thermal energy from the earth. Possibly to power whatever this is. Beyond that," he shrugged. "I need time to study it."

"Sir, the Regent?" a technician said.

Oh, right. The man who was trying to kill them wanted to chat first. With a deep breath to steady his nerves, John gave a nod.

The display morphed into video of the Regent. Hands clasped behind his back, chin in the air, calm assuredness on his face—their enemy struck an imposing figure.

He's a liar and a devil, John reminded himself. *And for now, he can't touch us.*

The Regent nodded. "General Carter, I presume. A pleasure to meet you, and my compliments on your survival thus far. Your tactics have made this a rousing game."

Despite the circumstances, John felt himself smirk. "Thank you, Regent."

The Regent gave an imperious nod.

"Not for the compliment," John said, "but for confirming you're no different than any warlord in history. Trading lives for power like it's a game, imagining you are destined for greatness. But even for the victorious, power only lasts so long."

"For them, perhaps. *My* rightful rule will be infinite. The traitors who opposed it will be less than a footnote, with no one to remember them." He took an ominous step toward the screen. "I referred to this as a game, general, not because it is trivial, but because you have already lost. I have the only pieces that matter, and my final gambit has begun."

"Indeed," John said, working to appear unshakeable. "I hope your pieces enjoy relaxing outside our shield, since they can't bring it down. Soon we'll clear them from the board."

Now it was the Regent's turn to smirk. "Why, General Carter, I am not going to bring down the shield. *You* are."

Sudden fear lanced through John. This wasn't empty posturing—the Regent was getting at something specific.

Externally, he forced himself to smirk. "I think not."

The Regent gestured to someone off screen. "Deploy Leviathan."

Before John could ask what Leviathan was, the ground trembled. A giant mechanical behemoth burst from inside the Pyre and flew into the sky. In the Command Center, a dozen jaws dropped.

It resembled a thousand-foot-long steel dragon. Like the serpent of legend, it undulated though the air, mechanical wings spreading from its impossibly huge body.

With an earsplitting roar, it sent a blast of flame down onto Emmett's Bluff. An entire neighborhood became ash, and the ground beneath it buckled and collapsed. Tyrathorn, Captain Armel, and all Chronauri in the Command Center grunted in pain.

"That fire is not natural," the captain said, clutching his temples.

"It burns Time as well," Tyrathorn breathed.

The mechanized beast lifted higher, turned, and flew eastward. It roared again, and a city block disappeared in flames. John stared after it dumbfounded, then shook himself back to his senses.

"Target lock," he said. "Keep an eye on it."

"Your century's weapons will have no effect," the Regent said, looking far too satisfied. "Only weapons forged of Time can threaten it, leaving you with two choices. Drop your shield and destroy Leviathan. Or do nothing and watch while your town, and then your entire eastern seaboard, are reduced to cinders. You have thirty minutes to decide, at which point Leviathan will depart and begin with Manhattan's destruction."

His transmission cut off, plunging the Command Center into stunned silence.

"I really hate that guy," Fred said. "When can I kill him?"

"You'll have to beat me to it, kid," Walter said.

"Drop the shield now, or let millions die in the hope of saving billions." John faced his friends. "We have minutes to decide, and whatever decision we make, history will hate us for it."

"Let history quibble with itself. We are men of action," Tyrathorn said. He brushed Winter's hand. "And women."

"John, you said the choices like there's a debate," Winter said. "Is there, though? We have a greater duty to protect the whole Timeline."

"With respect, my queen," Captain Armel interjected, "destruction of this magnitude would surely disrupt the Timeline. If I must, I will go out myself and stand in that thing's way."

"It's not just about the Timeline," Walter said. "The Regent is threatening the universe. Can we risk that to save a few now?"

"I'm with Armel," John said. "We can't sit this out and still call ourselves the good guys."

"We have thirty minutes to destroy the machine without lowering our shields," Tyrathorn said with a tone of finality. "Let's get to work."

Pitiful. The Regent watched Everwatch throw everything they could at Leviathan. As he had warned, conventional weapons were as effective as throwing water at a stone.

Twenty minutes had passed, and with each minute their desperation grew. He laughed as they crashed an explosive-filled hovercraft into Leviathan. What little damage the blast caused, his beast repaired.

Right now, the shield was still up. But the Regent knew the nature of heroes. It was only a matter of minutes.

"Project Rectify has succeeded," he announced. "Prepare the Praetorians."

John worked to project calm assurance. People could not follow a leader who fell to pieces. But the truth was becoming clear.

Their tricks were failing. Walter's exploding Sled idea was sound, but it had been futile. He and Tyrathorn were down in the hangar bay now, trying to rig another with higher-yield explosives, but it was little more than a desperate move.

The Ember Guard had examined Leviathan with their senses and confirmed the Regent's words. A temporal attack would be the only chance of taking it down.

Thank God we evacuated Emmett's Bluff, at least, he thought as Leviathan razed another city block. Buildings could be replaced.

Manhattan and the eastern seaboard, though, were far more than just buildings. He pressed down a wave of panic. But wait . . .

"The Empyrean Bridge! It has massive power." John turned to Armel. "Can we rig it to be some kind of weapon?"

"The Bridge powers the shield," the captain reminded him.

"If we try and the Bridge gets damaged, it's over," Winter said.

John pressed on. "There must be a way to do it safely. We have *minutes* before that thing flies away."

Armel hesitated. A shadow seemed to fall over him while he struggled to speak. John could relate. There were shadows over them all now.

"There is a way," the captain finally said. "It has not been done on such a large scale, but it could work."

"Good. How do we adapt the Bridge?"

Armel shook his head. "We cannot risk the Bridge. This is something different, a technique that Tyrathorn helped us develop. My people used it to infiltrate the Pyre."

"Will we need to drop the shield?" Winter said.

"Yes, but only for a moment." Captain Armel studied the Command Center now, as if memorizing the details, then faced John again. "There are risks, but I believe it is our best option."

They both turned to Winter.

"You're the queen," John said. "It's your call."

She swallowed, looking grim. "Do it, captain. What do you need?"

"A direct line from my comm to all Ember Guard."

John nodded. "Done."

"Good. I myself will be vulnerable preparing this maneuver." Armel looked to Winter again. "Will you guard me?"

As they locked eyes, John saw years of history and friendship pass between them. Sometimes he forgot that, while a few years had passed for him, these two and Tyrathorn had spent decades protecting Time together.

"I'll alert Tyrathorn," John said. "He'll want to help."

"No, please," said the captain. "Let my old friend continue his work. We can handle ours. How long do we have?"

John consulted the clock. "Eight minutes."

Captain Armel nodded, then stood straighter, looking every bit the warrior that he was. "When you receive the signal, drop the shield."

It's still beautiful from up here.

Captain Armel stood at the apex of the Eon Palace, over fifty stories high. Gazing out over the earth, he gave himself a moment to drink it all in. The surrounding countryside bathed in the golden light of the sun. He promised himself it was all going to survive.

He paused at the Pyre, noting the gaping hole in its side with a smile. Asha's sacrifice had decimated nearly ten floors.

Closing his eyes, he turned toward the soft breeze. His armored body couldn't feel it, but his face could. For a few seconds, he let it soothe him.

There was a click behind him, followed by footsteps. Armel savored the peace for one last second, then turned. Winter approached, flanked by four Watchers, all gleaming in their mechanized armor. She peered over the captain's shoulder and whistled.

"That's a *lot* of machines wanting to kill us," she said, referring to the horde gathered outside the shield. Thousands of Cyonics were backed up by Destroyers.

Armel glanced over his shoulder and grinned. "When this is over, we shall turn one of them into your throne."

Winter laughed. "A bed, too. Let's make it a whole set."

Growing serious, she squeezed his shoulder with affection.

"Strike true, Armel. And don't worry; nothing will get past us. We'll celebrate after."

He nodded his thanks. They parted, and Winter led her soldiers to the edge of the roof. Today they would be his shield.

Saying a silent prayer for their safety, he moved to the center of the roof and faced west. The Pyre dominated the sky. Farther south, Leviathan carved another fiery, earth-buckling swathe through Emmett's Bluff. He fixed that vision in his mind, promising himself it would be the last destruction that devil machine would inflict.

My heart, my sword will ever blaze

Armel opened his Chronauri senses and cast them out as far as he could.

For all of Time, for all my days.

Through the flows of Time, through the spiderweb of black, fiery cracks, Armel found hundreds of temporal signatures. The glowing points of light that were the Ember Guard. They were deployed throughout the Eon Palace and the surrounding grounds.

Warm pride filled him. To the last man and woman, they would give everything it took to defend the Timeline.

So would he.

He keyed his comm, knowing his voice carried to all of them. "Ember Guard, attention. Open your nexuses and prepare for a Corvonian Cascade."

"Who's in the chain, captain?" one of them responded, a Third-*sev* named Kewanee.

He steadied himself. "All of us. Channel through the Eon Palace to me. I am the locus."

"Captain," one of his High Protectors said, "please join me on a private channel."

"Negative, Liam."

"Captain, please! We can—"

"You have your orders, soldier. Please, just do it. On my mark, give me everything you have."

Taking hold of the nexus in his chest plate, Armel twisted. The device had been with him for decades. Now, with a series of clicks, it separated from his armor.

He went down to one knee. Setting the nexus aside, he placed his hand on the roof's smooth surface, palm flat and fingers spread. Even now he could feel the Eon Palace's internal clockwork realigning. It vibrated with the first faint bursts of Time.

Time had always felt warm wrapped around him. Like a favorite cloak.

He keyed his comm. "Ember Guard . . . now."

Removing the earpiece, he tossed it away and closed his eyes. Now the Eon Palace could fulfill its true purpose, and so could he.

Few people knew of it. The Ember Guard knew, and of course the Corvonians, but even they never believed it would need to be used. It never had, until today.

The day when the Eon Palace became a massive nexus.

Like a growing tidal wave, Time flowed from hundreds of Chronauri. It poured into the Eon Palace and rushed upward, toward the center of its apex where Armel now stood. He braced himself.

The wave hit like a furious thunderclap. Crying out, he clenched every muscle and brought all his will to bear on the energy.

The surface of the Eon Palace glowed like a star, brighter and brighter as the collective power of the Ember Guard flowed through it. That radiance gathered at Armel. He fought to keep it bridled like a wild stallion, letting it build to a crescendo inside him. When the moment came, he would be the lens that directed it.

"Now, Winter," he said through gritted teeth. "Drop the shield!"

Winter keyed her comm. "John, do it."

Armel sensed a subtle pressure release in the back of his mind. The shield was off-line, which meant the Cyonics would be charging. He must work quickly.

His people must have sensed it, too. They redoubled their efforts and another massive wave slammed into Armel.

He rocked back, nearly overwhelmed. Like an avalanche, Time poured into him, so much that it threatened to scour away everything he was, scattering him into particles. He clamped down tighter. *Just another moment, just last another moment!*

He couldn't feel his body. He couldn't think of the past or the future. Every shred of Armel's existence came down to this one moment and the raging light inside him. And, finally, to the mechanical monster flying over Emmett's Bluff.

Time was up. Leviathan was turning east and rocketing toward the horizon where millions would perish.

Armel's body held a thousand suns. With effort like moving a planet, he turned all that power toward the clockwork dragon.

"Strike true," he whispered. "For Everwatch."

With a shout, Captain Armel released a blast of Time that rocked the surrounding earth for miles. He gripped it tightly, focusing it like a temporal laser.

It struck Leviathan with an earsplitting *boom*. The beast writhed, emitting a mechanical scream.

Bending Time into a massive bubble, Armel trapped Leviathan inside. With every shred of will he could summon, he pushed the energy inside it to flow faster and faster.

The cells in his body were breaking down. He pushed harder, and finally the beast's armored shell began to age, turning to dust.

The Chronauri spark inside Armel burned away. Once he stopped channeling this massive flow of Time, his powers would be finished. A price he paid gladly.

Leviathan battered against the bubble, pitting its strength against his, fighting to survive.

With a scream, Armel gathered all of himself—everything he had been from his first day until now, every hope and dream, every golden memory of Everwatch and every moment of fighting for its survival—and channeled his will into one final blast.

Leviathan aged a thousand years in a microsecond. It gave a final, desperate wail, then burst into ash.

Triumph surged through Armel. With a last kiss of warmth from Time, he let go of its radiance and toppled onto his back.

Winter and the Watchers were fighting, keeping machines away from them. Distantly he could hear the *clangs* of battle. They were his people and he trusted them implicitly, which meant he could lie there in peace.

He could feel the breeze again, passing lazily over his face. He floated along, basking in its warmth.

So few people ever had the chance to fulfill their life's mission, to meet the very highest realization of their truest purpose and see it through to the end. Armel could barely feel his body, but he knew that he was smiling.

"I'm ready," he whispered.

The breeze stopped. The sounds of battle froze, and Armel felt a gentle hand on his shoulder. He cracked his eyes open.

His smile widened.

"I knew it," he said, his voice rasping and exhausted. "Somehow I knew."

A temporal bubble shimmered around him. Everything beyond it was still, as if locked in a single instant. A familiar face gazed down at him, smiling with pride and sadness.

"Everyone will know what you did, Armel," his friend said. "Your statue will stand across from Asha's in Meridian Square."

The captain laughed, incredulous. "Me, a statue?"

His friend nodded. "I've seen it. It's nice."

Armel appreciated the tribute. Still, it wasn't what truly mattered.

"The rest of them?" he said, grasping desperately at the hand on his shoulder. His body twitched and heaved—he didn't have long. "What happens? Will they survive?"

Armel felt fingers brush his forehead.

"Close your eyes, my friend. I'll show you."

Armel obeyed, and Time opened before him.

Tyrathorn rattled his head, clearing a sudden rush of dizziness. What had happened to Time just then? Shoving away the questions, he threw himself against the door and burst onto the roof.

Captain Armel lay prone in the center, waves of vapor rising from his body.

Winter and her Watchers fought furiously to keep the machines at bay. Clockwork debris flew as they fought. His wife caught sight of him and he could see her tears.

"I can't get to him!" she cried.

Tyrathorn gestured behind him. "Ember Guard, defend!"

A half-dozen Ember Guard barreled through the doorway and took position alongside their Watcher brethren. Winter broke away and joined Tyrathorn. Together they rushed to their friend's side and fell to their knees over him.

Armel's skin was badly burned. As they examined him, the soldier's eyes opened and fell on Tyrathorn.

"You're not supposed to be here," he chided weakly.

"Too late. I felt what you were doing," Tyrathorn said. "Why did you not tell me, Armel? I could have helped!"

The captain coughed hard.

"A kingdom needs its king," he said. "We all have our purpose, Tyrathorn. This was mine. It was always mine."

Tears streamed down Winter's face. Tyrathorn felt them burn behind his eyes, too. Armel grasped each of their hands.

"It's all right," he whispered. "I'm all right. Our friend came and showed me, let me *see*. Hard times come for you, but in the end . . ."

Winter choked back a sob. "In the end, what?"

Instead of an answer, Armel smiled. He drew in a breath and his chest heaved. He arched his back and gritted his teeth until the pain passed.

"My brother, and my sister. You're the only family I ever

needed." Gripping their hands tighter, he pulled them close. "Time is in your hands now. Look after her."

Tyrathorn wept openly. "I promise, my friend. We will carry on."

"To our last breath," Winter added. She caressed their old friend's cheek. "Be at peace, Armel."

With a grateful nod, and a last squeeze of their hands, Armel laid his head back on the roof of the Eon Palace and exhaled his last, victorious breath.

Tyrathorn sat back on his heels. His oldest friend, gone. What would Everwatch do without Captain Armel, the bravest leader they had ever known? What would he and Winter do without the counsel and companionship of their stalwart friend?

Hard times were coming, he had said that. But in the end, the space between Armel's words had conveyed hope.

Tyrathorn couldn't see it. All he saw was endless despair looming overhead. Sights and sounds beyond their circle were muffled and blurred, as if occurring in a distant nightmare.

Until a nearby explosion rocked him from his stupor.

Inside, Tyrathorn felt a terrible ripping sensation. A scream rang through the Timeline, as if the universe were crying out.

He shot to his feet and ran to the edge of the roof, looking down for the source of the blast. Like a hot lead weight, his heart dropped into his stomach.

"Merciful Eternity," he breathed.

At the far end of the palace grounds, amid a copse of trees, Praetorians surrounded a wide stone platform. The platform held the Empyrean Bridge.

Or it used to. Where the great machine had once stood, there was now a smoking crater.

Despair crashed into Tyrathorn. Trembling, he fell to his

knees. The Bridge had been not only their means of traveling through Time, but also the power source for their shield.

As he looked down, hordes of the Regent's machines poured onto the palace grounds. Now nothing stood between their enemy and the destruction he promised.

They would keep fighting. But in his heart, Tyrathorn knew the truth. They had just lost.

And Time would pay the price.

CHAPTER 43

Valentine was breaking.

She could feel it happening. Not a break like death or defeat. More like the slow cracking of a chrysalis.

Jaw clenched, she stood firm with Malcolm to hold back the Chrona's attacks. Pure energy assaulted them from all sides.

The Chrona wasn't attacking directly, which was baffling. Though she radiated a massive power signature, the energy didn't emit from her. It seemed to come out of nowhere, leaving the twins only fractions of a second to react to each volley. For the first day in many, Valentine was sweating through her clothes.

She had to admit it, the Chrona knew what she was doing. Not long ago, they wouldn't have survived this. Now they stood back to back, facing down a gale-force assault. Some attacks they deflected, some they canceled out, others they intercepted and absorbed.

They were also forcing their teacher to work harder. Caught in the throes of power, the Chrona closed her eyes and spread her arms, lifting into the air amid a swirling maelstrom.

Valentine gaped.

Malcolm whooped. "I told you she could fly!"

The cracking sensation had begun a week ago. It was as if Valentine had lived inside a shell her whole life, and only now begun to realize it. Malcolm had confessed to something similar, but neither knew what it meant.

The Chrona kept saying they were "not axial yet." Could it have something to do with that? The mysterious milestone she kept pushing them toward? Maybe if they *were* getting closer, she would finally—

Fiery pain lanced through Valentine's skull. She gasped, lost grip on Time and fell to her knees. Malcolm crumpled next to her. Even the Chrona dropped to her feet and grimaced, clutching her temples.

"What *is* that?" Valentine said.

The Chrona stumbled past them, intent on something in the distance. The twins staggered after her until she stopped, staring down at one point.

Emmett's Bluff. The tangled mass of cracks multiplied, searing ever-deepening wounds into the Timeline.

"Whoa," Malcolm said. "They've never spread that fast."

Cold fear pierced Valentine. "Something must have gone wrong."

They turned to the Chrona, whose eyes had turned unfocused and empty. Yet, beneath the emptiness was a manic frenzy.

"Oh, no," Valentine said.

Malcolm gripped their teacher's shoulder. "Stay with us. We don't know what to do."

"Helios," the Chrona mumbled. "Healing so quickly. I couldn't have known."

"Wait, are you saying he attacked *before* forty-six hours?" Valentine said. "We have to go back!"

"The Timeline will break."

"Look at this." Malcolm pointed to the cracks spreading beneath their feet. "The Timeline is *already* breaking."

"Not axial," the Chrona replied, shaking with terror.

Valentine threw up her hands. "Then show us how to *be* axial, whatever that means."

The Chrona looked up sharply. Valentine took an involuntary step back. They had witnessed her mental episodes countless times: the vacant eyes, the confusion. This one was different.

This one scared her.

It was as if Arsinoë drained away while a madwoman was poured into her body. The frenetic dementia now held control, and her confusion flashed into rage.

"Death and destruction," she said, her tone accusing.

"Excuse me?" Valentine said, trying to tamp down her unease.

"You only have breakthroughs amid death and destruction," the Chrona said. "Lucius Carmichael. Charlotte Corday. They killed and threatened to kill more. Only then did you grow enough to stop them."

Valentine began to object, but stopped. Malcolm looked taken aback, too.

"I guess that might be true," he said.

"Except, the Regent has killed," Valentine said. "So why haven't we grown?"

The Chrona spun on her heels and walked farther along the Aegis. The twins followed warily.

Each footstep carried them decades forward. Beneath the cracking crystalline structure, the future slowly unfolded. When the Chrona had moved ninety years into the future, she shuffled to the right and stared down.

"Here," she said. "Your final proving ground."

Valentine peered through the Aegis until the city beneath came into focus.

"London?" she said. "I don't get it."

"Final proving ground," Malcolm said heavily. "What does that mean?"

"The greater the power you need, the greater the threat it takes to unleash it. If you would finally let go and become who you truly are . . ."

The Chrona made a small gesture. Below them, Time began to *shift* at her command. Not a gentle redirection, but violent and thunderous. The flows turned back on themselves, slammed together, and twisted into something terrifying. In the skies above London in the twenty-second century, a temporal distortion filled the sky.

No, not a just distortion. Valentine cried out in shock.

"What are you doing?" Malcolm demanded.

The Chrona was suddenly at Valentine's side, gripping her shoulder. A second Chrona clutched Malcolm.

"Why?" Valentine pleaded.

It wasn't a Time distortion. It was a Time bomb.

They flashed forward. Shocked beyond belief, the twins failed to react. They now stood over London another ninety years in the future. The Chrona smashed together another bomb, left it hovering in the sky, and they flashed forward again.

Six time periods, all within a heartbeat. Six leaps of ninety-year intervals. Six bombs in the sky over London, capable of destroying everything for many miles.

They flashed back to their starting point. The first of the six, ninety years in the twins' future. Only one Chrona remained.

"Become what you must and save them all," she said. "Fail, and they will die because you did not protect them."

The Aegis opened beneath them. Valentine's insides leapt as they sank through. In a blink, the twins found themselves on the streets of London.

All around them, people stared fearfully at the sky. No one panicked—they didn't know what it was—but many went indoors. The busy street was already emptying.

Like a living thing, the bomb roiled, looping continually back on itself. The sky around it warped and twisted, too, as reality flexed around it.

"It's so huge," Malcolm said. "Even if we stop this one, there are five more waiting. How are we supposed to get to them?"

He was right. The power pouring off the Chrona's weapon was unlike anything Valentine had ever felt. The twins could absorb and channel more Time than almost anyone who had ever existed. Even still, she doubted it would be enough.

She shook her head, helpless, grasping for any wild thought that might give them a chance. Nothing. With a deep breath, she worked to quell her fear. Fear was a killer.

"I guess we just give it everything."

Malcolm faced her with a new glimmer in his eye. "Like with Lucius. We had nothing left, and everything to lose, so we gave it all."

"And suddenly we found *more* to give. Like with the Frost Hammer—she was winning."

"So, we gave it all and then . . . found more." He shook his head. "Could she actually be right about us?"

"Whether she's right or crazy, we're here. This city needs us."

They locked eyes, and understanding passed between

them. Mystical twin powers at work once again. In unison, they nodded.

"Okay," Malcolm said. "They die, we die."

Side by side, they faced the sky.

"When we get home," Valentine said, "I'm marrying John."

She expected Malcolm to gasp, or at least look shocked. He only smiled.

"You already knew?"

"Pretty sure I knew before you did."

Valentine couldn't help smiling. "Okay, then. Let's get me to my wedding."

As she spoke those last words, the sky screamed, and the bomb plummeted toward the ground.

The Gilbert twins became living conduits for Time. With the power of the universe flooding through them, they reached out and shoved against the falling bomb.

Valentine's power met the Chrona's and burst apart like waves on a rock face. Malcolm gave a huff as his own efforts failed. Panic gripped Valentine. She gripped it right back, squashing it and pushing harder.

The way they were using Time wasn't enough. It would *never* be enough.

As the microseconds clicked by, as the bomb hurtled toward them, she worked to expand her being farther and farther, absorbing and wielding more Time. With each attempt, she smacked up against that shell, the chrysalis that had always existed around her and that now refused to break. The one she had never noticed.

The Chrona's words came back to her. *Your first instinct is to act physically,* she had said. *You must come to see Time as a seamless extension of your will.*

Time, the Chrona had said. Not the Time she could absorb. Not the Time she could physically handle. Just Time.

In that instant, Valentine knew the secret.

The bomb loomed, so close now that it blotted out the sky.

She stopped trying to absorb bigger flows of Time. At its core, that was a physical act, which meant it would always be limited. Just as a nexus limited the power of Chronauri, Valentine's body had limited hers all along. So, she forgot her body.

Instead she summoned the deepest reserves of her will, a power as limitless as Time itself. Will could break free of the physical, accomplish what flesh never could.

A seamless extension . . .

Valentine reached for the bomb. With a scream of exertion, she called up every shred of will she possessed and flung it skyward.

The ground trembled. Lightning flashed between the clouds and thunder split the sky. And Time answered her call.

Her chrysalis shattered.

Time didn't flood into her as before because she didn't need it to. With her will extended, Valentine broadcast her wishes, and the Timeline obeyed.

As if reading her thoughts, Time moved as she willed it. Not the paltry streams that she had worked so hard to channel through her body, but the unfathomable torrents that drove the universe.

At her command, Time gathered around the Chrona's bomb and stopped it dead. She flexed her will again and the weapon unraveled, its energy reabsorbing into the natural flow of the Timeline.

"Holy . . ." Malcolm breathed.

Valentine understood now why it felt different when the

Regent and the Chrona wielded Time. Because they had transcended a limitation that no one even knew was a limitation.

And now, so had she.

"You can do it, Mal," she said, facing her brother. "I know you—"

"There are five more," he said.

Her heart sank. For a blissful moment, she had forgotten. How were they supposed to get to those without the Chrona or the Aegis?

But the determination on Malcolm's face could have shaken a mountain. Closing his eyes, he stretched one hand forward.

"You felt how I did it?" she asked.

"Oh, yes."

Malcolm's body tensed, and the ground began to tremble.

Now that the sky had returned to normal, a few brave Londoners were stepping tentatively outside. Valentine blocked them from her thoughts and refocused.

"It was there all along, right in front of us," Malcolm said through gritted teeth. "We never even realized. We thought we were strong, Val. But now . . ."

He gave a shout of exertion that echoed down the street. Valentine felt something around him crack, and then shatter. Again the skies burst with thunder and lightning. Gale-force winds whipped around them.

Malcolm clenched his outstretched hand into a fist. A vortex burst open before them, its energy a dazzling blue. Valentine could feel the portal stretching toward the day the Chrona's next bomb was set to appear.

"Whoa," she said. "I never imagined . . ."

Crackling with power, Malcolm turned a satisfied gaze on

her. "No more Time machines, Val. It's just you, me, and the universe."

She grinned. "Let's get the rest of these bombs. And then—"

"And then," Malcolm finished, "the Regent's going to have a bad day."

Together they plunged into the portal.

CHAPTER 44

Less than four hours.

The Ember Guard and Watchers were the best in the Timeline, and fighting in the Eon Palace gave them territorial advantages. The structure itself was equipped to fight alongside them. This had allowed them to slow the enemy's advance.

But even Everwatch couldn't fight an army ten times its size forever. As John analyzed the constant stream of tactical data, the weight on his shoulders grew heavier.

You're not playing to win, you're playing to survive, he reminded himself. *So, keep as many alive as possible.*

That's what Valentine would say. John paused, allowing himself a few seconds to remember her warmth. Her smile.

Saying he loved her wasn't enough. It would never convey all the ways he needed her. Silently he promised himself that, if they survived this, he wouldn't wait another day to start a life with her. Time was too precious for hesitation.

He had already taken what steps he could to keep their family safe. His first command today had been to conceal Neil and Grace in an armored chamber beneath the Eon Palace.

He had tried to send others, but they refused to leave his

side. Walter, Fred, and Callie had named themselves his personal guard, vowing to keep the Command Center safe so he could keep working. Tyrathorn and Winter had arrived soon after and joined them.

Even now, his friends guarded the doors behind his back. Half an hour ago, the machines had learned where their nerve center was located, and new squads appeared every few minutes. So far, they had all been reduced to scrap.

He keyed his comm. "Commander Maron, I'm sending a new waypoint. Direct your battle groups to move there, please."

"What are we marching toward, General?"

"I've prepared a trap. The machines are trying to get Destroyers inside. Show them the error of their ways."

"Consider it done, sir."

John cycled through more channels to deliver more orders. Managing one big battle had been hard enough. Now he was managing a hundred small ones.

The Eon Palace shuddered. Then shuddered again. That one had felt closer.

Cacophonous sounds echoed through the Command Center. Over John's shoulder, light and steel clashed as his defenders repelled another attack. When the last Cyonic fell, he could hear them working to catch their breath.

"Squads are getting bigger," Callie said.

"More coordinated, too," Walter said. "In my day, machines had the decency to obey humans."

"Pretty sure these do, too, dawg," Fred replied. "It's just the human they're obeying is a total jackass."

"Let them come," Tyrathorn said darkly.

"If there's a robot hell, we'll send them there," Winter added.

"Standing guard's cool for now," Fred said. "But without a real plan . . ."

"He's right," Callie said. "If the assaults keep escalating, we can't keep this up."

"Point taken," Walter said. "Got any bright ideas?"

"Actually, yeah," Fred said. "Gimme ten minutes. I'll be back."

Fred's footsteps moved away. The southern double doors opened and then closed.

John's comm crackled. *"Maron here, general. Your trap is ready."*

John called up video feeds from a large staging bay, where plasma fire was cutting through the wall from outside.

"Wait for breach, then strike," John said.

"Yes, sir."

The plasma cut a twenty-foot square. The wall imploded to reveal four Destroyers waiting to get inside the palace. John heard Maron give the order.

The barrel of the Verge swung into view and fired.

With a gut-churning *thrum*, a missile of sound smashed into the Destroyers. They disintegrated as if they were toys. Maron and his soldiers cheered, and so did everyone in the Command Center. Enough small victories added up to large ones.

"Consider the Verge under your command," John said. "Bring the pain."

He could hear the grin in Maron's voice. *"With pleasure, sir."*

"And remember to—"

The Command Center's western doors exploded.

Six Praetorian Berserkers charged inside. The nearest launched two missiles from its abdomen. Before John could blink, they slammed into the computer bank to his right.

Shock waves assaulted him. Light and sound overwhelmed him. The computers shredded in a burst of flames, and three of his technicians went flying.

The next thing John knew, he was on his back. His clothes were ripped. He bled from multiple cuts. He tried to stand, but his limbs were rubber. Breathless, he could only stare as the machines radiated destruction.

His friends fought ferociously, but these Praetorians were something different. If any machine could be evil, it had to be these.

John rolled onto his stomach and crawled toward what was left of his computers. The left bank still stood, but only one technician was conscious. He flicked his fingers to bring up emergency breach protocols, then saw that half the forward glass had shattered.

Pushing through the urge to pass out, John crawled toward a smaller display. The Command Center had a few surprises ready for—

A mechanical foot slammed down in front of him. Peering up, John met the merciless, unchanging eye of a Berserker. Then his vision filled with metal as the machine aimed a cannon at his face.

I'm sorry, Valentine. I tried.

The weapon's barrel glowed.

From out of nowhere, a giant battle axe buried into the Praetorian's chest. The machine stumbled back, plasma fire flying wide. John heard ancient battle cries as Techno-Vikings charged past him to assault the machine.

In disbelief, John rattled his head to clear the cobwebs. Pushing up to his knees, he witnessed the strangest, most beautiful thing he had ever seen.

It was Fred, at the head of his own little army of misfits. Criminal Time travelers, rogue Chronauri, villains from across the ages—they all charged into the Command Center on a wave of fury.

Fred emptied out the Pendulum, John realized. Home of the Timeline's worst offenders. Against all odds, they fought now for the good guys.

As they engaged the machines, John's own protectors gathered around him. They helped him to his feet before forming a line separating him and his computers from the fray. Two criminals even collected John's injured technicians for medical attention.

"If you ain't hurt, you can get back to work," Fred said over his shoulder. "Don't worry. We got this."

"I hope we do not regret this," Tyrathorn said. "They were locked up for a reason."

Fred shrugged. "Someone had to do what it took to keep us breathing."

"You told them what was happening?" Winter asked.

"Figured they wanna live, too," Fred said.

"And now our fight is theirs." Walter nodded. "Nice."

"Thanks, bro." Fred gestured toward the far wall. "Yo, who's that?"

A raven-haired woman fought with the ferocity of a tornado. With a blade in one hand and a pistol in the other, she laid into a Praetorian as if it had offended her personally.

Tyrathorn's eyes narrowed. "Masako Nakamura, from the twenty-third century. Her family was killed when thieves raided their village. She learned to fight, tracked down the thieves, and took their heads."

"Sounds like they deserved it," Walter said.

"Then she traveled back decades and killed their ancestors," Tyrathorn continued. "Then traveled back centuries to kill those ancestors' ancestors. If we had not stopped her, she would have wiped out entire bloodlines."

"Oh." Fred considered. "When this is over, think I could get her number?"

Everyone burst into laughter. Even John couldn't help joining in.

Winter wiped her eyes. "Oh, Fred, you idiot. I've really missed you."

Feeling bolstered, John turned back to his remaining computers. As he helped technicians back into their chairs, his mind began tabulating a new task list.

He would need to collect each battle group's status and redeploy as necessary. First task would be to reach out to battalion commanders.

John glanced through the forward glass and stopped short. "No, it's too soon!"

On the streets below, ranks of Cyonics opened to allow a lone figure through. Striding onto the Eon Palace grounds, the man stopped and stared up, right into the Command Center. Cold dread filled John.

The Regent had arrived.

CHAPTER 45

He looks like a king, John thought.

Even forty stories below, the Regent's presence filled the air with power and authority. It may have helped that a robot army surrounded him, ready to obey his every whim.

John opened all comm channels. "Everwatch, be ready. The Regent is here."

There were gasps from his protectors. He tried to ignore the noise and to focus.

The Regent had even upgraded his wardrobe. Where before he had worn a simple black suit, now he was wrapped in red and gold, his outfit cut like some far-future version of a formal military uniform.

Crazy as it seemed, the clothes told John what was about to happen. The Regent had dressed up for his big day.

Helios. Call him Helios. He's human, too. And humans, even powerful ones, could make mistakes.

The Regent—Helios—raised his right hand and made a slight gesture. John tensed, hands over his keyboard in preparation to defend. Then something behind him rumbled, and the floor quaked.

John glanced over his shoulder as half the back wall

collapsed. Cyonics poured in, a swarm of white and chrome. More Ember Guard and Watchers arrived on their heels, and suddenly the Command Center was the main battleground of this war.

He couldn't think about the machines. They weren't his job. Tapping a rapid-fire series of commands, John refocused all the Eon Palace's external countermeasures on their true enemy.

Helios issued no commands. Instead, his outstretched hand clenched into a fist.

Far to the west, there was a hint of movement at the base of the Pyre. John tapped his screen and zoomed in with an external camera. A doorway opened and a platform emerged, carrying a spinning ring and metallic coils. It was the ring array Everwatch had destroyed, good as new.

There could only be one reason Helios would deploy it: he was healed enough to power it. Everything they had dreaded was happening now.

Before John could shout a warning, fire lanced from the ring array like a laser beam. The flames burned across Emmett's Bluff and slammed into the side of the Eon Palace.

The palace rocked. Humans and machines alike toppled, disoriented. John stumbled to his knees. Chronauri cried out and dropped, clutching their heads in agony.

Warning Klaxons blared. Red lights flashed. The Eon Palace shook harder.

John consulted another data feed, and his jaw dropped. *It can't be.* His fingers flew across the keyboard to call up internal camera feeds from the first ten floors. *Dear God.*

The third mini-tower, the last one Helios needed to network his Pyres, had appeared inside the Eon Palace. Now, when their enemy powered up his final assault, the only people with any chance to oppose him would be the first to burn.

"Arsinoë."

John flinched back in surprise. Every device in the Command Center that could produce sound had come alive. Helios's voice emerged from them all.

"I have them, Arsinoë," he said. "Come to me now, or your cowardice will mean their destruction."

He paused. Nothing happened.

"Would you sacrifice the timeline you fought so hard to protect? This century will die, and in the new history there will be no memory it ever existed. But you can save them all."

As John listened, his fear was overwhelmed by disgust. He was sick of hearing this man's voice. He keyed his comm to broadcast on the same signal.

"She's not here, Helios. Hasn't been for two days. You're knocking on a door where no one's home."

Gritting his teeth, John stood. He wanted to look into this man's eyes, to let him see that he hadn't broken them.

"You want to fight someone?" He spread his arms. "Well, there's only us. So, either go back to hiding in your fortress, or shut up and bring it on."

The aggression in John's tone shocked even him. A rousing cheer went up behind him. Soldiers regained their feet and sounds of fighting intensified.

"Dude, awesome!" Fred called.

Forty stories down, Helios glared daggers. John couldn't help grinning. It seemed he had stolen his enemy's dramatic moment.

"Pity," Helios said. "Then you will die for nothing."

He dropped his fist, and the Pyre's beams of fire changed.

It felt like a great machine had been waiting on standby for days, and now it was waking up, summoning its true power.

The color and intensity of the flames deepened. The tremors that had rocked the Eon Palace now spread into the surrounding countryside. Searing, black cracks radiated from the fire beams, like spiderwebs that scorched the Timeline itself.

This was it, then. Helios really was going to end it all. John's only solace was knowing that Valentine was beyond the madman's reach.

"Goodbye, my love," he whispered. "I—"

In the sky above Emmett's Bluff, a red vortex burst open.

Two figures flew out. John could see the space around them warping as they moved. Puzzled, he aimed a camera and zoomed, and broke into a cheer.

He should have recognized the distinctive black jacket. Now he saw red hair whipping as Valentine flew. She flew! She spun to get her bearings, Malcolm at her side. They had come back early.

Aiming toward the Pyre, the twins took off like rockets. The sky split with a sonic boom as they broke the sound barrier. They reached it before John could blink.

Instead of stopping, the twins flew around the Pyre in rapid circles. Flashes of energy poured off them and slammed into the skyscraper from all sides, carving deep furrows into its structure.

More Time portals opened. The twins flew through them, then reappeared to fly more circles and unleash more fury at the Pyre. They flew through portals again, reappeared again and again, until multiple versions of them overlapped each other. Now dozens of Gilbert twins swarmed, and Helios's fortress quaked under their assault.

On a hunch, John quickly called up international video

feeds. Each skyscraper now had a portal in the sky next to it. Each was being swarmed by many Valentines and Malcolms, all leaping through micro-portals and reappearing in the same instant to multiply their attacking power.

The Pyres began falling to pieces. The twins were literally carving through them, reducing them to debris. As piles of wreckage fell, they were snatched from the air by some invisible force and sucked through the portals. The Gilbert twins razed them down to the foundations, leaving nothing, then split apart and rained the same destruction on the supporting mini-towers.

Behind John, others had caught sight of the spectacle and were joining him in shouting.

"Yeah, that's how we do it!" Fred shouted, pumping his fist.

With the doomsday machines in smoldering ruins, all portals winked out of existence. The twins' copies collapsed back into only the two of them. Glowing streaks in the sky, they raced across Emmett's Bluff toward the Eon Palace.

There was a blinding flash. Sounds like rock exploding and metal rending. A wave of dizziness swept over John. He glanced outside and saw that the ground below had been reduced to a deep, black crater.

He turned to check if everyone was okay. Only then did he notice the shimmering temporal bubble.

It extended over him and his friends, separating this corner of the Command Center from everything else. Outside, the battle between human and machine raged at one-tenth normal speed.

He exchanged puzzled glances with Fred and Callie, Walter, then Winter and Tyrathorn. Then . . . wait. Grace and Neil were standing there, too, blinking in surprise.

The bubble rippled. Valentine and Malcolm stepped inside.

"Jeez, guys, we only left two days, ago," Malcolm joked. "What happened?"

Valentine shook her head. "This is why we can't have nice things."

The next moments were a blur of happy reunions. Malcolm kept breathing little sighs of relief: they had come back just in time. Minutes later and the damage would have been done.

He came face to face with John, and for an eternal moment they stared at each other. Fear painted John's face.

He choked back sudden tears. "Malcolm, I . . . I'm so sorry."

Malcolm pulled John into a hug. A sigh of relief escaped his friend's lips.

"You did what you had to do," Malcolm said. "I can't imagine how hard that was."

When they stepped back, there were tears in Malcolm's eyes, too. But he was smiling.

"If Asha could have chosen her own end, it would have been that. Thank you for helping her save everyone."

John gave a grateful smile. "You're a good man, Malcolm."

The battle with the machines continued outside the bubble. Even at this speed, though, it was clear who would win. The Regent was still out there somewhere, but in this moment his army was being routed with extreme force.

Questions flew at the twins from every side. Valentine tried to answer as best and as quickly as she could. What was the Chrona like? Where had they gone? They could fly now—what's up with that? How did they come back early? It had taken all three of them, the Chrona using her power to literally hold the structure of the Timeline together while the twins traveled back.

They answered everything, savoring the moment while knowing it wouldn't last. This was a welcome reunion, but their work was far from done. They only had minutes.

Finally, Valentine and John found each other, and for a moment the rest of the universe faded away. She flung herself into his arms, tears burning as she kissed the boy she loved more than Time itself.

"I missed you every minute," he whispered.

John pulled back to look in her eyes. He stroked a lock of her hair, tracing down to the end and holding it between his fingers.

"Your hair has grown," he said. "How long were you with her?"

"Weeks, at least."

"Even months, maybe," Malcolm said.

Oma Grace ruffled Malcolm's long, brown hair. Valentine paused at that. *When did I start thinking of it as long?*

"Are you certain, dear boy?" Oma Grace said affectionately. "You look like some hippie friends I had in the sixties."

"You do look different," their dad said, gazing at them. "Both of you."

Valentine exchanged a look with her brother. Now that they were out of the Aegis, somehow the days away were coming into focus, as if their time away was now organizing in her mind. Their jaws fell open.

"It couldn't be," Malcolm said.

But it could, and they both knew it.

"Two years," Valentine said. "I . . . I think we were there for two years."

Their friends gave a collective gasp.

"Yo, it's been like forty-two hours here," Fred said. "That is crazy."

"It was the only way," Malcolm said. "The only way to have the breakthroughs we needed. It took every minute."

"And now you're back for good?" Callie asked.

Valentine nodded.

"So, what comes next?" Winter asked.

"We stunned the Regent, but he'll recover," Malcolm said. "We'll need to deal with him."

"But he's lost, hasn't he?" Neil asked.

A stray plasma bolt flew across the Command Center and crossed through the bubble. Absently, Valentine flicked at it with her hand. The bolt bounced away and struck the ceiling.

"His armies may have lost, but he was the real power behind them," she said without noticing the astonished expressions at what she'd just done. "And now he'll be angry and desperate."

"Then how will you deal with him?" Walter said.

The twins hesitated.

"Honestly," Malcolm said. "We don't know. He's going to be in a fighting mood. Short of killing him, I don't know. We'll figure it out."

"Just tell us how we can help," John said.

He slid his arm around Valentine's waist and pulled her close. She turned and gazed up at him, bursting with love. Nothing had ever felt more right than this. No place had ever felt more perfect than between his arms.

Her thoughts traveled back to the words she had said to Malcolm, about the future she wanted. As John Carter filled her vision, suddenly Valentine couldn't wait for it another second.

"The Regent's my second priority." Turning to face John, she grasped both of his hands. "This is my first."

Amid more gasps, Valentine sank to one knee.

"John, will you marry me?"

He beamed with joy, not hesitating for a second.

"Of course I will."

Kneeling with her, he pulled her close. Valentine reveled in the cheers of their family, then blocked them out enough to savor John's lips on hers.

"So, the town's burned down," he said when they parted. "Think the Aegis has a jewelry store?"

As if on cue, a Cyonic burst apart nearby, flinging internal clockwork into their bubble. With an ironic chuckle, John retrieved a sprocket and held it out to Valentine.

"Promise I'll get you a better one soon."

Valentine grinned. "I could not care less. I have you."

"Not to kill the cute moment," Winter said, "but John, you're literally wearing a ring on each finger."

They stared down at John's hands.

"Oh, right," John said. "I'm more tired than I thought."

As everyone laughed, John removed the smallest ring and slipped it onto Valentine's finger. For a moment of bliss, she just stared down at it—smooth, black metal set with a single jewel that glowed blue. It was the most beautiful thing she'd ever seen.

"Well, now we *have* to survive," Oma Grace said. "There's a wedding to plan!"

"Plan?" John said, gazing at Valentine. "I could get married right now and be happy."

Smiling, she stroked the side of his face. "If only, right?"

He nodded. "If only."

To the side, Fred cleared his throat. "Um, hey guys? Remember when I got back from traveling, and said I'd become an ordained minister?"

Valentine stared up at her friend in surprise. In the stunned silence, Fred shrugged.

"Just sayin'. If y'all wanna get married now . . ."

"We're in the middle of a battle, Fred," Neil said.

For the lives they lived, what could be more appropriate? Valentine looked to John. Instant agreement passed between them. They stood in unison.

"Let's do it," Valentine said. "Right now."

"Fred," John said, "we would be honored."

Just like that, their wedding began. Once the decision had been made, everyone fell in together to make it happen. They had only minutes before this war resumed for them all. So, Valentine and John would make the most of it.

In mere moments, they were standing before their friend. Behind them, someone pulled out their phone and began playing Pachelbel's "Canon in D," one of Valentine's favorites.

Fred adopted a pious, overly dignified air.

"A wise man once said, what is love?" he began. "Baby don't hurt me."

"Fred," Oma Grace snapped, "be serious, please."

Valentine laughed. "No, it's okay."

John laughed with her. "We knew what we were getting into. Go on, Fred."

Fred held up his hands. "Only joke, y'all, I promise. But I had to."

Taking a moment, Fred passed his gaze between Valentine and John. To her amazement, his goofy grin faded, leaving something earnest.

"I don't think about love all that often. When I do, though," he gestured at Valentine and John, "first thing that pops into my head is you two. World traveler and world-class player I may be, but across this whole wide world I ain't never seen two people more perfect for each other than you."

"Hear, hear!" Malcolm hooted.

"Y'all take care of each other. You're the same in all the right ways and different in all the right ones, too. Most people laugh when someone talks about love lasting forever. But most people haven't met Valentine Gilbert and John Carter. One of y'all has enough brains for five people, the other is a master of Time. If anyone's got a shot at forever, I'd say we're looking at 'em. But I promise you this: whatever life you build together, I can't wait to see it, because it's gonna be epic."

Valentine sniffed, tears sliding down her face. The good kind of tears today. John's eyes filled with his own. Even Fred sniffed and turned away to wipe his eyes.

John examined their friend. "Fred, are you—?"

Fred held up a finger. "Don't even start, dawg!"

Everyone laughed.

"Fred, you're crying over your own speech," Winter said.

"So what? Fight me, bro," Fred said. But he was smiling. They all were. Rolling his shoulders, he tried to get serious. "A'ight, ain't no thing but to do this thing. You two ready?"

Valentine and John faced each other. Clutching each other's hands, gazing into each other's eyes, they said the words. While battle filled the room around them, steel and fire flying outside the bubble, in here they promised their lives and their love for as many days and as many years as they could share.

It raced by in a blur, feeling like a dream. Before Valentine knew it, John was hers forever and they were locked in the passionate first kiss of their new life, cheers filling the air around them.

Oh my God, Valentine thought as their lips parted. *I'm someone's wife now.*

When this war ended, she would finally start the next great adventure with John Carter. The boy who had fallen through Time, into her life, then grown every day into an amazing man.

"I love you so much," she breathed, barely believing a person could feel so happy.

John kissed her forehead. "I will love you always, Valentine."

"I suppose the honeymoon will have to wait," Tyrathorn said with a grin. "At least, until evil has been vanquished."

Valentine giggled. "I think we can live with—"

She cut off as the temporal flow outside *shifted*. Before she could shout a warning, blast waves assaulted the Command Center. The outer wall cracked and burst, the viewing glass shattered. Time screamed in her head.

Valentine clung to John as their feet left the floor. It felt as if they spun for an eternity before tumbling back down in a heap. They slid to a stop, and she leapt to her feet. Not far away, Malcolm did the same.

As they faced the jagged opening, the Regent hovered into view, his visage twisted with hate.

"Very touching," he said. "Now you won't have to die alone."

CHAPTER 46

Valentine stood over her husband, shielding him from the Regent.

Helios, she reminded herself. *He's not going to rule anything anymore.*

But as she watched the man smirk, hovering before them with his arrogant entitlement, her blood began to boil. This would-be king was trying to take everything from her. Every part of her world, everyone she loved, every moment she had ever shared with them. And now she had her own family to protect.

Her hands clenched into fists. One way or another, this was going to end now.

Helios pointed at the twins. "Your deaths will—"

"Shut up!" Valentine spat, stepping toward him. "Shut up, shut up—"

"—you colossal jackass!" Malcolm finished, stepping forward with her.

Valentine snarled. "I've had enough of this."

The twins charged.

In the fraction of a second it took to close the distance, Valentine saw Helios flinch.

The twins leapt through the broken window and crashed

into Helios so hard that a shock wave rattled the Eon Palace. With the enemy gripped tightly between them, they shot like rockets into the sky. Emmett's Bluff fell away behind them until they crashed into the rocky hills north of town.

They hit the ground and skipped forward until they burst through a boulder. The three of them spun apart, leaving deep furrows in the earth behind them.

Valentine flipped onto all fours, dug hands and feet into the ground, and slowly scraped to a halt. Shaking with rage, she scanned for Helios. With her eyes, she examined the rocky hills with their ancient trees. With her Chronauri senses, she felt along the flows of Time.

Malcolm was over there, approaching fast. Helios was . . . *there*. Valentine had come to a stop in a valley between two hills, but Helios had spun away to the next valley over. A tall hill stood between them.

With a wave, Valentine opened a temporal viewing window. She peered through Time and space to watch Helios as he regained his feet. Shaking the dirt from his clothes, he looked skyward for the twins' approach.

Now it was her turn to smirk. *Not even close.*

She summoned flows of Time. They didn't have to channel through her anymore. Instead, responding to her will, they slammed into the hill separating Valentine from her prey. She dove in, flying through the earth with a rumble and then bursting through the other side in a hailstorm of rock and dirt.

Helios only had a chance to gape before Valentine struck with supersonic speed. All around them the hills shook and the trees rattled. He flew back as if he'd been tossed by a tornado.

His body tore through swathes of hillside, pulverizing rocks and trees along the way, until he finally hit the ground and sent mounds of earth flying. He came to a stop at the head of a smoking crater.

Valentine stalked toward their enemy. "All these years we've fought people like you."

Helios regained his feet. Suddenly his image blurred and skipped, blinking into existence and then away again at a hundred points around Valentine. Reappearing fully beside her, he struck hard enough to level a building.

Pain burst across Valentine's flank. She stumbled back, doubling over, and called a bolt of lightning from the clear blue sky. Helios collapsed.

"All these years," she said. "Getting clobbered by Time-traveling bullies while we only tried to protect."

Helios tried to stand. Malcolm appeared behind him. Ripping a huge oak tree from the ground, Malcolm swung like a Major League slugger and shattered it over Helios's head. The Regent went down to his knees.

"One day, we started getting stronger," Malcolm said. Then he disappeared.

Valentine stepped up in his place. "A *lot* stronger."

Conjuring a Time grenade like the glass bombs they used to use, she affixed it to her boot and delivered an earth-shattering kick to Helios's temple. In a burst of red energy, he flopped onto his back.

Valentine's heart leapt. *We're doing it!* She felt Malcolm returning and moved aside.

He reappeared overhead, carrying a boulder the size of a truck.

"So strong, we had to start holding back," he said. "So that when we fought all those villains, we wouldn't kill them."

He flung the boulder down. Helios actually cried out as it hit him like a thunderbolt and exploded into a million pieces.

Their enemy lay prone, gasping for breath, bleeding for real this time. Kneeling beside him, Valentine let herself envision what this man would have done to John. Then she grabbed Helios's chin and forced him to look up at her.

"But we don't have to do that with you, do we?" she said. "Because you can take it."

Valentine burst into the air. Flying high, she centered herself above Helios. Malcolm saw the move and knew to back away.

Now for the finisher.

Valentine cast her will out, summoning the culmination of all her days as a Chronauri. All her training, all her battles, every enemy she had faced in the fight to protect the Timeline and the people she loved. It all gathered around her, an unstoppable thunderhead of Time. The sky crackled and burst around her.

She focused it all, collecting it in the palm of her hand. In her mind Helios glowed like a bull's-eye, as if beckoning to her.

With a shout, Valentine unleashed everything.

Lightning and thunder. Ice and fire. Flows of Time big enough to wrap around the planet. She sent it all hurtling down at the man who would destroy it all. The weapon hit like a thousand thunderclaps.

Everything went white.

Emmett's Bluff shook hard enough to rattle John's teeth. The flash from the northern hills had been nearly blinding, the sound impossibly loud. When it dissipated, he peered north and his jaw dropped.

"Dude," Fred said, incredulous. "A bunch of hills are just *gone*. What's happening up there?"

John wished he knew. As if his gaze alone could sustain his wife (wow, *wife*), he stayed riveted northward. Until he saw her face again, his heart wouldn't beat.

Please live, he thought. *Come back to me.*

Valentine let her blood return to normal. Otherwise she would have kept pounding the Regent until he scattered to individual atoms. She stood over their fallen foe, Malcolm at her side.

"That was thorough," Malcolm said.

She breathed in deeply. "He had it coming."

They stood in a crater, as deep as if a meteor had struck the earth. Except that at the impact point, instead of a hunk of rock, there lay the world's greatest enemy.

"I hate to admit it," Valentine said, "but that felt great."

Helios still breathed, but hadn't woken. Malcolm prodded him with his boot, tense and ready to move. Nothing.

He gave a relieved sigh. "I can't believe it's over."

"Technically, it's not. We still have to figure out what to do with him. Then there's helping the Chrona fix the Aegis. Then—"

Malcolm chuckled, rolling his eyes. "Jeez, Val, savor the moment."

He did have a point. Looking down at the vanquished warlord, Valentine allowed herself to feel what this meant. They had protected the Timeline—the *whole* Timeline. She smiled.

"That's more like it," Malcolm said.

"I am happy. I'll just be happier when we find an unbreakable prison to drop him into."

"We'll probably need to build it ourselves. What kind of walls could hold him?"

He stopped, and their eyes met. A very specific type of *shift* was rippling through the Timeline. The twins turned as the Chrona stepped out of the Aegis.

"Well done," she said, her relief palpable. "You have surpassed all of this bitter old woman's hopes."

Valentine's heart warmed. Genuine, unqualified praise from the Chrona was a rare thing. The only thing better would be seeing John again.

"We were talking about what to do with him," she said.

"Yes, I know."

The Chrona marched past the twins, toward her nephew's prone form.

"Any suggestions?" Malcolm said.

"There is only one solution."

Staring down at Helios, the Chrona's face contorted with hate. She raised her right hand as Time collapsed into solid form, the shape of a dagger, in her palm. Something about it *twisted*, it felt wrong.

"Wait!" Valentine called. We don't—"

The Chrona swung. Her dagger hurtled toward Helios's heart, its blade literally slicing through Time. The very tip pierced his chest.

Helios's eyes opened.

He disappeared in a flash, and the Chrona's dagger buried itself in the earth. Before Valentine could react, the air rippled behind the old woman's back. Time folded, then unfolded. Helios stepped through, now standing behind his aunt with that deadly, glowing sword in his hand.

With a cry, the twins summoned their power. Too late. Far too late. Helios wrapped his free arm around the Chrona's neck.

Then he plunged the sword through her back and out her chest. The Chrona gasped in shock, flailing at Helios but unable to stop him.

He put his lips to her ear. "Your reign ends."

With a bitter snarl, he twisted the blade. The Chrona spasmed, her eyes wide. A shock wave of light, sound, and energy burst from her and threw the twins onto their backs. Disoriented, Valentine could only watch in horror.

Helios's power clawed deep inside the Chrona. As she gasped a dying breath, he ripped out her Chronauri spark and absorbed it. The source of her power paired with his own.

Before the twins' eyes, Helios of the Ptolemaic line became the most powerful Chronauri ever to exist.

Valentine met Malcolm's eyes and saw her fear echoed in him. It had taken their combined power to defeat this man before.

But it didn't mean they wouldn't try again.

"Well," Malcolm shrugged, "who else is there?"

Valentine shook her head. "Just us."

With a pause to gather their courage, they nodded once to each other and stood to face the man who would kill them.

The instant Helios turned on them, the fight was over. A storm of agony surrounded Valentine, lasting a moment and an eternity. When it passed, she dropped hard onto her back. Malcolm lay gasping beside her.

Helios loomed over them, vibrating with cosmic power. To Valentine's surprise, he carelessly flicked his sword away. The weapon disappeared before hitting the ground.

"You will not die," Helios said. "Not yet. Only when I take

command of the Aegis, only when you see all that you love un-ravel, will I allow oblivion to take you. Witness now as I claim my birthright."

CHAPTER 47

The Chrona is dead.

Lying on the churned earth, Malcolm blinked back tears. The eccentric, overly demanding, sometimes crazy, wonderful, amazing woman who had watched over the Timeline for so long was gone. She had taught the twins so much more than how to wield Time. She had shown them the endless, beautiful reasons it must be protected.

Goodbye, my friend, he thought. *I'm sorry we can't mourn you yet.*

Smirking, Helios backed away from the twins and peered up at the sky. A kind of peace crossed his face. Not the look of a man who wanted actual peace, but a man who knew he couldn't be stopped.

Leaning on each other, the twins managed to shakily stand. There was no way they were going out on their knees.

Helios paid them no mind. They were beneath him now. Closing his eyes, he spread his arms wide as if ready to receive a gift.

"At last," he breathed. "Everything is mine."

Malcolm felt Helios radiate the combined signatures of himself, what must be his sister Selene, and the Chrona into the universe, as if announcing his presence. Knowing what Helios was after, Malcolm wore a weary grin.

Helios's eyes opened. His gaze cast about suspiciously. Then he shut them again and redoubled his efforts. Still nothing happened. He trembled with exertion, refusing to give in as frustration mounted.

Finally, with a gasp, he stopped. When his eyes opened, they glared accusingly at the twins. He stalked back to them, projecting menace.

"What is happening?" he demanded. "I control the Chrona's power. Why does the Aegis not open?"

Malcolm only chuckled. Rage flashed in Helios's eyes. He swung, bashing his fist into Malcolm's temple with a sound like thunder. Malcolm rocked back, but his smile reappeared.

Helios pointed at Valentine. "You know the misery I can bring you. Tell me!"

"Oh, we were going to," Valentine said, amused. "But you just seemed so satisfied with yourself."

"Who were we to spoil your victory?" Malcolm added.

"I am losing my patience."

Valentine scoffed. "You have nothing left to threaten us with. Pain and death? Been there, done that."

"And we'd rather lose it all than let you rule it," Malcolm said.

"Tell me!"

Valentine said, "You thought it requires a temporal signature, like a lock with one key."

"When really," Malcolm continued, "It's a combination lock. Sure, you need the right signature, but it has to sense that signature coming from about fifty different days, hours, and places simultaneously."

Valentine cocked her head in mock curiosity. "You already know we're not going to tell you. So, how many combinations do you think you'll have to try before you guess the right one?"

Helios backed away in horror. "It cannot be. There is another way in; there must be! This is my right, you peasants!"

"In your dreams," Malcolm said.

"You may have won, Helios," Valentine said, "but you've lost where it counted. So, enjoy this victory now, because it's all you'll ever get."

With a shout of rage, Helios lifted into the air.

"The Aegis will be mine if I have to cut my way through the universe to get it!"

He rocketed into the sky. The sword reappeared in his hand, growing in size and brightness. Malcolm could feel his power coursing through it. When the Regent neared a low-hanging cloud, he stopped.

Drawing back, he swung the sword with all his might. Impossibly, the blade cut into the fabric of the universe and left a gaping tear in reality.

With a gasp, the twins fell back. Helios swung again, and again he cut a hole in the universe.

"What the . . . ?" Valentine said. "He's gone crazy! How is he doing that?"

Dread filled Malcolm. "It's fragile enough already. If he keeps cutting, you know what will happen."

"The whole thing's going to shatter."

"No more Timeline. No more universe."

"He wants to rule everything so badly, he'll destroy it in the process." Valentine shook her head in despair. "There must be some way to stop it."

Malcolm hesitated, knowing the risk of what he was about

to propose. Should it be up to them to take this kind of chance? To risk everything?

What's better? he asked himself. *Standing by while it's all destroyed, or trying to save it and possibly destroying it yourself?*

If he was wrong, history would judge the twins harshly. Then again, if they failed, there would be no history to judge them. *Okay, then.* Now to convince Valentine. He moved to speak.

"There is one way," Valentine said before he could. "But it's a last resort."

Despite the impending doom, Malcolm couldn't help sharing a smile with his sister. They had come up with the same idea, and each had been planning how to convince the other.

"So, how should we do it?" Valentine asked. "The direct approach?"

"Actually, I had another idea."

They clung to each other.

With the Pyre destroyed, the machine army had quickly drained its collective batteries and dropped dead. The Destroyer pilots had surrendered and been locked away. In every sense of the word, Everwatch's victory over the machines had been total. This was a day they would speak of for generations.

But no one celebrated. Instead they stood shoulder to shoulder, lending each other strength as they watched the spectacle in the northern hills. The only things holding back annihilation were two teenage twins.

One of them was John's wife. He stood with his new extended family, their hearts in suspended animation while they waited on Valentine and Malcolm. While they waited to see if the universe would go on existing.

Helios was in the sky now. Whatever weapon the man wielded, it must have been doing unnatural things to the Timeline. Even John, with no Chronauri ability, could feel the wrongness, like a ripping that wouldn't stop.

Please, Valentine, be okay.

Neil Gilbert pointed north. "What is that?"

Something was rising from the earth below Helios. An orb of red light, shining like a star and growing brighter as it ascended.

Two smaller stars orbited it, silvery light traveling in circles around the red. They spun slowly at first, but as the red star grew brighter, the speed of their orbit increased until John could barely follow them.

It was strangely beautiful. Hope filled him. If those two silver stars were what he imagined, maybe there was a chance after all.

Keep flying. Keep feeding it power. Almost ready.

Malcolm's power streamed all around him. Answering his call, it rushed constantly into the red orb the twins had created. On the far side, he could see Valentine with the same determined expression.

In unison, they pushed harder. The orb grew denser and more radiant, raw Time spinning inside it like a miniature star.

No, not a miniature star, a giant Time grenade.

The twins spun faster and faster, working to contain it from all sides. Soon they would have to increase the intensity even more. Malcolm feared what might happen then, but it was necessary.

"What is this?"

Helios had floated farther away, so intent on slicing the universe to ribbons that he hadn't taken notice of them. Until now. Malcolm's insides roiled as their enemy drew closer. He clamped down on his fear.

Focus. Do your job. Then, at the right moment . . .

Helios eyed their creation with derision. "This is your last resort? Your toys may have stung me before, little ones, but now I have ascended. *I have become a god.*"

He floated closer, wearing a half-smile as if he pitied them.

Wait for it, Malcolm told himself. *You'll know the moment.*

Within arm's reach of the Time grenade, Helios grasped his temporal sword with both hands and raised it high. One last time, Malcolm's eyes met Valentine's. *Get ready.*

"If this is your last hope," Helios said, "allow me to relieve you of it."

He swung.

Now.

As the blade pierced the Time grenade, the twins released their hold on it. The red energy unraveled, revealing that it hadn't been a Time grenade at all, but merely a convincing shell. Beneath it was another orb, this one made of deep, inky blackness.

A Night Blossom.

Helios's blade struck its shadowy surface and plunged through. The Night Blossom grabbed hold and sucked in the entire sword. Shocked, Helios kept his grip on the sword until it disappeared.

His hands, too, broke the surface of the Night Blossom. When he tried to pull away, he found that he couldn't.

Malcolm grinned. Helios cast about wild-eyed, searching for leverage while he yanked hopelessly on his arms. When his eyes met Malcolm's, they betrayed the one thing that shamed someone like Helios the most.

Fear.

The twins floated backward, increasing the space between themselves and the Night Blossom. With another burst of power, they spun faster than any human eye could follow.

The air whirled like a hurricane. Trees and boulders tore from the surrounding hills to orbit them. Clouds gathered from miles away and compressed into a storm head around them. Thunder cracked and lightning leapt from cloud to cloud, glancing off stone and earth.

In the eye of the storm, Valentine held a tight grip on the Night Blossom, using all her strength to manage its power. Malcolm held a temporal bubble around them all, ready to collapse it when the moment arrived.

In the center of it all, screaming defiance and terror, Helios sank further into the shadows. The Night Blossom clawed at him, relentless and unbreakable.

His arms had disappeared. He flailed, trying to kick at the blackness with his feet. His legs sank in, too.

He summoned all the Time he could, trying strike at the twins, to strike at the orb, determined to break everything in his struggle for freedom. The Night Blossom consumed that, too.

Helios's strength began to fail him. His chest touched the blackness, then his whole torso. Turning his neck as far as possible, he struggled while the left side of his face stuck to the inky surface. Inch by slow inch, he disappeared.

"I am a god!" he cried.

Malcolm floated closer until he could meet Helios face to face. He leaned in, making sure he would be heard.

"No," Malcolm said. "You're already forgotten."

Drawing back, he gathered swarms of Time and gravitation force around his fist and delivered a cosmic punch to the side of Helios's face.

Helios gave one final, desperate wail. The sound muffled as his mouth sank beneath the blackness. All that remained was one terrified eye, giving Helios his last look at the universe.

Then the Night Blossom took him.

Valentine released her hold on the orb. Gripping the bubble with all his might, Malcolm slammed it down into the size of a marble.

Like a thunderclap, the compression forced the Night Blossom to shrink and then collapse. Malcolm clamped down until the shadows disappeared. Whatever existed on the other side, it was separate from them again, and the Regent with it.

The twins lowered to the ground. Releasing their hold on Time, they sank to their knees. Once again, they leaned on each other for support. Malcolm's chest heaved with exertion.

"We just . . ." he panted. "We just . . ."

"I know . . ." Valentine clutched her chest. "He's really gone."

She laughed in disbelief. Malcolm couldn't help laughing, too. The kind of laugh that only happens after nearly dying.

"They're safe. All of them."

Closing his eyes, Malcolm placed both hands over his heart. "For you, Asha."

CHAPTER 48

Valentine closed her eyes, savoring the warm breeze on her skin.

"You hear that, Mal?" she said. "No one's trying to destroy the world."

"I could use more of that."

"No argument here."

Valentine knew they would have to get moving again soon. For now, though, she let the tranquility cradle her.

"I've been thinking," Malcolm said softly. "If Asha hadn't done what she did, the Regent would have killed us that day. There would've been no one left who could stand up to him."

"True."

"So, really, when you think about it, Asha saved the world."

Valentine opened her eyes. Malcolm wore a bittersweet expression, but there was a kind of peace underneath it.

She nodded. "In all the Timeline, I think there will only ever be one Asha Corvonian."

Malcolm faced southeast. They could see the Eon Palace in the distance. It was damaged, smoking, but it wouldn't stay that way for long.

"When things are settled," Malcolm said, "I think I'd like to visit Everwatch again. Just for a little while, to—"

The twins cried out in pain. Clutching their heads, they fell to their knees.

A ripping sensation tore through Valentine. Staring up at the sky, she saw what was happening and her insides went cold.

The Timeline was breaking.

She could see it—reality itself, coming apart at the seams as those burning, black cracks spread unchecked.

Valentine could feel the Aegis buckling under the strain. The flow of Time through the universe was turning chaotic. In a cruel twist of fate, it seemed their enemy might get his revenge after all.

"What Helios did," Valentine said. "All those holes he cut in the Timeline—"

"—pushed it over the edge," Malcolm finished. "It was weak already, but after that . . ."

As the initial shock passed, the twins' pain faded enough that they could stand. Every muscle in Valentine's body protested.

Together they stared helplessly up at the sky. The beautiful blue fractured more with each second, broken apart by the advance of the black cracks. As if in protest, lightning flashed and thunder rolled.

"Oh, God, Mal," Valentine said in horror. "The Chrona's gone. What do we do without her? There's no one up there to protect the Timeline!"

She cast about half-panicked, as if the surrounding hills might miraculously provide an answer. Some way to—

"Val."

Turning suddenly to face her, Malcolm took both of her hands in his. She had never seen this look in his eyes before.

"You and John," he said. "You really are perfect for each other. You're going to be so happy, I know it."

"What?"

"Look after Dad and Callie. I know they're adults, but still. They both need family."

"What are you doing?"

"And I don't want you to worry about me. It's okay. Whatever happens, just remember that it's okay. I *chose* this. I wanted to do it, for all of you."

"No!" She recoiled. "Mal, you're saying goodbye. Why? Stop saying goodbye!"

"Only two Sixth-*sev* Chronauri left in the universe, Val. Don't you see? It was always going to be one of us, and I understand now . . . it was always going to be me."

"Please don't do this. There has to be another way."

"It all makes sense now. Why I ran from love or attachment while you grabbed it with open arms. Why you've always known exactly what your life should be, but I was never sure about mine. It's so clear now. I could never see my place in this world because my place was never *in* this world. My future wasn't in one place or Time, but *all* of them. Somehow, I think I always knew it."

Valentine didn't know when she started crying, but now hot tears streamed down her face. She tried to speak and failed. All she could do was shake her head.

No, please, she begged the universe. *Don't take him, too.*

"The Timeline needs a Chrona, Val. You have a life here, a new family. This world, this century, they're going to need you and John to guide them." Malcolm wiped away some of her tears. "Let me do this for you."

He was right. Even through her protests, Valentine knew

it. The Timeline needed a Chrona, but she couldn't leave this place or this Time. Not anymore.

In the light of cold logic, it seemed inevitable. But Valentine couldn't be logical right now.

"But you can't just leave," she protested, waving toward Emmett's Bluff. "What about your friends? Your family?"

Malcolm gave her a smile tinged with sadness. "I'm already saying goodbye to them. Can't you feel it?"

She could. Swimming through her grief, Valentine sensed a series of temporal glows coming from the Eon Palace. Malcolm knew the Timeline didn't have long, so he was using their trick to be in multiple places at once. Their family were separated into Time bubbles, each with him inside.

She gazed at her brother, astonished. "You're already acting like her. And I mean that in a good way."

He gave a grateful smile. Valentine looked over her shoulder, her Chronauri eyes catching the distant glow.

"What are you saying to them?"

Malcolm and Walter Crane shook hands, the older man's grip as strong as ever. He really had found his place among the Watchers.

"I'm proud of you, kid," Walter said. "Always have been, always will be. I know Time will be in good hands."

"Thank you, Walter." Malcolm cocked his head with a grin. "You know, none of this would have been possible if you hadn't saved me from Lucius Carmichael all those years ago. So, in a way, you helped save the world."

Walter shook his head. "Don't blow smoke up by butt, kid. I'm just an old soldier doing his job."

He was smiling, though.

"No," Malcolm said. "You're my friend. Always will be."

Tugging on Walter's hand, Malcolm pulled him into an embrace.

"Goodbye, Malcolm," Walter said, his voice thick.

"Goodbye, Walter. Look after them for me, would you?"

"To my last breath, kid."

Tyrathorn was an enthusiastic hugger. Surprisingly, Winter squeezed Malcolm just as tightly. He couldn't help laughing.

"This isn't the last day we'll see each other, you know. Everwatch and the Chrona are supposed to work together."

The king and queen of Everwatch released him. Tyrathorn clapped him on the shoulder as he used to do in those early days, when he first taught the twins what it was to be Chronauri.

"We will be honored, Malcolm," he said. "No matter where, no matter when, you have only to call and we shall answer."

"Try to stay out of trouble," Winter said, grinning. "And maybe cause some while you're at it. Show the bad guys who's boss."

Malcolm grinned back. "I'll do my best."

He almost said goodbye then. But he couldn't—not yet. Though they had many meetings yet to come, Malcolm couldn't move on until he said it.

"Asha was the best of us, you know," he said, swallowing a lump in his throat. "I loved her so much. As long as the Timeline is mine to protect, Thorn, I promise you, she will never be forgotten."

Tyrathorn wiped away tears. "You are a better man than

this universe deserves, Malcolm Gilbert. I know you would have made her happy."

Malcolm held those words and Asha's memory in his heart. He knew that it would be enough.

"Dude, you're takin' over? That is *sweet*." Fred pulled Malcolm into a quick bro-hug, slapping him on the back. "I know you'll keep history cool."

"I'll try," Malcolm said, chuckling. *Classic Fred.* Yet, as he stood before his friend, he couldn't help growing serious. "I don't think I ever thanked you. Everything you've done . . ."

Fred waved it away. "Psh, it's cool. Don't worry about it."

"No, Fred, if there's any moment to say this, it's now. I know you play around because it's fun, but I also know it's sort of your shield. I want you to know I see the guy underneath. He's a far better person than you believe he is, and I think it's about time the world met him."

Fred stared down, his silliness fading. Malcolm saw his cheeks turn red.

"You really mean that?"

"Fred, look at you. You're a normal guy with friends who fell into a battle for the Timeline. Do you even realize how many chances you had to turn and run? But you stuck by us. You nearly died protecting us. You traveled the world, training just so you could help us. In any year, in any place, they would say you're a hero. And I would agree with them."

Fred looked up at that, staring at Malcolm in disbelief. His eyes were glassy.

"You and Val changed my life, you know. Changed *me.* All these scars . . ." He loosened his armor enough to expose his right shoulder. It still bore the mark where a long shard of glass had pierced him on the day he and Winter fought Lucius Carmichael's henchman. "I'd take a thousand more if it meant keeping y'all safe. I always knew the world would need you. Turns out I was right."

They shared a warm smile, enjoying the moment. Neither of them knew when they would get another one.

"One more thing," Malcolm said. "My perceptions of Time are already starting to expand. I don't know, maybe the Timeline knows what I'm about to do, or some future version of me is helping. Either way, I'm about to break a rule and tell you the future."

Fred brightened. "That's my boy. You know I love breaking rules."

"Oh, yes, I do." Malcolm said. "So here it is. In about a year, Winter and Thorn are going to come to you. They're going to offer you something. As the Chrona changes, so will the way we protect the Timeline, which means they'll need new ways to do it. They're going to ask you to lead a very special squad of Ember Guard."

"Yo, seriously? I ain't even Chronauri."

"I know. You'd be the first Watcher to lead Ember Guard. But if it's going to work, it'll need someone like you. *They* will need someone like you." Malcolm leaned closer, wearing a conspiratorial grin. "My advice? Take the offer, and thank me later."

Fred didn't even stop to consider. He just clasped Malcolm's hand and shook it.

"You got my word, bro. I'll do my best."

"I know you will, Fred." Malcolm pulled him into a real hug. "See you somewhere in Time."

They were a mass of embraces and tears.

Malcolm laughed through his own tears as Oma Grace, his father, Callie, and John all clung to him at once. It had taken several minutes to convince them that this had to be done, that it was the only way.

Now each of them alternated between crying and telling him how much they loved him. How proud they were. When they had calmed down enough, they began to talk.

"Who will look after you?" Oma Grace said. "Even a Chrona needs to be taken care of."

Her limitless caring warmed Malcolm's heart. If she could, Oma Grace would deliver chicken soup to the Aegis.

"I'll visit Everwatch," he said. "And I know I'll be busy, but, well, nothing says a Chrona can't come home occasionally."

"You'd better," Neil said.

"Or we'll come find you," Callie finished. "I still have a few tricks up my sleeve."

Neil said, "Just know we're proud of you. And we love you."

"I know. I love you, too." Malcolm turned to John. "Everyone's still alive because of you. Thanks for keeping them safe while we were gone."

"Of course, Malcolm. It was an honor."

Malcolm moved to speak again, but hesitated. "So, Valentine. The first little while won't be easy for her. Will you . . . ?"

John nodded. "I'll be there for her always, I promise. And if . . . *when* . . . we have a family, we'll make sure they know about their Uncle Malcolm. How he protects us."

Malcolm held back fresh tears. He hadn't expected that.

"I couldn't imagine her with anyone better," he said thickly, then forced himself to face the rest of his family. "I love you all so much. It may be a while before we see each other again, but trust me. This isn't the end."

Once more they pulled together, holding tightly for these last, precious moments.

Valentine felt the bubbles fade away. Malcolm faced her with tears in his eyes. She could see it all over his face—saying goodbye was the hardest thing he had ever done. Maybe the hardest thing he would ever do.

"Oh, no," Malcolm said, suddenly fearful. "Val, I've been saying all these goodbyes and making all these promises. But what if I'm not strong enough? I don't even know if I have the power to *be* the Chrona."

In this one thing, Valentine knew she was ahead of her brother. She had expected this and made a decision that even he couldn't have felt coming.

"Take mine," she said.

His head whipped toward her. "What?"

"My power, my spark, whatever it's called. Whatever makes us Chronauri."

He shook his head. "No, Val, I won't do it. I can't!"

"Yes, you can, Malcolm Gilbert. If you can make sacrifices to save the Timeline, so can I. We have no idea what it'll take to fix the Aegis. You need every advantage you can get."

He kept shaking his head, but Valentine saw the moment his resistance broke. As it turned to resignation, his head stopped shaking. She was right, and he knew it.

"Just leave me a little bit, okay? I do like being Chronauri."

That made him laugh. Good; they both needed that.

"Okay. I'll do my best with it, I promise."

"You don't have to promise," she said. "I already know."

Taking a slow, deep breath, Malcolm held up both of his hands. "Ready?"

She mirrored him. "Ready."

Clasping hands, they closed their eyes. Valentine opened her being as much as she could. She dropped all resistance and self-protection, giving Malcolm a clear path to where he needed to go, into the deepest part of who she was.

She felt his presence now, warm and soothing. Gently it moved downward through her, farther than she had thought possible, finally down into that one place no one could explain, not even Chronauri. The place that carried all that she was, the source of her power.

Malcolm's presence brushed Valentine's source. As if they resonated with each other, they both burst with waves of energy. Like twin stars they blazed side by side, not destructive but beautiful. A beacon shining across the Timeline.

Ever so slowly Malcolm's power cupped around Valentine's own. Ever so gently he guided it back with him while leaving her one tiny, vibrant spark.

She could feel it going now, like an old friend flying away over the horizon. As the power moved, her radiance moved with it. Her star's glow flowed to Malcolm. Then, between one breath and the next, what had been hers was now his.

That tiny spark inside Valentine still lived. She was still the slightest bit Chronauri, just enough to brush Time with a finger and feel its warmth. Just enough to sense its flow around her.

And enough, in this moment, to feel her power and Malcolm's combine, cascading off each other, multiplying beyond her dreams until he didn't just glow like a star but gleamed like the universe.

"Oh, wow," he breathed. "I feel it, Val."

She leaned closer. "Feel what?"

"Everything."

He opened his eyes and gazed at her. Behind them now, Valentine saw the depths of eternity she had once seen in Arsinoë. *He really is the Chrona.*

"I know what I must do, with the Aegis, the Timeline, all of it."

Her heart leapt. "You can fix it?"

To her dismay, he shook his head.

"The Aegis is too broken. It can't be fixed. Even if I did, it would be temporary. The problems I told the Chrona about wouldn't go away. Eventually we'd be right back here, watching it break all over again. No, if I'm going to save it for real, I have to do something more."

"Mal, I don't understand. What do you have to do?"

"I have to destroy the Aegis and make a new one."

Valentine couldn't hide her shock. Malcolm saw it, but instead of doubting himself, he gave a reassuring smile.

"It's what I've said all along. The Chrona built something to protect a perfect world. I'm going to build something to protect *ours*. An Aegis that will last forever."

Valentine's words failed her. Through all the conflicting feelings swarming through her, though, she realized a truth. Her fear wasn't coming from Malcolm's revelation. She wasn't afraid of the future of the universe. She was afraid of her future without her twin brother in it.

Malcolm bent to catch her eye again. "Val, just because I'm gone doesn't mean I'm *gone*. I'll watch over you and John and everyone." He paused, holding back tears. "And you're going to have just the best life. You're going to be so happy. I'm going to make sure of it. You won't always see it, but I'll be there."

Valentine smiled through fresh tears. She scrubbed at her cheeks. "But what about the rest of the universe?"

"Hey, forget about that," Malcolm said with a playful shrug. "You're the Chrona's twin sister. That should come with a few perks."

She laughed and she cried together. This time Malcolm didn't hold back his own tears. She pulled him in and they squeezed each other.

"I'm scared, Mal," she confessed.

"Don't worry," he said. "I'm here. I'll protect you."

"I love you, brother."

"I'll love you always, Valentine."

They pulled slowly apart. Still facing her, Malcolm took three steps back and stood straighter, his head high, his shoulders back like a king of old.

"How do I look?" he asked.

Valentine drew in a slow breath, working up the courage to say the words. Then, finally . . .

"You look ready."

What else was there to be said? The Timeline needed saving, now more than ever.

Malcolm burst into the sky. Like a shooting star he sailed higher until he was above the clouds.

Dizziness washed over Valentine. Light swirled around her, and then she was back inside the Eon Palace, side by side with John.

In the distance, the radiance that was Malcolm dove into the spreading, black cracks.

Being in the Aegis, turning in all directions to watch it fracture and crumble, only confirmed Malcolm's conviction. The Timeline needed a new beginning. Only he could give it one.

And there was no Time to waste.

"Live," he whispered. "Everyone live. For me."

Malcolm summoned every shred of his newfound power. Every scrap of his being. Every ounce of his will.

His consciousness expanded outward in cascades, drawing a vision of the Timeline in his mind. He could see it all, gathered around him yet stretching into eternity.

He was its master, its protector. Though he knew it before, now he could feel it. Every second of every day of every year, forever.

It all went back to Tyrathorn's first lesson on Malcolm's first day training. Summon your power. Envision what you want in your mind. With your will, drive your power through that vision. Shape it into what you need, then use it—and in doing so, protect the world with everything you are.

His mind was ready, his will as strong as mountains. His power was gathered and vibrating eagerly in his grip. All that was left to do . . .

I will not fail you, he promised them all. *I am the Chrona.*

In a burst of power that shook the universe to its foundations, Malcolm blasted out the full power of the Chrona. It traveled in all directions. As it swept across the Timeline, passing through past and future, the Aegis of old shattered like glass.

In that instant, it appeared to be a wave of destruction. But then a second wave followed, one that did not destroy but created. An endless wave that focused power into order, forming something new. Something shining and vibrant and alive.

For the people in it, whom he loved more than Eternity itself. That love, a power glowing brighter than Time, infused into the Aegis as it was born from Malcolm's fingertips. Trembling with exertion, he poured the deepest essence of his being into the expanse of his creation.

Until it was finished.

A new Aegis for the world Malcolm loved.

CHAPTER 49

Eldurfall (formerly Emmett's Bluff)
300 Years Later

"You sure you're okay, Oma?" The middle-aged man asked, scratching his beard worriedly.

"I am quite capable of looking after myself, you know."

Sitting up in her medical bed, Valentine gave him a smile, one chiding but tempered with love. She didn't mention that she'd forgotten his name again. Or where he fell in the family line. Squinting, she ordered her blurry eyes to focus. Was he a great-great-grandchild?

He had teenage children, she remembered that. One of the girls had long, red hair that brought back happy memories.

"Good," the man said with a smile that was just a little bit patronizing. "Well, the kids are here, and they'd hate to miss Oma Valentine. They'd like to say hi if you're up to it."

"Oh, of course, dear." Valentine waved him toward the door. "Give me a few minutes, please?"

"Anything you need."

As he turned to leave, she caught a familiar expression on

his face. John had worn a similar one at times. Her relative—her descendant, really—wore a bewildered look that many did in her presence.

She had broken the oldest living human record well over a century ago. Then, for reasons that baffled science, she had just kept on living.

Every branch and discipline had their theories. Even her old colleagues had visited to postulate ideas and learn from her. People she and John had hired long ago to work with them at the institute they had founded, the world's first center for research into temporal physics, which they had been uniquely qualified to spearhead.

Valentine and John—who lived more than two centuries himself—had never revealed the source of their long survival to the scientific community. They had entrusted that knowledge to family only.

In a great twist of irony, their descendants hadn't believed a word of it.

That had bothered her at first, family chalking up her stories to the ramblings of an old woman whose mind was surely fading. Blood should trust each other more than that!

Now, though, as Valentine sensed the last of her days swiftly approaching, she found herself content to let them believe what they wanted. It didn't change the truth. It didn't remove that tiny spark inside her. The one that flickered now, like a candle in a storm.

The door slid shut behind her descendant. To her surprise, it beeped an acknowledgment. It had been locked—not from the outside, but the inside.

The gray hairs on the back of her neck rose. Someone was

in the room with her, she could feel it. Her knuckles cracked in protest as she forced her hands into fists.

"I know you're here," she said.

She heard a soft chuckle, and then a man stepped out of the far corner. Valentine's sense of danger grew—there was no door near that corner. Where had this man come from?

"I never could fool you," he said.

At the sound of his voice, Valentine's insides rang like a gong. A torrent of memories rushed back to her. She brought a hand to her mouth.

"Oh, dear God," she gasped.

The man sat on the bed beside her and gently took her free hand. A cool wave of *something* washed through her. Suddenly she felt alert, and her eyes came into focus.

He appeared to be a man of about thirty-five. But she would have recognized that face anywhere, anytime. Lunging, she pulled her twin brother into an embrace.

"Oh, Malcolm!" she cried. "How long has it been?"

He gave a guilty smile, looking every bit the young boy she remembered. "Far too long. I've been busy, but I've missed you so much."

His gaze flitted to her side table. When he caught sight of the hologram hovering there, his eyes turned glassy. Reaching out, he brushed his fingers affectionately through the projection. It was a vintage photograph of Malcolm and Valentine Gilbert, Winter Tao, and Fred Marshall, standing with their arms around each other in front of Emmett Brown High School.

"I remember when we took this," Malcolm said, grinning from ear to ear. "Fred and Winter wouldn't stop punching each other behind our backs."

Valentine laughed with him. "They kept trying to get each other to make a stupid face—"

"—so it would be caught on camera. Perfect blackmail material."

They both laughed again. Then each grew quiet, lost in a pleasant memory. Finally, though, Valentine knew she had to speak.

"So, my day has come, then?" she said. "You've come to see me off?"

Malcolm looked uneasy at the mention of her death. She gave his hand a reassuring pat.

"It's okay; we don't need to discuss it yet. Tell me about your life. How old are you? What have you done all these years?"

"I'm . . . quite old, actually. Though in the cosmic sense I'm still pretty young. As for what I've done," he shook his head, eyes filling with wonder. "Val, it's more amazing than I ever expected. I mean, there are hard days, too. But mostly it's . . . well, I would make the same choice all over again."

Her heart warmed. How wonderful to see that he was happy. And his words . . .

"No one's called me Val in a very long time," she said. "Now, humor an old woman who used to be quite adventurous herself, and share a story with me."

Malcolm pursed his lips the way he always did when debating with himself. He was unsure about something. Finally, he nodded to himself.

"Actually, I'm here because there are a couple things I've been wanting to do. I was saving them for a special occasion."

"Why is that?"

"Because I wanted you with me."

Valentine leaned back against her pillow, caught off guard.

"What do you say?" Malcolm said with a grin. "Mind coming on one more adventure?"

She answered without hesitation.

That cool wave Malcolm had sent through Valentine was really doing the trick. Getting out of bed had been easier than it had been in years. She was seeing and hearing clearly, and when she walked, there was no need for support. Her back stood straight. A wonderful gift from her brother in her final days.

Hand in hand, they stepped through Malcolm's portal. He had just waved his hand and it had appeared. After so long, Valentine had forgotten how wondrous those abilities were.

When they stepped through, however, her smile faded. "Oh, Mal, I can't see this day again."

"Please, Val." Malcolm squeezed her hand. "I promise it's for a good reason."

"But won't he see me and ask questions?"

"You're phased slightly out of Time," he explained. "You can observe, but no one will see or hear you. Do you trust me?"

Of course he knew the answer, but it worked. Valentine suppressed her discomfort and placed herself in his care. Together they walked across the very top of the Eon Palace. All around them a battle raged, Winter and her soldiers fighting off Cyonics.

In the center, Armel lay on his back, smoke rising from his body.

Valentine stood back as Malcolm knelt by their old friend. He laid a hand on the soldier's shoulder. Armel's eyes fluttered open.

"I knew it," Armel said. "Somehow I knew."

"Everyone will know what you did, Armel," Malcolm said. "Your statue will stand across from Asha's in Meridian Square."

The captain grunted in disbelief. "Me, a statue?"

"I've seen it." Malcolm smiled. "It's nice."

"The rest of them?" Armel said, desperately grasping Malcolm's hand. His body twitched and heaved. "What happens? Will they survive? Will they be all right?"

Malcolm leaned closer and brushed his forehead.

"Close your eyes, my friend. I'll show you."

Armel obeyed, and Time opened up before him.

Even Valentine could see it. Malcolm showed Armel how the battle would end. How the Regent would be vanquished. Then glimpses of his friends' lives throughout the following decades.

Armel had given everything to ensure the ones he loved got a happy ending. Malcolm had come back to this moment to show him that he'd succeeded.

When it was over, Malcolm bade farewell to the brave old soldier and rejoined Valentine. Only then did she realize she was crying.

"I didn't believe I would say this," she said, "but thank you for bringing me here. For letting me see."

"Armel deserved the best ending I could give him. I just wanted him to die happy."

Valentine squeezed his arm, reassuring. "You succeeded, Mal."

He nodded his thanks.

"So. Ready for the next one?"

Her eyebrows raised. "Next one?"

"If you're willing, we have two more stops."

Valentine accepted his outstretched hand.

"Mommy!"

Maya appeared through the smoke, too small to have been caught by the attacks.

"Maya!"

As Callie reached out for Maya, a beam of distortion cut between them, forcing them back from each other. The armored man was pointing at a tall, shiny building a hundred yards beyond where they stood. The very air around him trembled.

"Maya, run!"

As the last word escaped her lips, the armored man unleashed his full power. The distortion beam grew, and as it did, the destruction spread wider around it.

Off to the side, invisible to all, Malcolm and Valentine stood among the maelstrom but were unaffected by it. Valentine cringed away from the tragic scene playing out before them.

"Mal, this is even worse. I can't—"

"Trust me," Malcolm said. "Just one more time, please."

Okay. For him, she could do it. Steeling herself, she turned back to face the scene.

"Maya, baby girl, please just run!" Callie pleaded. "Go! Go!"

Maya—so sweet and innocent, not knowing even the concept of destruction, just reached out to her mother, her eyes pleading for comfort, for safety.

"Mom!"

Malcolm lifted his hand and Time stopped. All around them, everything froze as if it were a photograph.

Gazing at Maya, Valentine breathed a sigh of relief. Malcolm had stopped Time an instant before the wave of destruction enveloped her.

"I do trust you," she assured. "But I have to ask, why here? Why now?"

He smiled cryptically. "I told you long ago, when you're related to the Chrona, there should be a few perks."

While she pondered that, Malcolm approached Callie's daughter and waved his hand. The city stayed locked in Time, but Maya unfroze. She looked around now, puzzled at the strange scene. He knelt and offered her a kind smile.

"Hi, Maya."

She scrubbed tears from her face. "Who are you? I want Mommy!"

"Actually, I'm a good friend of your mom's. She helped me when I really needed it, and I want to do something for her. Will you help me do that?"

Maya looked askance at him, then slowly nodded.

"Good. Now this may sound scary, but I need to tell you. The man who's making all this noise? He was accidentally going to hurt you. So, I came to take you somewhere safe. Now, your mommy's going to have to spend a little time thinking you're not around anymore. But if you come with me, I promise you'll see her again right away. Would you like that?"

Valentine's heart soared. What a priceless gift.

Maya didn't answer immediately, though, and Valentine's admiration for the little girl grew. So small, yet she was no fool. The wheels were turning in her head as she examined her surroundings. Her eyes fell last upon Callie, frozen in a scream as she reached helplessly. She seemed to make a decision then. Turning back to Malcolm, she nodded.

Malcolm's smile broadened. "Good. Just take my hand."

The little girl complied. With another wave of Malcolm's hand, a new portal appeared. As they stepped through, the Time they left behind raced back to normal.

Valentine heard Callie's scream as the portal closed behind them. With the timing of Malcolm's intervention, she would believe she had witnessed her daughter being vaporized. The thought made Valentine shiver. Having her own children now, she couldn't bear imagining what it would have been like.

"I wish I could erase Callie's pain, too. Everything it did to her. It kills me to let it stay." Malcolm faced Valentine, guilt painting his expression. "But the truth is, without that, she never becomes the person she is. She never comes back to our Time, never helps us defeat the Regent. We needed her. So I had to."

He seemed to be asking for her approval. Or at least her understanding.

"Just like we chose not to save our mother," she said. "Pain, yes, but for a greater good."

Malcolm nodded, seeming relieved. "I just . . . I didn't want you to think all this had changed me."

"Oh, Mal," she said, brushing his cheek. "I still know you, and I always will. You'll always try to do the right thing."

His real smile came back now. "Thank you. I needed to hear that. Ready?"

She gave an eager nod. "Oh, yes."

"Ready, Maya?" he asked.

She leapt for joy. "Mommy!"

Chuckling, Malcolm gestured and their portal reopened on a new landscape. He stepped out with Maya's hand in his, Valentine bringing up the rear. They had left behind a futuristic metropolis for a field with tall grass under blue skies.

Emmett's Bluff! Valentine turned in a circle, drinking in the sight. *Just as it was, so long ago.*

By the look of things, they had arrived one or two years after the Regent was vanquished. The town was on its way to becoming better than ever. And yes, more than ever it was known by the world as Home of the Strange.

As Valentine completed her circle, she caught a familiar sight in the distance and stopped short. Her heart leapt into her throat.

"That's me! And John, and Dad, and . . ."

Malcolm glanced back at her, grinning. "And everyone."

He was right. Valentine remembered this day. They had all come together for a picnic out in the fields by Oma Grace's house.

I'm so young! The Valentine of nearly three centuries ago walked with a dancer's lightness of step, wavy, red hair bouncing as she twirled into John's arms. *He's so young!* He was exactly the way she remembered, down to the last detail.

Malcolm tugged playfully on Maya's hand. "Maya, do you see your mother?"

Hopping up and down with excitement, she pointed. Valentine followed the little girl's finger until she found her father and Callie, walking out into the field. Callie had a picnic basket in her hand.

"Well, why don't you go say hello?" Malcolm said.

With a gleeful whoop, Maya set off running. As she did, Malcolm backed away until he was even with Valentine. They watched in anticipation as she closed the distance.

"Everwatch and I have worked together a lot," Malcolm said, "dismantling all the manipulations the Regent infected the Timeline with. He did a thousand things across more than a thousand years, all to manufacture a future where he was ruler. Which means that Maya's future shouldn't exist. As we keep fixing what he did, slowly the natural future will replace hers. So, I thought, if she happened to be rescued from a future that's disappearing anyway, would it really hurt anything?"

Maya was almost there. Because she was traveling through grass almost as tall as she was, though, she was hard to spot. As she looked on, Valentine was struck by a troubling thought.

"But if this is my past, too, why don't I remember her?"

Malcolm didn't look at her, but he wore a knowing smile. "Wait for it . . ."

Maya called out for her mother. Callie turned.

Her eyes went wide. The basket fell from her hands. She shook her head in disbelief.

Her little girl drew closer, proving to be real with every step. Then Callie's insides took over. Leaving everything behind, she scrambled through the grass as fast as she could, screaming her daughter's name over and over again.

As they finally embraced, a wall of memories hit Valentine like a tidal wave. Gasping, she fell to her knees.

"Oh, my God, Mal," she gasped. "I remember. I remember everything! Years of it!"

As she worked to process thousands of new happy sights and sounds in her mind, the reunion that sparked it all was happening in the distance. She watched in rapt attention, eager to soak up every second.

Callie clutched her daughter in the most intense embrace Valentine would ever witness. She sobbed as if, in one flash, the world was suddenly whole again. She kept saying Maya's name, barely stopping for breath.

The rest of the family was catching on now and sprinting to

join her. Valentine remembered it now! The day she first met her sister from the future. The day Maya's bright little light came into their lives. The day Callie found her old self again.

Questions were asked, and then Maya turned and pointed. The family looked far out into the field, where their eyes found Malcolm. As realization dawned on their faces, he held his hand high in the air.

A greeting from afar. The family knew what that meant by now. Sometimes Malcolm visited for real, and sometimes he just appeared from a distance, at the edges of their lives. They knew enough to trust his judgment.

So this time they waved, they shouted thanks. Standing with her daughter clutched in her arms, Callie let her gratitude shine out from her face as tears flooded down her cheeks.

Valentine was crying, too. How long had it been since she cried such happy tears? As Malcolm offered one last wave to their family, he turned. His own tears were falling.

"Come on," he said, taking her hand. "Time to go."

They walked through the portal together.

"Do you realize what a wonderful thing you did?" she asked.

He gave a noncommittal nod, but she pressed on.

"No, I mean it. We thought Callie and Dad were happy before? You should have seen them after today. It was like they were new people. Like all the scars had disappeared." She eyed him sidelong. "So, this is what you do with your Time, huh?"

Malcolm gave a little chuckle. "Well, some of it. Perk of the job."

"I can see how that wouldn't get old. Thank you, Malcolm, for letting me see that."

"Of course." He stopped and faced her. "Just one more thing

before we go back. Nothing like this, but I've been wanting to show it to you. Do you mind?"

She shook her head eagerly. "Lead the way."

CHAPTER 50

Malcolm smiled but didn't start walking again. Instead he released her hand and gently gripped her shoulder.

"I just need to lend you some of my sight," he said.

Another kind of wave passed through her. This one felt different; it opened her perceptions. Dizziness washed over her.

When it passed, she realized they were floating. With a yelp, she grabbed onto Malcolm. He laughed like he had when they were kids, and kept rising.

Something new glimmered inside him. She could barely feel it, but it was there. A heartbeat later they were in a familiar place, but a version that Valentine had never seen with her own eyes.

Malcolm's Aegis!

With his hand on her shoulder, she could see it stretching into eternal past and future. She admired the crystalline look, similar to Arsinoë's Aegis, but far more colorful and prismatic.

Where the old one had been rigid, this one gently flexed and breathed as if it were adjusting to changing conditions in the Timeline. That was better! The Timeline could withstand stress without cracking as it did before.

Then, as Valentine focused closer, she glimpsed what must

have been Malcolm's proudest achievement, a solution he had proposed since they had first learned about the Aegis.

"Mal, you built the Timeways!"

The closer she looked, the more obvious they became, each one like a silver thread weaving through the Timeline.

"I managed to do it," Malcolm said, and she could hear the pride in his voice. "We have new laws that govern Time travel, but more freedom, too. Some people try to abuse it, but that's what *they* are for."

He pointed toward a silver thread. Valentine saw a pinpoint of light traveling along it. Through Malcolm's senses she knew what she was seeing: a squad of Ember Guard on another mission to keep Time safe.

"Do you like it?" Malcolm asked.

"It's breathtaking."

"I couldn't have done it without you. Without what you gave me."

She turned to gaze at her brother. As she did, the Aegis faded slowly from around them. They stood once again in her room with the medical bed.

Valentine regarded the space wistfully. For a moment she had forgotten that her Time had come.

"Well, I *am* tired. That boost you gave me is wearing off." She sat against her bed, not yet ready to climb back in. Not ready for this to be over. "One last adventure. Thank you, Mal. I loved it so much."

"What will you do now?" he asked.

She sighed. "Rest, I suppose. I've lived a wonderful life. But even for someone like me, eventually it must end."

Malcolm stared down at his hands, fidgeting as if he were nervous. Then his head snapped up. He stepped closer.

"Well . . . what if it didn't?"

She tilted her head, puzzled. "What do you mean?"

"All these things I showed you—I didn't just want you to see them. I wanted you to see the things we could do . . . if you joined me."

Valentine leaned back, hardly believing. "Are you saying . . . ?"

"I've been thinking. The Chrona was originally three people, and two of them were twins. So why couldn't that happen again? If I can do this much by myself, imagine what a *dual* Chrona could accomplish. We could help so many people. We could witness infinite wonders together."

"Wonders?"

"Every moment in Time, every star in the universe."

"B-but . . . how? I gave up my power."

"Mine has multiplied many times over the millennia. I could easily give back what you gave me and never miss it. As the years go by, your power would catch up to mine."

"My old power . . ." The idea set her insides yearning. She had thought that desire long gone. "But for how long?"

Malcolm smiled. "As long as we could ever want."

Valentine touched her temples, dizzy at the whirlwind of possibilities. A universe of Time at her fingertips—not just to explore, but to help so many people. More than she could have with a thousand lifetimes.

One last thought rang through her mind like a bell. *Why on earth am I hesitating?*

"Yes," she said, barely able to contain herself. "Yes! Let's be the Chrona together."

He breathed a sigh of relief. She saw the excitement blossom in his eyes, too. Getting ahold of himself, he held up his hands.

Valentine remembered this part. She raised her own hands and grasped his.

Just as before, the touch of Malcolm's Time was gentle. She could feel his signature reaching out to her. Only now, instead of feeling her power fade, she felt it return.

It came slowly at first, then suddenly all at once. A rush of vitality. A burst of light. A crack like thunder.

Valentine's old Chronauri perceptions reawoke. Her old instincts returned in a flash. She could feel Time flowing across the universe again. She stood straighter, remembering the great power she used to wield, savoring it now as it embraced her.

As the light faded, sinking beneath her skin, she faced the floor-length mirror on her wall. With a gasp, she touched her face. Fresh, young skin. She tugged at her hair, once gray, now a long, vibrant red.

She could feel Time revitalizing every cell, turning back the clock to the very day she gave up her power to save the universe.

"I'm back!" Bursting with joy, she threw herself into Malcolm's arms. "All this power—I didn't remember the half of it. Mal, all the things we can do for people . . ."

"You're going to love it," he said. "This is only the beginning."

Frantic knocking rattled Valentine's door.

"Oma? Are you okay? We heard a strange noise."

"Oops," she said.

"Yeah, your transformation wasn't exactly silent."

Valentine trained young eyes on her brother. "Then we'd better not waste Time."

Catching her meaning, Malcolm grinned. "Where would you like to go first? And when?"

They knocked harder. "Why is this door locked?"

"I don't even know what to pick!"

Malcolm shrugged, enjoying himself. "We have all the Time in the universe."

They were pounding now, and shouting.

Right, she remembered. There was no pressure. Whatever they wanted to do, wherever they wanted to go, eventually they would get there. *So just pick a good start.* When she turned to her brother again, there was a twinkle in her eye.

"The Library of Alexandria," she said. "It's about time someone saved it. Don't you think?"

Malcolm grinned. "Take my hand."

She did.

"You ready?"

"You have *no* idea."

Malcolm laughed, standing straighter. Valentine stood beside him, ready for whatever the adventure would bring. He flexed just a fraction of his power, and Valentine felt the Timeline preparing to *shift* around them.

The door burst open. Generations of Valentine's family tried cramming through the opening, then stopped short at the sight.

The bearded man was in the lead. He looked puzzled at first. His eyes bounced between Valentine's old high school photo and the way she appeared now, not to mention her long-lost twin, standing at her side. Realization dawned and his eyes grew wide as saucers.

"Oh, my God, it's all true?"

Valentine just smiled.

She looked at Malcolm and nodded. He nodded back, eyes gleaming with eager anticipation. The Gilbert twins were about to be set loose on the universe! After everything they had been through, everything they had done, it only felt right.

Responding to Malcolm's will, temporal energy swirled

around them like a storm of light. Valentine reached out, unable to resist adding her power to his. Like an old friend, Time embraced them. The light reached its crescendo.

Time *shifted*.

The universe opened to them.

ACKNOWLEDGMENTS

This is a surreal moment. It wasn't so long ago that I was holding the manuscript for *The Year of Lightning*, having just received my one hundredth rejection, wondering if this world and these characters that I loved so much would ever see the light of day. Now here we are, celebrating the release of the conclusion of the entire trilogy. I'm extremely proud of *The Genesis Flame*, and eternally grateful to North Star Editions for giving me the opportunity to finish the series and share it with all of you.

Thank you to my family and friends for your constant support. Also, to the amazing crew of writers here in Phoenix, I'm proud to be among such awesome peers who work so hard to lift each other up. Beta readers like Allison Martin are also priceless and have my eternal gratitude for helping this book become the best version of itself.

To the teachers and librarians who work so hard to connect authors with young readers, thank you for your tireless support, and for encouraging children to open books and discover new worlds. Your efforts are not unnoticed, and they will not be forgotten.

If you're reading this, I want to thank you, too. By this point, you've spent about three hundred thousand words adventuring through Time with Malcolm and Valentine. I hope you've loved every moment of it. Rest assured, this may be my last book in the Time Shift Trilogy, but it is by no means my last book. I have many more worlds and characters to share with you.

So, stay tuned. Adventure awaits.

ABOUT THE AUTHOR

When he's not wearing a cape and fighting crime, RYAN DALTON sits in his awesome red captain's chair and thinks up fun stories to share with the world. A lifelong geek, a trained stage vocalist, and a pretty decent amateur chef, he knew since the age of ten that he would one day ~~take over the world~~ publish novels to stir the heart and spark the imagination. ~~And then take over the world.~~ Yep, definitely just the heart and imagination thing. Ryan lives in an invisible spaceship that's currently hovering above Phoenix, Arizona.